THE
OTHER
PEOPLE

THE
OTHER
PEOPLE

A NOVEL

C.B. EVERETT

ATRIA BOOKS

NEW YORK   AMSTERDAM/ANTWERP   LONDON   TORONTO   SYDNEY   NEW DELHI

ATRIA
BOOKS

An Imprint of Simon & Schuster, LLC
1230 Avenue of the Americas
New York, NY 10020

First Atria Books hardcover edition March 2025

ATRIA BOOKS and colophon are trademarks of Simon & Schuster, LLC

For information about special discounts for bulk purchases, please contact
Simon & Schuster Special Sales at 1-866-506-1949 or business@simonandschuster.com.

The Simon & Schuster Speakers Bureau can bring authors to your live event. For more
information or to book an event, contact the Simon & Schuster Speakers Bureau at
1-866-248-3049 or visit our website at www.simonspeakers.com.

Interior design by Kyoko Watanabe

Manufactured in the United States of America

1 3 5 7 9 10 8 6 4 2

Library of Congress Cataloging-in-Publication Data is available.

ISBN 978-1-6680-5830-5
ISBN 978-1-6680-5832-9 (ebook)

Hell is other people.

—JEAN-PAUL SARTRE,
No Exit

THE
OTHER
PEOPLE

PROLOGUE

Hello? I know you're watching . . . Yes, you, behind the mirror. I know you're watching me. Course you are. You wouldn't put a mirror in an interrogation room if you couldn't hide behind it, so I know you're there. I've sat here long enough, get back in here and talk . . . *Now* . . . Because you're wasting time. She's out there, dying, and I know where she is. You've got to find her. You can save her, if you get a move on . . . This is urgent, come on . . .

"Don't ignore me, *please* don't ignore me . . . I escaped from that house, came straight here, and . . . and all the others . . . all the others are dead. Murdered . . . All of them . . . And you've done nothing about that. *Nothing*.

"Oh, wait a minute, wait a minute . . . this paper suit you've given me, being left in here on my own, you don't think I'm a witness, do you? You think . . . you think I'm the killer . . . Is that it? My god, you think because I'm the only one left alive that I did it . . . And then there was one and it's me . . . The prime suspect. The *only* suspect . . .

"Well, that's bullshit, and you know it. I mean, for god's sake, I even told you who did it. One of the other people. Gave you their name and everything so why don't you go and arrest them? Get a confession. Go on, instead of doing this to me, go on . . .

"Stop pissing about in there! Stop ignoring me! Hello?

"Hello?

"Oh god . . . Fine. Fine. Leave me here, do what you want, just get back to the house. *Please*. Go to the house. With the bodies. Find the girl. That's all you have to do. Go to the house with the bodies, find the girl . . .

"Please, before it's too late . . ."

PART ONE

PART ONE

KYLE TANNER

The space I'm lying in is rigid and tight. Head to foot, shoulder to shoulder, no space for movement. It smells of fresh planed wood. A box. I look up. At first I can only make out darkness against darkness but I concentrate and eventually realize there's no lid to this box I'm in. I then differentiate the darkness above me, divide it into trees and night sky. Stars. A full moon. But distant, like looking through the wrong end of a telescope. Nearer to me are walls. They smell of earth, roots, loam. My heart flips as I work out where I am. In a coffin. In a grave.

I don't know how I got here, don't have the time or the energy to think about that now. Answers can wait. I just have to get out. Escape.

I try to wriggle my upper body free from the wooden confines, writhe, arch my back, and push my shoulders upward. I try to move my arms, get my hands free, work up to gripping the edges of the coffin, lever myself out that way. But I'm wedged in so tight I can't move. Like this coffin has been built around me while I slept. The more I struggle, the harder it becomes. Like the wood is pushing farther into me, tightening. I'm sweating and gasping but getting nowhere. I can feel myself begin to panic. Breathing becomes harder, movement more difficult. I pull and push, but the wood seems to move with me, expanding and contracting as I do.

Then the darkness above begins to move toward me. Fast. It hits me, hurts me. Increasing in weight and power all the time. I flinch, try to breathe, to see, but can't. Stones and soil and mud begin to cover me. Someone is filling up the grave.

My panic ramps up. I'm desperate to free myself. I scream for help, but the earth falls into my mouth, gets inhaled up my nose. I gasp, choking and coughing, spitting, more earth than air getting into my breathing passages. I move my head side to side to avoid the falling soil, but it's relentless. It's choking me. I try spitting it out, clearing my black clogged lungs. It just rains down, unceasing.

I have no idea how long I lie like this, could be faster than heartbeats, could be days.

My legs are soon pinned down by the weight of the earth. My arms also. I blink rapidly, trying to keep the dirt out of my eyes at least, get a glimpse of who's doing this, keep contact with that night sky. Because as long as I can still see the sky, the trees, there's hope that this will stop, that I'll be able to get out. That I'll be rescued, even. Then the sky and the trees disappear and with them all hope.

I'm going to die. The thought hits me with the force of a wrecking ball. I'm going to die. No argument, no bargaining. I just have to accept it. It's so unfair and I'm scared and it's not right because this is the kind of thing that only ever happens to the other people, not me. Never me. And I can't breathe anymore and I can't see and I don't know if my eyes are closed or open and it doesn't matter anymore and I'm holding my breath and I'm crying but no one can hear it not even me and I know I have to breathe out and if I do that'll be the end and I can't stop fighting but I know I have to breathe sometime even if there's nothing left to breathe in and I want to scream again one last time and so I try to open my mouth and breathe and scream and—

■ ■ ■

I wake up. And I'm screaming. Gasping for breath. A dream. Just a dream. A night terror. A bad one that had me pinned down and paralyzed, choked.

I struggle to sit up, my body slow to respond, getting signals it's still in the nightmare. Eventually I manage to prop myself on my side, panting. Shaking like I've run a marathon.

The room is dark, womblike. The bed soft, welcoming. I'm slipping down inside it. My breathing subsides and there's silence. And there's safety in that silence.

But not for long.

A sonic boom rips the world apart. The room is strobe lit in stark electric monochrome. The windows shake to near breaking point. A storm crashes overhead. Thunder, wind, lightning all at once. A nightmare of paralysis, then a storm. My two biggest fears. Like being pranked by a cruel god.

Another crash and I scream again.

Once more I'm paralyzed, but this time it's because I'm helpless. I burrow under the covers, keep my eyes tight closed. Pray to that bastard god for this to end. I try to do something positive. Counting the seconds between lightning crashes and thunder cracks is supposed to gauge the distance between them. The longer the gap, the farther the distance.

Lightning.

One . . . two . . . three . . .

Thunder.

Almost overhead.

I stop counting, it's pointless. So I just have to lie here. And then those images return and the memories with them. Summoned up from the depths of my mind, playing out once again on the insides of my closed eyelids. Movies I can't look away from. Storms always trigger that horrible time, that horrible place. Thunder and lightning take away my control. I just stare at the images, relive the memories. Plead for them to stop.

After what seems like agonizingly long years, the storm passes. I open my eyes once more, banishing those memories, shaking like I'm over-caffeinated. I'm alone once more. I remove the bedclothes from over my face. And something that I barely had time to register when the lightning lit up the room returns to me.

Where am I?

I get out of bed quickly. Look around as best I can with only the dim light of the moon. This is still the dream. It must be. I've jumped out of my night terror into . . . this. Yes. I'm still dreaming. I have to be. Because this isn't my bedroom. This isn't any room I've ever been in before. Beside the door there's a light switch. I flick it on. A large chandelier in the center of the room throws out illumination.

It's like a film set from an old Hammer movie. The kind of a room an unwary traveler stays in before something horrific happens to them. The walls are dark, wood paneled. An unlit stone fireplace at one end of the room. Intricately patterned rugs cover the bare floorboards. A lead-lined paneled window set in stone looks out into darkness. A heavily carved armoire dominates one wall. The bed has four massive posts at each corner. I had been lying under heavily brocaded and embroidered eiderdowns. The pillows are deep and downy. A large china washbasin and matching jug rest on a wooden console table. An ottoman is at the foot of the bed and on the bedside tables are candles. A central table holds a huge candelabra. I look up. The ceiling is bowed and covered with wooden struts. The whole room is heavy, oppressive, Gothic.

I try the door. Locked. I pull harder, an air of desperation in my grip. It still doesn't give. I turn and face the room once more. Something catches my eye. On the bedside table, exactly as it would be in my flat, is the book I am currently reading, *Tales of Mystery and Imagination* by Edgar Allan Poe. This room could have been re-created from within those pages. I turn around again, feeling like an animal trapped in a cage.

It's a dream. It must be. A more insidious night terror than the one I'd just had, but a dream nonetheless.

I do the thing I always do when I'm drunk and trying to decide whether I've had too much. I bite my inner lip. I read somewhere that if you do this when you've been drinking and you can't feel it, you've had too much to drink. If it hurts, you can still keep going. Student logic. I've lost count of the times I've woken up the next morning with a bleeding, chewed, and bitten inside lip. Figuring if I'm dreaming it won't hurt, I bite down. Hard. It hurts and I draw blood.

So if this isn't a dream, what the hell is it? And something else—and I can't believe I haven't noticed this before—I'm fully dressed. My jeans, boots, T-shirt, and hoodie.

I open the armoire. It makes the kind of creak you would expect. I stare at what I see. Inside are my clothes, neatly hanging up and folded on shelves. Shoes underneath. I have palpitations. I feel like I'm struggling to breathe. I can feel a panic attack building. Inside me, terror battles incomprehension. Who brought my clothes here? And my book? Who brought *me* here?

I look out the window. Darkness. The storm's gone, the rain's stopped. There's weak light coming from somewhere because I can make out a garden below. It's large, with different sections for trees, lawn, and flower beds, separated by high almost mazelike hedges. Something catches my eye. A flash of light against the darkness. A figure moving about.

I peer closer, cup my eyes against the glass, blot out the immediate light from the room, focusing on the scene below me. Definitely movement. Someone is dragging something heavy along behind them. I'm squinting now, trying to make it out, but the darkness doesn't help and the trees and hedges get in the way. Perhaps it's my mind playing tricks but it looks like the heavy item is . . . no. Just the trick of the light. Must be.

And then there's a flash of lightning.

I shout, jump away from the window. Wait for a few seconds, heart pounding. It wasn't close. Definitely wasn't close. Definitely. Or at least I hope so. But it did do something. It illuminated the scene in the garden before I jumped away.

Definitely a body.

THE BEAST IN THE CELLAR

This is a house of secrets.

This is a house of ghosts.

This is a house of hidden monsters.

This is a house of death.

And here's me, at the bottom of it. Literally. Everyone in the house knows I'm here. Either consciously or subconsciously. You mention the cellar and they all take a pause. They all think of what's there or what might be down there. Or what they're scared to find down there. Down here, I should say. None of them want to come down here. And see me. *None of them.* So they ignore me. Pretend I'm not here. What's that I've just seen out of the corner of my eye? Nothing. Didn't see it. What's that down in the cellar? Nothing. *Nothing.* There's no *beast in the cellar.* No monster. Didn't see it. *Didn't see it, right?*

So why would they do that? Pretend I'm not here when they know I am? Well, let's be honest. Wouldn't you? Of course you would. Just like them. Yeah, I know all this now. I've worked it out. I mean, I've had long enough down here all alone, I may as well have done something productive with my time. There's no Netflix down here to stare at.

Oh yeah, I know what Netflix is. I'm in the cellar, not the eighteenth century.

No. I've worked it out. It's because if they actually acknowledged me they'd have to acknowledge all the other monsters in the house. I mean, I'm just a beast. There are bigger monsters than me. And more ferocious, even if I say so myself. And these monsters aren't tucked away out of everyone's reach like I am. Behind a locked door and down a dark flight of steps into the scary, cold unknown. No. They're much closer to hand. Much *much* closer. These monsters can be touched, talked to, argued with, fought with, slept with. They can eat and drink. They can make small talk. And large talk, come to that. They can *mingle.*

They're here. In the house with me. With *us*. It's simply a question of identifying them. Or *it*. Might be plural, might be singular. Perhaps it's just one huge monster, acting alone. Or perhaps it's more than one.

But, hey, what would I know? Let's keep it light, or as light as you can when you're the beast in the cellar. The true monster at the bottom of the house.

All I'll say is this. If you want to know about monsters and what they're capable of, then ask me. But beware . . . (I said that like in a spooky old horror film voice. But you'll just have to imagine it. Because it's hard to write that kind of thing down. No nuance in writing, that's the trouble. Anyway . . .) I'm telling you now, you might not like the answer. And to get that answer you'll have to confront me. Worse than that, you'll have to acknowledge me. My existence. My relationship to you and the rest of the people in this house.

So do you still want to know who the monsters are and where they are and what they're doing? Really? Then you know what to do. And once you've done that, be prepared for what it'll cost you.

Or perhaps it's better not to know, to be willfully ignorant of what's going on. No acknowledgment leads to no confrontation equals no consequences. Don't ask, don't tell. Play it dumb, like all the rest of them.

Whatever. I have a tendency to ramble on. Just ignore me.

Pretend I'm not here.

And let other monsters go about their monstrous business.

KYLE TANNER

I don't know where I am. And I don't know how I got into this room. The door is locked and I'm not going to call down to whoever was in the garden. My only way out is the window. Climb down the side of the building and escape that way.

As I try the window frame I think of Jonathan Harker in *Dracula*, seeing the Count dragging his body down the side of the castle like some huge slug. I unlatch the arm, push. It's sealed shut. Somehow I'm not surprised. I try the door again. Still locked. I sit down on the bed once more. To stop me panicking further I try to mentally retrace my steps, hopefully helping me find out how I got here and where I am.

Okay. My name is Kyle Tanner and I have night terrors about being boxed up and paralyzed and I'm terrified of storms. I'm twenty-two years old, originally from Hertfordshire but currently a second-year student at Birmingham University. I'm studying English literature and film studies with a particular nod toward the macabre since my dissertation is "Representations of the Gothic in Western Postwar Cinema." My head's full of that stuff at the moment. I spend days watching old Hammer and Roger Corman films, reading academic and not so academic studies, short stories and novels, all on the same theme. The course has taken me over so much it's how I interpret things around me. Good for my degree, not much fun at parties.

I check my watch, but I'm not wearing one. That's not right. I've always got my watch on. I even wear it for bed. My ex-girlfriend used to complain that the last thing I did at night and first thing in the morning was check the time. There is something on my wrist, though, where my watch usually is. It's like a kind of Fitbit thing, a tight rubber bracelet with a rectangular piece of dark glass in the center. I try to pull it off but it won't budge. It may as well be welded to my skin. And it's the only thing in the room, apart from me, that looks out of place.

I check the Poe book at my bedside. It looks exactly like the copy I'm reading at home. In fact, it could be it, same creases and everything. The clothes in the armoire seem to be mine. But this gets me nowhere. I try to order my thoughts, think back.

What's the last thing I remember? Saturday morning. I woke up around ten, hungover (actually, still a bit drunk) from the night before. I got up about lunchtime, went downstairs to find my housemate Tom lying on our ancient sofa, half covered by a duvet, watching *Football Focus* and eating a bowl of Cheerios. Mike, our other flatmate, came and joined us. We chatted about the night before, made tentative plans for later, then I made myself a cup of tea and went back upstairs, thinking I was going to read some more Poe—I was up to "The Premature Burial"—but I ended up, like always, on my phone pissing about on socials.

And then after that—

There is no after that. That's the last thing I remember. And now I'm here.

I check through all my clothes pockets for my phone, check the floor of the wardrobe, the bedside table, anywhere else I can think of. No phone. I sit back down on the bed once more, awed about where I am but also terrified. Someone's gone to a lot of trouble and effort for all this. I don't know whether to be flattered they think I'm worth the attention or scared because of it. But I can't think of anything I've done to deserve it. Good or bad.

Tom, Mike, and I play practical jokes on one another all the time but nothing like this. Small stuff usually, like convincing Tom to eat the hot towel you get in an Indian restaurant by saying it's really a complimentary pudding, that kind of thing. The only big thing they've done to me was the night after we'd watched a really gory horror film. I tried not to let them see how scared I was by it but they knew. When I came downstairs the next day they were playing dead in the living room, covered in blood. They were sprawled all over the furniture, heads lolling back like they'd been attacked and knifed. I was totally convinced. I was about to call 999 when they both got up slowly and started groaning like zombies. That's when I ran into the kitchen to grab a knife and they pissed themselves laughing. I nearly killed them for real, then. They'd used strawberry jam for the lumpy bits and ketchup for the splatter effects. After I'd calmed down I got angry, told them they were cleaning it all up and if we didn't get our deposit back it was their fault and they owed me. They said it had been worth it to see my face. But they wouldn't go to all this trouble, would they? They had done that prank knowing gory films upset me, but I've never told them about my other fears, like storms. So if it's not them, then who? And why?

I check the door. Still locked. I sit back down on the bed. Wait. After a while I get up, look out of the window once more. The storm has long passed. The night dark and still. Washed, but not clean. No one is in the garden. Or if there is, they're hidden in the shadows.

And then I hear it. Faint but unmistakable. A click.

I cross quickly to the door, turn the handle. It opens.

My first thought was sexual trafficking. Waking up in a strange place with no memory of how I got here? Obviously. I came through the nineties when date rape drugs became ubiquitous and girls' drinks were all spiked. I grew up surrounded by stories of being raped while still conscious but not able to fight back or waking up in some cheap hotel in a bathtub of ice with a kidney missing. But I made sure that never happened to me then and I'm not about to let someone get away with that now. If they want me, they're going to have to fight me.

I mean, this wouldn't be the first time I've woken up somewhere I don't know with no functional memory of the night before and found myself staring at some snoring stranger whose name I can't remember but whose cock I could pick out of a lineup. God, no. But it's always been consensual. Now, as I get older (*hate* that word) the days of doing that are long gone. Well, not that long. I've just become more selective. And yes, that has been my deliberate choice. There are plenty of younger guys who love the attention of a cougar.

Yes, I am highly sexually oriented, so what? It's a big driver for me. Tried marriage, hated it. Don't want kids (had my tubes tied in my twenties). Tested regularly, don't want relationships. Nothing worse than when they get all clingy and soppy after a couple of dates. Please. You're fired. Gone. That's what ghosting was invented for.

And now I'm wearing a rather gorgeous little Prada number matched with what seems to be a very expensive necklace and I've left the bedroom I came round in and am walking down the hallway of an old dark house. If the attempt was to scare me, whoever you are, then you've wasted your time. If, however, your goal was to irritate and annoy me, then congratulations. Job done. I don't have the time for this kind of idiotic display. I have meetings to attend. A company to run. Deals to make. So I'm looking forward to meeting you to find out what all this is about. You, on the other hand, won't enjoy it so much. I haven't clawed my way up to the position I'm in (and, more to the point, stayed there as long as I have) without pointing out other people's faults to them. And when they make me angry, look out. The Hulk's got nothing on me. Yes, of course I know who the Hulk is.

My anger only increased when I was in, well, what I assume is supposed to be my room. It's clearly old but has apparent facsimiles of some of my bedroom furniture from my apartment and a selection of my clothing in the armoire. Whoever this is has gone to a lot of trouble for this prank but they've forgotten one important thing. My phone. It's missing. All I have is this ridiculous Fitbit thing on my wrist that I can't get off. It doesn't even look like it's working and it definitely doesn't have Wi-Fi. As soon as the door clicked open I was out of there. And here I am, striding as fast as my Louboutins will allow down the hallway.

Still, I can't help but be drawn in by my surroundings. It's like an old manor house, the kind that's been reclaimed and turned into an exclusive country retreat hotel. The floorboards are authentic but well preserved. Same with the wood paneling on the walls. Dotted here and there are old heavy pieces of furniture. Bookcases holding old leather-bound books. I was actually tempted to say "tomes" instead of "books," it's that kind of place. There are occasional recesses and nooks with lead-lined windows; I kneel on the heavy, brocaded cushions in one and try to peer out of the window, make out where I am. I can't see anything. Too dark. Waste of time.

I assume I'm heading down to dinner, since I'm dressed for it. I'm not hungry though—food isn't a great motivator for me, it's fuel at best and tends to get in the way of other activities—but I'm definitely looking forward to speaking to whoever's in charge.

I stop walking. Before me is an old elevator. The cage kind. It's not in keeping with what I've seen of the rest of the house but it's still archaic. I look around. No one else here. The stairs sweep downward but I see no reason to take them when I can spare my stilettoed feet and take the lift. I open the cage. The car is waiting for me like it knew I would be here. I get in, pull the door shut behind me. It's been well maintained. The gold inside is highly polished, the mirrors art deco. More modern than the rest of the house, admittedly. But still no Wi-Fi, my Fitbit thing remains blank.

I press for the ground floor and it starts to move.

As I descend, I look through the gaps in the cage. The walls are lined with paintings and there's something curious about them. They all look new but they're in a style centuries old. Like someone spent at least a week posing while the artist captured whatever they thought was there. They're all portraits but they seem, in a way, even more modern than this lift. The figures seem to be wearing contemporary clothes, holding contemporary items. I notice a young man depicted sitting in front of a laptop, his face lit by the screen, fascinated by what he's watching. An older man in contemporary military uniform taking command on a battlefield. Something dark that I can't make out. And then—

I gasp. No.

I hit the buttons on the panel, trying to make the cage stop. It won't, of course, but it doesn't stop me from trying. Instead I crane my neck, try to look upward, but it's too late. The gap has gone and we've been replaced by another floor. And now the lift stops. We've reached the ground floor.

Already I'm beginning to doubt what I just saw. It's ridiculous, can't be. Some trick of the light, a coincidence. I want to go back and check but I can see light coming from a double doorway off to the left. Someone is in there. Someone is going to get a piece of my mind.

The painting can wait until later.

I get out of the lift, cross to the room, swing the double doors wide open and stride in.

"Which one of you fuckers is responsible for this?"

I've always known how to make an entrance.

THE BEAST IN THE CELLAR

Don't you find it confusing when so many characters are introduced in such a small space of time? Yes? And you're expected to remember them all? Even though they haven't yet demonstrated an individual trait or said or done anything particularly character-defining or memorable? Sometimes there are so many characters all in one place you have to make notes just to keep up. Don't you find that irritating? Me too. So let's not do that here.

Oh, go on. Let's.

I'm sure you've worked out that the next part of the story revolves around dinner. So before we start on that, I suppose I should give you a quick rundown on who you're about to meet. Only the basics, of course, the rudiments of character so you can decide whether you think they're goodies or baddies, persecutors or protectors or anything in between. Beasts in the cellar, even.

You've met Kyle Tanner. Student, scared of lots of things, but likable enough as students go. (Sorry, shouldn't make judgments! That's your job.) Part of his degree's in what the more reactionary members of our dining party would call Watching Telly Studies. The film studies part of his BA that specializes in the Gothic. Yes, he does watch a lot of films—and read a lot of books, for that matter—but there's more to it than that. It's harder than you (or I) might think. Because he watches those films and reads those books critically. His course has trained him to look beyond what's being presented to him. See beneath the surface, beyond the text, either verbal or visual. He's learned not to take what's before him for granted. Subtext and context is everything.

And you've met Diana Landor too. That's not her real name, by the way. Janice Crewe. But she changed it as soon as she managed to disentangle herself from her roots. No one would take a glamorous PR executive based in the heart of London's glittering West End (as they used to say) seriously with a name like Janice Crewe and a turgid regional accent to match. But the beautiful, confident Diana Landor? That's a different matter. She's a masterpiece (mistresspiece?) of self-reinvention. She's an alchemist of identity, taking the most unpromising base material, combining it with pure ambition and an obsession with old episodes of *Sex and the City,* and transmuting it into something victoriously unrecognizable. No matter what's thrown at her, how much trauma she has to endure, she rises above it, coming out stronger, even more desirable. She projects her own perfection on the biggest canvas she can find. But can she ever truly overcome that past? Is that poor damaged child still locked away deep inside her? And to what lengths will she go to keep it hidden? Conversely, what kind of crisis would it take for that damaged child to emerge?

That's two of them. There are eight more (nine if you include me). And maybe some others we haven't met yet and might bump into as we go along. Who knows? I mean, it would spoil the fun if you knew everything up front, wouldn't it? What's life without surprises? So forget I said that and try to look surprised if and when it happens. Right. The other people.

There's Cerys and her baby, Monica. Monica doesn't say much, just sits there. A very sullen baby, doesn't play, doesn't seem curious about where she is or what's going on around her. Just watches blankly. And eats. And shits, presumably, since she's a baby, but thankfully, being down here, I don't have to deal with any of that. Never cries. Or I've never heard her. Or perhaps I have and I told myself it was foxes rutting by the bins outside. They can sound like screaming children. Now that I think about it, we do seem to get a lot of foxes round here.

Cerys always dresses frumpily, like she wants to be as unattractive as she can be. Possibly because the last time she went out dressed up she got pregnant. But she always looks torn, like part of her wants to get dressed up and go out and drink sugary vodka, dance, get off with guys (or girls, you never know these days) like any normal young woman but then realizes she's got this baby to look after and it's her responsibility alone. That kind of thing leads to resentment and self-hatred and possibly, in some extreme cases, abuse. She's holding it in check at the moment, but the anger's there, for sure. What if she was to turn it outward?

Have I mentioned Jimmy Saint? No? I'm laughing here at the thought of that. I know you can't see me but take my word for it. Although I am the Beast in the Cellar so it may not sound like laughter. Just say it's those foxes at it again. But anyway. Jimmy Saint. Or rather Captain Jimmy Saint, to give him his full title. He's probably got letters after his name and medals that he'd probably be happy to tell you about and how he got them, and there would be your day gone. No, that's wrong. That makes him sound vain and that's not right. Self-important is more accurate. A military man with a military man's bearing and outlook. A soldier. *A hero.* They mean the same thing to Jimmy. He's served with bravery, courage, and honesty in some of the world's greatest trouble spots. His men respect and obey him. He's a champion of fair play. He's Mister Terrific. Or Captain Terrific, rather. He sees things in binary absolutes: good and bad, black and white, right and wrong. And he's always on the side of right. The perfect hero. But can a man be as perfect as that? Really?

And then there's Sylvia Moult. Oh dear, Sylvia. Positively demonic in her outlook, the old girl. Well, I say old, I'm not actually sure how old she is. She seems to hail from a time when people knew their place and respected their elders and betters. Not like now. Of course, we all know that place and time only ever existed in the speeches of forgotten conservative prime ministers and Sylvia's imagination. Although if you consider imagination to be playing and joy and creativity and things of that nature, then Sylvia has more of an absence of it. Possessing those things is what's wrong with people today, especially young people, as she'll tell you at great length. She's the harridan of Human Resources. She hires and fires and enjoys half of her job. Unsurprisingly, she's single. Commitment, like so many things, is something Sylvia finds terrifying.

Don't worry, only another four to go. I'm afraid this has turned into a bit of a list. I know they're boring and hinder more than help information going in when you're reading, but it would have been more boring for you to read ten variations on: *I just woke up and don't know where I am. And there's a posh dinner, etc.* Over and over again. Dull! Dull! Dull! Assume that they've all experienced the same thing and they're all heading down to dinner. Don't worry, you'll get to know them. Well, most of them. But that's the nature of the beast, so to speak. (Not me. The other beast. The metaphorical, narrative one.) So onward. You can always come back to this bit if you want to. For reference. OK. Last four.

There's an old bloke here. Len, I think his name is. I say *think* because he's so unmemorable, as soon as he tells you his name, you've forgotten it already. He's probably got a surname as well. I'm mentioning him now because if I leave him to the end I'll just forget and then you'll be saying, who's this Len bloke? You didn't tell us about him. Or you might not because, as I say, he's so unmemorable. Anyway, Len. Wants nothing more than to be left alone in his allotment with no one to talk to, no responsibilities, and he can potter away to his heart's content, just him and his dog. It does make you wonder, though (if you give him any thought at all), why he wants to be left alone. Has he experienced something so horrible or traumatic that he just wants a little peace? Was it something he was responsible for? Or is he just too dull for words?

And then there's Iain, bless him. Every party has one, the almighty drunken bore. Not just a dull person but a dull person who's convinced he's the opposite of dull. His voice is louder than everyone else's and the more he drinks—and he drinks a lot—the more attractive and witty he gets. He believes. We've all met that person. Maybe, at times, we've been that person. (Not me, obviously, I'm just the Beast in the Cellar.) Everything in life has been provided for Iain, good school and university, the right friends and family; in short, the kind of advantages that even a moderately talented person could turn into a spectacularly successful life. Yet somehow Iain's managed to fail. He could have been prime minister—as some of his school friends have—and he would still have managed to fail. Ultimately he hates himself. But, bless him, he hasn't even got the self-awareness to comprehend that.

Now here's Ramona to brighten us all up. Ramona brightens everyone up. Everywhere she goes, talking with that Texas twang, batting her eyelashes, curling her long shapely legs under her as she sits down on any sofa, and those huge, round eyes. When they latch on to you, you feel like the most important person in the room. The *only* person in the room. In her life. On the planet. Distilled confidence in lithe-bodied perfection. Completely comfortable in her own, beautiful, skin. But like Jimmy Saint, can she really be that perfect?

I've kept the best for last. And by best I mean disgusting, sleazy pedo. The one you don't have to think about hating. Meet Desmond Blaine. Or rather don't. He's no doubt on several registers somewhere. The kind of person children are told not to talk to and to cross the street to avoid walking past his house on the way home from school. Because of course he lives next to a school. Or as near as he's legally allowed to. You look at him and you know he's wrong. He doesn't even have to speak, you can sense it. It emanates from him in waves, like repugnant cologne. And you're stuck with him in this house and you have to have dinner with him. Whatever you do, make sure he's never alone with Cerys and Monica. As I said earlier, there are monsters everywhere.

Everywhere.

So. There's the list. Sorry if it went on a bit.

Oh, something else. The stories I've told you about them? They might have different stories to tell about themselves. Stories they'd rather remain hidden in case you'd think badly of them. Stories they don't want anyone to know about under any circumstances. Stories that need to be protected. Because at least one of them is lying. *At least.* Remember that when they're giving firsthand testimonies of what's going on around them as they see it.

And now, take your places, please. Pavlov's gong has bonged and dinner is served.

Hi. I'm Kyle. Um, my name's here, next to you. Mind if I join you?"

More than OK, I should think. "Help yourself." He sits down. And immediately the party looks more exciting.

Apparently we're all programmed to do this thing of gravitating toward the most attractive person in the room in the hope of propagating the human race or at least getting a good night's fun out of it. Well, Kyle is young and handsome. And he's sitting next to me. And he is the most attractive man in the room. Although that doesn't say much for the rest of the room.

At least he's much better than Iain, the drunken bore with the wandering hands on my left. He thinks I haven't noticed his fingers creeping up my thigh or "accidentally" turning into a fondle when he admires my necklace. Or even worse, he's taken my silence as an invitation to continue. He's clearly rich and thinks that's an aphrodisiac in itself, but money doesn't excuse bad manners or bad behavior. As he'll discover if his hand goes any farther up my leg, because there'll be a fork sticking out of it.

"I'm Diana," I say to Kyle and give him my full attention. I can feel Iain glowering at me even with my back turned. Perhaps the fork won't be necessary after all.

Kyle leans in close, panic all over his face. "I've just got here. Like, I don't know, just woken up and I'm here. Wherever *here* is. How long's everyone been here? What's going on?"

Iain overhears him, thinks it's his way back into the conversation. "Not a clue, old chap. I thought at first it must be some chums of mine playing an elaborate kind of prank. Murder mystery dinner in an old dark house, that kind of thing. All hush-hush." He laughs. "Might still be. Who knows? The wine's very good, though."

He seems content in his own little world so we both ignore him. Kyle looks round the room, taking it all in. The heavy, brocaded curtains pulled tightly shut. The ornate chandelier. In fact, the ornate everything.

And before us our dinner settings, knives and forks on either side, a huge silver cloche covering each plate in front of us, wine and water glasses, filled. I have to admit—grudgingly—Iain has a point. The room is set for a murder mystery dinner.

Kyle lowers his head, speaks again, just to me. "Who . . . are all these people? D'you know them?"

"Never met them before in my life," I reply, leaning in close to him, making sure he can "accidentally" look down my dress, should he want to. He wants to. But his quick glance away tells me he's too polite to acknowledge it. "We've all got names on our place settings, though. That should help us remember each other."

Kyle's looking round again, trying to take them all in. And what a disparate bunch they are. Or rather, we are, I should say. Never met any of them in my life. Now that my anger has dropped a little I'm taking in the mood of the room. There's anger, of course, and bewilderment, obviously. Mutual distrust, too, judging by the looks everyone is giving. There's also this undercurrent of panic and fear, as if we don't get answers soon it could all kick off. I've got to say, now that I'm thinking about it, I'm not actually immune to that either.

The military man, Captain Saint, his place setting says, is questioning everyone.

"And who are you?"

"Kyle Tanner," he says. "Hello. I've . . . just got here."

"And you've had the same experience as the rest of us?" Saint continues, barking questions like he's in a parade ground. "Woke up here, no idea where you are, how you arrived?"

"Um, yeah."

The rest of the table murmur and nod.

"Can anyone remember where they were before?" asks Kyle.

"I've tried," replies a boring-looking old man somewhere to Kyle's right, so boring I can't even be bothered to look at his name tag, "but I can't remember."

"Neither can I," says the frumpy young mother with the baby sitting in a high chair next to her. "And where is this place, anyway?"

"Who knows?" says obnoxious Iain. "Perhaps we've all been taken to a foreign country. Held to ransom by Islamists."

He's so drunk the word *Islamists* comes out with no consonants.

"This is not a foreign country," says a middle-aged woman, who from her haughty manner seems to think she's above the rest of us. Sylvia, her name tag says. "This is most definitely an English country house."

"Might be Scottish," I say, and from the look she flashes me I can see I've annoyed her. "Or Welsh, even. They were good with castles and that kind of thing."

"Well, it's not America," says a glamorous young Black woman with huge eyes, a spray-on dress, and a loud southern drawl. "I would know."

She's immediately got Kyle's attention. Hello. Competition. She's got the captain and even Iain hooked too. I'll have to keep my eye on that young lady.

"You're American?" asks the captain, to which she nods. "How did you get here?"

"No idea. Same as the rest of you, I guess."

"This could be a foreign country," says Kyle, suddenly embarrassed to have the attention of the room on him. "I saw this film where people woke up somewhere, American people, assuming they were in America, and they were in some Eastern European country and they'd been brought there to be hunted down and killed."

A murmur goes round the room, and the panic notches at least one point higher.

I lean in to him. "Not what everyone needs to hear right now," I say.

"But this clearly isn't Eastern Europe," says Iain, raising his glass. "The wine's too good."

There's a creepy-looking middle-aged man sitting aside from the others. Not by choice, the two either side having pulled their chairs as far away from him as possible. He's ignoring everyone else, trying to pull the silver cloche off his plate. It won't budge.

They're all still talking but Kyle's leaned in close to me once more. He looks at my wrist. "You've got one of them as well. That Fitbit thing."

"We've all got one. We were talking about them right before you arrived. None of them seem to be working, though. And I can't get it off."

"Neither can I." He pauses, like that wasn't what he wanted to say. He continues. "Have you been outside?"

"No, not yet. Why?"

"Because . . ." Again, he pauses. Then decides to continue. "I think I saw someone dragging a body through the trees in the garden."

I stare at him. "A body?"

He nods, like he can't believe he's actually saying it. "Dragging it through the trees."

I don't know how to reply. I fall back on what Iain's just said. Because anything else would be too horrible to contemplate. "Perhaps Iain was right. Earlier, I mean, not about the Muslims. Perhaps this is all some elaborate murder mystery thing. Yes." I'm warming to my theme now, latching on to it like some kind of lifeline, like things might not be so bad after all. "And what you saw was someone, one of the actors or I don't know, stagehands? That's what they call them, right? Anyway, someone preparing the props. For later. Then we've all got to find the clues and find the body." I'm still talking but I'm not listening to myself. "It won't have been real, though. It can't have been."

Kyle says nothing. Perhaps I've convinced him. Perhaps I've convinced myself too. Or perhaps I was just nervously babbling.

"And maybe these things on our wrists are to monitor our heart rate while we're looking for clues round the house," he says. "Or timing us, or something? Quickest wins?"

"That sounds very plausible," I say. "Yes, I like that."

Neither of us speak for a while.

The grandfather clock in the corner of the room strikes eight. As the last chime fades away, the creepy middle-aged man, Desmond, succeeds in removing his cloche. And because he's done it, we all try it. And they all come away.

Captain Saint addresses the table. "Dinner, I presume, is served."

Fish tacos. What? How did they know—whoever they are—that my favorite food is Mexican and beyond that, fish tacos?

I look at everyone else's plate to see if they're all eating the same thing. They're not. They've all got something different. It actually makes me smile, for the first time since I got here. No two people are the same here, I get that. This is a disparate bunch, just like in a classic murder mystery dinner scene. And what better way to demonstrate their different personalities than by what they eat?

This is where the film studies student in me takes over and I direct the scene in my head. The military guy over there, Captain Jimmy Saint his place card says, is eating steamed meat pudding and boiled vegetables like he's back at his public school or in the officers' mess. This is easy. Establishing shot of him, knife and fork in hand. Quick cut to the knife, pulling the pudding wall apart, steam rising. Cut to the fork plunging in, extracting a chunk of meat, glistening, dripping, then straight into his mouth. Military precision. Shot of lips chewing, regimented number of chews, swallow, follow-up shot of him slugging red wine. Quick shot of him wiping the runoff away from the side of his mouth, close-up of the white linen napkin lying on the table as the red wine spreads through the fabric. And there we have him.

Iain is eating what appears to be a small chicken—guinea fowl, perhaps—with great relish. He has butter sauce smeared all round his mouth and he clearly likes the good things in life. Even if his slightly frayed cuffs show he can't always afford them. He's smiling while he eats, but he has a predator's eye as he looks round the table. Hunting for his next meal ticket, perhaps?

Next to me Diana has in front of her what could pass for a brightly colored minimalist art installation at the Tate Modern. She's looking at it like it's her enemy, pushing its components round her plate, the fork barely reaching her mouth.

After an initial collective surprise, everyone started to eat, and I'm no exception. I get stuck in to my fish tacos. They're just how I like them. Tilapia and shrimp with a lime, sriracha, and mayo sauce. And they're good. Really good. Washed down by a Gamma Ray Neck Oil, my favorite beer.

"They've done their homework, haven't they?" I announce. No one replies. "The logistics involved in doing this. Not to mention the research." Still nothing. "I mean the food. Has everyone got their favorite? I have."

"This guinea fowl is as good as Rules," says Iain. "In fact, it could have come straight from there."

I notice the matronly woman—Sylvia?—hasn't started eating. She's still cleaning her cutlery on her napkin. She has a plain meal in front of her. Omelet and peas. She stares at it disapprovingly. Suspiciously, even. It seems like her default setting.

"Not eating?" I ask her.

She looks at me, warily. "I don't trust it. It could be poisoned. I can't believe you're all sitting there and eating everything." Her voice becomes shrill, like she's building up to something. A high-pitched whistle, from the sound of it.

I look at her properly for the first time. She's not as old as I first thought. She just dresses old. And acts old. And, from what I've heard so far, thinks old. Or maybe I mean something else. Risk averse. Conservative. Small and big C, probably. She shares her disapproving look with the whole table. I watch her as she does so and realize there's something poking through that veneer. Her eyes give it away. Fear. Is that how she lives her whole life?

"Poisoned?" says Iain, his mouth full and laughing. "Well, there are worse ways to go. This wine's excellent too." He takes a huge mouthful, washes everything down.

"I believe you've already mentioned it." Sylvia's disgust at him ratchets up a notch. She shakes her head, unable to believe she's in such company.

"And where are you from?" I ask, keeping my voice low, trying to reengage Sylvia once more.

"Northampton. Kettering, actually." As if the distinction's big enough to be proud of.

"And you just woke up here as well?"

Her features cloud once more. She looks at me again with that mixture of fierce disapproval, as if I'm responsible for her situation and fears I might exploit it. "I assume I was invited. Along with everyone else. Why, I don't know."

"Same for me," I say. "And this thing on my wrist. We've all got one."

"It won't come off. I've tried." Sylvia shows me hers.

"I'm Kyle, by the way."

She nods, offers nothing in return. I wait. "Sylvia," she says eventually, her tone begrudging. "I'm sure there's a perfectly rational explanation for all this. And we'll get to it in good time."

She resumes her distrustful stare at her omelet and my audience with her is ended.

Diana has given up moving food around and placed her knife and fork on the plate. "Done," she says.

"Enjoy that?"

She makes a face that eventually forms into a smile. "It was OK."

She's barely touched it.

"Can you remember what you were doing before you arrived here?" I ask her.

"Yes, of course, I was . . ." She trails off. Looks at me. "I can't remember." Panic in her eyes. "I can't remember . . ."

"Neither can I. And I can't remember being brought here either. I mean, we must have been transported somehow but I can't remember a car, train, anything."

"They must have drugged us. Why would they do that? Go to all this trouble?"

"I don't know. I really don't know . . ."

Everyone's finishing up now. The food has gone some way to breaking down barriers. Everyone is talking to their neighbors. The young woman with the baby is talking to the old man on one side, and the hot American girl on the other. The baby is silent. The creepy-looking bloke isn't talking to anyone, just watching. His lips are moving though, as if he's talking to himself or some imaginary friend. No. Himself. I don't get the impression he has any friends, even of the imaginary kind.

I drink my beer. I try to think about how I got to this place, what I was doing beforehand, the dream, the storm, but nothing fixes. There's too much happening all at once for me to think properly. And the more this goes on, the more I feel my life before this house start to recede. It seems to be increasingly a long way off and getting increasingly distant. The strange or at least unexpected thing is, I feel like I'm just accepting it.

Then the lights go out.

Sorry. That was a bit dramatic . . . sorry. I didn't mean . . . didn't mean to do that . . ."

The light goes on again. A woman strides from the light switch by the door and stands at the far end of the room, away from the diners. She stands bent over, hands on knees and out of breath, taking in all of the guests.

"Give me a minute . . . had to run to get here . . . had to make sure they weren't . . ."

There are murmurs of shock. She gets her breath back, straightens up. Looks anxiously at the doorway she has just entered from.

"I haven't got long. So you need to listen. I'm sure you've got loads of questions but it's important you listen to me. Please." Her hands are raised, imploring. She gives another anxious look toward the door. "Hello. There's a lot to tell you."

"Why haven't you got long?"

"What's going on?"

"Who the hell are you?"

"No time for questions, just listen."

The urgency of the woman's tone quiets the diners down.

She is in her early thirties, and with raven-black hair and clothing to match, she looks like an aging Goth. The collection of skull rings and other assorted silver jewelry only adds to, and indeed confirms, that impression. She is clutching a heavy black tote bag. She is unsmiling, serious. When she is sure she has everyone's attention, she speaks again. Her voice carries round the whole room. Either the room has good acoustics or she's used to being listened to.

"Right. My name's Amanda. And I'm sure you're all shocked and disoriented to be here. If there's any time left after I've finished talking"—another anxious glance toward the door—"then I'll try to answer any questions you've still got. Or as much as I know or can tell you, anyway."

The assembled diners wait. Expectant. Frightened to exhale, like the air has been sucked out of the room.

"First, do any of you know each other?"

They look at one another, strangers, shake their heads.

"You sure? Never met before? Seen each other before? Mutual friends or anything? Work together? Relatives? Any kind of connection?"

"Look," says the captain, "what's all this about?"

An admonishing hand is raised. "Please. So none of you have ever met before. No links to each other." Amanda nods. To herself. "Right. OK." Then looks back at them again. "Good. Now. I'm sure you want to know who brought you here. And why. And obviously how, because that was a logistical nightmare. We'll get to that. But there's something more important you need to know first." She looks round the room again, making eye contact with them all, waiting until she's sure they're listening before proceeding. "Brace yourselves. This is big. And unpleasant. And there's no way to sugarcoat it. No time, either. So try not to, you know, freak out. Take it as well as you can." She takes a deep breath. Exhales. "Right. OK. There's someone in this house who wants you all dead and is trying to kill you."

Predictably, chaos breaks out. Loud voices are raised, some stand up, declaiming.

Amanda gives them a few seconds to let this news sink in, but before chaos threatens to take over, she raises her hands to calm them down. "Please! Listen! Listen . . . please . . ."

Calmer heads calm the less rational and gradually order is restored.

She lowers her arms. "Thank you. Stay where you are, don't go running around. I've still got more to tell you, including how you can get out of here. Yes, you're locked in. Don't run for the doors, they're locked. You can try them later if you don't believe me, but for now take my word for it. Same with the windows. Since you've come down from your rooms they've been sealed. You can't even look out now, never mind get out. You're all trapped in here."

A noisy tension rises once more.

"Please . . ." Silence is grudgingly restored.

"Who wants to kill us?" The student this time.

"Good question. Let's start there." Amanda gives a quick glance toward the doorway once more. Then back to the room as if deciding how much she can tell them. "This house belongs to a man named Charles Boyd. Do any of you know him? Heard of that name?"

Blank faces all round.

"You sure? No bells ringing?" She pauses. "OK, then. He owns this place."

"And it's this Boyd chap who wants us all dead?" The captain again.

"Might not be Boyd himself. Might be a, shall we say, friend of his. Or even a couple of friends acting together. I'm not sure."

"And are they hidden in the house somewhere? Watching us?" Diana this time.

"They could be."

"Or is it one of these people here?" The middle-aged matronly woman, Sylvia, pointed at everyone else. "Is that what you're implying? It could be someone sitting at this table?"

"It's possible, yes. Very possible."

They all now eye one another with a new suspicion. If not outright hatred.

"But why? Why would anyone want us dead?" Diana again. She looks round the table, points at the old man, Len. "You. Do you want me dead?"

Len looks surprised. "I've only just met you. I don't know you well enough to want to kill you."

"Exactly," says Diana. "None of us have ever met this Boyd person before, we've not even heard of him, so why us? Why does he want to pick on us?"

"That's something you'll need to discover for yourselves, I'm afraid," says Amanda.

"This is bullshit," says the student. "Absolute bullshit. It sounds like something out of Agatha Christie, like we're all somehow responsible for someone's death and have to be punished, one by one. Revenge for something none of us know we did. Pathetic." He laughs.

"Yes," says Sylvia, "but it's not Agatha Christie, is it? This is real life. No matter how strange it might feel, it's real life. It's here and it's happening." Her voices rises in pitch.

"Please," says Amanda. "Giving in to hysteria won't help." She pauses, reestablishing control. Continues. "Perhaps you all did contribute to someone's death. Or are responsible for some wrongdoing. Or are going to do something that has to be stopped. I don't know."

"Really?" says the American girl. "Even me? I'm not even from the same continent as everyone else."

"Well, it might be something else, then." Amanda's getting exasperated. "You'll have to work that out among yourselves."

"So, to reiterate," says the captain, "we're trapped in here with people we don't know and we all may or may not be responsible for some calamity that may have befallen some person as yet unknown to us. Is that correct?"

"I said I didn't know if that's the case. It might be. Or there could be something else that binds you all together."

"I don't have time for this bullshit," says Diana. "I've got work to do."

"But the one thing you do know," says the captain again, ignoring Diana's outburst, "is we're trapped in here with no way out and a madman—or men, or women, or any combination—is on the loose trying to hunt us down and kill us? Is that right?"

"I said you were all shut in here. I didn't say there was no way out."

The mood in the room changes as hope rears its duplicitous head among the guests.

"So there is a way out?" asks Sylvia.

"Context. Or at least a bit." Amanda takes a laptop out of her tote bag, a USB stick from her jacket pocket, and inserts it into the laptop, attaching it to a cable on the floor connected to what they now see is a projector. The curtains at the far end of the room are lit up. She perches on the edge of the table and hits a key as an image appears on the curtains. The face of a young blond woman. Smiling, happy, out with friends who have been cut from the image. The kind of photo that could have been taken from a social media account, that seems innocuous enough on its own.

"This is Claire Swanson. Nineteen years old, a university student. She disappeared from her home last night. She's the fifth girl to go missing in as many months. And if you want to get out of here, you have twelve hours to find her."

"Us?" says the student. "How?"

"Please. Watch and listen. You'll now see photos of the four others. Please study them closely and see if you recognize any of them."

A slideshow follows. Four faces appear, all looking similar to the first young woman. As each appears, Amanda reads off the corresponding names. "Carrie Phillips. Lucy Tollund. Jamie Morgan. Danielle Ward."

The images linger on the screen, long enough to imprint their faces on the viewers. To see details at the edges, get a sense of a life lived, of them as human beings, rather than faceless victims. Real people whose absences create terrible, unfillable voids in others' lives. High school, college, or family snapshots. All blond, all happy. Young girls enjoying their lives.

"These are the before images. Now here's the afters."

New images appear. In stark contrast to the initial photos, these are official police photos. Naked bodies being pulled from shallow graves, the whiteness of their skins contrasting with the dark, rotting earth around them, close-ups of wounds. Then shots of them lying on mortuary slabs waiting to be cut open.

"Carrie Phillips. Lucy Tollund. Jamie Morgan. Danielle Ward. Please, no questions yet."

Amanda pauses while the diners make their expected horrified reactions. Not replying isn't sitting well with the guests, but they manage to stay silent. She continues.

"You'll notice they're all similar. Young, blond, white, pretty. The killer's type. A lack of obvious marks of a struggle suggest the perpetrator somehow gains the trust of each of their victims. Then they drug them. While in this state they're tortured, sexually assaulted, and their still-sedated naked bodies are buried alive in a shallow grave. They're wrapped in plastic sheeting and given a breathing tube attached to their mouths, which is connected to a canister containing a limited, measured supply of air. Enough for twenty-four hours. The perpetrator then contacts the police, leaves rudimentary clues and puzzles as to where the bodies are located, and gives the time remaining in which to reach the victims before their air runs out."

She pauses, making sure the information is being absorbed.

"The riddles this person leaves are deliberately obtuse. Despite the police's best efforts, no single girl has been found alive. For the third victim, Jamie Morgan, the puzzles were cracked and her location found. But she was dead by the time police arrived on the scene. Her killer turned off the air supply prematurely. And now the perpetrator has Claire Swanson. And this is where you all come in."

"Twenty-four hours," says the student, Kyle.

"You've been paying attention," she replies. "But you're half right. He *keeps* his victims twenty-four hours. He's had her for twelve. There's twelve left."

"Want to fill the rest of us in?" asks Diana.

Amanda moves her fingers over the laptop keys, makes another image appear. Grainy CCTV footage. A young woman walking down what looks like a dark suburban street. Trees, pools of light, houses either side. Old. Edwardian or Victorian. The video quality indistinct.

"This is Claire Swanson. Walking along a street beside where she lives, near the university." A blurred figure enters the screen, face obscured by what could be a hoodie, rushes toward her. Blurred action follows. Claire Swanson's arms raised in surprise or resistance, the figure doesn't allow her to retaliate. She is then subdued and dragged off. The street reverts to its previous calm self. The speaker closes the laptop and the screen goes blank. Amanda returns it to the tote bag and turns to the assembled group once more. Before she can speak, the old man, Len, asks a question.

"Where did you get that footage? That should be with the police."

Another glance toward the door. "I can't tell you. But let me just say . . . Twelve hours. That's the time you've got to find Claire Swanson."

The captain's straight on to his feet. "What are you talking about? This is a job for the police. How are we supposed to find this woman? We're stuck in this house."

Others begin to take up his cause, start to become vociferous.

"Please . . . please . . . you don't have time, listen . . ."

"Shut up," shouts Kyle, "listen to her."

The group, surprised at hearing another voice back her up, quiet down.

"Thank you," Amanda says, rather surprised. Then she gives another look toward the door and her actions become panicked once more. "Sorry, I've got to go. I've said as much as I can. Just remember this: find the killer and you'll find the girl and you'll find the way out. Or find the girl and avoid the killer and you'll find the way out. Twelve hours." She gives another anxious glance toward the door, gets up off the edge of the table. "I've told you what I can. It's a risk even saying this much. If they find out . . ."

"Who? Who find out? I mean, who even are you?"

"Doesn't matter. Find the killer, find the girl, find the way out. But avoid . . . well. Whatever."

"Whatever? You mean there are traps as well as a killer?" asks the captain.

"This isn't Agatha Christie," says Kyle, "more like *Saw*."

Amanda gives another anxious glance toward the doorway into the hallway. "Please just—"

She doesn't get to finish the sentence. A single gunshot rings out and her body is blown backward. Someone screams. The room is plunged once more into darkness.

Then there's uproar.

Get the lights! Somebody get the lights!"

I think that's me shouting. I certainly do shout, but there's suddenly so much noise it's impossible to tell. I'm on my feet along with everyone else, so it may have been someone else, or even everyone else. Some just screamed. But the lights are turned back on. By the old guy, I think, although I can't be sure.

"Nobody move! Everyone stay exactly where you are!" That's the other thing being shouted. I think that's the army guy but no one is listening to him. Everyone's all over the place.

The main thing people are doing is running for the door, hiding under the dining table, trying not to be the next one shot.

The woman called Amanda is no longer where she was standing. I run toward where she was to find the army captain already there. He's kneeling down over her prone body, checking her neck for a pulse. The carpet's quickly staining red, the gaping, ragged wound in her chest pumping blood out like a grotesque fountain. Her head's back, eyes unfocused and glassy. Empty. She's gone. The head shake the captain gives confirms it.

Realizing that the lights are on and there's no more shooting, people emerge from their hiding places and begin clustering round the body. Someone, the middle-aged woman—Sylvia, I think?—starts to shriek. I turn.

"Get her away, keep back. All of you, keep back."

Diana puts her arm round Sylvia's shoulder, not particularly tenderly, guides her away.

The American woman, Ramona, kneels down, joining the captain and me. "Dead?"

I nod, still keeping my eyes on Amanda's body.

"Pretty powerful handgun to do that."

"Well, you would know," says the old man—Len?—from behind her. "Being American, I mean."

She stands, turns to him. "Meaning what?"

"Meaning you're used to this kind of thing. Americans. Trigger-happy."

Ramona squares up to him, eye to eye. I notice that Len doesn't seem too fussed by the sight of a dead body. More about who did it.

I step between them. "Please. Someone's just been shot." I can barely believe the words coming out of my mouth. "Can we keep the dick measuring for later?"

Ramona raises an eyebrow, smiles. Len looks angry. But they both, reluctantly, back down.

The captain stands up. Shakes his head. "Dead before I reached her. Sorry."

My head is bursting with questions. More than questions. Practicalities. So, I presume, is everyone else's.

"Did anyone see anyone holding a gun?" I say to the assembled room. Naturally no one answers me. "Anyone?"

"We were all looking at her," says Diana, pointing to the dead woman.

"She did say there might be more people in the house than us," Cerys says.

"Obviously," says the old man. "Like she said, someone made the food and delivered it, someone must have rigged up this projector system. And that dinner gong didn't ring itself."

"And someone killed her, old chap." Iain, the drunk, is swaying as he talks.

"Is anyone here a doctor?" I ask, realizing I should have asked this earlier. Head shakes and mumbles. No one is a doctor.

Before anyone can say anything else, I feel a sudden buzz from my wrist. I glance down. My wristband has come to life. Red numerals appear on the black glass screen.

12:00:00
11:59:59
11:59:58

I look at the others. The same thing's happening to everyone.

The countdown has begun.

THE BEAST IN THE CELLAR

Told you, didn't I? Told you I wasn't the only monster in this house. Although strictly speaking I'm a beast and not technically a monster. However you might disagree. Semantics. Potay-to potah-to, your mileage may vary and all that. Anyway. That's by the by. Let's put a pin in that one, as they say in the more boring office meetings. At least I assume that's what they say. I wouldn't really know. I'm just a beast in the cellar, etc., etc.

Anyway, I digress. Because there's something else I should tell you. And it's this: I'm nowhere near the worst in this house. Beast, monster, whatever. Nowhere near. As you'll discover.

However, even as I say this you might think I'm lying. And I might be lying. Or I might not. Here's a little story to help you make your mind up. Or not, as it were.

When I was a child (Yes, I was once a child. I wasn't born as a beast in the cellar. It's not something one aspires to. But more of that later.), we went on a family holiday to Scarborough on the Yorkshire coast. You could go on this boat, the *Hispaniola* from Treasure Island. It would take you to Treasure Island itself and once there you had about twenty minutes to dig in the sand for doubloons before you went back to the mainland. I was with my dad and I had my bucket and spade with me. When we reached the island, there were old pirates wandering around, doing pirate voices and limping with wooden legs while an unseen parrot screeched about pieces of eight. I was totally convinced and got to digging. I found a doubloon or two. And I was happy. I'd been on the *Hispaniola* to Treasure Island, met pirates, and dug up doubloons. A great day out.

But as we stood in line with all the other dads and kids, waiting to board the *Hispaniola* and return to the mainland, the pirates showing their hooks for hands and Ah-Harr-ing to the crowd and making the kids laugh, I turned round. And wished I hadn't. Because there was one of the old pirates taking out a handful of plastic doubloons from his pocket and throwing them down on the sand, covering them over with his foot. And another one was resetting the tape of the squawking parrot and checking the hidden speakers. I checked my doubloons. They had Treasure Island embossed on them but they were only painted gold. Plastic. Not real treasure at all. Then I noticed the pirate waving his hook at us had a real hand underneath. You could see it at the end of his shirtsleeve. These weren't real pirates. They were middle-aged men who'd probably answered an advert in the local paper for unskilled seasonal workers. They weren't limping because they had wooden legs; given their ages, it was more likely to be arthritis and gout.

And when we headed back to the mainland, while all the other kids were counting their treasure and laughing about the pirates, I looked round to see where we'd come from. It wasn't an island, cut off from the rest of civilization, populated by pirates and parrots and reachable only by boat. It was just a spot farther along the coast dressed to appear like that. There was even a car park behind it.

That day stayed with me. Shaped me. I had allowed myself to be seduced by the trappings. I had succumbed to the illusion. And at the time I was upset to discover that something I had believed in was a lie. But as I grew older I kept that example in mind and I vowed to never fall for something like that again. The trappings, the setup, the execution. All real, all believable. So now, when someone tells me to look one way I look the other. Or at least I would if I wasn't shut up in this cellar. There's text and there's subtext. Remember that as you read on. Or don't. As I said earlier, it's up to you what—and who—you choose to believe.

CAPTAIN JIMMY SAINT

Now just a minute, just a minute . . . let's not panic, now . . ."

My voice is used to being obeyed. In my profession it can be the difference between life and death. I may not have been blessed with natural authority but by god I've worked at it.

"Remain . . . remain in your places. We need to . . ."

First the body and now the wrist things. The panic in the room has intensified to the point where no one is listening to me anymore. Staring instead at their neighbors with fear and distrust and in some cases outright hostility. My own soldiers are trained to listen and obey me. But these are civilians, unused to discipline and order. I shall have to remedy that. For their own good.

I unholster my pistol, aim it at the ceiling. And fire.

The sound reverberates around the room. I turned away as much as I could to deflect the blast but I'm still temporarily deafened in one ear. Plaster rains down over what remains of our meals, into wineglasses, and onto plates and heads. Plaster dust coats the dead woman's body, making it appear as some dusty heirloom for which I can only apologize to her. But I don't look down. I don't look up and see the damage I've incurred. I keep my gaze steady. A still point in the confusion. There is an imperative at play. These people need leadership, and they need it right now.

"Thank you," I say, once I have their attention. "Let us all remain silent. We now have one casualty, we're locked down into our positions; so it's important that we retain clear, cool heads. We need to think, strategize. We need a plan of action. We will not be helped by letting our emotions get the better of us."

Near silence falls over the room. The baby is sobbing. Its mother is cradling it, staring at me.

"Look what you've done," she says and there's no mistaking the anger in her voice. "You've upset my child. Put that gun away. What the hell's the matter with you, you mentalist?"

I realize I'm still holding my gun. Brandishing it, one might say. Waving it about to make a point. I also realize immediately how that might appear to civilians so I holster it. "I apologize," I say. "But it was the swiftest way to get your attention. We can't just panic."

"Why not?" The mother again. "Did *you* shoot her? You're the only one here who's armed."

Murmurs of discontent build at her words. Others find accusations in their voices. Right. Nip this in the bud.

"Stop, stop, all of you. No, I did not shoot her. This is a revolver." I hold it up for them all to see. "With only one bullet fired. Up there, in the ceiling. Whatever did that to . . . to . . . was a much more powerful gun. Much more powerful. As I'm sure our American friend can attest to."

I look toward this rather attractive American, who had previously spoken. "What is wrong with you people? First the old guy, now you. You think I did it, just because I'm American?"

"No, I—"

"You know how insulting it is? Not to mention tedious and stereotypical."

"I was just—"

"Who elected you leader, anyway?"

It's the woman with the baby again. Rage builds inside me. Some people have a problem with authority. This frumpy female's clearly one of them. Well, I'm trained to deal with this sort, the entitled, those who only think of themselves and can't see the bigger picture. I know how to get the best out of them.

"This is clearly an emergency situation," I say. "And as the chronometers on our wrists demonstrate, we have a mission and only a finite amount of time in which to complete it. We have to find this poor young girl before the time is up and get out of here."

"And what about who killed that woman?" The drunk this time. Liam? Iain, I think.

"It would appear everyone in this room is accounted for. So the shot must have come from someone else, agreed?" Get them to reach consensus. We'll get nowhere until I do.

The student crosses to the curtains, peeks behind them. "Someone could have shot her from here. We never thought of that. The bullet coming from the other side." He looks down at the body. "Is that the kind of mess being shot in the back would leave?"

"How do we know?" The hysterical middle-aged woman again. "We've already established none of us are doctors." She is ignored.

"And how did they get out again?" Diana, is it? The one with the clingy dress?

"In the general confusion, I suppose." The student again. "It was dark, everyone started screaming and running, easy to get away."

"If you know where you're going." The old man.

"And what about the . . . the body? We haven't mentioned the body . . ." The middle-aged woman again. Trying not to look at the body but unable to help herself. "We didn't even know who she was . . ."

Time to reestablish my authority. Again. Before the whole room descends into an unrecoverable anarchy. "Her name was Amanda. She told us that herself." They quiet down at that. My voice drops, deepens. "We need to move forward with a clearheaded plan. There's nothing more to be done for her now." I point to our casualty. "And since we don't know much about the layout of this house I suggest leaving the body here until we can find a place to put it. Her. Sorry. And then at the first opportunity, we inform the relevant authorities." I look round the group. It's important they take in my words. And act on them. "There's nothing more we can do for her. But we have a mission. Find this Claire Swanson woman and the absolute beast who has her."

"And what happens then?" It's the mother again. "I'm sorry, I don't mean to be insensitive, but to us, I mean. What if we don't find this Claire woman? Are we stuck here? Will we never get let out? Do we end up like her?" The last couple of words choked off.

I can't keep referring to her as the child's mother so I cast an eye at the place card where she sat but can only see half of it. I hazard a guess at the rest of it.

"Listen, Carrie—"

"Cerys."

"Cerys. Sorry." I pause. "Are you Welsh?"

"Does it matter?"

"Just trying to . . ." Build a rapport, like I've been trained to do. "Cerys. Right. And all of you. None of us know what will happen when the twelve hours are up. But that gives us the impetus to investigate, surely?"

Someone gets up from the table, leaves the room. It's the posh drunk. Liam? Iain. "Where d'you think you're going? Come back here. Now."

He doesn't. We hear him trying the main door in the hallway without success. Then we hear him hammering on said door, screaming and swearing at it. He returns to the dining room even more flushed than when he left.

"She was right, the bastard thing's locked. We're locked in . . ." He resumes his seat, reaches for his wineglass, and drinks, ignoring the sections of ceiling in it.

"So we're locked in," I continue. "And time's running out. You're right," I say, gesturing toward Cerys, as a concession toward humility. "I haven't been elected but I do have experience with this sort of thing." Then I do the thing I hate to have to do. Open it up for discussion. I know this sort appreciate the semblance of involvement, so I make a show of encouraging that. Even though the final plan will have to be mine. It's quite a skill and even though I say so myself, I'm quite the dab hand at it. "Has anyone got anything constructive to add?"

"Yeah."

It's the student. Always the first to go, that kind. Thinking a book-learned education makes them instantly more knowledgeable than a life lived in the field.

"Yes . . ." I squint at the name tag. "Ken?"

"Kyle, actually." He continues before I can give him the floor. Ill-mannered. "I saw someone before, out in the garden. It looked like they were dragging a body, on the way to bury it."

This brings a response from the table. Questions, gasps. I rush to take control again.

"Are you sure you saw this? Not a trick of the light?"

"Definitely not a trick. And I definitely saw it." He turns to Iain. "The doors are locked?"

Iain nods.

"Then," continues Kyle, "we have to find a way to get out into the garden and find it. But first we should search the house. Perhaps whoever it was brought the body in here."

"That's a good idea, son," says the old man whose name I can't see and don't know. "What about getting into twos? Searching round the house, then all meeting back down here at a prearranged time?"

"Seems sensible," says the woman in the clingy dress, Diana? "We can't just sit here and do nothing. At least that way, we'll be together and be able to keep an eye out for any . . ." She shudders. "You know."

"Right," says Kyle. "Let's do that, then. Who wants to—"

I stare in disbelief. The civilians are taking over. This is anarchy. I need to restore order. Immediately.

"Wait!" I shout. "Wait. We can't go running off willy-nilly. We need a plan. This can't be left in the hands of civilians."

"Civilians, are we?" I know who this is from the shrill tone of her voice. Sylvia. The middle-aged hysteric. I made that woman for trouble the minute I set eyes on her. "And we should leave all this to you, should we?"

"I am trained in these matters, yes. Therefore I consider myself best suited to take charge in a situation of this nature."

"Been in many locked old houses with a nutter on the loose?" asks the old man, making the student smirk. I could slap that stupid smile off his face. But I calm myself down. Don't let it show. Remain in command. There'll be time for recriminations later.

"We'll split into groups of two," I say, regaining the initiative. "Search the house. You—" I point at the student. "And you—" I point at Sylvia. "Check the ground floor."

"I'm not going with him," Sylvia says, making the student grin once more. "What if I don't come back? What if he's the murderer?"

"Then the rest of us'll know who to watch out for, sweetie," says the American. "Either that or he's had enough of you."

Sylvia looks about to burst.

"Fine," says the student, laughing. "I'll go on my own."

"I shall accompany Diana," announces Sylvia.

Diana seems somewhat shocked at this. "No, you won't," she says.

"Just . . . just go with the student," I say, trying to rescue the situation.

Sylvia stares daggers at me, at the student. Then reluctantly relents. "Fine. But I want you to know I'm not happy about this."

"Noted."

"I'll go with Cerys. And her baby. Make sure they're safe."

We all as one look at the creepy man sitting apart from the rest of the group. It's the first words he's spoken since sitting down. He's spent the whole of dinner eating slowly and staring at each of us in turn. Giving some of us more attention than others, I noted. And I noted which ones, too. All the while smiling a secret smile to himself. Very unpleasant. Not to mention unnerving.

"I'm fine on my own, thanks," says Cerys, visibly shivering.

"I'll come with you, honey."

It's the American girl in the revealing clothes. Ramona—I'm not good on accents, they all sound the same to me, but I think that twang's Texas. Not unattractive. Like everything else about her.

Cerys smiles. "Thank you."

Ramona nods. Desmond, the sleaze, looks very angry indeed.

"I'll poke around on my own, then," he says. No one jumps up to accompany him.

"Good man," I say. "So who does that leave us with?"

"Me, old chap," slurs Iain.

"You come with me," says the old man. Les? Len?

"Very well," says Iain, laughing. "We're all in the captain's regiment now."

I don't rise to it. He might be hilarious in some gentlemen's club in Mayfair among his own type but he certainly isn't here. "I think that's everyone sorted."

"Poor woman." The student again, glancing down at the body. He moves the dinner debris to one side, pulls the tablecloth from the table. He steps toward Amanda's prone body, drapes it over her. As the linen settles, blood soaks through the white material.

"Oh god . . ." Sylvia.

"Right," I say, to break the mood, focus the minds.

"Where you going to be then?" asks the student.

"Searching the house, of course." I feel that anger rise once more. I shouldn't be questioned. Especially not by the likes of him. I don't normally take an instant dislike to anyone but I've made an exception with him. However, for the sake of group harmony, not to mention expediency, I let it go. For now.

"OK. You've all got your assigned tasks."

"Yes, sir," says Iain, mock saluting.

I ignore him and continue. "I don't need to remind you all how serious this is. So let's get out there and save a life."

"And the sooner we do that, the sooner we can go home," says Sylvia.

"Hopefully," says Cerys.

They all file out, going their separate ways. And I'm left with a feeling of anger once more. That I've been outwitted somehow but I can't put my finger on how.

"Our timepieces have been synchronized for us. We'll reconvene here in twenty minutes," I call. "Twenty minutes, everyone . . ."

I'm sure they heard me. Of course they did. Because whatever else, the last word should definitely have belonged to me.

DESMOND BLAINE

So he thinks he can shut me down, does he? That jumped-up army man, that uniformed imbecile? With his slim hips and his strong jaw, and his commanding voice and his . . . his . . .

No. No. Don't let him get to you. He's nothing. *Nothing*. Don't let it show. Keep your face like stone. *Stone.* Stone. Don't show *anything*. That's it. There. That's better. Just get up with the others, rise and follow. Rise and follow. You don't need him to tell you what to do. You don't need them. Any of them. You just need yourself. The only one you've ever needed. Rely on yourself for now, for always. And most importantly, for what you're about to do.

No. Don't smile. Don't. Don't let them see that. This is supposed to be serious. An important thing. A serious moment. You know how to do this, Desmond, you've watched them, you've learned from them. Learned to mimic the way they behave. Laugh when they laugh. Look upset when they look upset. Cry when they cry. Well, that last one's still a work in progress, but no matter. It's all mimicry. Like the monkeys in the zoo having a tea party. Watch, learn, then copy. And they'll never notice the difference. So stop smiling while they're all around you. Wait until you're alone. And then you'll have plenty to smile about.

I spotted them straightaway. I always do. The limping ones at the back of the herd, the weakest in the pack. They give off an aura, a smell. One or the other. It's either chemical and I can smell it or it's something else, the essence of a person and something within me responds. It's either science or magic, I don't know. I've spent a long time thinking about it and I still haven't decided. Maybe I don't want to know, just enjoy the mystery. Having a definite answer would be like knowing where the magician hides his rabbits and playing cards and flowers. There would be no magic anymore. And with that gone I might not enjoy it so much. So I don't pry. And in the meantime, when I need my skill, my smell, my aura, it's always there.

They're leaving the room now. I dawdle by the door, trying to look like I'm deciding which way to go while hiding what I'm really doing. Which is watching the weakest walk away and letting enough time elapse before I can follow at a safe distance without one of the other busybodies trying to stop me. I'm not going to let anyone stop me from having my fun. Not this time. Oh no. The feeling's too strong within me now. The smell. The aura. And it has to be indulged.

I watched them all through dinner. But I was very clever about it, no one noticed me doing it. If anyone looked at me they would have seen me as the perfect dinner guest, attentive and interested in what was going on around the table, in the moment, as I've heard them say, and none of them, *none of them* would have guessed what I was really thinking. I've gotten so good at it it's frightening.

Because I know what they all are. Especially the women. I don't need to talk to them, to ask them. They tell me. Oh, not with anything as boring as words, but with gestures, implanted thoughts, imaginings. They telepathically let me know what they *really* are. They can't help it. They give off signals and I'm a receiver.

There's that one with the clinging dress sitting next to the student. I know right off what she is because she tells me. With her mind. Her signals. Slut. Bitch. Whore. And that's all I need to know. She has nothing I can possibly want. Oh, she looks good in her finery, but she can't hide what's really inside her because I can smell it. Oozing out of her like pus from a diseased organ. It disgusts me. Almost put me off my ham and chips.

Then there's the old maid, Sylvia. There's nothing oozing out of her. Nothing liquid at all. I smell only desiccated skin and dust. The dust of old leaves and dead pages. Forgotten tomes in cold wooden shelves. That's what she reeks of. I see her where she belongs, in the dark. Not the wonderful, myriad darkness that envelops and bewitches, but the other dark, the cold, flat dead one. The only sounds heavy breathing and occasional footsteps echoing away to nothingness. She thinks she has conquered the body, embraced a life of the mind. It's a belief that's almost pathetically laughable. Because all she's done is hide from life in that darkness, scared to come out, existing only behind the covers, among the shelves. And her knowledge has brought her nothing. She has so much hatred. It shimmers from her in raging waves like a desert mirage. And she thinks she's smarter than everyone else in the room. She looks at the rest of them—and me, too—with disdain. But that just makes me smile. Because I see what's behind that mask of disdain. Fear. It's quite arousing, actually. Later, for fun, I might put it to the test.

I file her away and move on to the next ones.

There's Ramona, the American. She's everything the slut isn't. Young, beautiful, dark and alluring. The kind that ensnares. The kind to beware of. Even if I can't sense her aura I know she's a trap. And I'm not going to fall into that.

But she's gone off upstairs with the mother and baby. And now we're getting somewhere. Cerys and the baby. The mother isn't interesting although she could have been once, not so long ago. But she's too far gone now. She's not a trap like Ramona, but she could be on her way to being a slut like Diana. I get that aura, that smell from her. She's young to have that but I'm very rarely wrong. Not as strong as the other one, of course, but left alone it'll build. Nature, that sick, crippled thing that goes from birth to decay on our planet with monotonous, daily regularity, has already seen to that.

So that leaves just Monica. The baby of the group.

The doll. That's what she is. A perfect little doll. A tiny human, not yet infected by all that corruption and sin. There's only an aura of light around her. A smell of purity. I can't explain what purity smells like but I know it when I smell it. It's the opposite of the disease and decay the others have. It's light and innocence. It's alive with possibility. It's the most beautiful thing in the world to experience.

She sat quietly throughout dinner, eating diligently, refusing eye contact with the other diners. I was content to just observe, bask in her reflected light. I will talk to her soon, though. And she will reply to me. Not with words. But we will communicate. And we will understand each other. We will share a communion on a deeper and richer plane than anyone round this table with their boring, dull minds and lives can ever imagine. It will be the most intense and perfect experience of her young life.

The ultimate experience.

And now she's gone upstairs with her mother and that American.

From a discreet distance, I follow.

I am the shadow flowing unnoticed. I am the knife glinting in the darkness.

I must remember not to smile.

Sylvia and I leave the dining room. Waves of resentment emanate from her like an overpowered radiator. I'm tempted to say something to annoy her but I stop myself. After all, my wishes have been overridden too. We decide to search the ground floor because Sylvia declares if we use the elevator we might miss something, but from her expression and tone it seems that elevators, even ones with open cages, are on her list of things she either disapproves of or, as I suspect, is fearful of.

"Let's try the front door." Surely she can't argue with that. But apparently she can.

"Iain tried that. It's locked. That woman told us it was locked. Besides, we don't know what's out there, or where we are. Or who's out there waiting for us."

"No, we don't. So let's see if we can open it and find out."

It's a double door. Huge, old, wooden. Exactly the kind you would expect a house like this to have. I grab the huge worn circular metal handle and give it a twist. It doesn't budge. I pull harder. Nothing.

"Is it locked? It's locked, isn't it? Of course it's locked. I told you that was a waste of time."

I keep pulling but nothing else happens. Me against this door, even if it weren't locked, would be an uneven contest so there's really no point in persisting. I check the edges to see if there's a bolt or anything holding it shut. I can't find anything. I stand back, look at it.

"Well, that's that. Let's go back and rejoin the others." She's visibly relieved.

"We haven't even started. Come on, this way."

"What if I don't want to?" Sylvia can't hide the fear in her voice now. It's broken through the layer of indignation.

"Stay here, then. Or go back to the dining room with, you know."

"That's a horrible thing to say."

I round on her, barely keeping my temper in check. "I don't want to be here either, okay? I'm pretty shocked by what I've just seen, to put it mildly. And for all I know you could be a murderer. But I want to get out of here. And the captain's right, this seems like the best way to go about it. So are you coming?"

I move away. I'm halfway down the hall before I realize she's not with me. I turn. She hasn't moved, standing there with her head down, shoulders gently shaking. She's crying.

I'm too embarrassed to move. I just stand there, looking at her. It's like I'm intruding on a kind of private grief, even though I know I caused her upset. And I feel bad for that. But there's a part of me that thinks it serves her right. If she can't take it, then she shouldn't go round dishing it out. But then I remember the fear I glimpsed behind her eyes and understand her a bit more.

I walk slowly toward her. "Sorry," I say. "That was . . . I was out of order. It's . . . It's been a day." I try a smile, hoping she'll respond.

Eventually she nods, takes a handkerchief from the sleeve of her blouse, wipes her eyes, blows her nose, replaces it.

"Come on," I say, much quieter now. "Let's keep going."

She nods once more. The silence between us is uncomfortable. I can sense she feels badly about letting me witness her breakdown, her weakness. So I say nothing further, deciding it might be more use to just try to act like nothing's happened.

We walk through a set of double doors into what seems to be a lounge or drawing room. I find a light switch on the wall, flick it on. A dusty, discolored chandelier pushes out weak yellow light from above. Overstuffed brocaded armchairs and sofas dot the space. Looks like a cloud of decades-old dust would erupt if you sat down too hard on them. Every inch of wall is taken up with bookshelves. Old, dark, heavy. Mahogany, I'd say. Solid enough to have been here for centuries. The shelves are crammed with books. Most look as old as the shelves, leather-bound and weighty. Equally old rugs cover the dark floorboards, expensive and vibrantly patterned, presumably plundered mementos of Western expeditions to the once mysterious East. The whole room smells musty, like it's been closed off, left to decay. There's nothing here that identifies the owner of this house, though. No personal keepsakes or knickknacks. It's

impossible to say who lives here. Apart from Roger Corman–era Vincent
Price, of course. He would fit right in, sitting, legs crossed, in one of those
armchairs, wearing a smoking jacket and cravat, nursing a large globe of
brandy, and planning some deliciously camp cruelty.

The room does, however, have windows. Or I presume so, as there are
huge closed wooden shutters all around the bay.

"Is this a library, d'you think?"

"Well, it has books in it, Sylvia, so it's as good a guess as any."

"I don't need that kind of impertinence, thank you."

She seems to have recovered. I cross to the bay window. "Why don't
you have a look at the books? See if there's anything there that tick-
les your fancy." I hear her huffing behind me as she moves over to the
bookcases.

I try one of the shutters. It's stuck as fast as the front door. I pull harder.
Nothing. Like the shutters are bonded to the window frames. I try to prize
one corner away, just to get a glimpse beyond. Nothing. I may as well try
to move one of the walls. Precisely like Amanda said.

"Someone definitely doesn't want us to see out. Or get out," I say.

I look around the room. Sylvia is still staring at the bookshelves. Having touched a book, she's searching for something to wipe her hands on.

"Any good titles?"

"No."

"Oh, come on, there's usually something in these old books. Stuff like
A Queer Summer, or *Biggles Takes It Rough*, something like that."

"There are no titles of any kind. Not even your puerile ones. On any
of the books. See?"

She gestures toward the shelves, not wanting to get too near in case
the books carry something contagious.

I look for myself. She's right. There's nothing on the spines to identify
what's in the books. I take one off the shelf. A cloud of paper dust ac-
companies it. I open the book. Nothing. The pages are blank. Touching
them they seem old, but there's nothing printed on each page. I examine
it closely, thinking that perhaps the ink has faded over time. But that's
not the case. No indentations of any kind. There's never been anything
on these pages.

"Why do this?" she says. "Why go to all this trouble?"

"I don't know," I say as calmly as possible, trying to counter the rising hysteria in her voice. "It's like they're film props, or something. Stage props. Not real. Is *any* of this real?" I replace the book, check round the room. I don't know what I'm looking for but there's nothing else there. No surprises. No secret trapdoors or passages that I can see. "Let's move on."

We leave the room by another door. And find ourselves in a hallway. I'm trying to get my bearings. This seems to be leading toward the rear of the house. It gets darker the farther we go, the light from the study receding into dimness.

"So d'you think we could be related, Sylvia?"

She actually harrumphs in response. "I doubt that very much."

"Just, you know, seeing if there might be a connection between us. Something that could tell us why we're all here. You never know, we might be distantly related. Where you from again?"

"Kettering."

"Where's that?"

"If you don't know where it is, then I doubt you have any family there. You would know."

I'd know if they were all like you, I think, *and I'd never visit.*

"Anyway, that's ridiculous."

"What is?"

"Any of us being connected."

"Really?"

"Are you honestly saying I could be related to that Black American trollop? Fanciful rubbish."

"Yeah, well," I say, trying not to let my anger show, "earlier today if you'd said I'd be stuck in an old, dark house with nine strangers and a dead woman searching for a missing girl, fanciful wouldn't have covered it. But hey, look at us now."

She's clearly getting annoyed with me. "Can you find a light switch? This passageway is too dark to see in."

I let my fingers crawl across the cold plaster. I want to find one, too, but part of me doesn't just to spite her. As it happens, it's a moot point. "Can't find one."

We walk on, the dark encroaching farther. We're going to run out of light soon.

"There must be a light switch somewhere." I can sense Sylvia's getting desperate.

My fingers brush something. I stop, alight on the object, grasp it. A candelabra. "Got a light?"

"Of course not."

I haven't, either, and I'm about to give this up when my hand touches a small box at the base of the candelabra. Matches. I quickly light all five candles. It throws out a scrawling, spider light against the wall, giving us glimpses of our surroundings.

We must have wandered into a completely different wing of the house. In fact, it looks and feels like it could be a completely different house. A much older one judging by the architecture. There are no carpets, only huge stone flags. They feel worn, rounded and smooth from centuries' worth of feet walking on them but they gleam as well, as if they're new and have just been aged artificially, if that makes sense. The walls are half wood paneled to about waist height, plastered stone the rest of the way up. The ceiling is massive, curved wooden slats and struts, like the inverted hull of a huge old ship. I'm getting that film set vibe again. But this one is more historical Poe, medieval, all tights and codpieces and pits and pendulums. We keep walking.

"I refuse to believe I have anything in common with anyone else in this house," Sylvia says, continuing the previous conversation as we walk.

"So why d'you think you're here, then, Sylvia?"

"I haven't the faintest idea. I don't know what I've done to deserve this."

"Could it be a game, d'you think? A test? We've all been brought here to play a murder mystery game and whoever solves the puzzle wins?"

"With someone having already been killed? If this is a game, then whoever devised it has a sick mind. And I want nothing to do with them. Just let's find this girl and get out."

I check the watch on my wrist. Over ten minutes gone. Before I can speak further I hear a noise. It stops me in my tracks. A girl crying. Wailing.

"Can you hear that?"

"What?"

"A girl. Crying. There she is again."

"I can't hear anything apart from you blathering on about—"

"Shush. There it is again." Definitely a girl crying, sobbing. I can hear the hopelessness in her voice. It sounds like it's far away but it can't be because I can hear it inside this corridor. She's asking for help. No, begging for help.

"It's coming from somewhere along here," I say, and I start knocking on the wooden paneling, seeing if there's a hidden door somewhere. "Here, hold that." I pass Sylvia the candelabra.

She scurries along behind me, almost allowing the candles to go out. "You must be imagining it. And if you're not, if you're doing this to upset me, then I'll regard that in very poor taste." Anger rises in her voice but I have no time to consider her now. I need to find the source of the voice, find the girl.

The paneling gives up nothing, but eventually we reach a door. It doesn't seem like it leads to the outside but in this house I can take nothing for granted. I turn the handle. It opens. I look at Sylvia. "Shall we?"

Her face betrays her inner turmoil. She doesn't want to step through, confront whatever's on the other side. But neither does she want to stay in the dark hallway by herself. She disguises her fear and lack of options with angry bluster. "Come on, then. Let's get it over with."

I step over the threshold. Sylvia follows. Another room. Cold, dark. I search for a light switch on the wall, find nothing. Sylvia sweeps the candelabra round.

"It's a kitchen," she says.

I step father in for a closer look. It hasn't been used in ages, if at all. I start examining things.

"Well, they certainly didn't cook our dinner in here, that's for sure."

"No," I say. She's correct. A huge Victorian-type range dominates one wall. The cupboards all seem to date from the same period, as far as I can tell. The bare, unfinished floor also. Utensils hang round the walls, pots and pans cover the worktops. The kitchen is big enough to house a whole army of cooks to serve an awful lot of guests. But there's something else. Something clearly not right.

I pick up one of the pans from a worktop. "Check this out," I say. "It's never been used. In fact it couldn't be used. It's like dollhouse stuff. Look."

I hand her the pan. Sylvia puts the candelabra down, takes the pan as if it's about to bite her. Examines it. It's rough, unfinished. Clunky. Like an afterthought. The whole kitchen is the same. One wall's even unpainted. Then I hear it again. That faint sobbing. I look around, trying to pinpoint where it's coming from. Not in the room. But at the far end is a door. The kind that leads outside.

"Come on." Before Sylvia can object I move to the door. If she wants to remain in light, she has no option but to follow. She does.

The door is old, heavy and wooden, as expected and, of course, sealed shut. I turn to Sylvia. "This must lead out to the garden, where I saw someone dragging what looked like a body earlier."

"Or thought you did. Like you said, this just might be an elaborate game." The desperation of wanting to believe her own words.

"Maybe. But I definitely heard a voice before we came in here, even if you didn't." I stand still once more, willing the voice to return but it doesn't.

"Well, it's gone now, whatever it was."

I'm straining to hear but she might be right. I can't hear anything.

"We'd better get back to the others," says Sylvia.

I stare at the door. "Suppose that makes sense."

We turn and walk away. Through the kitchen, back to the corridor.

As we go I start to hear it again, faintly and becoming more so the farther away I get, a girl sobbing.

What I saw on the stairs before dinner unsettled me. But I didn't want to say anything to the others until I'd had a chance to confirm it closeup. Make sure I was right. And I hope I'm not. I hope what I glimpsed—and it was just a glimpse through the bars of the lift cage so that's my get-out—isn't what I thought it was.

I don't get far across the main hallway before stopping to take off my shoes. Louboutins are incredibly beautiful but ridiculously high, belonging in a design museum rather than on my feet and definitely not the kind of thing one can bear to wear for long or to walk any length in. They do scream power, however, and give my legs great shape so I consider the pain worth it. And they look even better in the bedroom. But that's beside the point. My feet are cold and make echoing slaps as I walk but I don't care.

I carry them in my left hand and smooth down the hem of my tight little black Prada dress with my right as I start to ascend the stairs. My outfit is rope-tight around my thighs, hugely constricting and keeps rising up. Not practical in the least but I know how much couture goes for and I don't want to tear it because whoever set this whole thing up is not getting it back. It fits perfectly (Thank god I didn't give in and gorge at dinner!) and it's leaving this house with me.

I reach the first landing. The portraits haven't started yet so I've still got a ways to climb. It doesn't take me long but I'm dragging my feet because obviously I want to put this off as long as possible. But I suppose I have to find out, one way or another.

I reach the paintings. I'm shaking from more than the climb and the lack of food. I'm trembling with the thought of discovery.

I look at the first one, the last one I saw from the lift cage. It's a military man all right, in full gear standing in what he probably thinks of as a heroic stance, holding his gun in one hand, commanding his soldiers forward toward the enemy with the other. A platoon? A squadron? I don't know what they're called but they're all running behind him. He looks the part, like he's really at home on a battlefield, ordering people about in life-and-death situations. He appears confident too. Like his word could never be questioned. Like he's right and he knows he is. And, yes, you've guessed it. It's Captain Jimmy Saint.

I examine it further, in close-up. It's been done recently, although it's not in a contemporary style. Oil on canvas, with an attention to detail like the old masters.

I move to the next one. It's Kyle, the student. Sitting in what I presume to be his apartment or room in a shared house, looking intently at his laptop, his features lit by the screen's glow. Behind him the walls are covered with old film posters and crammed bookshelves. He appears studious, erudite. And his clothes are . . . it's hard to explain. You know in Hollywood films when movie stars play ordinary people and wear ordinary clothes yet still make them look like the kind of thing movie stars would wear and make you think, ooh, I should get some jeans like those? Yes. Like that. Stylized? I don't know. Like he's a perfect example of a student, just as Jimmy Saint is of an army officer.

My heart skips as I see whose painting is next. Me. This is what I saw from the lift. When was this done? How do I not know about it? The others I could accept, because I don't know anything about them and they could have something to do with this house, but not *me*. Never set foot in it before in my life. So how can my painting be here among all the others? It doesn't make sense.

I study it. It's a sideways view of me in my office, behind my desk, and I'm leaning back in my chair on the phone. Through the glass windows and doors you can see people running around, but I'm perfectly still. The eye of the storm. Despite the circumstances, the situation, I have to say I quite like it. Then I change my mind. Because the way I'm stretched out, the way I've been depicted, makes me look fat. Immediately I feel depressed and hate myself even more for what I did actually eat at dinner.

I park that and try to see it more objectively. Like the other two it looks like I've posed for this and for quite some time given the painstaking quality of the brushwork. But I haven't. I know I haven't. I don't think I've ever posed for a photographer in that position and yet . . . there's something niggling in my mind. Now that I've seen the painting and confirmed that it's me and despite it being almost impossible, it feels like, on some kind of hidden or unacknowledged level, I do know about this painting. Somehow, somewhere, I remember it in some way. Like a repressed memory coming back.

"Interesting, aren't they?"

I jump. And scream as well, I think.

"Oh, sorry, I didn't mean to startle you. I thought you knew I was there."

I turn to see who's behind me. It's the old man. Les. No, Len. He's smiling at me, standing at the entrance to the hallway. He doesn't look sorry.

"I didn't . . . didn't see you there."

He nods. "No, it seems not. The older you get, the more invisible you become."

I frown. "Aren't you supposed to be with Iain?"

He sighs and smiles at the same time. "I get the impression Iain prefers his own company. Rather a lone wolf, so to speak." He continues before I can reply. "Imagine you were quite taken aback seeing these." He examines the paintings. "I know I was."

"You're in this lot as well?"

Another nod. "We all are. Here, I'll show you."

I follow him up the stairs as he points them all out.

"There's me, in my allotment. Holding some leeks, I think." He laughs. "Wish I could grow them that size in real life. There's the dog next to me. And next one along there's Sylvia, sitting in her living room with a cup of tea."

Sylvia is surrounded by what I can only describe as a floral hellscape. She's trying to smile, but perched on the edge of an armchair with a dainty bone china cup and saucer that she seems more scared of breaking than drinking from, it doesn't look likely.

"Ramona. She's a one . . ."

Len stares at this painting for a longer time than the others. I can see why. The American girl is near naked and pole dancing (God, I'd kill for her body.) It makes an interesting juxtaposition next to Sylvia.

He was right, we're all there. Cerys and her baby, Monica, out at a park. They look happy but Cerys seems to be watchful, as if expecting someone she doesn't want to see. Or fearful of someone taking the child away.

Iain with his bow tie undone and a drink to hand at a roulette table in some swanky casino. Smiling, of course, even though he's losing. Which I can't tell from the painting, I just presume he is.

And then there's the last one. Desmond. I recoil even looking at it. He's sitting in an old armchair in the bay window of a squalid living room. Behind him, filthy, rotting net curtains obscure the view outside, bringing the viewer's gaze back to the depressing interior. The carpet looks like it hasn't been vacuumed in years, every surface filthy with dust and detritus. There are magazines strewn on the furniture and DVD boxes on the floor. He's dressed in joggers and a stained old vest. And he's smiling. Smiling like he's the happiest he's ever been, ever could be. An emperor in his empire of dirt? A lord in his manor of filth?

"God, that's horrible," I say.

"Yes," says Len, and it's the first time there's a lack of cheer in his voice. "It is." He sighs.

I inch closer to Desmond's painting, trying to make out the titles of the magazines and DVDs.

"Oh my god . . ."

"What is it?"

"Look at the magazines. The titles. They're all . . . child porn."

"Oh. Oh no. The DVDs as well. Oh. That's horrific." More than a lack of cheer in Len's voice now, an edge of anger.

"Let's get away from here," he says. "There's no sign of anyone along this corridor. All the doors seem to be locked. Should we try another?"

I look down where he's indicating. It's long and dark. The kind of hallway where unknown things loom out of the shadows. The kind of hallway a stranger who's just appeared beside me and might be lying about who he really is would want me to walk down. I glance at the timer on my wrist. That gives me the excuse I need not to accompany him.

"Time's getting on. Maybe we should be getting back to the dining room. See if the others have found anything."

He shrugs. "As you wish." He starts off down the stairs.

I follow him. Seeing that painting of Desmond is even worse than discovering the one of myself. A truly horrifying depiction. As I walk I try desperately not to look behind me.

I know it's only a painting, but I feel those eyes watching me as I go.

RAMONA O'ROURKE

This girl, Cerys, with the kid seems kind of dumbstruck. And I'm stuck with her. She hasn't said anything, just looked around like she can't believe she's here. You and me both, sister.

But that's OK. She seems kind of vulnerable. She wouldn't be the first vulnerable kid I've been stuck with and had to take care of. I have to say something, break the ice with her. "So how old's Monica, then?"

It's like Cerys is in a trance and my words have hardly penetrated.

"Monica?"

"What?"

"Your kid. How old is she?"

"Oh." Cerys has to think of an answer. She peers down at Monica, little legs swinging in her chest papoose, looking everywhere and taking everything in. Even if her mother doesn't seem to be. "Nearly two. No, just over two. Had her birthday recently."

"Two? Isn't she a bit big for that papoose?"

"I don't have her pushchair with me. So it's this or nothing."

Good an answer as any, I suppose.

We're only on what the Brits in their fussy old way would call the first floor, or what I would call the second floor, walking along a hallway above the dining room. Cerys said she didn't want to go too far with the baby strapped to her.

We walk, trying doors, finding them locked, the kid watching the whole time, fascinated but not speaking, when I notice Cerys is looking at me. No, not looking, staring. Fascinated, like I'm something in a zoo that she hasn't seen before. It's uncomfortable.

"You OK?" I ask.

My words snap her out of her spell. "Oh. Yeah." She smiles. "Where are you from? Your accent . . ."

"Texas. Lone Star state. Yee haw, and all that."

"You lived there all your life?"

"Not yet," I reply and laugh. That seems to do something to her, move something inside her, and she joins in. It's a proper laugh. Really out of place in this house.

"You've got a lovely laugh," she says. "It's real. Makes you want to join in when you hear it."

"You just did."

She smiles. "I just did." Then frowns, like she wants to say something else. I wait. "You're a warm person. I like that. I like being near warm people. Sharing their light."

"OK . . ."

She blushes. "Sorry. That sounds a bit weird. I guess I mean, you're safe. To be around, like. I can feel it."

"You sure I'm not the murderer?"

Another shy laugh. "I think I'd get a vibe, and I don't. And your voice is warm. Not like this house. Cold and dark. I hate the cold and I hate the dark. I like light and warmth."

"And that's what you're getting from me?"

She doesn't reply, just shyly nods. I know that look. I've had it before. I don't say anything.

We continue on. She keeps talking. She's opening up now. "What d'you do? For work, I mean?"

I smile at her. "Stripper."

She tries not to look at my body but it's too late. I catch her doing it. "Oh. Right." Head down again. Blushing.

"Oh, come on," I say. "I've got a master's in Business and Finance from an Ivy League university. I can pick and choose what I want to do. And what I want to do at the moment is show the world my physical confidence. Or at least those who can afford it. I don't work for free."

"Oh. I thought strippers were all . . ."

"Oppressed? Forced into it? Trafficked? Exploited?"

She blushes again. "I was going to say prostitutes."

Telling people my job is a good way to gauge if we're going to get on or not. I've heard all the responses. Some people get angry, think I'm disgusting. What I do is disgusting. Some get kind of pervy about it, talk to me like I must be sexually charged the whole time, always ready to fuck.

Cerys just seems a bit naive. It's quite sweet, really. "Yeah. Some of them," I say. "Maybe. But it's a job like any other. You work at it, you get good, you get paid. I've got a nice body and I like showing it off. I know what the men are thinking when they're watching me and I also know they're too scared to do anything about it. Dancing onstage in front of a paying audience is a power relationship. And I'm the one in charge. They're the ones who are being exploited. Not me."

"Sounds like you've said that speech a lot."

"Different variations of it. Handy to remember it."

Cerys gives a nervous laugh, looks down at herself. "I must admit," she says, voice quiet and hesitant, "I feel very dowdy next to you."

"Why?"

"Well, you're . . . you know. You've got that glow. Confidence, and that. And I—"

I stop. Take her chin in my hand, stare her straight in the eyes. "You're beautiful as well, kid."

And she is, genuinely. She can't meet my eyes. Pulls away.

"Surely your husband tells you that? Boyfriend, whatever?"

She shakes her head.

"Girlfriend? I don't judge."

"I . . . it's just me and Monica. When I had her, I gave up everything else. She's my full-time job now. Don't have the energy for anything else. Any*one* else." She sighs. Then kind of realizes where she is, who she's with. "I'm sorry. Sorry."

"What for?"

"I've only just met you. You don't know me. And here I am, telling you my boring life story. You don't want to hear me babbling on. Sorry."

"I think you're a bit lonely. And you've got someone to talk to."

"Yes, yes. You're right. It does get kind of lonely bringing up a kid on your own. I'm not used to it, this talking to a grown-up."

"Don't your family help out?"

Her features change, harden. "No. They don't. It's just me and her. I have to protect her. I'm her . . ." She pauses again. "Mother."

She falls silent after that, staring at one of the doors at her side, like that's the end of the conversation, or she's said more than she wants to. I can take a hint. Change the subject.

"So did you just wake up in your room too?" I ask her, not waiting for an answer. "And I guess we're in England. Or Scotland or Wales. Wherever."

"That student said we might even be in Eastern Europe." She sounds scared saying it.

"That's even farther for me. I mean, the airfare from Texas to England would be huge enough. Not to mention the time it would take, I mean, how would they keep me out for over ten hours? I presume they must have done that. Drugged me to get me here. God knows what with. And before that they'd have to get me in and out of airports, check my passport . . . Jesus . . . All that happened and I don't remember a thing about it. What about you?"

"Yes, I woke up here too. Monica was in her cot at the side of the bed."

"Same here. One minute I was . . . I dunno. In my apartment? Yeah. That's the last thing I remember. Next thing, I'm waking up in the room here, which even looks kinda like my apartment at home. And they haven't just brought me, they've brought some of my stuff too. Clothes, you know." I shake my head. "This is some next-level weird shit."

"Why would anyone go to all this trouble? That's what I can't work out. And why us? Why me? I'm nobody special. I don't know the others and I've never met you before. I'd remember that. And you. You don't seem scared. Or fazed by any of this, confused even. You're taking it all in your stride. Accepting what's going on. Even someone getting killed in front of us."

There's something about this girl that brings something out in me. Not a maternal instinct, fuck no. But I do find myself wanting to be strong for her, protect her. I guess she's about my age but she seems younger, more naive. No self-confidence at all, bless her heart. I don't think telling her I'm scared, too, and just trying not to show it will make her feel any better. "Life's for living, girl, it's all an adventure," I tell her. "Yeah, that death was awful but be honest. We didn't know her, so we can't really grieve for her. Or I can't. We all dodged a bullet there. Literally. All her death did, and excuse me if this sounds callous, is make me even more determined to get out of here. And we need our heads straight for that. Once we've found this missing girl and we're out, then we can grieve. Hey, who knows? Maybe none of this is real, even that death. I mean, how do I know you're not an actor? How do you know I'm not? We could be giving Netflix its biggest viewing figures ever. They might even have to vote for their favorite to not be killed." I make air quotes with my fingers, showing her I'm joking. She smiles. I readjust my top, pulling it even lower. She stares at my tits and her eyes widen. I'm in no doubt now what she's feeling for me. I give her my killer smile. "That being the case, I'm doing my darndest to make sure it's me they're voting for, honey."

I laugh and she joins in, but stops abruptly, suddenly self-conscious.

"Aren't you scared, though?" she asks. "We just saw someone get killed and . . ."

I laugh again. "And here we are walking round in the dark. Like I said, honey, we don't know what we saw. They can do all sorts of things with special effects."

Cerys seems like she's searching for the right reply. "I'm not an actor," she says eventually.

I have to smile. She looks so sincere when she says it. It's like she's led a sheltered life and this is the first time she's been away from her hometown. There's something very attractive about that kind of innocence.

"But I do feel safe with you." She touches my arm. Smiles. Then realizes she's gotten too close and drops her hand. Turns to the nearest door, clearly embarrassed. "Let's take a peek in here," she says. "Oh. This one's open."

She enters, I follow. It's not what I expected and, from her expression, not what Cerys expected, either. It's a nursery. But not an old nursery, the type you'd think an English (or wherever) country house like this would have, all tin spinning tops and blank-faced porcelain dolls, a dollhouse, and a rocking chair. It's modern, contemporary, like the kind of place I could imagine Cerys having for Monica. There's a cot with a mobile overhead, walls papered with cute smiling animals helping one another and having adventures, handmade toys made out of wood.

"I think Monica's got some of those toys," she says.

A line of storybooks on top of a brightly painted chest of drawers for a parent to read aloud. Cerys looks at me, a kind of guilt in her eyes. "This is like the perfect nursery for Monica. If I could afford it."

"And the complete opposite of anywhere else in this house," I say. "We got our rooms, I guess Monica's got hers."

Cerys straightens her back, lets out a sigh of pain.

"Back sore?"

She nods.

"Take the papoose off, put Monica down in the cot. Do you both good."

She does as I suggest. Sets Monica down in the cot where she just lies there, staring at the mobile. She seems happy enough. I check out the room.

"Anything interesting in that wardrobe?"

"Nothing. Unless you want baby clothes. Oh, look at this."

I've found a door in the side wall.

"A connecting door?"

"Might be. Let's see." I cross to it, turn the handle. It opens. "Yeah, come and see."

Cerys goes to pick up Monica again.

"Leave her there. She'll be fine for a minute. We're only going next door. Save your back."

Cerys looks down at the kid. The kid smiles back. "You're right; she'll be fine," Cerys says. "She's got this private language that she uses, plays this little game in her own little world between herself and her toys. Or even herself and her fingers sometimes, if she hasn't got toys to play with."

"Kids are imaginative."

"They are." Cerys keeps looking at Monica. Smiling down at her. "She'll make up little stories with her fingers, bend them into shapes, give them characters, get them to interact with each other. I have no idea what she's talking about or makes them talk about. But she gets totally engrossed, sometimes even gets angry with them. But usually she's just laughing."

I want to keep moving, but this seems like something important Cerys has to say. Maybe she doesn't get much of a chance to talk to anyone.

"I mean, I thought it was odd at first, how she would play her little games all by herself. I'd try to join in, ask her who the finger people were, what they were saying. But she would clam up. Sit there silently until I went away. Then her face would change and she'd start playing again. Like her little world closed down when I was there and opened up again when I left. So now I just let her get on with it. It's who she is and what she does."

She stares at the kid, content with her own company, her own space, and the kid looks back up at her as if to say, *Go on, I'll be fine. You'll only be a minute.* Cerys smiles, Monica smiles back, and, cynic though I am, it's a genuinely lovely moment.

"OK, then. Coming."

We go through the door.

What? What is it?"

I enter the dining room, stop. Jimmy Saint is standing there, looking like he's seen a ghost. There's terror in his expression. He startles at my words, jumping almost.

"It's . . . she's gone." He points to the spot where Amanda's body had previously been lying. There's just the crumpled bloodied tablecloth there now.

I try to make sense of it. "Amanda? So she . . . wasn't dead, then? Only wounded?"

"She looked pretty dead to me." And here's Sylvia, ramping up the hysteria again.

Surprisingly, the captain agrees with her. "And to me too. And to you, Kyle. She had no pulse, did she? No pulse. You checked. I checked. Nothing."

"So you're saying she got up and walked? A dead body?"

"Obviously not. That would be ridiculous. But maybe we got it wrong. Maybe in the heat of the moment, the surprise of the moment, we only thought she was dead. And now she's crawled off somewhere."

"Who's gone where?"

I turn. Diana has entered the room, followed by Len. She's visibly shaken, the carapace of confidence she wore at dinner chipped away like day-old nail polish.

"That woman Amanda," says Sylvia. "She's gone."

"What d'you mean gone?"

"Apparently walked off, so Captain Jimmy thinks," says Sylvia again, unhelpfully.

Then Iain turns up, scanning the room for any remaining booze. "What's happening, then? We found her?"

"No," says the captain. "But the woman, Amanda, her body's gone."

"Oh," says Iain, shrugging. "Perhaps she wasn't as dead as we thought."
Everyone ignores him.

"If she did get up and walk," I say, "or more likely crawl, where's the
trail of blood? I mean, she was very wounded at the least. Terminally, I'd
say, since she had a massive great hole in her. And, apart from the tablecloth, there's no blood anywhere."

"Perhaps someone carried her off," says Jimmy Saint.

"Or aliens."

"Thanks, Iain, that's really not helpful," says Diana. "Go and get yourself a drink."

"Righty-ho." He doesn't need to be asked twice. He crosses to the table
where there are replenished decanters. That's when I notice something
else.

The dining table has been cleared. It's completely bare, with no trace
that we recently all ate dinner in here. Not only have the decanters been
replenished but there are glasses and a jug of water on a side table.

"The table's been cleared. The whole room's been cleared. Could
someone have come in and taken Amanda's body away too?"

"Who?" asks Diana.

"Well, none of us, because we weren't here."

"Perhaps she wasn't really dead," Len says.

"Yes," says Jimmy Saint, exasperation showing. "That's what we've
been saying."

"No, I mean the whole thing was staged. Fake blood and everything."

I just stare at Len. He continues.

"Cornstarch and food coloring, apparently. That's what they use now.
Saw a program on it." He points to the tablecloth, then to me. "Give that
a lick and see."

"You give it a lick."

Before he can reply, and judging from his expression he's not happy
with my response, Jimmy intervenes.

"Did any of you see anyone with the body?" Jimmy scans the group
of us. "When you were exploring the house. None of you?"

"Did you?" asks Sylvia with the tone of a professional interrogator.

"No. I came back here to stand stag." He checks his wrist. "Not quite
time but enough of us here for a debrief."

"We're not all back yet," says Diana. "There's still—"

"Yes, I know, the woman with the baby. And her . . . friend." *Friend.* Clearly Ramona has made an impression on Jimmy. Or stirred something within him.

"And Desmond," says Len.

Jimmy Saint doesn't even bother to answer him. Just continues as if he's not there. "There are enough of us to begin. Who's up first?" He points at me. "You."

"So we're not going to look for Amanda? We're going to pretend it never happened?"

"And what about these things on our wrists?" says Diana. "Shouldn't we be getting a move on?"

At dinner I thought there was something warm about the captain. Yes, he spoke loudly and declared himself group leader without consulting the rest of us but he seemed, I don't know, decent. A word he would no doubt approve of. But since we all came back into the dining room he's ramped up the officiousness, turned down the bonhomie. Perhaps it's the shock of the missing body. Perhaps he's scared. But it seems like since he's leader he doesn't need to get us on his side anymore, just expects us to obey him because he says so. He also doesn't reply to me or Diana, which kind of proves my point. I'm not going to let that go. "Hello? You just going to ignore the missing body?"

He stares at me. It's not pleasant. He's clearly not used to having his orders disobeyed.

"Anyway," says Sylvia, "where have you been in all this, Captain Saint? It's all very well you wanting to know where we've been, why don't you tell us where you've been?"

"I told you. Standing stag," says Jimmy, clearly angry now.

"We don't even know what that means, old chap. Army jargon, is it? Not for the likes of us civvies," says Iain, laughing. I can almost hear the alcohol sloshing around inside him, like water in a wheelie bin.

Saint turns his attention to Iain. Then looks round the rest of the group.

"Ooh, you going to get your gun out again, Jimmy?" Diana this time.

"Steady," says Iain, "we're all going to be court-martialed."

"As I said," says Saint, "I came back to stand stag. Guard duty. That's when I found the casualty gone." He clearly hates being a figure of fun and now seems like he wants to shoot us all.

"You didn't do too good a job, did you?" says Diana.

"And where were you before that? Which floor?" Me this time. I can tell he doesn't like me, if he ever did.

"Upper. Top, I think. I took the lift. Nothing there. Locked doors. Now. You."

He's pointing at me. I look at Sylvia but she's doing that thing again of being too scared to talk and hiding it by letting proceedings appear to be beneath her. So it's down to me.

"We went round the ground floor. Started in the room over the way, I think it's a library."

"Not an ordinary library," says Sylvia, finding her voice. "All the books are blank."

"Then we went down a hallway to what I think is the back of the house. I heard a woman crying, sobbing, really. Asking for help."

"He heard it. I didn't."

"Yeah, thanks, Sylvia. You made it clear you thought I was imagining it earlier. Then we found a kitchen, went inside. It was unused. Wherever we got our dinner from it wasn't cooked in there. The pots and pans and everything weren't functional at all. They're props, like the library. Then we came back here."

"I had a good look around," says Iain. "Couldn't find her. Tried some doors, locked. Nothing else to report. Sorry."

"I found something," says Diana, jumping in ahead of Jimmy Saint replying, which clearly annoys him even further. "On the walls going up the stairs. There are paintings. Of us."

"Paintings?" says Jimmy Saint. "What kind of paintings?"

"Oil, I think. Len saw them too."

Len nods.

"They're of all of us, everyone in this house. I think they're new as well, even though they're painted in an old style."

"Traditional I'd call it," says Len. "Not like modern rubbish where you can't make out what it's supposed to be."

"What are we doing in these paintings?" asks Sylvia.

"I suppose it's our normal lives. Kyle's studying, I'm working, the captain there is charging into battle, that kind of thing."

Saint visibly preens at the thought of that. "We should go and investigate."

"Yeah, that's right, Jimmy," I say. "Don't go looking for the dead woman but check that your painting's a good likeness."

He rounds on me. "I've had quite enough of your insubordination and answering back . . ."

I can't help but laugh. "Insubordination? Mate, I've got news for you. I'm not in the army. You're not my boss. I don't answer to you. You're just a bloke, bit mouthy, bit up himself, wearing a uniform that makes him think he can dish out orders to whoever he likes and expect them to be done. Well, it doesn't work like that."

A drop of water hits me on the head. I ignore it, wipe it away.

Saint looks ready to kill me. His hand twitches, moves to his holster.

"You going to shoot me? Is that it?"

Another drop of water. Another swipe away.

"Crack on, then, mate," I continue. I spread my arms out, laughing but angry. "Here I am, take your best shot."

Another drop of water, then another. I'm caught up in this confrontation, I haven't got time to deal with this as well. I swipe them away. Then another. Faster, heavier now. And another swipe.

"What?"

Jimmy Saint has stopped moving. He's staring at me. He's not angry anymore. He looks horrified.

Another drop. And another.

I turn to the rest of the group. They're all staring at me, same horrified expression on their faces.

"What? What you looking at?"

Another drop. And I see it this time. It's not water falling on me.

It's blood.

I look up. I'd moved into the center of the room when I was arguing with Jimmy, not noticing there was blood beginning to seep through the ceiling and work its way down the chandelier. By the time it dripped off and hit me on the forehead the initial trickle had become a much heavier flow. Now I was beginning to get drenched by it. I move away.

"Where's that coming from?" says Diana, voice edging into hysteria.

"What's above this room?" Sylvia this time. She pauses. "It couldn't be *her*, could it?"

Jimmy Saint just stands there, staring. Contributing nothing but a slack jaw.

Someone has to take the lead. "We won't find out standing here. Come on."

I make for the door, into the hall and up the stairs. The lift will take too long. I try to take the stairs two at a time, but their depth defeats me. I'm aware of the others following behind.

I reach the first floor, try to work out which hallway will take me directly above the dining room.

That's when I hear the scream.

It's nothing like the crying I heard earlier. That was soft, hopeless sobbing. This is strong, fierce. The sound of a person confronted by horror. Working out that there's a better than even chance that the scream is coming from wherever the blood is, I follow it.

It leads me to a doorway. I run straight into the room.

It's a nursery. Cerys is the one screaming. She's standing at the far side of the room in the frame of a connecting door, being held by Ramona. My sudden appearance hasn't stopped her screaming. When I follow her eyeline I can see why and I don't blame her.

There, lying on the floor is one of the most hideous sights I've ever seen and I know no matter how long I live I'll never be able to scrub the image from my mind. It's Desmond. Or what's left of him. Lying in the center of the room, blood pumping rhythmically through the floorboards in tune to his dying heartbeat. His body has been hacked to pieces. His insides are also his outsides. His assailant has . . . oh god.

I turn away, trying not to vomit.

His eyeballs have been squeezed out of their sockets. One is missing. His face has been sliced up until it's only a mess of flesh and broken teeth.

The rest arrive. I think I attempt to call to them, tell them not to enter.

Cerys is still screaming.

"Monica . . . Monica . . ."

That's the first time I notice the baby. She's in the cot, sitting there, taking everything in. Her hands are covered in blood and she's playing with something.

The missing eyeball.

"Monica . . ."

She hears her mother's voice, looks at her, and smiles.

THE BEAST IN THE CELLAR

Well. Weren't expecting that, were you?

Oh, what am I saying, of course you were expecting that. Why else would you be reading this if you didn't want to see some sudden, surprising—and let's be honest, horribly gruesome—death? Or two, in fact. And the first one was bad enough but the second, well . . .

Now, you're saying to yourself, they're going to kill them off one by one and we have to work out who the murderer is. But we won't be able to do that because there'll be a twist at the end that no one could see coming. It'll probably be someone who died earlier, you'll be saying, who just faked their death and is still hiding in the house, knocking the rest off one by one. Well, if that's the case it's not going to be Desmond, is it? And if it is him, then he's gone to some admirable lengths to throw suspicion off himself, including losing an eye, his face, and most of his internal organs. So I think we can rule him out.

So who, then? Well, you're probably thinking it's the mysterious Amanda because her body's disappeared. Or is that too obvious? Or is it so obvious that it's a double twist? Or has someone just carried her away? And if so, why? Well, that's not for me to speculate. I mean, obviously, I know what's going on. I may be in the cellar but I do get about a bit. In a manner of speaking. So is it me? Am I the killer? What do you think? You might be thinking that or you might even be thinking I'm the missing girl. Or I'm a red herring.

By the way, since I mentioned it, do you know what a red herring actually is? I mean, yes, we all know it's a false clue to throw you or the detective or whoever off the scent but do you know where it comes from? Its etymology? Would you like to? Here goes. It's from the 1800s and it first appeared in a story by William Cobbett, who wrote about dragging some strong smoked fish along the ground to put hunting dogs off the scent of their prey, a hare. (Off the scent. That's where that phrase comes from too.) Apparently the story was allegorical, as it was meant to be a criticism of the press, who had been quick to publish false information about a supposed defeat of Napoleon but the phrase caught on. So there you go. Every day's a school day.

RAMONA O'ROURKE

Jesus Christ. Jesus Christ. Jesus . . . This is real. No, really real. I mean, not a game. Not makeup and acting, not . . . no. Really real.

That creepy guy is lying on the floor, eviscerated. And poor Monica . . . God, that kid's going to have problems. I'm holding Cerys in my arms to stop her screaming. It doesn't work. She wriggles out of my grip and runs to the cot, picking up her baby, throwing the eyeball on the floor, where it lands with a cartoon splat. She looks like she doesn't know which way to turn or what to do so she comes back toward me. Her expression breaks my heart. Poor kid looks lost. I reach out to her once more. I think I'm on autopilot, trying to take in what's in front of me.

By this time her screams have alerted the rest of them and they're trying to pile in through the door all at once. Or at least they are until they see what's in front of them. That changes their minds. Some of them scream, others gasp. It's too confusing to say who and in which order.

I expect the army guy to take charge, but he just stands there, struck dumb like the rest of them. At least he doesn't scream.

The student steps forward. He looks at the body, then at me. "What . . . what happened?"

He's got blood on his head but it doesn't appear to be from an injury. More like a bird shat blood on him from above. I really don't know what the hell is going on here.

"We came in and found him there. That's it."

The student seems to have a bit more sense about him than the others. That's usually me. I pride myself on being the rational one in the room, taking charge, asking smart questions. Being unafraid, being confident. But there's a horribly mutilated dead body on the floor in front of me and it's kind of distracting, you know?

The student's staring at me. Like he's trying to work something out. "Did you kill him?"

It's the right question to ask. The perfect question to ask. And then I see how this must look to the rest of them. Two women, a baby, and a creepy guy. Sorry, dead creepy guy.

"No," I say. "We were in this other room and we came in to find him like that."

"Who was in the room with him, then?"

"Monica. Why, you think she did it?"

"Did you hear anything? Screaming, anything like that?"

"Nothing. Which I guess is kind of unusual, now that I think about it. Old houses have thick walls, I guess."

He looks down at the body once more. Then back to me. When he speaks his voice is low, serious. "Well, if he attacked the kid, I doubt anyone would blame you."

"I saw his painting on the wall," says the tightly dressed woman. "He was in his living room. There was child pornography all over the place."

"If that's the case, you should have a medal," says the drunk.

I look at them all then, really seeing them. And I know what they think of me. What they *really* think of me. Normally I wouldn't care. But things are different now. "I didn't kill him. Cerys didn't kill him. And I really doubt that Monica went to town on him, then removed his . . . Anyway. We were in a different room and we're not armed. So it wasn't us. What about you?"

"We were all downstairs," says the hysterical older woman. I should learn their names. "All of us. Together. When the blood started dripping through. And before that Kyle and I were together. So that rules us out. So it must be . . ."

"It might be the dead woman."

"It might be whoever shot the dead woman."

"This isn't very helpful." The army guy seems to have found his voice. "We should get this mess cleaned up and the, the   body disposed of. Then we can discuss the whys and wherefores."

"Good idea," says the student. Kyle? "Is there a rug in the next room?"

"Yes, I think so."

He nods at the army guy. "Come on, Jimmy. Give me a hand."

Kyle walks toward the doorway I'm in. Jimmy, the army guy, follows him, taking an order rather than barking one out, which is surprising.

Maybe he's not the natural leader he thinks he is. I move aside for them. Cerys has stopped sobbing now, just clinging on tightly to Monica. I move her gently out of the way. The old guy steps forward.

"Why don't I take you both downstairs, get you a drink, or something?"

I thought at first he was talking to me but he's addressing Cerys. He has to say her name a couple of times before she responds, then she numbly allows herself to be led out of the room. Kyle and Jimmy reemerge with the rug. Throw it over the body and roll him up in it.

"Just like Cleopatra," I say.

The old woman gives me a dagger of a look. "This is no time for frivolity."

I ignore her. "Where you taking the body?"

"There's a kitchen at the back of the house," says Kyle. "It seems unused. We'll put it there for now."

"Okay, sure. Why don't the rest of us meet in the dining room?"

"Maybe not the dining room. That could do with a mop as well," Kyle says. "There's a library opposite."

■ ■ ■

Which is where I find myself sitting, along with all the other dinner guests minus one, fortifying ourselves with spirits fifteen minutes later. Anyway. We're all here and we've all calmed down. And now it's time for the postmortem. Kind of literally.

"So," says Jimmy, apparently believing he's back in charge, "anyone want to confess now? Saves time in the long run."

"I . . . I can't be here anymore," says Cerys. "I want to get out. I need to get out."

"We can't," says the mutton-dressed-as-lamb woman. "The door's locked. So are all the windows. We're all stuck in here together, I'm afraid."

"Then I want to go to bed. And take Monica with me." Cerys hadn't put the baby down since we got in the room, letting it cling to her. The baby didn't seem to mind.

"There are a few things we need to know before you do anything else," says Jimmy. "How long was the baby alone in that room? Did you hear—"

"Oh god, stop it, already," I say to him. "There's a second body. In a much worse state than the first one. It's taken one hell of a toll on Cerys, and Monica might have been hurt. Let it *go*."

"But I need to talk to her—"

"Whatever." I turn to Cerys. "Want me to accompany you to your room?"

"Steady," says the drunk, "the murderer might still be out there."

"Or it's one of us." Sylvia answers him. Shrill, like a kettle summoning up the will to boil. "It could be one of us. It could be."

"Yes, it could be," I say, sighing.

She sits back as if I've just proved something. "There. You see? There. Doesn't care at all. The Black girl clearly did it. Clearly." That kettle coming to the boil now.

I stare at her. "Black girl?" Suddenly, Sylvia's eyes can't quite meet mine. But I'm angry now, I'm not stopping. "You think I killed both of them? Amanda as well? You think I pulled a big old American gun at dinner, in full view of the rest of you and shot her? Then you think I switched the gun for a knife and killed that guy? Really? Why, because I'm *Black*?"

She doesn't answer. Just as well the mood I'm in now. Looks anywhere but at me. The room feels uncomfortable.

"I'm going to let that slide this once because you're upset. We're all upset. But let me tell you something. You know nothing about me. My life, how I think, feel, respond, anything. So you don't have the right to make any assumptions about me."

Sylvia rolls her eyes, trying to regain some of her indignation and momentum. "Confident little thing, aren't you?"

"Oh, I'm confident, baby. And let me tell you, that confidence is hard-won. I made sacrifices to be who I am."

"What sort of sacrifices?"

"None of your goddamn business."

Silence in the room. And not the good kind, either. I have no intention of breaking it. Not my job. Eventually the drunk clears his throat, ready to speak.

"Who was the chap, anyway, do we know?"

"Desmond, I think his name was," says Jimmy, happy to have something else to focus on.

"Do we know anything apart from that about him? I mean, I certainly wouldn't leave my child alone with him, if I had one." The drunk chuckled. Actually chuckled. "Although you never know, with my track record . . ."

Kyle rolls his eyes. "Shut up, Iain. No, we don't know anything about him. We don't know whether he was the one who kidnapped this girl or not. Or killed anyone."

"According to his portrait, he was a pedophile." The mutton-dressed-as-lamb woman.

"Be that as it may," Jimmy again. "If it was him, then it looks like we've lost our last chance to find out where this Claire Swanson is."

"How could it be him?" says the old man. No idea of his name. "Granted, he's the most likely candidate for the killer but someone's offed him. Still, you know what these things are like."

"What things?" I asked.

"Murder mystery things. It's never the one you suspect, is it? Could be a red herring, something to put us off the scent. Never the most obvious, is it?"

The mutton-dressed-as-lamb woman, Diana, I think, is getting angry. You could tell from the energy change in the room what kind of anger it was. Useless, impotent. But also the kind that's so useless it's infectious. "You think this is all just a game? After everything you've seen, this is just a game to you?"

"Well," says the old guy, "you have to admit, there are elements of that here."

"It's not a game . . . it's not a game . . ."

I was right about the anger. Cerys is building up to joining Diana. Sylvia might even put her kettle on to boil again.

"I think we can safely say this has gone beyond a game now," says Jimmy, and for once I can believe he's a captain. I take him in. He seems tired. I mean, we all are, but it's like the burden he's given himself, self-appointed leader, has worn him out. Or he actually isn't very good in a crisis, as he proved upstairs.

"Maybe it's like that film *The Most Dangerous Game*?" Kyle's greeted by blank expressions. "This eccentric millionaire brings people to his island just to hunt them down for sport. And there's *Hostel*, anyone seen that? People are lured to this hostel where they're imprisoned and tortured and rich people pay to watch. Actually, there's been rumors of that going on for real. Red rooms, they're called. You can access them on the dark web and if you've got enough money, you can watch the people in them being made to do whatever you want. It's like—"

I've had enough. I stand up. "I'm going to bed."

"Bed?" says Kyle. "We've got less than twelve hours to find this killer, get this girl, and get out of here. We haven't got time to go to bed."

"Yes," says Sylvia. "And how can you sleep with all this going on?"

"I need sleep. We all do. It's been a tiring day. And none of us know how long a day it's been." I hold up my wrist. "This thing is still counting down and I've got a headache. If we're going to find this girl we need rest and some time apart from each other." I look pointedly at Sylvia when I say this. "Some more than others."

"But one of us is probably the murderer!" And the kettle boils over.

"Unless it's not. Unless whoever killed that Amanda woman and this Desmond guy is hiding in the house somewhere, ready to pick us off one by one. In which case we're all as safe as each other. Or as unsafe as each other. Either way, I'm tired. Nighty night, y'all."

"No," says Jimmy. "We need to stay here. Stay together. The killer can't get us if we're all together."

"Fine," I say. "Let's work through the night. But if we're getting all Scooby-Doo, then I'm getting out of this dress, putting something more appropriate on." From the expression on his face, I'm sure Iain wants to come and watch me change. "Yeah, I see you, King Leer."

"I'll come with you, if you don't mind," says Diana, checking her wrist. "And it must be nearly midnight. We've only got eight hours left and I need to change."

"Fine by me. Cerys? Want me to walk you upstairs?"

She nods, stands up.

"Come on, ladies." I smile and sashay out of the room. And yes, I know I'm doing it. I always know when I'm doing it.

"Safety in numbers," says Diana as we make for the elevator.

"Sure is, honey," I say. And I'm right. Because no one knows I stole a steak knife from the dinner table and I've hidden it about my person in a place I can reach but no one else would ever get to.

So yeah. Whatever happens next, I feel pretty safe.

THE BEAST IN THE CELLAR

Well. Things are hotting up nicely, aren't they? And I'm sure you have loads of questions. So many questions. And none of them to do with Napoleon or red herrings or anything like that. In fact, I already have a few questions here that I could go through with you, if you like. Just imagine I've had letters from readers or listeners or whatever, and this is my mailbag feature. Ready? Here we go. Let's make it atmospheric.

Hi there. You're listening to Beast in the Cellar FM. That was Curtis Stigers there with his great version of ("What's So Funny 'Bout) Peace, Love and Understanding." Well, what is so funny, I ask you? Anyway, as we're coming up to the big old witching hour, I thought it would be a good time to go through some of the many letters I've been getting from you, my loyal listeners. Here's one:

"Dear Beast in the Cellar, love your show, but I'm a bit confused as to what's going on. When Kyle and Sylvia reached the kitchen they found it hadn't been used and even said it couldn't be used and that it had dollhouse furniture in there. Are they stuck inside a dollhouse, is that it?"

Well, thank you . . . oh. There's no name on this. Well, thank you anyway for your question. Are they in a dollhouse? Is that what's happening? Here's another question from . . . no name on this one either. What, are you all scared of letting the other listeners know who you are?

"Hey Beasty!" Beasty, indeed. Kinda like it, though. It continues: *"Love the show, never miss it. But I noticed something and I think I'm the only one. The books in the library are blank. What's all that about?"*

What indeed, my anonymous friend? Here's another. It's from . . . no name. Very rude. This is becoming a pattern.

"Love the show, but I have to ask you. What age is Monica? And is she a creepy kid?"

A creepy kid? All kids are creepy, whoever you are. Don't you know?

That's why they turn up in so many horror films. Some people. Moving swiftly on . . .

"*Hi you gorgeous great Beast . . .*" Please. Flattery will get you everywhere. "*How come they all had something different to eat for dinner and the kitchen wasn't working? Is there another kitchen somewhere in the house? That dinner had to be made somewhere. And who cleared up after them? Love the show, keep it coming . . .*"

The kitchen again. What is it with you people and food? Obsessed by it, the lot of you. Another one here.

"*Howdy Beast, old chum.*" Not a promising start. I'm sure I've never met them. "*What's the deal with the dead woman, Amanda? It looks like no one in the room shot her and now she's disappeared. How did that happen? Was she ever really there in the first place?*"

Well, who can say? Are we all here, really, in the corporeal sense? Or is life just one huge dream or program in the Matrix or whatever? Makes you think, though, doesn't it? Here's another.

"*Never miss a show, great fan.*" Well, that's lovely, whoever you are. "*But I do have a question.*" Course you do. "*Why is Kyle frightened of storms? Did something bad happen to him during a storm in childhood? Is that it?*"

Honestly, all of you. Does everything have to relate to childhood trauma? Think about what good old Ziggy Freud said. Sometimes a cigar is just a cigar. Sometimes a storm is just a storm. And sometimes . . .

Well, that's it for the postbag tonight. Lots of questions but I'm surprised that no one's asked the big one. The elephant-in-the-room-size one. There's actually a young woman's life at stake here. Her name, in case you've forgotten, is Claire Swanson and time is running out for her, second by second. Like tick follows tock. But no, you don't mention her. You're all, who's the killer? What's in the kitchen? When are we going to get something to eat and what's for dinner? So selfish. Really. I mean, I'm laughing while I'm saying this but still, the point stands. This isn't a game. This is genuinely a matter of life or death.

Anyway.

I should imagine they've all overcome their shock at what's happened and managed to clean up the room by now, as well as find somewhere to stash poor Desmond's body. I don't know about you, but if I were one of them I would want to get as far away from the rest of the houseguests as possible after that, barricade myself in my room, and wait until morning. It seems like this lot won't get the chance, though. But there's still one thing they need to see before we hit the "End of Part One" break. Or at least one of them does. And that'll be coming up next.

But in the meantime . . . You're still listening to Beast in the Cellar FM. We're well past the witching hour now, so here's Julie London with that haunting—and I mean that in every sense of the word!—old torch song, "Cry Me a River" . . .

Ramona walks me to my door, which I tell her is unnecessary but she insists. I wait until I'm sure she's gone, then step out into the corridor and, lightly as I can, start walking.

Well. That was easily the worst evening of my life. Not even the shoes, dress, and necklace make up for it. Nothing else has come remotely close. Not even . . . Anyway. The dead woman at dinner, the paintings, that was bad enough. Then running into that nursery, seeing the body on the floor, the baby sitting there . . . I . . . I couldn't. My eyes took in too much at once, my brain couldn't process it all. I was overloaded. I just stared and stared. I couldn't speak. Couldn't move. Rooted to the spot. A cliché, I know, but what's a cliché if not an overused truth? I wasn't even aware of the others around me, only what was bombarding my retinas.

I don't know if I screamed. I probably did, I can't remember. I don't know if I cried. It was like being in a car accident, your adrenaline goes off the scale and your heart becomes a steam hammer. I can understand why people faint or go into shock in a crisis. It's nothing to do with weakness. It's the body protecting itself. That's why the whole thing is a blank.

We must have moved the body. We must have got the baby out of there and cleaned her up. We must have put the body somewhere no one could come across it. We might have even cleaned up the room, stopped the blood dripping through the floor to the ceiling below. I don't know. Like I say, it's a blank. And I'm happy for it to remain that way.

I do know that afterward we sat in the library and confronted one another. And it got heated and it got tedious until Ramona provided me with an excuse to get away from the rest of them.

Before all this happened, I had entertained hopes that Kyle might join me in bed at some point. And while I stood there in the library, suddenly tired but wanting to keep going, there was a part of me that still wanted him to. But, as had been pointed out, the killer might be one of us. Not me, of course, but one of the other people. So it was best to come and get changed on my own.

As Ramona and I took the lift up I saw something on the stairs. Glimpsed it like before and a huge, shuddering shock wave hit me. But I said nothing. Didn't want to alarm her. Not before I'd checked it out for myself.

And that's why I'm now creeping around the house in the dark.

And I wish I wasn't.

■ ■ ■

I make my way slowly down the corridor. I've lit a candle and brought it with me. The flame throws out a surprising amount of light but it's quite delicate so I have to keep it protected with my hand. This makes my progress even slower.

I reach the landing. Start my descent.

As I walk, I realize I'm still hungry. I don't eat a lot usually. In my business so much is dependent on looks and the older a woman gets, the harder she has to work to keep in shape. And you have to keep in shape. Because there's always someone younger and thinner and prettier coming up behind you. I'm getting to the stage where I'm going to have to pay someone to take a knife to my face to keep me in the game. I mean, I've had plenty of treatments already—I've been pumped so full of Botox and fillers that I could claim it as tax-deductible—but soon I'm going to have to think hard about serious knife work. And that terrifies me. Because I would hate to end up as one of those cocktail-party-haunting living skeletons that everyone else bitches and laughs about behind their backs, at the ridiculous lengths they've undertaken to stop aging, the fear they have of being old. But that's for future me to think about. Tonight there's something much more immediate on my mind.

When I looked out of the window in my room, I didn't see the expected gardens Kyle had mentioned. All I saw were shutters. It was disorienting, not to mention frightening, and I immediately panicked. I tried pulling at the window latches, trying to get them to open. Yanking as hard as I could. Nothing budged. Not only were they shuttered from the outside but the windows wouldn't open inwardly, either. I thought of picking something up, trying to smash the glass and push the shutters but didn't because somehow I knew that the shutters wouldn't move, either. That whoever had done this didn't want us looking—never mind *stepping*—outside and they had damned well made sure of that. I'll have to mention that to the group.

I walk slowly down the stairs. Thankfully, whoever packed for me remembered my trainers as the Louboutins have just about ruined my feet.

I reach what I want to see. Hold up the candle.

I say I want to see it. But I don't really. I don't know if confirming what I think I saw will make things better or worse. For me, for all of us. But I can't not look. I mean, I don't know how much sleep I'm going to get in any case but I'll definitely get none if I don't look.

I look.

And my stomach does roller-coaster flips.

Desmond's painting, the one of him sitting in that squalid living room, isn't there anymore. Well, it is, but it's not the same painting. He's still sitting there, same filthy armchair, same fetid room, but his body is different. Exactly like it was upstairs. Guts all over the place like it's party night at the abattoir. And his eyes . . . just two black holes in a face of meat. Does he still have a smile on what's left of his face?

It must be a different painting. Must be. Someone must have substituted this one for the other when he died. But if that's the case, then someone must have been expecting his death. And if they were expecting his death, they must have another painting for all of us.

I'm hyperventilating. I feel faint from more than a lack of food.

I want to go home.

And then I hear music. Faintly, from a distance, but definitely coming from somewhere within the house.

It's an old song that I've heard before. The kind of sad slow song you play in the middle of the night when you've come in from a party and you're sobering up and realizing you're all alone. In your apartment, in the world.

"Cry Me a River."

And then it disappears into the air, like it was never really there.

PART TWO

A wise man once said that the world is a tragedy to he who feels and a comedy to he who thinks. So which one's me, you might ask? And you might think, even from our brief time together, that you know. Well. To answer that fully, I've never been much of a thinker. But I'd also rather die than let anyone see that something had upset me. Doesn't fit with the self-image, see. The devil-may-care roué. The twinkle-eyed rogue. Having said all that, events in this house were starting to upset me very much indeed. Not that I'd let it show, of course. Time to get what I want and skedaddle.

Which I'm currently working on. I suppose you'd think, considering the amount of alcohol I've put away last night, that I'd be out like a light or at least roaring drunk. Not a bit of it. What's my secret, you may ask? Practice. Simple as that. Eventually it becomes a way of life. Protective camouflage, you see. We're all just beasts in our own particular jungle.

And, I suppose, one could construe that this kind of setting, milieu if you like—big house, people milling about, everyone distracted and taking their eye off the ball—*is* my kind of jungle. I can move through these kinds of gatherings largely unnoticed, standing at the back, making the odd quip, keeping myself topped up, but always with my eye on the prize. Yes, sometimes there's a little consolation in the shape of a willing filly and that's all very momentarily satisfying, or sometimes disappointing, depending on the alcohol ratio, but I never forget what I'm actually here for. Never. So once they're all suitably distracted, in I swoop, take what I want, and off I go. And nobody's ever any the wiser.

What am I talking about? Why, I'm a thief. That's what I do. Or rather, what Iain Wardle-Roberts does. There's no such person, obviously. Or there never used to be until I dreamed him into existence. The name on my birth certificate and passport is Kevin Baldwin. Kevin was a street thug, an unimaginative plodder, an unsuccessful criminal.

And deathly dull to boot. So how did Wardle-Roberts come about? By accident, really.

I was inside once more, short stretch this time, street robbery, but I knew that if I messed up again I was looking at some serious time. And I was also getting pretty sick of being unsuccessful. Of relying on unimaginative morons for support and failing every time, no matter what we tried. Something had to give. And it was while I was inside I got this idea. I never read anything on the out but inside I was always in the library, every chance I got. Martina Cole and picture books of the countryside, that's the most borrowed stuff in there. But I got myself interested in some old books that no one else seemed bothered about. *A. J. Raffles, Gentleman Thief: The Complete Collection*, by E. W. Hornung. Like a kind of Sherlock Holmes in reverse. Instead of solving posh people's crimes he committed them. And that got me thinking. What was to stop me doing that? Getting myself all ponced up in fancy clothes and robbing the rich? I'd done a bit of acting at school, I could talk posh, so why not?

Once I was out I stole myself a new set of clothes, got some decent luggage and a smart haircut, and said goodbye to low-level, criminal-failure Kevin Baldwin and hello to successful gentleman-thief Iain Wardle.

And it was so easy. *So* easy. That's the thing about affluent people. They're so fucking gullible it's easy to convince them of anything. There's some party, gallery opening, launch for a book, whatever. They're always there. The monied leeches. And wherever they are, there's me. My jungle prey. In I walk, drunk and overfamiliar. They all think they've met me somewhere. Or someone like me. Or they don't want to appear as if they don't know who I am because I might be important. So because I've got the right clothes and the right accent I'm accepted. They think I'm one of them.

It's only after I'm long gone that doubts may arise. And even then they won't linger. What, Iain, they say? A thief? Never. Bit of a rogue, bit of a character but a thief? Must have been one of the servants. And it's all smiles when I turn up again. They never learn.

And that, murderer or no murderer, missing girl or no missing girl, is what I'm going to do here. I spotted that necklace Diana was wearing at dinner. Must be worth a pretty packet. That was her main attraction. I intended a bit of flattery, some smooth talking, woo her into the bedroom, and bang. Necklace in my pocket and off I trot. Of course, things didn't go as planned. But I refuse to be thwarted. And who knows? Perhaps there's a reward for finding that missing girl too. I'm sure I could wangle some way to pocket that as well.

Yes, I know there's a murderer on the loose. But I'm hardly the target like that big unpleasant chap was, am I? I'm clever. I'm shrewd. And I won't allow myself to give in to fear. In fact, I'm positively perky. Must be the thought of those pretty little sparklers being in my pocket that does it.

I let a certain amount of time elapse after the women went upstairs, then wandered out of the library. I don't think any of them missed me particularly. I've now found a shadowy alcove to hide in. This house isn't exactly short of them. And from there, a simple matter of waiting until Diana leaves her room and heads off back downstairs and I'm in. Raffles couldn't have had it easier. And if, in the unlikely event I'm stopped and questioned by our very own Boy Scout, I'll tell him I thought I heard a scream, something like that, point to the opposite direction of where I'm headed and by the time the dear lady finds herself parted from her jewels I'll be long gone, thank you very much. Because you know, that French playwright got it right when he said hell is other people. I mean, at first I thought he meant hell is other Frenchmen, which is fair enough, but on reflection I realize he meant everyone and, my god, he was spot-on with that. Being among this lot is such hard work. But at least I won't be here much longer.

Right. She's gone. Off I go.

Quick glance round, check I've got the corridor to myself, cross to her room. It's not locked, which is good although I do carry a set of lock picks with me. They're quite handy, not just for separating belongings from their rightful owners. They've also helped me to extricate myself from several rather embarrassing situations involving willing, or possibly unwilling but always inebriated, wives from the sudden and wholly un-expected appearances of angry cuckolded husbands. Although thinking about it, you could say that, too, involves separating belongings from their rightful owners. All part of the fun, isn't it?

But this is just a lady's empty room and I have all the time in the world to go through her private belongings and walk away with at least one of them.

Now please don't get me wrong. I'm not one of those perverts who gets his kicks from doing unmentionable acts with ladies unmentionables. I have nothing but revulsion and condemnation for that sort. Having said that, however, I must admit I'm not averse to the odd rummage through the old knicker drawer. Just to satisfy my curiosity. It can often help in putting together an accurate picture of the fair thing in question. What undergarments she chooses to wear can be an indicator for what kind of person she is in private. That sort of thing. Beige and bland tends to mean the same personality-wise while frilly and lacy ... ooh la la. We're off to the races. It might sound simple, reductive even. But it's never failed me yet. And it's not always the ones you suspect, either. It can often be surprising, eye-opening, in fact. Seriously, psychologists should make a proper study.

So what is the fair Diana like in reality? I'm coming to that. Don't be impatient. This isn't about her, it's about me. First let me set the scene. And then go on to amply demonstrate my dazzling prowess as a gentleman thief. Think Cary Grant in that old film, all tanned and urbane and well-dressed. That's me. Or at least how I think of myself when I'm on the job.

The room. It's quite like mine, I suppose. A typical old bedroom in an old house. Hers has a few more modern touches than mine, though. There's a contemporary bedside light and more, shall we say, modish furniture scattered throughout. It's just more *her*. Like she's managed to personalize it in the small amount of time she's been here. She's not very tidy, however. Her dinner dress is thrown on the armchair, the shoes kicked off beside it. And if the pile of discarded clothing on the bed is anything to go by, it looks like she changed her mind several times before settling on whatever it is she's wearing now. It shouldn't, but it always surprises me when I see that women can be untidy. Knocks them off their pedestals somewhat.

But that's of no consequence now. The necklace. Where would she keep the necklace? The obvious place, I think, would be in the drawer of the bedside table. If, of course, she hasn't thrown that somewhere random as well. So that's where I check first. I don't bother with gloves on this occasion as I'm never going to see these people again after today and they're not going to be able to find me where I'm going. Which, in case you're wondering, is as far away from here as possible.

I open the drawer. And there it is. The necklace, just sitting there.

Simple as that. No flourishes, no hidden safes, nothing. Not looking the proverbial gift horse in the smacker I pick it up and pocket it so quickly I could make a convincing argument for it never having been there in the first place.

I'm all set to leave, on my way across the floor to the door, when I pause. If she had that necklace, and it was so easy to find, what else might she have hidden away in the room?

I smile to myself. Clever old Iain. I open the armoire. Her remaining clothes are hanging up neatly, as if someone else has put them there for her. I rifle through them, checking for any jewelry-shaped bumps and lumps. Nothing, sadly. I even upend her shoes and check them. Nothing.

I open her drawers and go through her nether garments. Nothing there, although they do tend toward the racy and lacy side so part of me is rather disappointed that I won't get the chance to take things further.

Seems like the necklace is all I'm getting. Well, beggars can't be choosers. And once I've negotiated with my usual fence I'm confident I'll get a good price for it. Enough to keep me in martinis somewhere warm for the next few months.

All I need to do now is get out of this house.

The window is of course shuttered, as mine now is. They won't budge. I push incredibly hard but end up losing my breath and dignity. I look around for some kind of weapon to smash through it but can't see anything. Also, a noise as great as that would alert those downstairs. And there's no sense in getting away with half a job only to be caught doing the other half. No. I need to think of something else.

I run through the options. The front door is locked. We established that earlier. That wouldn't be a good way to exit in any case as I'd have to pass the library and the dining room downstairs. There's no way I could casually stroll past them. So. I could go exploring again in the hope of finding an exit that hadn't been locked. But I might be all day looking for that. And of course, there's still the question of this murderous nutter on the loose. I don't want to get away from all the others only to find myself in the arms of that one, thank you. No. I need another way.

And I've got it. It's a really stupid idea but in a sense the most obvious one. If everywhere else is locked up, get up on the roof and climb down the outside.

Yes, I said it was stupid, but it's not if you think about it. These old houses have all sorts of crenellations and battlements and whatnot and with a bit of effort I could certainly do it. Never been scared of heights. That's one thing in my favor. And let's be honest, it won't be the first time I've had to shin down a drainpipe to escape someone's clutches. Oh, the stories I could tell . . .

But that's for another time. Right now I have to get out of this place.

I leave her room and glance down the hallway. No one about. So what would the most likely route to the roof be? The stairs, obviously. Unless of course there's some secret passageway I don't know about. And if I don't know about it, I doubt it's going to be much use to me. So the stairs it is.

Or the lift. It's there in front of me as I walk along the corridor. No one else is about so I could take it to the top and those downstairs would be none the wiser. I press the button. Wait.

"Off back downstairs, are you?"

I nearly jump out of my skin. I probably do scream. I turn. It's the old man.

"Sorry," he says, "didn't mean to make you jump. Thought you knew I was there."

He looks like he's on holiday. He should be wearing a beige flatcap with a rolled-up *Daily Mail* under his arm. He's even smiling when he speaks. Is he enjoying all this? "Yes, well, I do now. Bit jumpy, obviously."

"I'll come down with you, if you don't mind."

The last thing I want, obviously. I'll have to get rid of him. Use my famous interpersonal skills.

"No, actually, I think I might see the rest of the house first. Have a wander. Tempers were getting a bit frayed. Get a bit of exercise, you know? Clear my head." I do a small bit of jogging on the spot to indicate what I mean. It just about exhausts me.

"In the lift?"

Bugger. "No, you're right. I'll . . . I'll take the stairs. Do a bit of . . . of running up and down. Get the old, the old . . . whatever going again."

The old man shrugs. "Leave you to it, then."

"Yes. You do that."

And off I go up the stairs. Exercise is anathema to me but I have to make it look like I'm enjoying myself so I jog as briskly as I can until I'm out of sight, then stop. Bloody hell. I'm winded. And I've got however many floors after this to go as well.

I won't bore you with the details or the state I get myself into, but I eventually reach the top of the house. And it's pretty much as I expected. These big old houses tend to get less and less ornate the higher they go, and smaller and smaller too. Obviously the servants would be housed in this part and no one ever expended much money or effort to make servants' quarters fancy. Quite right too. This top floor is sparse, even by the most austere of servants' digs. As if it's hardly finished. Someone get fed up decorating and even building. Very rudimentary. Plain, undecorated, with a single uncovered bulb hanging down.

There's an old wooden staircase with an old wooden door at the top of it. The attic, I presume. The staircase is old and rickety and as I place my feet on each board it lets out a horror film creak. And is it just me, or is the light starting to go? Even with the bare bulb it seems to have gotten suddenly dark.

I look down behind me. Yes, it's dark. The bulb's low-watt radiance doesn't touch it. As if the night is washing in like a tide on a shore. I can almost see it rolling away.

I look upward. The door is still there. But it seems farther away, as if the number of steps I have to climb to reach it have increased. And I notice something else. A small window set into the sloping roof to one side of the door. And it doesn't seem to have a shutter behind it. Bingo. If I can just reach that, grab the frame, pull myself through, I'm home and dry.

I keep climbing the stairs. The dark below me is impenetrable now, as if telling me I only have one way forward, that there's nothing to go back to. If I stopped to think I might find it scary. But I don't stop. I keep going. I reach out from the step I'm on, place my hands on the lip of the window and make another discovery. There's no glass in it. It's open. Emboldened by this finding, I lunge at it, fully committing myself, ending up hanging from it. It's at times like these that I wish I actually had devoted more time to physical exercise as it'll make the next part so much easier.

I try to pull my body up, get my hands over the edge of the sill. It's a struggle, but I'll manage it, because the alternative . . .

I'm sweating and somewhat giddy, presumably from the alcohol. But my hands are right over the edge . . .

I can't see the bottom of my legs now. They've been enveloped by the black fog. It's rising. My heart is hammering. I'm sweating and this time it's from more than alcohol.

I just need to use the power in my arms, pull myself farther up . . . farther . . .

That's it, nearly there . . . nearly there . . .

Then I hear a noise. I look up.

I open my mouth to scream.

And—

Has anyone checked out the dining room?"

Kyle, Jimmy, and Sylvia are in the library. They all look up when I enter. It doesn't seem they've been talking much.

"No," says Kyle. "Why?"

"Someone's set it up for us to keep going through the night. If this is the night, of course. Snacks, tea, coffee, water, fizzy drinks . . ."

"When?" Sylvia, this time.

"You didn't hear anything?"

"No. We've all been sitting here. We would have heard something if someone had done that." Clearly Sylvia is rattled.

"Maybe it was the fairies," says Kyle.

"You're a very tedious young man," Sylvia replies, anger rising. "Has anyone ever told you that?"

Kyle gets angry in response. "Has anyone ever told you what you are? Would you like me to?"

Jimmy Saint stands up, gets between them. "This isn't helping anyone. We have rations. Good. We shall need them if we are to continue our search." He turns to me. "Are the others on their way down?"

"I don't know. I came by myself. There's something you should know, though. Desmond's picture. It's gone."

"Gone? Where?"

I turn. Cerys and her baby have appeared.

"I couldn't sleep. Neither could Monica. Too nervous."

Cerys has changed. Obviously she couldn't keep wearing the same bloodstained clothing, but she seems to be wearing something altogether more figure-hugging, showing off her curves. And is she wearing makeup? It's like she's deliberately tried to undowdy herself. Ramona then enters, looking casually radiant. Not just radiating beauty and youth but also health and confidence. I notice in that moment that everyone stares at her and that gives me a pang of jealousy. Not to mention anger. And then I see how Cerys is staring at her. Even harder than the others. And immediately know what, or rather who, her makeup's for.

"Anyone else got shutters in their rooms?" asks Ramona. "Can't budge them. Or the windows."

"Yes, me," says Cerys. "Thought I was the only one."

"Me too," I say.

Sylvia sighs. "This place gets better and better."

"But like I was saying—"

Jimmy Saint is still standing. "We need to move this on. More recces. More expeditions. Now—"

"I was *speaking*." I'm getting furious now.

Jimmy Saint stares at me. Clearly not used to being interrupted. Especially not by a woman. I stare at him.

"Thank you." I check my bracelet. "We need to get moving, you're right. I have places I should be, meetings to attend, and the sooner we get out of here the better. But before we do I need to tell you about Desmond's painting. It's—"

I don't get the chance to speak. A scream comes from somewhere in the house.

We all freeze and stare at one another.

We automatically begin a head count. See who's missing.

The old guy.

And Iain.

He went thataway . . ."

Len is standing by the lift on the second floor when we all run up the stairs. He's clearly distressed.

"Who?" asks Jimmy Saint. "Who went where?"

"Iain. Said he was off for a wander round the house. Bit of exercise. Not sure I'd want to do that, but there you go. Each to their own. Then I heard the scream, same as you."

"And you didn't go after him?" Jimmy says.

Len stares at him with steel in his eyes I hadn't noticed before. "So am I to stop anyone from going for a walk when they feel like it? He seemed in a bit of a hurry, anyway."

"And you didn't go after him when you heard the scream?"

"I just heard it now. Anyway, why are you—"

"We haven't got time for this." I run past the pair of them, trying to take the stairs two at a time but failing as they're old and wide and all I do is tire myself out prematurely.

I reach the third floor, call out. Nothing. I run up the next flight. The stairs are becoming much less grand with each floor I travel up. By the time I top the fourth floor it's positively spartan. Looks like the part of these kinds of old houses you'd put servants' quarters in, I guess. Although servants seem to be in even shorter supply than ways out.

And then I see Iain.

Sprawled out at the foot of another flight of stairs, this one wooden and as functional as could be. Leading up to a closed wooden doorway. An attic?

I look down at him. Oh god . . .

His hands. They're missing. Just two wrists combining to be a blood pumping fountain. Iain's face contorted in agony. I bend down. He's no longer breathing. The blood flow weakens, stops.

"He's dead," says Jimmy.

"You've got a great skill for stating the obvious," I say, keeping my eyes downcast.

"Oh my god . . ." He's noticed the hands now. "Was he like that when you found him?"

I nod. "Exactly like that. I haven't moved him." I look from the position of his body to the position of the stairs. "What's that up there, a window? What's that on it?"

"A window?" says Jimmy. "More like a guillotine."

He's right. Judging from the position of Iain's body, it looks like he was reaching for the window when the shutter came down. Hard, judging by the two bloody smears on it.

"Oh god. What's . . . ? Where are his . . . ?"

I turn round. Sylvia, panting like a marathon runner, has arrived.

"Behind there, we think," says Jimmy, pointing to the shuttered window.

"But who would do that to him? How?" Diana, this time. "There was nobody up here. Only Les. Len."

"How could Len have done that? It looks like Iain was reaching for the window when the shutter came down. Taking his hands with it."

Sylvia makes a squeaking sound, turns away.

"What's that? Did I hear my name mentioned?" Len chooses that moment to arrive.

Jimmy rounds on him. I can see the terror in his eyes. He's trying to hold on to a sense of order to keep his fear in check. Without order, without discipline, I can imagine him turning into Sylvia.

"You were the only other one not in the library. Apart from . . ." Jimmy points to the body.

"Iain," I say.

"Yes, I know." Jimmy is furious. "I was trying to give him some dignity."

"Oh. Thought you'd forgotten his name again."

"Stop it, both of you. Just stop it . . ." Diana sounds wrung out. "A man is dead . . ."

"Yes, he is," says Len. "And I had nothing to do with it. I saw him by the lift, I just told you. Bloody ridiculous. I . . . . Jesus, what's happened to him? His hands . . ." Len peers down at the body. "Horrible. Really horrible." Then he looks up. "So that's him gone, then."

Sylvia rounds on him. "How can you? How can you stand there like that and say that? A man has just died. With no hands. How can you . . ." She breaks down into sobbing. Diana comforts her. Silence falls.

This is all getting too much. I want to sit down somewhere, on my own. I check my wrist. The Fitbit tells me over four hours have gone. "We've got less than eight hours left to find that girl and get out of here. We need to focus. Come on."

"You're right." Ramona. "Think of that girl. We don't find her, we fail her. So let's go. Could someone have gotten behind that window up there and actually done that to him?" Ramona points upward.

"Well, not me, that's for sure," says Len.

"What about that door?" says Ramona. "Anyone know what's behind it?"

Someone has to make a move, and with everyone else playing statues it looks like it's me, putting what I just said about needing physical action into practice. I step over the body and start to climb the stairs. "Let's see what's here."

"Careful," shouts Diana.

I reach the top. It's an old, rough wooden door. Barely finished, which brings to mind the kitchen Sylvia and I discovered. There's a doorknob. I give it a twist.

It opens.

I turn to the others. "Well, color me shocked. Given our collective experience with doors and locks so far in this house. This one's open."

Some of them draw back when I say that. A couple lean forward, intrigued. And it's not necessarily the ones you think it would be. Len and Ramona seem interested, Diana, too, to an extent. Jimmy Saint looks like he should be interested but I can see, even from here, the conflict raging within him. Which makes me wonder if that's the only conflict he's ever seen.

I stare ahead of me into the dark space. Turn back once more to the others.

"I'm going in. Who's coming with me?"

Silence. Then: "Ah, one . . . one minute . . ."

Jimmy Saint. Obviously.

"If, ah, if anyone is going on this recce, then it should be, should be me . . ."

Yeah, mate, I think. *Your mouth's saying one thing but your eyes are saying another. Anything to try to keep command. Not lose control.* "Come on, then, up you get."

Jimmy steps gingerly over Iain's body and makes his way to the stairs. "Wait . . ."

I turn. Diana's kneeling over Iain's body. Overcoming her distaste, she's got her hand in his pocket, pulling something out. She holds it up for us all to see.

"My necklace . . ." She looks round at everyone, asking for help in finding answers. "How did my necklace get in his pocket?"

"Ah." Len nods. "Explains why he was in such a hurry, then."

"What d'you mean?" she says.

"I tried to talk to him, accompany him downstairs. But he was having none of it. Off for a walk? Ha. Trying to get away from me, more like."

"Away from all of us," says Ramona. "He must have waited for you to get changed and go back down, crept into your room, and stolen your necklace. Then tried to find a way out."

"But why up here?" Cerys now, holding Monica unconsciously on her hip as if the baby was actually attached. "Why come to the top of the house?"

"Because everywhere else was locked," says Jimmy, and it's the best contribution he's made so far. He looks up past me at the open door. "He must have been trying to find a way out through there . . ."

"And then that window took his hands off," says Len. "Terrible accident."

"If it was an accident." Everyone stares at me and I can't believe I actually spoke those words out loud. "Sorry," I say. "But didn't that Amanda woman say something about traps?"

Diana looks down at Iain's body. "Poor sod."

"I mean," says Ramona, "he was a thief and a bit icky, but . . ."

"You think that means he deserves to die?" Sylvia again, nearly hyperventilating.

"Not at all. I'm just wondering if there's any logic to this. First one's a pedo, second one's a thief. Who else is keeping something hidden? Who's next?"

Sylvia's even more horrified. "You think that's why we're being picked off? We deserve to die if we've got . . . flaws, or something? Things other people don't like. Or secrets. Is that what this is about? Is that what they think we all have in common?"

"I don't know," says Ramona. "I'm just theorizing."

Sylvia sighs, tears gathering. "All I want is to go home . . . back to my living room, drink a cup of tea, listen to *The Archers* . . . that's all I want . . ."

This is getting out of hand again so I hold my wrist up, flashing the Fitbit thing. "OK. Horrible though it is, we need to crack on. Find this girl and get out of here. Time's running out. We can mourn him properly later when we've found her." I look at the door, back to the rest of them, down to Iain's body. Then back to the door. Jimmy is standing behind me on the next step down.

"Ready for an explore, Captain Saint, sah?"

He's not but he says he is.

We go through the door.

CAPTAIN JIMMY SAINT

This is out of my comfort zone. Seriously out of my comfort zone. The training ground, the battlefield, theater of war, yes. All of that. Yes. What I know. Black and white. Right and wrong. But this . . . skulking about in the dark, cloak-and-dagger . . . not me at all. Leave that to Intelligence. Obviously I'm going into the attic. Confront whatever's in there. Because I'm an officer in His Majesty's army. And we're bred to face danger. Proud of it. Plus, the rest of the guests look to me to set an example. No matter what my feelings are about them.

But even so . . . give me a desert or a jungle anytime. Give me an opponent I can understand and outwit. A terrorist or a bomber. Not . . . whatever's waiting for us in here. Or worse, what *might* be waiting for us in here.

"You still behind me, Captain?" Kyle the student, stepping through the attic door.

"Right behind you. On you go." Even if I'm not up front I'm still the one giving orders.

He turns to me again. "You got your gun with you?"

"I do."

"Come on, then."

He enters. I follow. First thing I notice is that it's dark. The only light seeps in from the staircase behind us.

"Is there a light switch?"

"I'm trying to find it . . ." A dusty bulb bursts into some kind of half-life overhead, throwing out weak radiance. "Found it."

We both look round, wary of something or someone rushing us from the shadows. And there are plenty of shadows. The place is practically constructed from them and the light bulb only makes the situation worse.

It's a patchwork of gray and black. There are lighter patches of gray where I presume the windows and bays are. Darker blacks for the corners and distant eaves on the far side. I know the human mind is programmed to see faces in things, find bodies. A survival mechanism since we were in caves, spotting predators. In this attic there could be predators lurking in the corners. There are anonymous shapes everywhere, lumpy and misshapen. Any one of these abandoned items could potentially be a standing or crouching murderer just waiting to pounce. My heart's hammering, I don't mind telling you. But I'm trained to be stoical and that's what I'll do.

I turn, and something leaps out at me. Instinctively I cry out, going for my gun, but it seems to be stuck in the holster and I can't get it out. I'll have to defend myself with my fists. I jump forward, pummeling my attacker, shouting as I go, trying to overwhelm them, knocking them to the ground.

I step backward, feel someone behind me also, turn and begin punching. Straight into a wooden tea chest.

I turn, regaining my breath, look down at my beaten assailant. It's an old dressmaker's dummy.

The student is almost bent double, laughing at me. My hands are still curled into fists. I want to start on him next. I hate his stupid, vapid face.

"You got him, Jimmy, you got him . . ."

I'm so angry now. "Oh, that's funny, is it?" I'm shouting, I know. I've still got my fists up. I'm really tempted to punch him, consequences be damned.

"Sorry," he says, trying to get control of himself once more. "But . . ." He starts laughing again, walking back over to the doorway and calling out, "It's OK, just Jimmy fighting with himself. Nothing to worry about." And more laughter.

I hate being a figure of fun. *Hate* it. I take in the room. The anonymous shapes are just boxes, pieces of furniture, a birdcage. No standing or crouching murderers. I could slug him, I really could.

"I'm going to look through those boxes," I say. "When you've quite finished, perhaps you'll come and join me?"

I don't wait for a reply, head right over to the shelves. The boxes are all old, dusty, well-worn. Abandoned. I pull the first one out.

"Yeah, you do that, Jimmy," says Kyle, laughter finally subsiding. "I'll check over here for anything."

Kyle goes off somewhere else in the attic and, left alone, my anger starts to fade and I'm overwhelmed by embarrassment. Ashamed of myself. I shouldn't have reacted that way. And my anger at the student laughing at me? It's beneath me. I should be better than that. I *am* better than that.

Jettisoning those feelings as much as I can, I concentrate on the task at hand. Rummaging through the box. Toys. Old, broken, worn toys. Played with, then discarded. I pull a few out. A teddy bear, threadbare with an eye missing. An old model kit of a Spitfire, hand-painted in camo colors but scratched, brown at the seams where the glue has hardened and aged. Missing a wing. I drop it back in, replace the box. Then notice something.

Written in felt-tip on the side of the box: PROPERTY OF CHARLES BOYD.

Charles Boyd. The person whose house this is. I suppose it makes sense that his things are here.

On the shelves next to the boxes are some board games. Monopoly, Mousetrap. That kind of thing. A very tattered and obviously well-used edition of Cluedo. As old and dusty as everything else up here. I pull out another cardboard box, again with the same name on it, stick my hand in. Find some old magic tricks, whatever magic they once possessed now gone. Reach in farther. There are some discs at the bottom. I pull one out. A plastic coin. I examine it in the weak light. A doubloon from Treasure Island, it says.

I sense something at my shoulder and begin to turn. It's a doll.

"Hey," says Kyle, "I've found you."

I look at what he's holding up and showing me. It's an Action Man in army gear. Showing the rank of captain.

I turn to him. "Look at this." Cross back to the shelf, show him the writing on the box.

"Charles Boyd. Proves this is his house if nothing else."

"If that doll is all you've found, then we should be getting back to the others. Time's moving on."

"It's not," Kyle says. "Come and see."

The floorboards creak under our feet as we make our way from one side to the other. Kyle keeps up a commentary. "It's like an abandoned life up here," he says. "Toys over there, a dismantled bed over there." He gestures to where pieces of a brass bed frame lie propped against one wall. "Boxes of clothes . . . furniture . . . books . . ."

"Anything pointing to our adversary? Or the missing girl?"

"Nothing so far. But this is what I wanted to show you. Come over here."

Kyle leads me to the far end of the attic. It's almost pitch-black, the light from the weak overhead bulb barely penetrating this far through the detritus and shadows. I can make out the pattern of chimney bricks and that's about it. "What am I supposed to be looking at? I can hardly see anything."

"Here," he says, and I can feel him leading me toward the wall.

I put my hand out, feel nothing but brick.

"Not there, here."

Kyle guides my hand along to where the brick ends and the roof beams start. Then down. The wall is different here, the eaves feel filled in, not open like the other side of the attic.

"There's something here, I think," he says. "Can you feel it?"

I run my fingers along the wooden surface of the eave. I do feel something. A join, a gap in the wood. "What is it?"

"Press it and see." He laughs. "I want to see if I'm right and not imagining things."

I do as he says. Press the wood inward. I hear a click and the wood moves slowly outward. I turn to him. "It's a cupboard."

"That's what I thought when I found it just now. But I felt inside. And there are stairs going down. I felt them. It's only small but I think it gets wider. It's not a cupboard. It's a secret passage." Kyle can barely keep the excitement out of his voice. "Shall we see where it goes?"

Everyone stood still, as if Kyle's last, shouted words rendered them mute and immobile.

"We've found a secret passageway. We're heading down it . . ."

After that he'd appeared at the attic doorway to tell us that he and the captain weren't coming out again and we shouldn't worry. At least not yet. Then he disappeared. So we're left standing, some of the others moving their lips like they want to speak but can't find the words. And there's still a dead body at our feet.

Someone has to make a move. "OK. Let's do this." My words make Sylvia and Diana jump, like they've been asleep or in deep meditation. I continue. "We've got to move this body. We can't just leave it here."

"Why not just leave it here?" Sylvia, obviously. "We won't come up again. We'll stay downstairs."

"And what if we have to?" asks Cerys, baby still glued to her hip.

"Why would we have to?"

"They say there's a secret passage," says the old guy. "Who knows where that leads? We might need it. And if that's the case, Ramona's right. We should move the body. Besides, it's not very Christian, is it? Leaving a dead body lying around."

"Not very tidy, either," says Diana. "Someone could trip over it."

She's fingering the necklace Iain stole from her as she speaks so I guess she's not remembering him in a compassionate way. Certainly not a Christian way. And the way she's staring at his body makes me think she might like to trip over it. Several times. As hard as possible wearing steel toecaps. I think it's fair to say Diana's recovered from the shock of finding him there.

"Let's put him where we put Desmond," I say, "and then see if we can find some keys to the locked doors in this house. And maybe by doing that, we find Claire."

Cerys shivers as I say that. I can see from her eyes she's reliving the events of last night. Seeing that creep's body again, finding her baby play-ing with his eyeball. I can't let her slip back into that. Or any of them. This is a volatile situation and we're all pretty volatile people. Fear and panic will spread like an airborne disease in this house.

"OK," I say. "Where did the last one go? Desmond?"

"In the kitchen," says Sylvia. "The kitchen that's never been used."

"Who's going to give me a hand?"

Diana's still staring at the body like she wants to do it some harm. "I will."

"OK. Sylvia, you know where this kitchen is, right? You can lead the way."

It's clearly the last thing Sylvia wants to do, but she sees she has no choice.

"Let's get him to the elevator."

"I think Cerys needs a strong drink; I'll take her to the library for one. Meet you there when you're done," Len says. I nodded my head in agreement.

I take Iain's head and get my arms under his, Diana his legs, and we kind of pull, kind of drag him down the narrow wooden staircase toward the floor below where the elevator sits. Aware of the snail trail of blood we're leaving, neither of us wanting to get it on our hands or clothes. Obviously there are only stairs up to the servants' quarters. The kind of people who have servants think—if they think about them at all—the extra walk will improve their circulation. That elevators will make them weak. And are too expensive. Jesus. Your class system. Not saying we don't have similar in the States, but my god, y'all take some beating.

"Watch his head," I say. Diana's pulling hard at his legs, which takes him from my grasp and makes his head bump off the bare stairs like a wooden ball hitting a coconut at a fairground. She's pulling so hard it sounds metronomic.

"Sorry," she says. She isn't.

We reach the landing with the elevator. Diana lets his legs drop, opens the cage door.

"Come on, Sylvia," I call. "In here with us."

From the appalled look on her face I've either invited her to witness the horror of her last night on Earth or indulge all her private desires in the greatest orgy ever. Both options seem repulsive to her. But, to her credit, she puts that aside and joins us in the elevator.

I pull back the gate, press for the first floor. Or ground floor. Whatever.

I see Cerys's terrified face as the elevator descends, Len putting a protective arm around her, the baby staring ahead.

And then we're going down. None of us speaking. Not much to say. Until Diana screams.

"Stop . . ."

She reaches over to the control panel, pressing the stop button as hard as she can. The elevator shudders to a halt so quick it feels like we're swinging in the shaft. I look at Diana for some explanation, but she's staring through the bars of the cage; something's caught her attention.

"What's the matter?" Sylvia almost shrieks the question.

"There," says Diana, pointing. "The *painting*."

We both follow her finger. Iain's painting has changed. Last night it showed him standing in a casino, smiling and failing to win. It's still the same casino scene, but now Iain's body is slumped over a roulette table, arms out, hands missing. Blood pooling on the red. The other casino patrons don't seem upset. If anything they're laughing at him.

"It's a different painting," says Diana, turning back to us. "Completely different. I mean, if someone was defacing them or painting over them or taking them down I could understand that. But like with Desmond last night, it's been replaced with a completely different one. One that shows what's happened to him."

"Like it's been planned," says Sylvia. "But who could do that? We've all been upstairs, who could have done it? And how could they know?"

"I don't know," says Diana, clearly struggling to keep her composure, "but it means . . . it means there must be a stack of hidden paintings somewhere, and someone knows how each of us is going to . . ." She grasps her chest like she's having a panic attack.

"*If*," I say, "not how. Come on. Get a grip." I'm not going to let their fear infect me. I'm not. "We'll dump this body, find the missing girl, and get out of here, right?" I look between their faces. Neither seems to believe me. I up the volume. "*Right?*"

They both mumble in agreement.

THE OTHER PEOPLE   119

"Come on then. One thing at a time. There's a poor kid locked up somewhere, waiting for us to rescue her. The paintings can wait for now."

I press the button and the elevator resumes its descent.

We reach the ground floor. Yes, I said ground. I open the cage and we drag the body out.

"Which way?"

Sylvia shows us.

Iain's pretty heavy by this time and I can see Diana's struggling. I pride myself on my core body strength—regular sessions on the pole see to that—but even *my* arms are starting to seize up and shake. Luckily Sylvia tells us we've arrived.

"This is the door," she says and turns as if she's going to disappear on us.

"Don't run off," I say. "Open it, please."

It's clear she doesn't want to do that, knowing what's waiting for her inside, but she does so. Turning her body away as the door swings inward, closing her eyes so as not to see anything.

Diana and I drag Iain's body inside. We straighten up, look round.

"You sure this is the place, Sylvia? Where they left Desmond's body?"

Sylvia opens her eyes. "Of course I'm sure. I'm not likely to make a mistake, am I?"

"OK," I say, not wanting her to start arguing again, "but have a look in here."

"Why should I?"

"Just do it," says Diana, clearly tired from the exertion and in no mood for Sylvia's shit, either.

Sylvia steps inside. "Oh."

"Yeah," I say, "Oh."

It's apparently the right room, but it's empty.

Desmond's body has disappeared.

Well. Shock follows shock as surely as tick follows tock round here, doesn't it?

I mean, that's a given, really, when you think about it. So much so that we shouldn't even be discussing it. So let's not. If you want to, we could look at other things that have just occurred. Detective Beast in the Cellar could don his (or her, I'm quite fluid about these things) deerstalker and we could examine what those of you of an investigative bent might like to call "clues." If you want to. I mean, you've probably spotted things you want to discuss. And I won't stop you. But wouldn't that spoil the fun? Isn't it best to be surprised? Follow things to see how they unfold, where they go, rather than try to fit everything into your one-size-fits-all narrative?

Well, I think so.

But first, an apology. About Iain. Or as I should say, Kevin. Maybe I should have mentioned that earlier. Thing is, I didn't know. I only had the information I was given. And that said he was Iain Wardle-Roberts. So that's what I told you. I don't want you to think I was lying. *He* was lying. Which poses another question. If someone in the house is a liar and is exposed as a liar, does that automatically make them a killer? Or just more likely to be a killer? Hmm. Something to ponder.

And here's something else I've been thinking about lately, and I'd like to share it with you. Imaginary friends. We all had one, didn't we? At some time or another. Someone in childhood usually, to share games with, talk to when things were tough, celebrate when things were going well. And then, like Kipling said, and like you've just seen in the attic, it comes time to put away childish things. No. Wait. That wasn't Kipling. It was the Bible, wasn't it? Yes, of course it was. 1 Corinthians 13:11, to be exact, for all you fact fans out there. Of course, it's a bit rich the Bible coming out with that, isn't it? Especially the part about childhood's end consisting of getting rid of imaginary friends. Which reminds me of a story I once heard. It's a long time since I heard it so I might get a few things wrong but the spirit'll be there. Here goes.

One night a man had a dream. He was walking along a beach with God next to him. Or Jesus, or whoever he was being that day. Anyway, the man could see in the sky all these scenes from his life playing out. And there were two sets of footprints in the sand—one set belonging to him, the other to God. With me so far? Great. Now, when the last scene of this man's life flashed before him, he looked back and noticed that occasionally there were only one set of footprints in the sand. He also worked out that this one lot of footprints coincided with the worst, lowest, saddest, most wicked horrible times of his life.

Well, this made him angry. And since he had God next to him and thought that God owed him something he called him out on it.

Oi, God, he said, *you told me that if I did all the things you wanted like being a good person and living a good life and that, you'd take care of me always. So what's all this about? When I've gone through the absolute worse parts of my life, you left me on my own to deal with it.*

He got really upset saying this. Because, to be honest, he had actually gone through some terrible shit that hadn't been his fault, even if at the time he had been forced to believe it was and it had given him an unhappy life for years afterward. In fact, in his darker moments, he doubted he would ever overcome it.

So God looked at him, spread his arms out like he's supposed to do, and smiled. *Well*, he said, *more fool you, you fucking idiot.*

This wasn't what the man had been expecting to hear and told God that. *What d'you mean? Aren't you supposed to console me and tell me those footsteps were yours and you were carrying me or something? Make me feel less alone? Feel wanted and needed?*

Jesus, how old are you? said God. *What's that bit I put in the Bible about putting away childish things? Don't you think imaginary friends come under that heading?*

The man was confused. *But that means . . . you're not real.*

No, mate. Course I'm not.

So how can I be talking to you if you're not real?

Because this is a dream, dickhead. Remember? Imaginary friends won't help you in real life. Not even the popular ones like me. No one'll help you.

Good things happen to bad people, bad things happen to good people. Get used to it. There's no great cosmic point to all this, no lesson to be learned or wisdom to be gained. There's just you. Alone in the universe. And you can do what you like, you won't be judged. Not by me, at any rate. No, you were born alone, you'll die alone, and that's that. What you do to fill in the bits in between is up to you.

And then God, who had never really been there in the first place, disappeared. And the man woke up and went on with his life. Alone.

So there you go. I told you I'd have to paraphrase a bit but you get the gist. Imaginary friends. Childhood's end. All of that. Alone in the universe to do what you want.

And God? As usual, that fucker's nowhere to be seen.

KYLE TANNER

The stairs continue down. It's cramped in here and both the captain and myself have to contort our bodies to make any progress. Whoever made this wasn't thinking about comfort. Or regular-size people.

"Perhaps it's some old priest hole or something," says Captain Saint from behind me. "Where they used to hide Catholic priests back in Elizabethan times."

That doesn't strike me as being right, somehow. I'm not getting that vibe. "You think the house is that old?"

"Some of it, perhaps, might be. This part, for example."

I can't excuse his logic. The steps are wooden, basically made. The walls and ceiling from a similar wood. It's cramped and it's dark. The weak light from the attic has disappeared now, and there's no light penetrating anywhere. As you've seen previously, I'm not great in enclosed spaces and this place is no exception. Actually, I hate enclosed spaces. I have extreme claustrophobia. When I was a kid on school trips, I'd get panic attacks if I had to go up a stone staircase in a tower. I would always think I'd be entombed there, especially when the steps became smaller as we got nearer the top. The worst was St. Paul's. Up in the dome they have a corridor that tourists can try to make their way along. It's tiny. Cramped on either side and from top to bottom. There's barely space for one person to make it along. When we went, people were coming up at the same time. No one would give way. Impasse. We were stuck. I thought I was going to be trapped there forever and felt myself start to faint. To this day I still don't know how I got out.

"Kyle? You all right?"

I blink, breathe as deeply as I can. Feels like the small space is robbing my body of breath. "Yes." Hope my voice doesn't shake. "Why?"

"You've stopped moving. Thought there must be some kind of barrier up ahead."

"No, no, just . . . having a breather." *Come on, Kyle, don't crack up now, especially not in front of this one.* "Checking the time." I look at my wrist. We've been in here for less than fifteen minutes. I thought it was much longer. "Right. On we go."

I start moving down the stairs again, the captain following, the darkness and confined space a kind of sensory deprivation chamber. We continue wordlessly until I notice the hallway begins to shrink to an even smaller, more cramped size. I have to bend down just to keep going.

"What's wrong? Have you found something?"

"Feel the walls," I say. "They're closing in, it's like . . . Oh."

"What?" I can feel the captain trying to reach over my shoulder. "Is there a door?"

He's annoying me even more now and I'm about to let him know it. "Can you not . . . it's hard enough to stand in here without you pushing me out the way."

He stops but he's unhappy about it. "Yes, of course, yes. So why have you stopped?"

I feel ahead of me. Just smooth wood. Around to the sides, the same. Above, ditto. "Because we've run out of stairs," I say. "It's a dead end. There's nothing here."

"We'll have to go back." There's rising desperation in Jimmy's voice. He sounds as scared of this tiny space as I am.

I feel him try to turn round, huffing and puffing as he does so. He stops, his breathing becoming increasingly heavy. "I can't, there's . . . there's not enough room to turn . . ."

Bent nearly double now I can feel a panic attack coming. I'm back in my dream again, earth being thrown on me, unable to move from my shallow grave, my restrictive wooden coffin. I close my eyes hoping those visions will disappear. They don't.

Behind me the captain's movements are becoming increasingly erratic and desperate. "I just . . . If I can get round here to . . . I have to . . ."

Jimmy pushes into me, both of his feet in the small of my back, taking away any semblance of balance in this small space and flattening me against the blank wall ahead. I have the presence of mind to put my hands out as I go so it's not my face being squashed against it.

"Idiot, what are you . . ." I can barely get the words out as my body is crushed against the wood.

As I move my hand I feel something move beneath it. A click. Like the one that opened this passage in the first place.

"Just a minute," I say, "I think there's . . ."

The floor gives way beneath me and I fall through.

"What's happened? Where are you? Are you all right?"

"It was a . . . fuck . . ." The wind has been knocked out of me and I'm on my back. I'm more surprised than hurt, though. The fall wasn't far. "Fuck . . ." I try to stand. Decide not to, not yet. "It's a trapdoor," I manage to croak.

I hear scrabbling from above. "There's a ladder here. Why didn't you use that?"

"Yeah, thanks, brainiac," I manage. "If I'd found it, I would have done . . ."

"I'm coming." I hear Jimmy climb down.

I push myself up from the floor. Try to look at my surroundings. No light, not even coming from any chinks from anywhere. I press my Fitbit thing so that the glow from the screen illuminates where I am. All I can make out are rough stone walls. It smells damp, feels shivery. I put my arms out in front of me, make my way over slowly to where I see a wall. I trace my fingers along it, searching for a light switch, a candle, anything that might help. I find a light switch. Screw my eyes closed, so painful is the sudden light after so long in the dark.

Gradually I open my eyes. Let what I'm seeing form before me. Process it. This is a room in the house I haven't been in before. From the captain's expression, neither has he.

"Good lord . . ."

"Jesus . . ."

"What the hell's all this?"

The captain bends down, examining the first thing he touches. A shovel. And next to it a pick sporting a heavy-duty head. Both recently used, gathering from the drying dirt clumped on the shovel's blade.

I've got a bad feeling about this. I turn away, checking what else is in the room. My bad feeling intensifies. Gas canisters. Heavy, standing upright. Tubes attached. A breathing mask fitted to the end of the tubes.

Plastic sheeting, folded neatly, some still in its original packaging. And on the far wall, the clincher.

Photos. Lots of them. All young girls, all more or less the same physical type. I remember them from the video presentation Amanda gave us earlier. Some of the actual photos she used are here. All smiling. None of what they look like after he's finished with them.

"This must be his lair," I say, back to Jimmy. And when I turn to face him, I stop dead.

He's pointing his gun at me.

"What?" I say.

"That's far enough. Don't move."

And then I realize. It's him.

Before I can say anything else I hear it. Again. That noise.

The girl. She's crying, terrified. Sobbing to be set free.

CAPTAIN JIMMY SAINT

"Can you hear her? There. There . . ." Kyle flits around, pressing his ear against this wall, that wall, the floor. Panting frantically with excitement. "There . . . she's . . . no, there . . ."

Well, I didn't expect this. Denials, yes, lies, obviously. Even an explanation. But not this.

"*Stop it,*" I say. "Stop that and look at me."

After all this whirling dervish action, Kyle eventually comes to rest in the middle of the room but he doesn't stop because I've commanded him to. In fact, he's ignoring me, which obviously annoys me further. He holds his hand up, fingers out, shushing me as if I'm making too much noise. Since you shouldn't interrupt sleepwalkers or madmen, I say nothing, do nothing. Just stand where I am, watching him. As I have done since he started his performance. With my gun still on him.

And the thing is, I don't hear what he's heard. I can't actually hear this Claire girl crying.

There's silence in the room while he stands frozen, eyes staring like he desperately wants to believe something to be true.

"There's no one there," I say. "And you know there isn't. Now stop playing for time and stand still."

Kyle stares at me then, as if only noticing that I'm holding my gun on him. He looks from the gun to me. "What are you doing? You going to shoot me?" Some kind of realization comes over his face. He smiles. "They'll know it's you. When you come down on your own, they'll guess."

I frown. "What are you talking about?"

"Your gun." He's shouting, as if he wants his voice to be heard above the noise. Except there isn't any. "Clearly you're going to kill me. Like you did the others. And all while that girl's crying out for help. Is that it? Because she's crying? I'm getting too near so you have to kill me?"

I still can't hear anything. At first I'm confused about what he's saying and then I get it. And smile. "Clever. Very clever. No. I'm pointing the gun at you because this is your lair. You gave yourself away when you entered. Went straight for the light switch."

Kyle's looking at me incredulously now. "What? I fucking fell in here, you regimented moron! I could have killed myself!"

"Staged, of course. You knew you wouldn't hurt yourself."

"Bollocks. I had no idea. And I only found the light switch by running my hand along the wall. You'd have done the same if you'd been the one in front."

"But I wasn't, was I?"

"No. Because you clearly knew where we were heading." Kyle gestures to my gun. "That gives it away."

We stare at each other, saying nothing. He closes his eyes.

"Please stop . . . stop crying . . ." he says.

"There's no one there, Kyle."

Silence once more and then he sighs, drops his shoulders. Opens his eyes. "You're right. She's stopped now. I can't hear her anymore."

"There was never anyone there. There was no girl crying in the first place."

Kyle looks round quickly, as if I've tricked him. Then smiles. "You would say that, wouldn't you? I heard her before, when Sylvia and I discovered the kitchen. And I heard her just now. We must be beside the kitchen. Am I right? Have we come down that far?"

"I have no idea. You tell me."

"No, *you* tell me."

I'm getting exasperated with him. To put it mildly. "I am not the killer. Clearly. I have an alibi for all three deaths. I was even with you for Iain's. And I was with you when Amanda was shot. Clearly I didn't do that."

"Your accomplice did it."

"Or yours."

I pause, thinking about this. Have I made a mistake? "What about this room? How did you know where the passageway led?"

"I didn't," Kyle says. "Same as you. We were with each other, you know that. Like I said, I just happened to be the one in front."

I say nothing. Just keep the gun pointed at him.

"Think about it," he says. "If I'm the killer, why would I go to all this trouble to bring you into my secret lair? Wouldn't I just have kept it secret?"

I have to admit, that does make sense.

"And then what was I going to do? Confess, or something? Then kill you? And tell the others what, exactly?"

I have no answer to that.

"And now you're holding a gun on me. Doesn't that make me think the killer's you?"

"It's definitely not me."

"And it's definitely not me," he says. "Which leaves us at a bit of an impasse, doesn't it?"

One of us has to take a chance. Trust someone else in this house. And it looks like it's going to have to be me. And if I'm wrong, then I've still got my gun. Which I now return to its holster. We both breathe a sigh of relief.

"I'm sorry," I say. "Sorry for wrongly accusing you."

Kyle gives a weak smile. "And I'm sorry for wrongly accusing you too."

The atmosphere in the room changes again. As if with that unpleasantness out of the way and acknowledgments made to each other we can move on. Like this misunderstanding has created the basis for some kind of bond between us. A kind of trust.

Kyle searches for something to sit on, finds a pile of plastic sheeting, plonks himself down. He sighs, rubs his face with his hands. "But I definitely heard her. Didn't you?"

I find an old tea chest to sit on too. "Sorry, old boy, I really didn't."

He sighs. "Then why is it just me that can hear her?"

"I don't know, but maybe you're not the only one. Maybe one of the others can hear her and they're not here to tell us about it. Maybe . . ." I stop. That's thin gruel, even to my own ears.

"Maybe I'm imagining it." He sighs again. This time when he speaks, it's not as he's spoken yet in the house. Quiet, thoughtful. The bother with the gun seems to have allowed us to talk on a deeper level. "I'm sure I heard her, Jimmy. Sure. But . . ." Another sigh. "I'm on edge. I mean, we all are, but with you pulling the gun one me, and at that storm when we first got here. I hate storms. Hate them."

I nod, but I don't know what he's talking about. What storm? "Why . . . why do you hate storms so much?"

"Because of . . . you know, some people have phobias? Like snakes and spiders? Irrational fears, really. Yeah, you'll meet a spider sometime, lots of them. But they're not going to kill you. Maybe in Australia or somewhere, but even then you shouldn't fear them. Just be wary of them. Prepare for them. Oh, I don't know what I'm saying." Kyle looks up at me and there's a softness in his eyes. It's the first time I've seen it. Softness and . . . something else. Fear? No, that's too melodramatic. Honesty, perhaps? Whatever. It makes me feel ashamed for blaming him for being the killer. "You know what I mean, though. Some people are scared of snakes. Well, I'm scared of storms."

"I see." This is all out of my wheelhouse, I'm afraid. I consider myself a man of action, not contemplation. And I'm certainly not a therapist. But it's what Kyle seems to need right now. And we are stuck here and we do have an obligation to help out our fellow man and all that. But there's something I'm not getting. "Sorry, old boy, but what has this all to do with hearing that girl?"

His eyes shift down to the floor. Thinking, apparently, before answering. "It all seems bound up together. To me, at least. I've always hated enclosed spaces. Being trapped in them. Unable to move or get out. And I had a dream about that when I was first here. The first time I looked out the window and the lightning flashed I saw someone moving what I thought was a body through the garden."

"Yes, I remember you saying."

"And after that, when we went exploring, I heard the girl crying for help. And then again now. So . . . I suppose it might not make much sense to you . . ." He laughs. "I mean, god knows it doesn't make much sense to me, but it feels like everything is tied up together somehow. My nightmare, my fear of the storm, the girl crying . . . I don't know."

I nod and say nothing. I don't know what to say that would help.

"Maybe it's . . . I don't know. Sounds stupid, but maybe it's got something to do with what I'm studying? The Gothic? Interpreting all my experiences through a Gothic frame of reference? Imagining all these things just to help me cope with what's actually happening? Could that be it?"

He wants an answer this time. One I'm not able to give him, I'm afraid. But I try. "I . . . well, yes. It could be, yes. Why not?"

Kyle nods and eventually looks up, directly at me. "What about you?" he says. "Don't you have any fears, phobias? That have maybe manifested themselves since you arrived in this house?"

I'm about to tell him not to be so stupid, of course not, but I don't. Because that isn't actually true. I have been beset by something since being in this house. And since this young lad has shared something of himself with me it only seems right and proper that I should share something with him. He's displaying a sincerity I haven't previously seen. But then I suppose none of us know anyone else, not really. We all contain multitudes, and all that.

"Fear," I say. "Fear of losing myself. My authority, at least." I sigh. It's hard work, this opening-up lark. I can't seem to find the right words. "Is that the problem? I don't know. I'm used to being listened to. Taking command. I'm a straightforward kind of chap. Not the kind that goes in for that psychology mumbo jumbo. At least not outside the context of my work in the field. I'm . . ." Should I share this with him? I suppose I should tell someone. "I'm not really a captain. My actual rank is second lieutenant, the most junior rank you can have as a commissioned officer on entering the armed services. So I've never been in charge of a regiment; in fact, I've never actually been in charge of anything. Or anyone."

"So why are you dressed as a captain?"

I look away, shamefaced. "Because that was the uniform waiting for me in the wardrobe when I got here. Naturally I put it on. Obviously I wasn't going to let on that I wasn't a captain. And then when we were all together and things became serious, I took command because that's what a captain would do in that situation."

"And shoot a chunk out of the ceiling."

I can't meet his gaze now. "Yes, well . . ."

We sit there in silence for a while. Until I break it to explain myself further. "It's hard work, taking command. I thought the uniform would give me a natural authority. Command respect. But it seems not."

"Especially with this lot."

I look up. Kyle's smiling. I, too, manage a smile. "Yes, you're right. So what shall we do next?"

"You're asking me?"

"I'm a second lieutenant, not a captain. I'm used to taking orders."

"Right, Second Lieutenant Saint. Let's find a way out of this room and get back to the others."

We both stand up. Before we make to leave, I place a hand on Kyle's arm. He looks at me. "You, ah, won't be telling everyone else about my little deception, I take it?"

"Will you be telling everyone about my bad dreams, phobias, and delusions?"

"Fair point. And let's not mention that business with the gun."

He nods, as if to say, our secrets are safe.

"Captain, let's get out of here."

We file into the library, one by one. No one speaks. No one can think of anything to say. And we certainly can't explain what we've just seen. Or haven't seen.

Len is sitting on his own in an armchair, eating a pastry, cup of tea on a table at his side.

"Thought you were bringing Cerys here for a stiff drink?"

"Didn't want one. Said she was going to get her head down instead. How did it go in the kitchen, then?"

I leave the library, go to the dining room, get myself a coffee. Leave Diana and Sylvia to explain that one.

"Gone?" Len is saying as I return. "What d'you mean, gone?"

"As in not there," says Diana. "Gone. Like Amanda's body was. And he definitely didn't get up and walk."

"You sure you didn't make a mistake?"

"Of course we're sure." Sylvia this time, her voice modulating on the most annoying frequency possible. "We put it there and now he's gone. We left Iain there, though. We had no other place for him."

"But Desmond's gone?" Len says again, his head back, frowning, like he's trying to come up with theories. He doesn't say any more, but I can see from the look on his face that his mind's working away. I sit down on one of the overstuffed sofas and watch him.

Something about what he's doing, the expression on his face, it's not like the old man we've seen previously. This one is more calculating, shrewd. When he thinks no one is watching, his eyes dart round the room, studying us all, making decisions about us. I've got good instincts when it comes to men. And I don't think I trust him anymore. If I ever did.

"I couldn't sleep with all this going on. What's happening? What have I missed?"

Cerys enters, with Monica still strapped to her. The baby once again an immobile extension of her. Cerys looks round the room, too, and despite the fear in her eyes, when she sees me, she smiles.

I pat the seat next to me; she comes and sits down. I tell her what's happened. And straightaway she bursts into tears. "Disappeared? How can he just disappear?"

"I don't know, dear," Sylvia replies. "We went to deposit the latest one and Desmond was gone." Her final word cracks and it's clear she's barely holding it together. She struggles, tries to tamp her emotions down. "We don't know anything more than that."

"But if he's disappeared, then . . ."

"Then he may be still alive," says Len. "And perhaps, just perhaps, he may be the one behind all this." This is a different Len who's just spoken. Stronger. More in charge. Younger, if that's at all possible.

He's gotten our attention. He continues.

"It's obvious, isn't it?" he says. "He kills that Amanda woman, hides her body, then becomes the first one of us to go, and he plays dead, so he can creep round the house and watch the rest of us. Fake his own death, make it as grisly as possible so we don't question it. A classic ploy."

"Says who?" I say.

"Says ex-Detective Inspector Len Melville, that's who."

"You're a cop?" I say. Kind of surprised, but it also explains his recent change.

He smiles. "Question: What does an invisible man do best? Answer: anything he likes. He can't be seen. You thought I was invisible, didn't you? Poor old Len, sitting in the background, not saying anything, wanting to go back to his allotment, bit senile, probably, bless him.

"You think I wasn't doing that on purpose? When people don't really see you, you can watch them unobserved. And that's what I've been doing with you all. Watching. Observing. The way you all talk and act when you're together and especially when you think no one's looking at you."

"That's fucking creepy," I say.

"That's good policing," he replies.

"A policeman. Excellent. Now things will be sorted out." Sylvia wriggles in her chair with excitement. At least someone's happy with Len's news.

"I'm an ex-copper. Murder Squad. And while this may be a bit more fanciful than what I usually encountered in my time south of the river, it's not out of the realm of possibility. Think about it. When we found Desmond's body last night, what did we think? Were we shocked?"

"Of course we were bloody shocked," says Cerys. "My daughter was playing with his . . ."

"Yes," says Len. "Yes. I know. His eyeball. Or a very elaborate prop. Which was disposed of instantly if I remember correctly, so we can't check it out now?"

No one answers. He continues.

"So. All he had to do was to arrange a convincing body with plenty of gory trappings so we would immediately fear the worst and lie still long enough to be disposed of. Then once we've left him, he has free rein of the house. To go anywhere and do as he pleases. Don't you all agree?"

Sylvia, nodding, clearly does. Diana and I exchange uneasy glances.

"But we saw the body," says Diana. "We *smelled* it. He was disemboweled. Slashed all over. Blood everywhere. It was like an abattoir in that room. There was barely anything of him left intact. He was dead, no doubt about it." She looks round the room, asking for support with her eyes. "Wasn't he?"

"I didn't say he didn't use real meat," says Len. "That's what you smelt and saw."

"I agree with Len," Sylvia says proudly. "It's quite clear that's what's happened. He's the killer, the one we should be searching for. Now we know what he looks like we can set about finding him. If we all stay together, we can do that."

I look directly at Sylvia. "Well, listen to perky Paula, now."

"Oh, trust you to be negative. Someone's trying to help and all you can do is be negative."

"This is . . . this is like one of those shows on TV where all these people get gathered together and they're . . . they're dead, or something . . ." Cerys says.

I see Sylvia roll her eyes. She's about to say something—no doubt derogatory and hurtful—when Len jumps in.

"That's right," he says. "We're dead and people keep dying. That makes perfect sense." His sarcastic manner and dismissive shake of the head show what he thinks of her. I really dislike him now.

Cerys is clearly embarrassed by his words but red-faced and to her credit, she answers him back. "Well, maybe not, but I just thought . . . thought this could be a game. On TV. Hidden cameras, like *Big Brother*, or something."

"You've got a valid point, Cerys, but I doubt it's the TV idea," I say. "If Len is right, then Desmond being killed would rule that out."

"But it might still be a game," says Cerys. "Like puzzles we have to solve. Or the deaths could be tests, or . . . I don't know."

"I think you've said enough for now, dear," says Sylvia.

I turn to Sylvia. "Aren't we getting away from the fact that there's a vulnerable, scared girl in fear of her life that we should be looking for?"

Sylvia gives me that hideous condescending smile of hers. "Of course we know that, dear. But none of us want to suffer the same fate, though, do we? We have to look after ourselves."

"Whatever," says Diana, holding up her bracelet thing. "We need to do it quickly. Time's running out." She turns to Len. "What you're saying about Desmond, he wouldn't have been able to do all this on his own. Wouldn't he need an accomplice?"

"You mean someone in this room?" Len smiles. A smug, cruel smile, confirming something he's been thinking. "That's a very plausible idea."

"But who would do that?" asks Diana.

"Could be Len," I say, trying to hit back at him. "He's the one came up with the idea. Is he trying to shift suspicion from himself?"

Len stares at me like looks could kill. I hold his gaze, return it. It's a long time since I allowed a man to intimidate me.

"Don't be ridiculous," he says eventually. "I'm ex-police. I'm on the right side. But someone in here could have done it."

"Who?" asks Diana.

"Well, I do have someone in mind . . ."

Before anyone else can say anything there's a noise. A shuffling sound, like muffled footsteps. We all look at one another in alarm.

"Can you hear that?" I say.

"Of course we can hear it," says Sylvia, snappy and tense.

Then we look around the room for the origin of the noise.

There it is again.

"It's coming from the bookcase," says Diana. And she points, rather unnecessarily.

We all turn to stare. And with a soft click the bookshelf moves. Opens into the room like a very large door.

Sylvia, giving vent to her barely hidden fear, starts to bleat. "It's him. It's . . ."

The bookshelf door opens fully. And out steps the army captain and the student. No one speaks, just stares at them as they enter the room.

"Right," says Kyle. "You'll be wondering why I've asked you all here . . ."

Well, I thought it was funny.

"Sorry," I say, "couldn't resist. I saw the looks on all your faces and . . ." I shrug. What else can I do? I laugh. Actually laugh.

Sylvia, predictably, is the first one to respond. On her feet, finger wagging, the lot. "You think that's funny, do you? Here we all are, in this room while murders are going on left, right, and center, and you think it's time to make a joke?"

"Oh, give the guy a break," says Ramona. "You're reacting like he's just fingered your mother."

Sylvia is so stunned she can't speak. Which is a good thing, but I know it's only going to be temporary and when she does speak, it's going to be stratospheric so I interject before it can reach that stage.

"Captain Jimmy and I have found a secret passage. And a couple of other things." I turn to Jimmy. "Captain?"

He follows me into the room, looking at me in alarm when I mention his rank. I give him a small, reassuring nod to say his secret's safe with me. He gives me a grateful smile in return, closes the bookshelf behind him. Of course it leads into the library. Of course it's a bookshelf. If I'd been designing a house like this, it's exactly where I would have put a secret passage.

"Right," says Jimmy, taking center stage. I notice Len seems disappointed by our arrival. Angry, even, if I thought his emotional range extended that far. "As you know, Kyle and I found a secret passageway in the attic. We also found a set of boxes containing the childhood belongings of Charles Boyd."

"The man who's supposed to own this house," says Diana.

Jimmy continues. "We followed this passage down to a secret chamber. In it were all the things you'd need to bury a body and keep it alive."

"Shovels, plastic sheeting, air canisters." I can't resist joining in.

"All of that," says Jimmy. "And also another secret passageway leading here."

"Are there any others?" asks Diana.

"I suppose we must assume so," says Jimmy. "It's not like these old houses to have only one."

"Well, that makes sense, I suppose." Len, this time. And I don't know if I'm imagining it but he seems to have a much stronger voice than earlier. One that commands authority.

"How does that make sense?" asks Jimmy.

Jimmy sits down while Len fills us in on what we've missed while we've been on our little adventure. Desmond's body disappearing, all of it.

"I helped get rid of that body," I say. "We could barely carry him he was so badly mutilated. Bits kept falling out. It was a struggle to keep him whole. And now you say he just got up and went walkabout?"

Len gives me a smug smile and a patronizing shake of the head. "When you've seen the things I have, son, you'd not be so easily fooled."

I think of Desmond's slippery organs falling through my hands as I carried him, how I repeatedly swallowed down vomit to keep going, the frequent stops we had to make just to hold his body together long enough to get him to the kitchen. "Bollocks."

There's that smug smile from Len again. "With all due respect, son, you're much easier to fool than me."

"What about me, then?" says Jimmy. "I carried the body too. Am I easily fooled?"

Len doesn't reply. He just turns to the others. "Think about it. The woman is shot, then disappears. Then Desmond. We all took it for granted he was dead. Maybe that act did most of the imaginative work for him."

"What about the pictures?" Diana again. "Desmond's was the first to change."

"Which proves my point," says Len, smugness in overdrive. This new Len might be more dynamic but he's a bit of a prick. "What better way to throw suspicion on someone else?"

"Amanda didn't have a picture on the wall," says Diana. "Are we discounting her?"

"She wasn't one of the guests," says Len. "She told us as much. But Desmond couldn't have done this alone. He would need an accomplice."

"And who might that be?" I ask.

Len smiles. "I don't have a name. Not yet. Just conjecture."

There's a silence in the room then. I look at Len. Really observe him. I'm expecting him to say that it was Amanda who was Desmond's accomplice but his eyes say something else. They're roving around the room. I watch where they're going, hoping he'll give himself and his thinking away. And he does. He's staring at Cerys. And smiling to himself. Cerys? *Cerys?* Oh wow. He's really lost the plot now.

"So what are we going to do, then? We can't sit here and wait to be killed." Sylvia again, building up to another explosion.

"I agree," I say. I check my wrist to see that time's ticking down and am about to speak but Ramona gets there first.

"Any of you heard of the Stanford prison experiment?" Blank faces. "OK. This university took a whole bunch of volunteers, divided them up into prisoners and guards, and watched what happened. Supposed to be a psychology experiment. It lasted less than a week before they stopped it. The ones who'd been given guard uniforms were abusing and torturing the prisoners. The authorities had to step in."

"So what's that got to do with anything?" asks Sylvia.

"Just thinking," Ramona says. "We were saying this might be a game but it got too nasty for that. What if it's an experiment? What if we're all here because someone's watching us to see how we behave in a stressful situation? How we cope? Anyone thought of that?"

"And what if it is?" asks Len, clearly unhappy, if not angry. "How does that help us, exactly?"

"I don't know. Something else to consider, I guess. If someone's putting us under the microscope, it might help to be prepared for anything that might happen."

"Very practical," says Len, dismissive once more.

I'm beginning to wonder whether he has a problem with women in general rather than just the ones here.

"Look," says Diana, checking her wrist. "Time's getting on. We're over five hours into the twelve hours we've been given. And we're no further forward. We need to get looking round the house again."

"We need keys for the locked rooms," says Len. "Can't do anything more till we get them."

"You got a theory where they might be, then?" I'm letting my anger with him show and I don't care.

"Monica was playing with some keys upstairs," says Cerys. "Got them here in my pocket." She delves into her jeans pocket, comes out with a set of keys. "Don't know if they'll fit . . ."

"Where did you find these?" asks Ramona.

"Dunno. Monica found them. Among those toys in the room, I think."

"Or they may have been on Desmond's body," says Sylvia. "After all, that wasn't the only thing she was playing with belonging to him, was it?"

"Anyway," I say, to head off another one of Sylvia's confrontations, "let's see if they work." Cerys passes them to me. There are three keys, all the same, like they fit the same lock. Promising.

Jimmy, having been sitting in silent contemplation for some time, rises slowly from his armchair. He's clearly feeling the need to take charge. I think after our time together in the room that I understand him more. And if he wants to play captain, I'm not going to argue. Time's running out. We all need to be on the same side now.

"I suggest," says Jimmy, "that we split up once more."

"Oh no," says Sylvia. "We all need to stay together. Desmond could be anywhere. Anywhere . . . Especially if there's two of them now."

"Jimmy's right," says Ramona. "We'll cover more ground if we split into smaller groups. Not too small, though. We can still watch each other's backs."

"I'll come with you," says Cerys, straightaway.

Ramona turns to her. There's some kind of conflict in her eyes. I can't tell whether she's happy about that but she accepts it. "Okay."

"And I'll go with the two of you as well." Len stands up to speak. There's an awful glint in his eye as he begins. That and the way he was looking at Cerys a few moments ago makes me think it's not going to be a very harmonious group. "Keep an eye out for you."

"What, us poor, vulnerable girls?" Ramona says, ramping up her Southern belle voice, then dropping it just as quickly. "We're more than capable of taking care of ourselves."

Len just shrugs. "Whatever you say."

"Fine," says Ramona. "Do what you want." She turns to us. "I guess you're going to have to make your own groups."

"I'll go with Kyle," says Diana.

Jimmy stares at Sylvia. He doesn't need to speak. His face says it all.

"And I have the captain." Well, at least one of them seems happy.

"All sorted, then," says Len. "We'll take the top level."

"Yes, boss," says Ramona with undisguised distaste.

"Then we'll start at the bottom," I say.

"In that case, I suppose we'll work round the middle," says Jimmy, reluctantly.

I distribute the keys.

"Right then," says Jimmy. "If anyone needs, there are provisions in the dining room so stock up on them first. And— Oh. Forgot I had this." He takes out a whistle from his side pocket. "How about if I discover something I give two sharp blows?"

"What about the rest of us?" asks Ramona. "What are we supposed to do?"

"Scream loudly?" I say. "OK, Captain, let's go."

"Let's get it done, then," says Len. "Let's find that girl."

Murmurs of assent.

"And let's not get killed." Sylvia's shrill contribution.

No one replies.

We all file out.

THE BEAST IN THE CELLAR

So off they go on their quest again. Into the valley of death rode the six hundred. Or at least the eight of them. And it's not really a valley. It's a house. And there aren't any cannons to the left or the right of them. Or at least none that we know of. But you get the gist. At least I hope so. It's come to something when my humorous asides need footnotes.

So did you expect that? Desmond disappearing? Yes? No? Well, let's examine it in further depth with Professor Beast. I mentioned it before, the body disappearing, so what d'you all think? A cliché? Something boring and tired and used too many times before and shouldn't be attempted now at all? Or is it a trope? Something that should definitely be here because it fulfills part of the form and function of the story. And let's be honest, does it really matter either way? Isn't that just a way of examining things to stop being affected by them? An intellectual rather than an emotional response? All it really says is, aren't I clever for spotting a trope, or even aren't I clever and feigning boredom for spotting a cliché? The important thing is, it was a surprise. It did surprise you, didn't it? You weren't expecting it to happen and it happened. That's the main thing.

Or maybe you were expecting it, or anticipated a twist or something. Who's to say? Not Professor Beast. I'm just stuck here doing what I'm supposed to do. Fulfilling my role. Me talking, you listening. So shush. Because there's a lot happened since last we met.

Len's come out of his shell for one thing. And that may have surprised you. Not to mention Iain being a completely different person to the one we all thought he was. And this is all interesting, don't you think? No, don't answer—*please*—it was a rhetorical question. We start off thinking one thing about one person, having an opinion based on what we first see and experience of that character, then that opinion might change as we get to know them. It's always like that, not just in this house. And sometimes it's for the better, sometimes not. Sometimes we find a person we initially thought boring interesting, an interesting person ultimately dull dull dull. Fun, not so fun. I mean, those are all diametric opposites, most people aren't really like that. They're just people, that's the thing. And people don't have one defining characteristic, one thing about them that makes them who they are. That would make them one-dimensional. And one-dimensional people are boring. Deeply, deeply boring. No, we're all multifaceted, even me.

And I find that fascinating, I really do. I mean, here's me, a Beast if ever there was one, sitting in a cellar, the way beasts are supposed to. But in the short time we've known each other (and I'm using the word *known* in the loosest sense, because after all, can we ever really, truly know another person? Really? Which is kind of the thing I'm talking about here), have I done anything particularly beastly? Yes? No? I don't think so. But that doesn't stop me from being the Beast in the Cellar. Because that's who I am. So you might think, the Beast hasn't done anything beastly yet but they might because they're a beast and that's what we expect them to do. Fair enough. Or alternatively, that Beast is just lulling us into a false sense of security and is going to do something so bad it'll be the most monstrous thing ever. Because that's what beasts do. Well, yes, that point's valid as well. And I suppose that's what I'm getting at.

They say that if you want to see what someone's really like, give them what they want. It'll accentuate their real character. Especially if you give them money. And power. That's why so many famous people behave like arseholes. Because they can. And they think there's no consequence to their actions. So what about Ramona's idea? That this is all one big psychological experiment? Could she be right? That everyone in the house is being observed to see how they cope with extreme stress? That way we could really see what people are truly like.

Kurt Vonnegut said we all wear masks. And we should be careful about which masks we choose to wear because those masks will eventually become us. Or something like that. I'm paraphrasing again, but once more I hope you get the gist. (That could become my catchphrase.)

We've met all the houseguests now. And we thought they were one way, but then they started opening up about themselves. And we find things aren't so black and white about them as we first thought. Some are nicer than we first imagined, some are not. Some are sadder, some aren't. And we get to understand people more, the way they behave, what choices they make, when we see them as rounded people. And that's good, that's right, that's how people are meant to be and how people really are. Not all good, not all bad. All just shades of gray. To quote the Monkees song. (Google it, youngsters.)

Hey, Tennyson and Vonnegut and the Monkees. Professor Beast's crammed a lot of knowledge into such a short space. Go, me.

Well, I won't hold you up any longer so I'll just leave you with this thought:

Even the villain believes they are the hero of their own story.

CAPTAIN JIMMY SAINT

Now that the ordeal of the secret passageway is over, not to mention being out of that hideous chamber where this devil stored his evil apparatus, and therefore not feeling quite so desperate, I feel rather ashamed about a couple of things. First, accusing Kyle. And then trusting Kyle with my confession. It was the kind of thing a chap does when he doesn't expect to be going much further, the kind of thing one blurts out in desperation. However, I did feel better once I'd been honest about my predicament. And to be fair to Kyle, he took it in a much more mature manner than I had expected. And despite my fears, he didn't mention it to the others once we'd reconvened. Fair play to the boy. It's a daunting experience having something like that hanging over one's head, a secret that could be trotted out at any moment and used against one, but I'm afraid I have to hope the boy keeps his word and we can all get out of this house and away to our separate lives once more none the wiser.

And now I had better concentrate on the task before me, because experience has taught me that all this introspection does one no good at all.

We take the third floor, Sylvia and I, leaving the others to their appointed tasks. Sylvia, alone from the others, seems a little more cheerful. Or at least slightly relaxed. Although I suspect she's not the kind of person who can manage total relaxation. On reflection, I'm not sure she can be cheerful, either. I suppose the word I'm looking for is *quieter*.

Again, I should know how to get the best out of a person like this; after all, a regiment is composed of individuals and man-management is paramount. Not to mention placating warlords in conflict situations. Not that I consider Sylvia a warlord, although she does have her moments. But she's not currently hysterical and for this relief much thanks.

The third floor is composed of a set of long corridors with locked doors on either side. Like a Gothic hotel, you might say. The key we have seems to be a skeleton key, as it opens all the rooms. We're going room to room together. I open the door, pop my head round, give Sylvia the all clear and we both enter. We've found nothing of any importance so far, at least not pertaining to the matter in hand, no young woman waiting to be rescued.

It strikes me that, beyond the bare bones, we still don't know anything about her, this woman we're trying to rescue. But what, I suppose, do we need to know, beyond those bare bones? She's a young, attractive woman, and her life is in danger. And for those reasons alone we should put aside our differences to rescue her from her fate.

But that in itself brings up another conundrum: Would we be so energized to find her if she weren't young and attractive? Does that matter? It shouldn't, obviously. But, personally speaking, and I know this is an awful thing to say, the more attractive the victim, the more effort will be made to find her. And it's always a her. And she's usually a blonde. This brings up some unpleasant truths within myself that I'd rather not face at present. So I'll continue to concentrate on the matter at hand. Leave these thoughts for another time.

What we have before us is a variety of different bedrooms, the majority of them decked out as if a specific person were living there. Not, I should say, for any of us gathered together. From what I gather, most of our rooms are all on the floor below. These rooms appear to be set for different people, perhaps people we haven't encountered yet. The one we're currently engaged with checking seems to belong to a teenage boy, with posters of footballers on the wall, piles of homework on a kind of makeshift desk, and a computer with a games console attached. It looks like a suburban room in which the occupant has just left. There's the feeling he'll be returning any minute.

The previous one was done out like a beach house, all bare blond wood and chunky blue-and-white ornaments. Dried starfish hanging from old twine, bleached painted driftwood repurposed as objet d'art. Books on the shelves denote a female occupant. There's an artist's easel set up, facing out at what one would presume to be the view if not for these damnable shutters. From the aspect of the room one would expect a sea view, not whatever is actually out there. Although we don't know for sure there *isn't* a sea view, if I take that thought to its logical conclusion.

"Not your kind of room?" I had asked Sylvia.

She recoiled from the very thought of it. "It looks like it belongs to an artist." The amount of distaste carried in the words she may as well have said child molester.

"Not fond?"

"If this woman, whoever she is, has time to paint, she has time to get a job. Waste of a life."

And with that the subject was pronounced closed.

"We haven't seen the people we assume these rooms are for." I'm looking round the teenager's bedroom, musing aloud.

"No, thank god. There are enough people in this house running round causing trouble as it is, without bumping into any more."

"D'you think they might be in here somewhere and we just haven't met them yet?"

"Let's hope not."

She turns her face away from me as she speaks. I catch the fear in her voice, if not her face. I'm not one for all this psychology lark, but I think it's fair to say that even I can tell that not only does Sylvia not like other people, she fears them too. In my experience of this kind of mindset it's the fear that comes first.

"I suppose you wish there were more people in this house," she says. "Like those ones downstairs or upstairs?" Clearly she hasn't finished yet. And I'm in no mood to listen.

"Go through the drawers and what have you. Check for anything that might give us a clue. I'll check under the bed and in the cupboards."

She does so with no complaints. Perhaps, despite the bluster, she's the type who needs to be given orders.

We find nothing.

"Onward, then," I say.

I open the next door, pop my head round. "All fine," I say and we enter.

It's like a box room, the near-redundant third bedroom of a suburban semidetached. The kind that can barely get a bed inside so is used to store junk or turned into a home office. This one's a home office. Cheap office furniture and an old computer on the desk. Cheap shelving with box files. I'm not a great one for atmosphere but even I can feel something depressing about this room.

"Bit bleak," I say.

"Go back to the artist's room then," says Sylvia, that ever-present disdain in her voice. "Wait for the woman who lives there to come back. You're practically salivating at the thought."

Now I'm usually a tolerant man, but I really have had enough of her attitude. With the others she was slightly more bearable because they could drown her out. But a little of her goes a long way on her own. "Now, look. We have to work together. And I have to say I've had enough of your snipes and barbed comments. Perhaps you'd like to keep your opinions to yourself and concentrate on the task at hand? That way we might make quicker progress and find this poor girl."

She stares at me like I've physically assaulted her. Stands there, mouth open, like I've slapped her.

"What . . . ?"

She's unmoving. "You check the box files, I'll go through the desk." Still unmoving. "What is it?"

When she speaks there are tears in her eyes. "There's no need to . . . talk to me like that . . . I . . . I'm only trying to help."

I sigh. More from irritation than anything. Apparently she can happily dish it out but crumples as soon as someone gives her a taste of her own medicine in return. And it was barely a taste. A soupçon, if anything.

"You look in the box files, I'll check the desk. Come on. We have work to do," I say again.

Clearly unhappy, she does as she's told.

We find nothing.

"Next one."

Silently, moving like a stroppy teenager, she enters the next room. She doesn't wait for me, just opens the door and steps inside. I have no option but to follow her.

"You didn't check to see if this room is safe—" I stop. She's not listening to me. She's staring ahead. "What's wrong?"

She doesn't reply at first. But eventually she turns to me. And there are tears in her eyes again. I don't know what for this time, I've said nothing to upset her.

"This room . . ."

"Yes?" I say.

"It's . . . it's my room . . ."

She's right. It's the room from the painting on the stairs. Midcentury decor, all Ercol and Scandinavian wood. Flowered walls, a flowered sofa and matching armchairs, with a smoked glass coffee table dominating the center of the room. On the sideboard is a radio. She picks it up.

"What are you doing?"

"Seeing if it works." She examines the back, checking it's plugged into the wall socket, switching the thing on and off, turning the dial. "There should be something . . . there." She sets it back on the sideboard, turns to me, and smiles, her eyes lit by an ugly triumph. "Well, I've kept my opinions to myself and managed to make the radio work so perhaps an apology might be in order?"

"I can't hear anything."

She looks at me as if I'm an idiot. "It's Radio Two. What's the matter with you?"

I have a sudden flashback to being stuck in that room with Kyle hearing the girl crying. Is it me? Am I just not sensitive to these things? Or is it them?

And then the expression on Sylvia's face changes. "No . . ." She stares at the radio. "That voice, I know it, it's . . . No, no, no . . ."

"What is it? What's the matter?"

"It's . . ." She points at the radio. "No, it's . . . that's . . . no . . ."

She makes to run from the room. I grab her, stop her.

"What's the matter?"

"Get off me, get off . . ."

She turns to the radio again, hearing something I can't. And screams.

So the best thing to do, I think, is open as many doors as possible in as short a space of time. That way we might find the girl and a way out in one go. And get away from the killer while we're at it."

Kyle's talking as he's walking. Down the darkened corridor of the ground floor and I'm rushing to keep up with him. It's all very *West Wing*, really. Yes, I've watched something other than *Sex in the City*.

We've tried the kitchen, which is on the left side of the house, so we're going in the opposite direction to see where it leads us. I'm getting a bit breathless now but I don't want him to know. My Pilates class didn't train me for this. Instead I say, "Shouldn't we be examining things as we go? Mightn't we miss something speeding along like this?"

"Like what?"

"A door?" I'm trying not to state the obvious. "The kind you're looking for? Secret or otherwise?"

He stops, turns, looks at me. Smiles. "You're right." Then frowns. "You OK? You sound out of breath."

"I'm fine," I say, although glad of the rest. "Yes, I want to find the girl and get out of here, but I don't want to go so fast that we miss something, that's all."

"Fair enough."

There's an old carved wooden chest against the wall. I sit down on it. "We haven't really stopped to think about what we're doing, have we? Because of the ticking clock things on our wrists we've just gone blundering off again. We should have more of a plan."

"We've got a plan. Find the girl, find a way out, avoid Charles Boyd and Desmond. So what more do we need?" As he says this, he sits down next to me. "What are you thinking?"

I check the thing on my wrist. It says we've got less than half the time left to find Claire. "Even with this thing giving me a countdown, I have no idea of what time it is. I mean, is this still nighttime? Are we working through the night? We assumed so because we assumed we had dinner in the evening. And it feels like it because it's so dark, but it might not be because we can't see out. I just think, I don't know, time seems to have stretched or something since we got here."

"Yeah," he says. "Dinner seems like a week away. Longer. Like we've been in this house . . ."

"Forever?" He seems disturbed by that word. I immediately take it back. "Maybe not forever. But for a long time. Longer than it says on our wrists."

Kyle nods. Then looks at me as if wanting to say something he's unsure of. I wait, hoping my silence acts as encouragement.

"Is your . . . do you feel like your life, before you came into this house, does it feel like it's fading away from you the longer we're in here? Like, I don't know, a dream?"

"You mean my life was a dream and this is real?"

He's embarrassed now. Drops eye contact. "Sorry. That's ridiculous."

I don't reply. I think about what he's said. And he's right. My life, everything before this house, who I was, what I did, feels like it's getting lost in some kind of fog. When I woke here I was angry, but mainly because I wanted to get back to my life. I had meetings to attend. Proposals to give. The longer I stay in the house, the less important it becomes, the more distant all that is.

I get up off the chest. "Let's keep searching. Find Claire."

He looks at me, unmoving. Studying me. "You feel it as well?"

I'm suddenly embarrassed. "Let's do something. This is getting us nowhere."

"Do you?"

"Yes . . ." Louder than I intended and I immediately regret it. "Yes, I do." Much quieter now. I sit back down again. It feels as if I've suddenly got nowhere to go.

We sit in silence for a while longer. The darkened hallway doesn't scare me anymore. It feels quite welcoming now. I risk a look at Kyle. He's lost in his own thoughts. I smile.

"I've been thinking," I say.

"Yeah?"

And now I feel awkward saying this. But I go on. "Well, I was just thinking there, about the three . . ." *Say the word.* ". . . murders."

Kyle turns to me. I have his attention now. "What about them?"

"Well, the whole way they happened. It was Iain's death that got me thinking. You know, a thief losing his hands. That's what happens, isn't it? Punishment for thieving in some countries?"

"You think someone punished him for stealing your necklace?"

"Well . . . it sounds a bit ridiculous when I say it out loud."

"What about Desmond? He was . . ." Kyle's eyes light up. "Penetrated. In a frenzy. D'you think that's kind of a metaphor for, you know?"

"You think they were killed because of what they wanted? Or what they were?"

"What was it Sylvia said?"

"God knows. I block her out."

"No, she said something about the thing that we have in common, or that we're being killed for, is the secrets we've got. Or desires. Or wants." Kyle shakes his head and I can tell he's energized. "Like we're being killed off because of the things we are, or the things we want . . ."

"Sylvia said that? Wow."

"It's the only thing I've heard so far that makes sense."

"So what about Amanda? Why was she killed?"

"I don't know. For talking to us? Telling us too much?"

"OK. So where does that leave us? What are our secrets? Our wants?"

Worry crosses his features. "Hadn't thought of that."

We fall into silence once more. And because the hallway's dark and in that moment there's a connection, I say something I perhaps shouldn't.

"You know at dinner? When you sat next to me?"

He nods.

"I . . . before all this started, I was going to make a pass at you."

He laughs. "Going to?"

My turn to laugh now. I feel slightly embarrassed and I'm now glad the hallway's dark so he can't see my face. "Yes, going to."

"But then people started getting murdered."

"Yes, and the other thing."

"What other thing?"

"Well, it's all wrapped up in what you said. About feeling like we've been here forever." I didn't want to use that word, it just slipped out. But now it feels appropriate. And I don't think I like that. I continue. "I couldn't do that now. Make a pass at you. Because it feels like we've known each other for—"

"Forever?"

I nod. "Yes. It just feels weird now that I would ever have thought that. It doesn't seem right any more. Incestuous, even."

I don't need to look at Kyle to know he's staring at me, open-mouthed.

"Sorry, I didn't mean that. That's wrong, that's the wrong word. But close. I can't explain how. Or why. I just, feel it."

He says nothing for a while and I assume it's because he's somehow embarrassed or even disgusted with me. But eventually—after how long I don't know because I no longer trust time in this house—he speaks.

"I know what you mean," he says. "And I don't think it's just you. It's . . . I don't know. Don't you feel like these people aren't strangers anymore? That we all know one another somehow?"

"Maybe because we feel we've been here so long. Or extreme situations make those kind of connections happen quicker and we only think we know one another. Trauma bonding."

"Maybe," he says. But he doesn't sound convinced.

This talk is too intense for me now. "Come on. We'd better keep going."

We set off down the darkened hallway once more. We follow turns that we both believe are taking us away from the library. We should have a ball of string or breadcrumbs so we can retrace our path back in case we get lost. Although Kyle seems to be remembering our route.

The feel of the place changes once more. It becomes more like the kitchen area and the upstairs. Rougher, unfinished. No particular architectural or historic style. Just old.

We stop.

"Look at this," says Kyle.

"A door."

Set into the wall, as rough as its surroundings. Kyle tries the handle. I want to tell him to be careful but I'm sure he's doing that. The door opens. He looks at me in surprise, then back to the door. Peers round it, comes back out again.

"Well?"

"Stairs going down. I think it leads to a cellar."

We've only been up here for a couple of hours, walking round the unfinished rooms at the top of the house, but it feels like so much longer. In fact, if I didn't have this thing on my wrist counting down the time, I wouldn't believe it. And all I can think of is that poor, locked-up kid we're trying to save. What she's going through right now. How she's feeling. And the responsibility we've got toward finding her. Well, that's not *all* I'm thinking about. There's also Cerys. I know the signals she's trying to send me. And let's just say I'm not immune to them. Not that we can do much about it with Len the limpet tagging along.

But it's more than tagging along with us. He's got that look on his face again, where he's working things out for himself. His detective look, I guess you could say. All the way up in the elevator, then walking the last flight to where Iain's body was found, his eyes never leaving Cerys or me. Hardly blinking, as if he'd miss something important if he did. I can't take a step without him taking one too. Like an ancient shadow. Then when we reach the top floor his behavior gets worse. Still staring, but moving his lips, talking to himself, nodding when he thinks I'm not looking at him, smiling at something I say or a movement I've made. I thought he was harmless before, a little old man keeping himself to himself, but he's not. There's something much worse about him, and I know from her expression that Cerys can see it too. She's scared of him.

"You take that room over the other side of the landing," I say to Cerys. "I'll search this one. Len, you take the one next to mine."

"We should all stay together." A statement from Len, not a question. "Safety in numbers. No use going off on your own, no telling what might happen."

"I'm fine on my own," Cerys says, clearly not wanting Len anywhere near her. "I'll shout if I find something."

"And I'm fine on my own too, Len," I say, twisting his name, stretching it out to two syllables, putting on a little girl lost voice. "But don't worry. If us poor little defenseless girls need your big man help, we'll scream and scream."

He doesn't like being spoken to like that, which is obviously why I did it. But he just mumbles something under his breath that, thankfully, I can't hear, then goes into the room I suggested. I'm aware of Cerys looking at me, kind of open-mouthed.

When she speaks, there's a kind of awe in her voice. "I can't believe you talked to him like that. And it worked. How d'you do it?"

I just shrug. "I don't take shit from angry old men, honey. You should try it some time."

"Wish I could."

I smile at her. "You can, honey. If you want to."

She smiles back at me. There's no mistaking what that expression means.

"Come on," I say. "We don't want to give that old fuck the satisfaction of standing here doing nothing."

I turn and enter my chosen room. I hear a noise behind me, pivot. It's Cerys. She closes the door behind her, locks it, leans against it, looking at me. She's got the kid in her papoose and she's asleep. Cerys is breathing heavily.

"Why have you followed me?"

"There's . . ." She tries to talk but nothing comes out. She just stares at me, eyes wide.

"Why are you looking at me like that?" I have a feeling I know the answer.

Before I can say or do anything else, she grabs my face with both hands and kisses me. Full on the lips. It's not easy with the papoose but I have to say, she manages.

I taste her lipstick, her hot, soft lips. She puts her tongue inside my mouth, desperate to connect with me.

I close my eyes, then stop myself, pulling away. "What are you doing?" I say.

She steps back, stares at me. Scared, like she's done something wrong. "I'm sorry . . ."

"Why?"

She drops her head. "I've shocked you."

I smile. "Honey, it takes a hell of a lot more than a kiss to shock me. A pretty good kiss, too."

"I . . ." Again, she loses the power to speak. The embarrassment is coming off her in waves. "I'm an idiot. Sorry. Forget I did that."

She turns away from me, makes to leave.

I place my hand on her wrist to stop her.

"Hey. You don't get to kiss me, then just walk off. Don't you think we should talk about this?"

She stares at me once more. "You're not angry with me?"

I smile, a bit confused. "Why would I be angry with you?"

She keeps staring at me. I know that look. I've been on the receiving end of it a fair few times. Even done it myself when I was younger.

"I . . ."

I let her take her time. I think I know what's coming next.

". . . I think I'm falling in love with you."

"OK."

I'm still holding her hand, but she tries to shrug me off and move away. "I'm sorry, I'm sorry . . ."

I don't let her go. In fact, I grip her a little harder. "Cerys, you've done nothing to apologize for."

I stare at her this time, seeing what's in her eyes. Honesty. Passion. Good things.

"So you think you're falling in love with me," I say.

She nods. "And I . . . I want you." Her voice is a hoarse whisper.

"And I guess you're not going to move on until you've had me, huh?"

"I just know that we, we may never see each other again when we leave here. And I . . . I couldn't, I want to be . . . to be with you."

"You know we've got a girl to find. A girl who's in danger of losing her life."

"I know. And I really want to help her. Honestly. But I've been brave enough to tell you this. And I may never get a chance again. I might be the next one who . . . you know. And I couldn't . . . couldn't . . . you know, without being with you."

I study her some more, taking in what she's told me. I check my wrist, see how much time's left. We're over halfway down in the countdown, but she does have a point. We may not see out the night.

"OK," I say. "Check the door is locked."

She does so.

"Now take off the baby."

She does that, too, careful not to wake Monica. She places the papoose gently down on the floor. Angled away from us, but so she can still see the kid if she wakes up.

Outside, I hear Len shouting, calling us all the names his little mind can think of. I block it out. It seems to come from a world away.

"That's better," I say to Cerys. "Now come here."

I open my arms. She falls into them.

Can't you hear it? What's the matter with you?"

That stupid man is just staring at me like I've grown another head. What's wrong with him? Surely he can hear that voice coming out of the radio. It was *The Archers* at first, just like I wanted, but now it's this voice, asking me questions. Not only that, but demanding I answer them. It's a woman's voice. Familiar, somehow.

"Sylvia? Can you hear me? Hello?"

I look between him and the radio. He's still holding me tight, stopping me from running. But why can't he hear it?

"Sylvia?"

I want to scream again.

"Sylvia, come on. It's time. Talk to me."

The captain remains mute. I can no longer bear the sight of his stupid, dull face.

"Why are you gaping at me like that? Can't you hear that? Do you recognize it?" A thought comes to me. "Or are you both in it together, is that it? Just pretending you can't hear, the both of you playing a trick on me. Well, it won't work. I'm not going to fall for it. You hear me?"

"Sylvia, there's no one there. I honestly can't hear anything. Honestly. Please . . . please stop this nonsense," the captain says.

"It's not nonsense . . . I can hear . . ."

"Who are you talking to, Sylvia? Who's there with you?" asks the voice on the radio.

"You hear that? That question was about you." He's starting to look scared. "Or are you hearing something different that I can't hear? Is that it? Oh, I don't *know*."

"We need to get out of this room, Sylvia. Come on." He tries to steer me toward the door.

"No. This is my room and I refuse to leave."

"I can hear someone else there with you, Sylvia. Who is it? What does he want?"

I turn back to the radio. "It's the army captain, Jimmy Saint. He's trying to drag me out of the room. *My* room."

"Don't do that, please, Sylvia. Stay here. We have to talk. We *need* to talk."

I turn back to him. "You hear? We need to talk. Without you being here."

"Well, then . . ."

"Please, Sylvia. I need to talk to you." The voice from the radio sounds calm and soothing. I must be getting over the initial shock because I'm now listening to what she has to say. "I won't upset you. We'll just talk, that's all. And when we have, you can go. Simple as that. Can you do that? Please?"

I'm still in the captain's grip, my body rigid, ready to run. I relax myself, show him I'm no threat. "Yes," I say to the radio. "But there's a killer out there . . ."

"I'm well aware of that," says the voice. "But you'll be safe, here in your room."

"What about the captain?"

"He can go. I need to talk to you alone."

I turn back to him. "You hear that? You can go. This is my room, and I'll be safe in here."

He stares at me, clearly not understanding anything that's going on.

"I said, you can go. Let go of me and leave the room, please."

"I can't leave you in here on your own."

"I'll be quite safe. I have her word on that." I turn back to the radio. "Don't I?"

"Absolutely. You'll be quite safe in here for as long as we're talking."

Back to the captain. "See?"

"No. I don't."

"Now let me go, and get out. Out, go on."

He releases his grip on me, staring as if I'm still some kind of sideshow curiosity. Unwilling to leave. He probably thinks he's being chivalrous.

"*Go.*" I say it so firmly Jimmy leaves the room. He wants to get the last word in but I won't let him. I turn back to the radio. "Right. I'm alone now. I don't know how you can talk to me through that thing. Or why he couldn't hear you. But you've given me your word that I'll be safe in here so I'm holding you to that. Understood?"

"Totally. Why don't you sit down? Make yourself comfortable."

I do so. And feel immediately at home. There's a cup of tea on the coffee table in front of me. Hot and steaming, it looks freshly made. And the mug, it's exactly like my delicate bone china at home. I take a sip. Hot. I'll let it cool. I smile to myself. This is all I've wanted since I came into this house. Peace and quiet surrounded by my own things.

"This is the nearest I've been to home since I got here," I say to the voice.

"Good. I'm glad you feel settled."

"What do you want to talk about?"

"You, Sylvia. I want to talk all about you."

Oh. I don't like talking about myself. And I certainly don't let strangers know anything about me. People who know too much about you can turn that knowledge against you.

"No. I don't think so."

"Why not?"

"I'm not sure I want to talk about myself, thank you very much."

"I understand." The voice is very soothing. Like a doctor who actually listens. And lord knows there are precious few of those about. In, out, take these tablets, come back a week later if things aren't better and if you can get an appointment. But this one seems sympathetic. She's still talking. "We don't have to talk about anything you don't feel comfortable discussing with me."

"Good." I take a sip of tea. Ah. Exactly how I like it.

"But remember, this room is a safe space. Whatever you say in here won't be used against you outside of here. Not by me or anyone else. OK?"

"Right." My guard's still up, but I'm relaxing more. I mean, what can happen to me in my own room?

"So, Sylvia. Tell me something about yourself."

"Like what?"

"Where you're from, what you do, that kind of thing."

"Kettering. Do you know it?"

"A small town in the Midlands. What's it like?"

"Well, like everywhere else in this country, not as good as it used to be. Gangs of youths roaming the streets and Muslim no-go areas, too, I've read."

"And what do you do for work?"

"I'm a stock control clerk at a very large and successful tile warehouse."

"Responsible job."

"Indeed it is. I'm indispensable there. And they know it."

"I'm sure you are and I'm sure they do. How do you get on with your co-workers?"

I bristle. "What has that to do with anything?"

"Just a question. That's all."

"Well. There are very few that have my professional standards, if you must know. Especially the younger ones. Spend half their time playing about and making jokes. Filthy jokes. And filthy language. Horrible. There's no need for that. And I tell them so. Often. They all benefit from me taking charge. I show them the right way to do things. And they never put a foot wrong after that. Some of them don't stay for long but the ones that do realize who the boss is. Well, Mr. Bexley, but after that, me. And that's the way it should be. I've given my life to that firm, to Mr. Bexley, and I know how to make it run for the best. And I make sure everyone else does too." Another mouthful of tea.

"I see. And are you married?"

I'm bristling once more. "None of your business. Why are you asking these questions?"

"I'm asking everyone in the house these questions. Don't worry. It's all routine."

"No one else has mentioned it."

"I haven't got through everyone yet. It's nothing sinister. So please. Are you married?"

"No. I'm not." More guarded now that she's getting personal.

"Have you ever been?"

I know this voice. "Who are you? I know your voice. Where do I know you from?"

"You'll remember soon enough. Let's just keep going with the questions. So you're not married and you never have been?"

"*No.*"

"That was quite emphatic. Do you not like men?"

"I don't see that that's any of your business."

"Fair enough. So you live alone. And you always have done. Would you say you're the kind of person who likes everything ordered? A place for everything and everything in its place?"

"Of course. It's a shame that more people don't share my outlook. The world would be a much better place if we did." This tea is really nice. Loose leaf, obviously.

"Let's talk about the house. How did you get here?"

"I have no idea. And I'm not happy about it, either. When I get out, I shall be complaining in the strongest possible terms to whoever is behind all this."

"I don't doubt it. And how have you found your houseguests? Agreeable? Not so much?"

"Not the sort of people I'd want to spend any time with. Even the ones I thought I might like have flaws and have let me down. Like the captain, for instance."

"What's wrong with him?"

"Weak. You can see it. A military man shouldn't stand any nonsense. He should be strong, lead by example. This one spends all his time asking others what they think. It's not a manly trait."

"Right."

"And don't get me started on those girls. Urgh. Disgusting. All of them. Especially the Black one, although can you still call them that these days? It's so tiring trying to keep up with them. They take offense so easily. The American one, then. But I can still call her what she is. That uppity prostitute. She wouldn't get a look-in at the firm I work for. Flaunting her body so all the men can gawp. And the mouth on her. Awful. I tell you, she wouldn't last five minutes if she were under me. Not that I would have her, of course. Mr. Bexley doesn't take just anyone on at his company, I can tell you. Oh no. And I'd have to vet them first. I don't let many past and if someone is appointed without my say-so I make sure I let Mr. Bexley know what I think. Oh yes. 'What would I do without you, Sylvia?' Mr. Bexley always says and smiles when he does. 'I couldn't get rid of you if I tried, could I?' And I always say, 'Oh no, Mr. Bexley, I'm not going anywhere.' And he just laughs and shakes his head and walks away. He's a good man, Mr. Bexley. And the best boss to work for."

"I'll not get you started, then. What about things in common. Have you discovered anything yet?"

"Certainly not. And I wouldn't want to, either. Nothing worse than being considered one of that rabble." I take another sip of tea and take in the room. How long have I been here? I seem to have lost all track of time. Has the room gotten darker or was it always as dark as this? And if so, how could that be? The curtains were drawn when I entered. It feels like I've been here for a long time. I'm actually getting quite tired. "Is this going to take much longer?"

"Probably not. Just a few more questions."

"What do you intend to do with this information? You had better safe-guard it. This is sensitive and personal. Anyone could use it against me."

"As I said, this room is a safe space. You've got nothing to worry about."

I want to argue with her but I can't see the point. Plus I really am getting very sleepy. Another mouthful of tea and I've drained it. Pity. I was enjoying it.

"Ask your questions, then. Come on."

"Did you kidnap Claire Swanson, imprison her, intending to rape, torture, and murder her?"

Well, that woke me up. "Of course not. How can you ask such a thing? Why on earth would I do that? The very idea is despicable. Here I am, trying to find that wretched girl, and the person who owns the house, this Charles Boyd, is it? And you have the audacity to ask that?"

"It's a serious question. I'm sorry if it upsets you. But it needs an answer."

"Well, I've given you one. No, I did not. And I'm disgusted that you could ask. Now if you'll excuse me—"

I stand up, ready to leave. Or try to. My legs feel like they've had the bones removed. I can't put weight on them. I immediately fall to the floor.

"I have to ask, Sylvia. Because it seems like you might have a motive."

I'm crawling across the carpet now, hoping that the captain is still outside the door, waiting for me.

"You clearly hate women. Especially young women. Is this because of repressed lesbian tendencies? A severe, perhaps abusive upbringing that might cause you to act out in that way?"

I open my mouth to call for help. No words come.

"A desire to hurt and humiliate young women because you wish they would find you attractive?"

In my head I'm screaming. In the room all I can hear is that voice. Accusing me of things I would never commit. Never.

"Are you sure it isn't you, Sylvia? Are you sure?"

Something in my body tells me I'm not going to make it to the door. That I'm not even able to open my mouth to cry out for help, or even to counter these baseless allegations. That I'm never going to be able to get up again. I'm tired. So tired. And it's getting very, very dark now. In my room. My lovely room.

This is it. I know it. And I'm sad. And I'm sorry for everything. I wish I'd gotten out of this room more. I wish I had lived more.

"Are you the killer, Sylvia?"

No! I scream. *No.* But no one can hear it but me.

Mummy doesn't need me anymore. But the finger people do. They'll show me where to go.

And I can play with them forever.

RAMONA O'ROURKE

Cerys smiles, eyes closed. And I suppose I'm smiling too. I should be. I had a good time. The frisson of imminent death will do that to a girl.

I turn toward her, observe her unaware. She's so much more attractive than she thinks she is. Underneath all those shapeless, cheap, style-free, baggy clothes her body's *smoking*. You'd never know she's had a kid. And her face? Cerys thinks it's plain. It's not. Just not made the best of. She's got it all, this girl: bone structure, perfect skin, beautiful eyes, lips . . . if she had self-belief and the courage to do something about it, she'd be dynamite.

I stretch out under the blankets, feel those residual tingles leaving my body, our sweat dry on my skin. Yeah, it was good. And she was hungry.

I'm pretty much always up for sex. There's nothing slutty or wrong about wanting sex and having sex. It's just enjoying your own body and someone else's. And it's not just for procreation. It's a natural bodily function. You're hungry, you eat. You're thirsty, you drink. You're tired, you sleep. You're horny, you fuck. Sure, some uptight assholes have a problem with that but you know what? Fuck 'em. They think they have to do what their imaginary friend in the sky tells them to do. Their book tells them not to have any fun or they'll burn forever, so they're too scared to enjoy themselves. But their terms and conditions sure as shit don't apply to me, because I'm having my fun and they can't stop me. I'll fuck whoever I connect with. If we click, we get it on and enjoy ourselves. What we were put on this Earth to do. And don't let anyone tell you different.

So yeah. Cerys is asleep and smiling. I presume her kid is sleeping peacefully in the corner where she carefully placed her papoose. I can't actually see her, the light in here is so dim. Just a candle we found and lit on the bedside table. It's burning unevenly, casting dancing shadows on the wall. Funny thing about that kid, or one of the many funny things about that kid, I should say, is that she does seem to disappear. Like when

Cerys is quiet or just holding her, not saying anything, content, it's like the kid's not there. Not real disappeared, like gone, just like you forget about her, like she's wiped from your mind. Cerys has said all she does is look after that kid, like it's her only role in life, so I guess that not noticing she's there means Cerys is doing her job properly? I dunno. Me and kids don't get on so great. So a silent, invisible kid seems to me like a good kid.

But Cerys. I could get to really like her. She seems real sweet, bit of a lost soul. Just needs some guidance. Like a plant that needs extra care before it can fully bloom. If that isn't too hippy-dippy for me to say.

She opens her eyes, rolls over toward me. Her smile widens when she sees me.

"Did I nod off?"

"Guess so." I smile back at her and she gives me an even bigger smile in return. This is getting kind of sickly sweet. Time to get up, I think. But Cerys puts her arm round me, stops me. Swings her leg over me, grips me, hard. I can't say I don't like it.

"That was . . ." She sighs. I don't know if she's looking for the right words or if the sigh is expressive enough. I guess it's enough. I know what she means.

"Your first time? With another woman?"

"First time full stop. Well, apart from Monica's, you know, father. If you can call him that."

The grip of her legs lessens a little, her eyes flick away to somewhere else. She's getting lost in memories, I can tell. I think she's going to share some personal history. Not sure I need that on a first date. We've had fun, both got what we wanted, and now we need to get back on it. Why can't that be that?

She's frowning now. Still cute, though. Time to head this partner off at the pass. "Feeling good?"

"Yeah," she says, eyes back in the present. "Better than I've felt in a long time. Years. Better than . . ." Her eyes flick away somewhere else again. "Probably the best I've ever felt."

"Wow."

She grips me hard again, staring intently at me. "All because of you. And your magic . . ." Her fingers trace a line down my body. I know where she's going. Holding eye contact and she looks absolutely filthy.

"I don't think I recognize you from the woman who came in here," I say.

"I don't recognize myself." Her fingers reach where they want to go.

I'm smiling again. "You're a quick learner."

"I had a good teacher . . ."

Her fingers keep working on me and her head moves down my body to join them.

From far off I hear something that sounds like a whistle.

What the hell. A few more minutes isn't going to change anything.

What's happened? What—"

I don't need to say any more. I can see what's happened. Sylvia's lying on the floor with some kind of yellowish froth round her mouth. A teacup and saucer lie beside her, whatever liquid that was in the cup now sinking into the rug and sizzling away nicely. Or rather not so nicely.

I look at Diana. We're both breathless from running. She stops in the doorway, surveying the scene, hand over her mouth, like people do in films but I've never seen in real life. But then I've never seen people get picked off one by one in an old dark house in real life, either. So I guess anything goes.

Jimmy's sitting in an armchair, unmoving, staring at Sylvia's body, whistle in hand. He barely registers Diana and me. He's off somewhere else.

"What happened?" I ask again, this time more quietly, more focused.

He eventually looks up, sees us both there, blinks like we're imaginary. He looks away. His eyes can't keep away from Sylvia's body for too long.

"She's dead."

"I can see that, Jimmy. Be more specific."

"She's . . ."

"Don't just say she's dead. Tell us what happened."

My words must have finally penetrated as he begins to speak. "We found this room. She said it was like her living room. *Was* her living room. And she said she could hear the radio." He points toward an old-fashioned wireless at the far side of the room. "Said she could hear a voice coming from it. Talking to her, saying her name. She . . ." He drifts off again for a few seconds. I'm about to prompt him when he returns, picks up his thread. "I couldn't hear anything. Just . . . nothing. Like you can hear Claire crying but nobody else can. And then she got quite agitated.

Angry. Then the door slammed shut and I couldn't open it, even with the key, and she was locked in. I tried to listen to what was going on but the door, old wood. Too thick. Just heard muffled talking."

"Was anyone answering her?" asks Diana.

"No," says Jimmy. "Just her voice. And then she became more, well, shrill, really."

Shrill and angry. I can imagine.

"Then she started to scream, then made another sound, choking, then . . ." He sighs. "The door unlocked itself and I ran in, found her like this. Blew my whistle." Looking at it in his hand as if it's a conduit back to a different world, a safer world.

"It must be poison." Diana has overcome her revulsion and is crouching next to Sylvia's body.

"That'd be my guess too," I say. "And whatever it was was in that cup." My turn to sigh. I sit down in another armchair. "Shit."

Jimmy looks lost. "What are we going to do?"

Before either Diana or I can answer, another red and breathless face appears at the door.

"What's going on? What's happened?" Len.

"Sylvia's dead," I say. Rather unnecessarily, in hindsight.

"What happened?"

We run him through the details. He listens, nods. Eyes on Sylvia's body the whole time. When he's heard enough, he looks up.

"Where were you, then?" Accusatory, harsh in tone. Not like previous Len.

"We found a cellar," I say. "Diana and I."

"And what did you find there?"

"We'd only gone down the stairs to the bottom when we heard the whistle."

"We didn't go any farther, we came straight here." Diana this time. "Where are the others?"

Len sneers. Honestly, sneers. I didn't think people actually did that outside of films. It's a day of firsts. Ones I never want to experience again.

"They won't be joining us," he says.

"How come?"

"Gave me the slip, they did. Little . . ." He's about to tell us what he thinks they are, but a quick glance round and Len decides to keep his opinion to himself. He's seething, though.

"What d'you mean, gave you the slip?"

"We were checking the rooms at the top. Then they disappeared. I tried the other doors but they were all locked. So they were either hiding in one of them or they'd run off somewhere. Just what I'd expected, really."

"Or someone took them," suggests Diana.

Len sneers again, but there's nothing funny about it. You wouldn't want to be on the other side of the table in an interview room when he does this. It feels like a precursor to something awful happening.

"Oh no. They've been waiting for an opportunity like this. To get away from me. And now Sylvia's dead." He nods, a look of sick triumph on his face. "Knew it was them. All along. Fucking slags."

Diana and Jimmy stare at him. "Can we have the old Len back, please?" I say. "He seemed less of a twat."

"You sanctimonious little shit." Len's almost shouting now. "Can't you see? They're behind it. Or at least the Welsh one is. I had my suspicions but that's all they were, suspicions. Well, this proves it, doesn't it?"

"What?" says Diana. "I thought you said it was Desmond doing this?"

"I also said he had an accomplice." Talking to Diana in a condescending manner. This new Len is a real nasty bastard. "And I said I knew who it was." He throws his arms wide. "Case solved."

"Cerys? Are you mental?" I say. "Utter bullshit. Never in a million years."

"Oh. And what qualifies you to disagree with me? I've got a lifetime of service in the force, don't forget. What have you got?"

"Common sense, of course. Ramona and Cerys aren't here."

We all turn and look. Jimmy has spoken, made it to his feet, standing at his full height, back straight. He looks angry. He looks like the military man he's always wanted to be.

"Listen to me, Len Whoeveryouare, I don't care how much experience you have as a detective. You weren't here and I was. There was no one else involved. Not the girls, not Desmond. *No one.*"

"There could be a secret passage in this room, they could have—"

"Yes, and so could you. You were by yourself, by your own admission. No witnesses. You could have found your own secret passage, come down here, killed Sylvia, made your way out again and then come running in as you did, out of breath and blaming the people who aren't here to answer for themselves." Jimmy crossed toward him. "So with that in mind, why couldn't it be you, Detective Inspector?" He really sneers that title.

He stares right into Len's face. Diana and I daren't move, even breathe. Len stares back.

Impasse.

Len is the first to break. "Who the hell do you think you are? Eh? Accusing me of this? Who the hell d'you think you are?"

"You just said," says Jimmy, features impassive, "one of us is lying. Why not you? Maybe you know your way round this house, know where all the secret passages are. And all this shouting's meant to throw us off."

"We have found you hanging out on the stairs a couple of times," says Diana.

"Yes, looking for clues." Len's face is almost purple, like he's ready to explode. "You think this is me? After the career I've had? All the criminals I've put away? If you think—"

"Oh, give it a fucking rest, Len." Diana this time. "We're all on edge, we've all had to cope with stuff we never in our lives thought we'd have to go through, and all in the last few hours. We're tired, we're scared. No, we're terrified. We have a missing girl to find and a house to get out of. And we don't have time for all this. You didn't do it? Fine. Great. Just stop accusing people when you don't have proof. OK?"

He stares at her now. "You want proof? I'll get you proof. Oh yes, I'll get you proof."

"You do that." She looks beyond tiredness, beyond anger. "Because in the meantime you sound like any other misogynist cunt."

I don't see the slap coming. Neither does anyone else, especially Diana. She stumbles to the side, head whip cracking round with the force of it.

I just stare, open-mouthed.

Jimmy doesn't. He steps forward, his arm moving even quicker than Len's. His fist connects with Len's face and the old man goes down. Hard.

I have to intervene, because Jimmy's standing over Len, waiting for him to get up so he can knock him down again. I put my arms around his body, move him away.

"Come on, come on, Jimmy, have a sit-down now, come on . . ." He doesn't want to go but I make him.

Once he's settled, I help Diana to her feet. The side of her face is one huge blazing welt. "You OK?" She nods. She's close to tears.

I then turn to Len, who's still on the floor. His hand goes to his mouth.

"My tooth is loose . . ."

"You deserve more than that, you twat."

He says nothing in reply but the anger in his eyes is off the scale.

"Get out of my sight, Len," says Diana. "Now."

He gets to his feet, slowly, still staring at the three of us as he does so.

"You'll be sorry," he says. "All of you."

We just stare at him.

"Did no one notice Ramona take that knife from the table after dinner? Really? No one? Am I the only one around here awake?" He laughs. "It's going to be your turn next. Believe me."

He turns and leaves.

I watch him go, then look down at Sylvia's body. I feel I have to say something.

"Sorry."

I'm suddenly very, very tired.

THE BEAST IN THE CELLAR

Well, that was a close one, wasn't it? Dodged a bullet, you might say. If that wasn't too much of a tasteless thing to say round here.

Sorry? What am I talking about? The cellar, of course. Kyle and Diana going down the stairs but not getting any farther. Hearing Jimmy's whistle. Lordy do! Think what might have happened if they'd found me down here! That would have been messy, wouldn't it? Would have become a completely different story.

What? Oh. I see. Sorry. You're right. I am being quite insensitive and thinking only about myself, you're absolutely right. Yes, I know Sylvia's just died and the fallout has been intense. And, yes, perhaps it might be inappropriate for me to be wanging on about myself considering everything else that's happened in the great scheme of things. Sure, absolutely. And I'm sorry. Sorry.

Still, could have all gone tits up then, couldn't it?

Actually, that brings me to an interesting point. Mourning the victims. Especially when we didn't know them. Jimmy Saint made a good observation. The best victims are always pretty, young blond girls. When I say best, I mean that in the eyes of the media. They always get reported on the most because they play best with the general public. If, say, Claire hadn't been much of a looker or even—the horror!—from an ethnic minority, there wouldn't have been, broadly speaking, as much media outcry. Not that there has been in this case, time being of the essence and all that, I'm just making a general point about the society we live in.

So what happens when someone is murdered that we didn't particularly like? Should deference be given to anyone, regardless of who they were? Or should that only be done if they were likable? Should we even be glad to see the back of them?

I mean, I'm just asking the questions here, don't expect me to come up with the answers. That's your job.

You see, we always go on about the killer. Who's the killer? Why is he/she doing what he/she does? What drives them? What went wrong in their life to make them turn out the way they have? Questions we always ask, that we're always interested in. Always. Because no one wants a killer who just kills because they're a killer, do they? We've gone beyond that. We want to know the whys and hows. We want to get inside their mind, to *understand*.

Why? Does it make us feel cleverer or more superior? Us armchair psychologists diagnosing, then going off for a cup of tea, pleased in the knowledge of what we've done, the conclusions we've reached?

Again, just asking questions. You can supply your own answers.

And does it always follow that there has to have been some deep, dark trauma to create a killer? Does everyone who experiences trauma become a killer? Perhaps some go a different way, you know; they might even try to understand what happened, ensure it doesn't happen again. To themselves and others. Or they might try to get on with their life as best they can, put it behind them, slog on.

Which kind of brings us back to earlier. Sylvia seemed like a bit of a mess, didn't she? Horrible opinions, obnoxiously expressed. And now she's dead. So the question to ask is, do we mourn her? Or rather, do we mourn her as much as someone with more palatable opinions more delicately expressed, had they been killed the same way? Which then begs the question, did Sylvia experience some kind of trauma to make her the way she was? Perhaps it wasn't one thing, it may have been cumulative things. If indeed she experienced anything. Maybe she was born that way. Like killers apparently used to be before we started analyzing their origins and ascribing cause and effect to their motives.

Lots of questions. Lots and lots of questions. Probably too many, if I'm honest. In which case I'm sorry. Sitting down here I have a lot of time on my hands, lot of time to think and reflect. Lot of questions to ask. And I can't give myself all the answers. Maybe we just have to react the way we want to. Maybe what we feel and how we feel is the right way to feel about losing someone, irrespective of whether it's sadness or whatever. It's just us and how we respond to our own feelings. It's how we are and we can't help how we are. Or can we? Grief and guilt are like two sides of the same coin, in a way. They're both these kinds of cancer that hollow you out from the inside. Grief is what you feel when you lose someone you loved. Guilt is what you feel when you lose someone you think you should have loved.

But grief can disappear in ways that guilt can't or won't. Or if not fully disappear then at least you can find ways of coping with it, or coping with a life that contains grief. Processes to go through to enable you to move forward. But guilt is the opposite. It sits there inside you. Oh yes, people tell you that you've nothing to feel guilty about, that you have to forgive yourself and move on, try to give you permission—which never works—then say ultimately only you can free yourself and you have to give yourself permission to move on. And you say fine. OK. Great. And you try that. But it never works. That guilt is still there, sitting inside you, gnawing away, always trying to find a way out. And it will find a way out. Often in ways you don't expect.

Anyway. Back to the story.

But before I go, one more thing.

Dodged a bullet, didn't I? You've got to admit that.

You're smiling again," I say to Cerys.

And she is. Beaming. Like she's using facial muscles she's never used before. Or at least not for a long, long time. She snuggles farther into me.

"It's you," she says. "What you do to me."

I laugh. "It's what you've just done to me, too . . ."

Cerys laughs too. It's such a surprising sound coming from her, like she's forgotten how to do it. She's lying on her side, stroking my shoulder, looking at me intently. Her touch is great. Warm, tingling, really lovely.

"You set fireworks off inside me," she says. "No one has ever made me feel like this. *No one.*"

"So you like girls, then?" I say.

"Seems so. I like you, anyway." She sighs and it's a happy sigh. Contented. "It's like I already know you. Touching you now, stroking your body . . . like it's meant to be. Like *we're* meant to be."

"Careful, hon. You'll be getting attached."

"Would that be so bad?"

This is what I was worried about. Why I kind of hung back at first. I could tell this was what she wanted—*I* was what she wanted—right from the start, and part of me didn't want this to happen because I wasn't sure she could cope. But part of me wanted this to happen because she's just so damn hot. And fun. When she lets herself be.

"You're about to say something to me and it's not going to be good."

"No, I'm not, it's just . . . you should know I'm not the exclusive type. That's all."

"OK." Her eyes drop away, she stops stroking me.

"Hey, I thought you knew that. Don't want you to go getting your hopes up if you're wanting, I dunno, something—"

"Long term?"

"I was going to say exclusive again but . . ." I shrug. "Same."

She removes her hand from me. Stares ahead at the ceiling.

"You've gone quiet."

"Yeah," she says. "Well, I suppose I should have figured that, really. I mean, you're . . . you're perfect. You wouldn't want me for, you know. More than this." She's touching me again but it's different this time. Like she can't stop. Like if she does stop, she'll never get the chance to touch me again. I'm concerned for her. This wasn't meant to happen.

"Hey, look," I say. "Come on. We're friends. Lovers. We had fun. We might have it again. That's what sex is for."

Flat on her back Cerys can't look at me. Still stares at the ceiling. "Not that I would know." Another sigh but not a happy one this time. "I only ever had it once. Hated it. It was horrible and it resulted in Monica. Then she became my life. And that was that. Parents threw me out when I got pregnant. Called me a slut, a whore, everything. They were chapelgoers, see. Proper religious. Fire and brimstone, and all that. And they had a whore for a daughter."

"They threw their own daughter out? Jesus."

"Yeah. Jesus is right. And he hates me for what I've done."

"Your parents tell you that?"

"Everyone at chapel. Went there from when I was tiny. And a boy from the chapel got me pregnant. Didn't even like him, really. He was my boyfriend because my parents liked him. Sang in choir. All that. Everyone loved him. And then when we were walking home one night after singing practice he started putting his hands all over me. I told him to stop, that I didn't want him to do that, but he kept saying that it was in the Bible, that we were going to be married and that a wife had to submit to a husband's needs. So in some bushes just off the path on the way home he made me, you know, submit to his needs."

"Shit."

"Wouldn't speak to me after that. Ignored me. Told me I was a slut and he wasn't going to marry me anymore. How could he marry a slut who let boys do that to her?"

"So he raped you, then ignored you."

"Nobody called it that. Not in the village I grew up in. You never talked about things like that. If it happened it was always the woman's fault for leading him on, asking for it. A man's right, it was."

"And then you found out you were pregnant. And it was nothing to do with him?"

"Exactly that. Not his baby. He wouldn't get a girl pregnant, he was one of God's chosen. My parents wouldn't believe me, they took his side. No matter what I said."

"You poor kid."

"Don't pity me. Please. I've done what I've had to do for my baby. Lived in some terrible places the last few years. Homeless shelters and hostels with people just out of prison and druggies and I don't know what else. Eventually I got a flat from the council. And I've lived there, just me and Monica, bringing her up as best I could." She stops talking, puts a hand to her face. She hasn't realized she's been crying while she's said all this. "Sorry," she says.

"You got nothing to apologize for, kid. Nothing at all. Your folks, on the other hand . . ."

Cerys lies there in silence. After what she's just told me, I can't not be honest with her. I guess this kid's becoming important to me. "We're not so different after all, you and me," I say.

She doesn't reply.

"You see . . ." I pause, unsure whether to continue or not. I do so. Cerys deserves my honesty. "I had kind of a similar upbringing. In Texas. My folks were ultrareligious. Went to one of those megachurches. Gave all their money to pastors with shit-eating grins who gave lip service to the bits of the Bible that suited them. And yeah, I got pregnant too."

I've got her attention now, she's up on one elbow, listening. "Really? What happened?"

I'm not used to talking this way, to opening up in front of other people. But I have to. I *feel* I have to. "Well, I figured I had a choice. The kid who got me pregnant was from the church as well. And, yeah, he tried to blame me. And, yeah, I felt like it was the end of my world. That God hated me and I was never going to heaven and the guilt was crippling. Christ, the fucking guilt."

"I've still got it, too," Cerys says. "Carry it with me always. Everything I do, every decision I make, it's like my parents are standing behind me telling me everything I'm doing is wrong and I'm damned whatever I do."

"Yeah, I hear you. And I could have gone down that route. Easily. But something happened. I don't know. I just . . . found strength. Decided I wasn't going to put up with their shit. So I had an abortion, which let me tell you isn't an easy thing in Texas, gave a mighty fuck you to the whole lot of them, and walked. And never looked back."

"Wow." Cerys can't keep the awe out of her voice. And I'm not saying I don't feel I deserve it. "I wish I'd had your strength. I really do."

"Wasn't easy. It took a hell of a lot to find it. But long story short, I became my own person. Got educated, could have done anything I wanted. But I kind of fell into stripping. And you know what? I liked it. I liked the power. The feeling of being up there on a stage with men staring at me, knowing they hated me, feared me, and there was nothing they could do about it. I had something they wanted and they were never going to get." She laughs. "And oh yeah, plenty of people from the church came to watch me. Regulars. Even the kid who fucked me. Even my own father." She's smiling now. It's a cruel smile but it makes me proud of Cerys. "Yeah. My own father. And I danced for him, and I took my top off and took my panties off and swung round the pole and opened my legs right in front of him and I stared at him. Didn't blink. And I laughed in his face."

"What happened?"

"He ran out." My turn to stare at the ceiling now. "Heard from someone that a few days later he took his shotgun and sucked on it till it blew the back of his head clean off."

Cerys doesn't answer. I don't expect her to. We lie like that for I don't know how long. It's not uncomfortable.

In that silence I sense the moment change, as acceptance grows of who we both are to each other. And what we could be. A warmth shared through secrets overcomes us. "So I guess deep down we're the same. We just went different ways, that's all. But you recognized it in you. That's why you wanted to fuck me."

"What?"

"You wanted to fuck me because you saw something in me that you knew was in you. What you could have become if you'd gone a different path. You fucked me because you want to be me."

I'm not being arrogant when I say this, it's just a statement of fact. Cerys smiles.

"Yeah, but there's something more than that."

"What?"

"I wanted to fuck you because you're hot as well."

I laugh. Just can't help it. "Goes without saying."

"I didn't just want you. I wanted to be consumed by you."

"There's tribes used to think if you killed your opponent you took their power and all the people they had killed into you as well. They became part of you."

"Wow. That's . . . intense."

I smile, play my finger gently down her neck. "And hot as well. Wanting to be wanted so much. I'm very OK with that. You?"

She's thinking. But the look on her face tells me she's happier about things than before. "Yeah. I feel good about that."

"And about yourself?"

Cerys frowns. Nods eventually. "Yeah. For the first time in years, maybe ever."

"Feeling guilty?"

"Guilty?"

"In a religious way?"

Her turn to smile. "No. I don't. Not at all. I'm not even upset about you not being exclusive. I'm with you now. And I want to stay with you. For . . . however long that might be. I'm OK with that. Are you?"

I smile at her again. We seem to be doing a lot of smiling at each other, but she's a very, very special kid. And while she's told me how good she feels with me, I don't think she realizes how good she makes me feel.

"That's very OK with me."

She sighs, happily this time, stretches out. "I don't think I've ever felt this happy before. Even in here, this house . . . so happy."

I say nothing. It doesn't need an answer. We lie like that for, well, I don't know how long.

Eventually, I look at my wrist, see that plenty of time's gone by. And something else. "Monica's very quiet. I thought kids wake up after a while."

"She's an easy kid. She sleeps a lot," she says. "Probably playing with her finger people."

She glances over at where she left the papoose on the floor. Frowns, gets up.

"You OK?"

"I'll just check on her." Sounds like something's not right.

She crosses to the pile of clothes and pick ups the papoose.

It's empty.

The baby's gone.

Oh. Oh dear . . . That's, no, that's not right . . ."

I'm stating the obvious, I know. But this is the kind of thing, the kind of happening, that makes you want to say something. And the only thing you can say, really, *is* the obvious. I've opened the door to the unused kitchen to leave Sylvia's body here. And Iain's body has disappeared. Just like Desmond's.

"What's happened?"

Kyle is at the other end of Sylvia. Diana declined to join us, going instead to look at the paintings on the staircase. So the student and I once again did the decent thing. Or as decent as possible under the circumstances.

"Iain's gone," I say. "His body. It's gone."

I'm trying to be matter-of-fact about it because if I deviate from facts and begin to speculate, I feel my newfound confidence in overseeing this mission to a successful conclusion will disappear forever. This . . . whatever it is in front of me, it's just . . . it's out of my wheelhouse entirely. I have to admit at least to myself that I may not be able to cope.

Kyle places his half of Sylvia's body on the floor, presumably as gently as he can, then comes to join me at the door.

"See for yourself."

He does. Then turns to me, frowning. "Has someone been down here? Messing us about?"

"Your guess is as good as mine."

He looks back inside, just as I did, hoping this is an optical illusion, a prank, willing the body to appear once more. And bring the first one back with it. "So this might mean Desmond has nothing to do with whatever's going on. Perhaps someone's taken his body as well? I mean, Iain was definitely dead. There was no coming back from that. So someone must be doing this deliberately." He shakes his head. "Maybe Ramona was right.

Maybe this is a psychological experiment we're in. See what we'll do in extreme circumstances."

Kyle is becoming too conjectural for me. I need absolutes. Now. I step inside and kneel down on the floor, examine it. Bare, old boards. Nothing more. Not particularly scratched or chipped, just old. And certainly no evidence of bodies having been stored here.

"But there's no blood, marks on the floor, nothing," says Kyle. "Like they weren't here."

I stand up, turn. "But they were here." I try to keep the panic from my voice. "They definitely were here. Both of them." My heart is beating faster. I'm shaking somewhat. I'm losing control. I *can't* not be in control. I attempt to wrest back some degree of command within myself.

"We, we can't . . . we've got to put her somewhere and this place is as good as any."

"Can't carry her forever," agrees Kyle.

Yes. Practical action. Exactly what's needed. I pick up the front end of Sylvia, Kyle gets the other end, and we take her over the threshold. Place her where the others had been. Straighten up.

"See how long *she* lasts before she disappears," says Kyle.

"How can you be so flippant?"

He doesn't look at me as he replies. "Because Diana's not the only one fucking terrified." He continues before I can speak. "Speaking of which, let's see what she's found in the paintings." He shuts the door, ready to be away.

I place my hand on Kyle's shoulder, detain him. He turns. "Could we have a moment, please?"

I must present a sorry sight. I certainly feel like I do. All my certainties, everything I've ever built my character on, my beliefs, literally everything that's made me who I am is crumbling away and taking with it my capacity for rational thought.

I find an old sideboard or something to perch on. My head spins. I feel somewhat nauseated. I close my eyes, try to breathe.

"You OK, Jimmy?"

I try to keep the nausea at bay before answering. My first response is the usual one. *I'm fine. Just need a minute.* But instead I'm honest with him.

"No. No, I rather think I'm not."

"What's up?"

Kyle sounds concerned but I see him checking his watch thing on his wrist. I don't blame him, obviously, time is of the essence, but it's hard not to think that with that gesture he regards me as a burden.

"I'm beginning to suspect this . . . this mission is beyond me."

"Join the club. I think it's beyond all of us."

I attempt a smile, but it's so weak it dies before it reaches my face. "I deal in regimented things. Absolutes. Orders given, orders carried out. This is all just . . . I can't cope anymore . . ."

My head is in my hands now. It feels like my insides are slowly turning to lead, slowing my body down to a stop and I can't or won't move. The nausea makes my head spin. My left hand shakes uncontrollably now. I cover it with my right but it's no use. There's something inside me going on that I have no control over. It's unmooring me. Setting me adrift. Un-anchoring the solid part of me.

"Oh god . . ."

I'm breathing heavily, images speeding through my mind, fast but jerkily, like one of those flicker books we had as children. Glimpses through a magic lantern, my life as phantasmagoria.

"Jimmy? Jimmy?"

"This is not . . . I'm not . . . together anymore . . ."

"Jimmy, come on." Kyle's voice is insistent, breaking through my mind. "We need you. Don't go to pieces now, there's still too much to do. C'mon, mate. C'mon."

I open my eyes and he's looking at me. Intently. But compassionately.

I sigh. The air leaves my body like a last breath. I feel empty inside. Hollowed out. Whatever defined me has departed.

"Iain's body is gone. So is Desmond's. And we have to work out why. We need your mind for that. Your talents, your organizational skills, your leadership. C'mon. Take a minute, get your breath back. Then let's get going. Yeah? We need to work out what's going on."

Another sigh from me. "I have no clue what's going on." And now that I've admitted that, I realize it's what I've been thinking, feeling, for hours. "Really. No clue. I don't know if we're still looking for that poor girl, or something to lead us to her, or this Boyd character, or the missing bodies or what. I just . . . don't know anymore."

"It's all that, Jimmy. But we have to keep focused, we have to find the girl."

"We don't even know that she exists. It might all be some hideous game, or experiment."

"We've found the stuff Boyd uses to keep his victims alive. So there must be more clues to be found. And hopefully those'll lead us to the girl herself." His voice drops. "Come on, Jimmy. Don't check out now. Not when we need you the most."

My eyes have been all over the place while Kyle's been talking, mainly inside myself seeing things he can't possibly see. But I look at him and see sincerity. I dredge up a smile. This one lasts slightly longer than the last one.

"That's the spirit. C'mon, mate. We need you, Captain. You've got a mission to complete."

I stand up. Sway on my feet. Kyle grabs my arm.

"Steady now. Let's find Diana."

I allow myself to be led away but stop before we get too far, holding up my hand for emphasis.

"What?" Kyle can't hide the impatience in his voice.

"One thing. Let's just check."

I turn, free of his grasp, and make my way back to the kitchen. I open the door, peer inside.

"Oh no . . . oh god, no . . ."

Sylvia's body has gone.

I accompanied Jimmy and Kyle to the lift, and Sylvia, too, I suppose, and helped them into the cage. The door slid shut with a sense of finality and they descended. I watched until they disappeared. I heard them reach the ground floor, the door of the cage slide open. I let them go. I've got my own thing to do.

I walk slowly down the stairs, anxious all the time, alert for sharp sudden movements, things or people that shouldn't be there. I'm tired. And hungry. My stomach wails and screams like a haunted castle, desperate for me to put some meat on these old bones. But I've refused to eat any of the snacks laid out for us, as I don't want to lose my edge, don't want to get fat and sluggish and tired if I need to run for my life. Stay alive, stay hungry. Hungrier than the next person. Even if the next person's a killer shark who's younger and thinner and thinks they're prettier than you and after your job. Can't see why I should change just because I'm in here. It's kept me at the top of the heap and ahead of the pack. And it'll keep me safe in here too. When the time's up, I'm walking out of that door, missing girl or no missing girl. Killer or no killer. And you can take that to the bank.

I walk slowly down the stairs, alert as I go. No sudden movements, no sounds out of place. The faint noise of Jimmy and Kyle huffing and puffing with Sylvia's body drifts up from the ground floor. I block it out. Can't think about that as well. One thing at a time. Down one flight, step by cautious step. I reach the paintings. They're all still here, most of them as they were originally. Not Desmond, though. Not Iain. I find Sylvia's. And my heart somersaults.

Before, it depicted her sitting in her living room, perched on an armchair, cup and saucer in hand. That maddening symphony of florals, chintz, and stultifying neatness surrounded her. She was staring at the painter, looking angrily superior.

Not anymore.

The cup and saucer was gone, rolling on the floor, a stain spreading on the once immaculate carpet. Sylvia herself was sprawled beside it, reaching out for something, what we'll never know. Just as we found her upstairs. All details perfect, down to the wallpaper and the radio.

I stare at it, transfixed. What am I feeling? I suppose it should be panic, fear even. Like when I discovered the last two paintings, saw how they'd changed. But I'm not. I feel more like a viewer in a gallery, studying the work before me. Looking at the brushstrokes, the technicalities, which shades of what colors had been mixed for which specific effect. Framing and composition. I'm expecting to feel something, something negative, horrible, but I'm not. I don't feel anything. Not a thing. Just . . . numb.

So I study the lifeless body of a woman who not forty minutes ago had been alive and barking orders and insults in equal measure. And I still feel nothing. It's only when the tears slowly running down my cheeks tickle my face that I become aware I'm actually crying.

I swipe at them with the back of my hand. Batting them away like they're annoying insects. I'm sniffling as I do so, my movements getting more frantic. The wetter my hand gets, the more my tears keep coming. I get more and more annoyed and irritated with myself; for crying, for allowing emotion, the wrong kind of emotion, for this woman who I barely knew and hardly liked. And then I realize I'm crying for more than that. I'm crying for me, for this situation, this house, for all of us. The fear, the stress, everything. And when I acknowledge that, the numbness I told myself I was experiencing finally reveals itself as self-delusion and I fall to the stairs, sobbing.

I'm too heavy to stand, too tired to bear everything that's happening. I can't hold myself together anymore. I'm a heap. A ragged, crying, spent, useless heap of utter, total despair. I've given in. I've given up.

Don't know how long I stay like this, don't care. I've fallen so low in such a short space of time. It's so exhausting trying to keep going and sometimes it just feels like it's not worth it. This is one of those times. But that's the rational part of my brain explaining. What's really happening is me sobbing and screaming for this whole ordeal to end, for the dead to come back to life, to be free. I'm crying for everyone; the missing girl, everyone who's died. Myself. For my life. Just crying because I never have done so. Not since I escaped that dead-end dreary life and re-created myself as someone new. I vowed never to cry about anything, to never show weakness. And I managed to do that, for years. Or thought I had. But really I was storing it inside, bottling it up, ready for something massive, seismic, to allow it to come crashing out. Like this.

Eventually the wave rides itself out and I'm too exhausted to move. Right now, a big knife-wielding maniac could come and skewer me and I'd be too tired to fight back. Or even care. I'm spent. Nothing left. A slumped lump, spread almost boneless over the stairs.

"I suppose it gets to all of us, doesn't it, in the end. In different ways."

Jesus Christ. I scream, jump, you name it.

I fumble about, try to get up, body immediately into fight or flight but too shocked to decide which. I push myself away from the voice, and my back hits the wall, my head smacking painfully against it. I look up to see who's spoken.

And wish I hadn't bothered.

It's Len standing there, staring down at me.

Fear and confusion immediately turn to anger. Both with him and myself. Letting myself be vulnerable like that. Too wrapped up in my own self-indulgent little world. Stupid cow.

"What d'you want?"

Len doesn't reply, just stretches out his hand. I stare at him.

"I'm trying to help you up."

"I don't want to get up. I'm happy here." I'm trying to sound defiant but to my ears I just sound petulant.

Len gives something like a sympathetic near smile. "I doubt you are," he says. "I heard you crying."

"Big fucking deal."

Obviously I do want to get up, I want to get as far away from him as possible. But my head's ringing from the wall smack and I can't go anywhere for a few minutes. And I certainly don't want to be beholden to this bastard. I want nothing to do with him.

Len drops his hand and, with a great effort of huffing and sighing, sits down on the stairs. Keeping his distance but as near as he can get. "Mind if I join you?"

I instinctively shuffle away into the wall. "Why? Want to get close enough so you don't miss this time? Or you just going to throw me down the stairs?" I try to stand but the pain in my head's still hurting.

Len casts his eyes downward. "Look, I'm sorry about that. Tempers got heated, things got said that shouldn't have been said. And I should never have hit you. Never. I should never hit any woman."

Something in his tone makes me think it's not the first time he's done that. "Really? You had practice in that department?"

He sighs and I know I've hit a bull's-eye. I feel a slight thrill at exposing him but also a shiver at being so close to him.

He keeps his head down, eyes away from me, and says only one word, quietly. "No."

And I know he's lying.

"Really." And now he knows I don't believe him.

He sighs again. "Ex-wife. Kept taking my work home with me. Drinking too much." Another sigh. "Loads of excuses but no reasons. They told me that at AA. There's never a reason. And I should never have hit you. I can't apologize enough. I can never apologize enough."

I say nothing.

"I'm disgusted with myself. It's this place. Getting to us. In different ways."

I don't want to accept his apology quite yet, in case it's a ruse or comes with a *but*.

"But you have to admit," he continues, "I do have a point. About the two women."

And there it is.

I struggle to get to my feet. Still can't manage it. "Why them? What have they done to you? Why not Jimmy? Or Kyle? What do they have in common, Len? Oh. They're women."

He shakes his head, closes his eyes, gestures with his hands like he's being misunderstood. "It's not that. Not anything like that. I was a copper for years. You develop an instinct for these things."

"So why them? And how come none of the rest of us can see it?"

His voice hasn't softened any. "Well, it's obvious they're not kosher. Especially the one with the baby. Not the first time I've seen someone carry a kid as a prop. Probably not even hers. And the other one? Well. Just look at her."

"You have been. Since dinner. All of you."

He smiles like I've proved his point. "Exactly. Too obvious, isn't she?"

I can't reply. Can't argue. Can't fight back. Can't even move.

He sighs again and his anger subsides. "I just want to get this over with and see my boy."

"Boy?"

"Kenny. Chocolate Lab. Lovely lad. Would never upset me or hurt me. People'll let you down but dogs never will. Never. Sometimes I think I prefer their company to humans." He laughs. Again, more to himself than to me. "Sometimes? Always, more like. I just want this to be over and be back at home with him now. I thought for a minute there I was back on the job. Working again, feeling all those synapses zing. But I'm just an old man who should have known better."

We sit like that in silence. I don't know how much time passes. I don't even look at this thing on my wrist. I do know that my head's feeling better.

"Anyway," he says eventually, eyes on the step below him. "I'm sorry. I became that person I promised I'd never be again. I'm disgusted and there's no excuse. And I don't blame you if you can't forgive me."

I say nothing.

He nods to himself. "In fact, I'd rather you didn't. Serves me right."

Another silence. I break it this time.

"Come on. We've still got a girl to find." I stand up, hold out my hand to him.

He looks up, wary. Then takes my hand. I help him rise, slowly and painfully. He's heavier than he appears. He acknowledges the help with a nod.

"Up or down?" he asks.

"Down," I say, knowing that Jimmy and Kyle are down there and feeling safer in that knowledge.

"Righty ho."

We start down the stairs, but something catches my eye. I stop. "Wait."

"What?"

"There, in the painting."

He squints. "Can't see anything."

"Exactly." I turn to him. "The picture of Cerys and Monica. Cerys is still there, but look. The baby's gone."

Cerys . . . Cerys . . ." The poor kid can't hear me. She's lost in herself.

Tearing the room apart, looking for Monica. In the battered old wardrobe, crawling inside it, standing up, hammering on the flimsy wooden walls until they threaten to splinter, squeezing her whole body under the bed. Pulling at the floorboards, checking for loose planks, cracks Monica could have fallen through, no matter how improbably small. Not allowing an inch of space in the room to go unexamined. Not allowing the evidence of what's before her eyes to get in the way of the desperate hope of finding her child.

Can't blame her. Guess I would do the same in her position.

"Cerys, hey, honey, hey . . . stop, listen . . ."

She's deaf to me, to the rest of the world, and frantic in her actions. Like some naked force of nature, fingers into claws, ripping everything before her apart.

I'm out of bed, hands round her shoulders, trying to stop her. She just shrugs me off.

"She's here, she's here, she must be here . . ."

She checks the door again. It's still as locked as we left it. But that's not good enough for Cerys, who rattles away at the handle, pulls it, rattles it again, confirming what she knows but refuses to believe.

"She's got to be somewhere . . . She has to be somewhere . . ."

I stand in front of her, plant my feet so she can't ignore me, can't move me. "Hey, Cerys, stop. *Stop.*" Can't dodge round me, either. So she comes to a reluctant halt, allowing me to grab her and stop her physically but her eyes never give up, roving all over the place, never resting on any one thing, checking every shadow, every corner, every nook, no matter how tiny, no matter how many times she's already done it. Eyes like a swallow trapped in a barn, flitting everywhere, anywhere.

Anywhere but at me.

"Cerys, she's gone. She's not here." My voice is as quiet, as reasonable as I can get it. Like a parent talking to a child. I imagine.

"No. *No . . .*"

She's trying to break free, to continue her frantic search, but I can feel her body weakening in my grip. Moving on to the next stage. Some kind of weary acceptance.

"She's gone. I'm sorry."

I take my hands away, and she's calmed down enough to not instantly move away from me. Slowly her eyes come into focus. And she's looking at me now.

"Where is she, then? My daughter, *where is she*?"

Her eyes aren't kind. They're accusing, building up to anger.

"I don't know. She's just . . . gone." I place my hand gently on her shoulder, to draw her to me. "Come on, let's sit down."

The frantic eye-darting begins again. There's an even more manic quality to it. "Did you do this? Did you take her?"

"What? How . . . I've been with you all this time. In bed. We haven't left each other's sides. Why would I do that?"

She quiets down, thinking about what I've said. I manage to lead her to the edge of the bed where we sit. "Come on. Let's think this through."

"We've got to go and look for her. She must be . . . she can't be far away. She must have found one of those secret passages or something. Woke up while we were . . . were in bed . . . and gone through it. We have to find it. It's here somewhere, it must be."

She allows me to hold her. Like part of her wants me to take charge, tell her it's all going to be all right, find her daughter for her. Like she's become the child and I'm, Jesus, her mother.

"Cerys."

She looks at me. Waiting. Expectant, like the next words out of my mouth are going to make things good again.

"She's not in the room. Maybe she left and we didn't hear her."

I realize that what I'm saying is impossible, that a small child couldn't have let herself out of the room and managed to lock the door from the inside after her but I'm hoping that Cerys doesn't notice and will calm down. She's still quiet, listening. Good.

"Let's get dressed and go and find her. That's the best thing we can do."

THE OTHER PEOPLE   195

Cerys nods.

"Come on then."

And yeah, I should have noticed the look Cerys gave the bed we'd recently occupied. Saw it as more than just a casual glance and for the filthy, sour stare it really was. A game changer of a stare. And also made more of the way she avoided looking at or even accidentally touching my body when she dressed. Like it was pathological. And how she covered hers up fully. But, hey, it's easy to say all this now. Hindsight's a bitch.

What I should have really noticed, though, was that my knife was missing.

It seems darker in the library now. The old wooden bookshelves with the fake books more overpowering. Like they're folding in on us. The furniture harder, older, somehow. Like everything's starting to fall apart. I know how it feels.

I'm sitting in an armchair hitting the whiskey while the rest of them are talking. I see their mouths move but can't hear what's coming out. Or rather I'm not listening to what's coming out. They've not asked my opinion and I've not offered it.

All the bodies have disappeared and the paintings keep changing. We haven't found the girl, Claire, and according to the watch on my wrist we've only got just under three hours to do so. We're exhausted and we're scared. And I don't know what to do anymore.

Kyle told me to lead and that's what I'm trying to do but I can't. Lead them where? Do what? I was bred for this, trained for it. Give orders to those below me, take orders from those above. A chain of command, respected, followed. Regimented. And that's what I've implemented because it works. But not this time.

We should have found Claire by now but we haven't. And everything I've tried has failed. *I've* failed.

They're deep in discussion, Kyle and Diana. Len lingers on the edges, listening, processing. I spot his type now. Should have done so before. I fell for the old man act, like everyone else.

I shouldn't have told Kyle my real rank, either. That honesty has gnawed away at me ever since. It felt like the right thing to do in that awful room, when we didn't know if we were going to find a way out. To share confidences. Secrets. A moment of vulnerability that I don't intend to repeat. But now he knows. Perhaps he won't share that fact with the others, but it leaves him with power over me. And that I don't want.

Like boarding school. Being constantly on guard in case one's intimacies get used against one. Weaponized. Boys can be vicious, murderous. It's why we send them to war.

Another mouthful of whiskey. After Sylvia's demise I should be scared to drink this. But I don't feel that's the way out for me. And besides, it's good stuff. I'm not much of a drinker but this doesn't burn, it slips down smoothly and the warmth inside is comforting. It whispers to me that perhaps things aren't as bad as I've made them out to be. I can understand why so many get hooked on this stuff.

"D'you agree, Jimmy?"

I startle, a rabbit in the headlights. "I'm sorry, what?" The words dribble out from the sides of my mouth.

Kyle's talking to me. I focus on his mouth, try to make out the words coming out. The whiskey's hit me harder than I thought. I look at the decanter. It was nearly full when I started. There's only about a quarter left. Surely I can't have drunk all that much just now? Really?

"We're talking about what to do next, Jimmy." Kyle can't keep the exasperation from his voice. And then I see myself as he sees me. A drunk, tired, prematurely old man in an armchair, a leader who, by his own inadequacy, can no longer lead.

And it makes me—unreasonably, I know—angry.

"It's Captain," I say, "Not Jimmy. Captain. You'll address me by my rank, thank you."

I manage to stand while I say that. The glass seems very large and cumbersome in my hand and I can't help spilling some whiskey down my trousers. "God, look what you made me do . . ." I put the glass down, sloshing a bit more over the sides, and try wiping the wetness away.

"Captain? Really?"

I try to focus. Kyle is staring at me. A voice—my own?—tells me to back off, keep quiet, but that voice can go to hell. "Yes," I say, rounding on him, "*Captain.*" I stagger toward him, stare him down. Like they taught us to do in officer training. "Captain to you, Captain to all of you."

My voice is too loud for the room but I don't care. Who's he to question me? I want my armchair and my drink. My temporary happiness, my warm little cocoon where things make sense. Or are on the verge of making sense. One more drink, and everything will be fine.

"Now if you've quite finished," I say, "I just want to be left alone."

I sit down again. Ignoring their stares.

He laughs. Not a happy laugh, because god forbid there should be any humor in this house. I ignore him. Pour myself some more whiskey.

"Yeah, you just sit there, *Captain*, don't mind us. Enjoy your drink. Excuse us if we don't salute. You'd need to be a higher rank for that."

That penetrates. Gets me immediately angry. I'm up, grabbing hold of the little shit by the front of his shirt. Pulling his face into mine.

"What did you mean by that?"

He's angry now too. "You want me to tell everyone?"

"Try it . . ."

"Get your hands off me . . ."

He pushes me away. My arms flail about uselessly and I fall backward toward the armchair. I hit it, knocking the whiskey decanter onto the floor, where it smashes. I slump into the armchair. Stare up at him. "Now look what you've done . . ."

"I think you've had enough, *Lieutenant*."

I feel my face redden. "You little shit . . ."

He turns to the other two. "Yes, old Jimmy here, our *captain*, is nothing of the sort. Just a second lieutenant who found the captain's uniform in his wardrobe and couldn't resist putting it on and pretending. Isn't that right?"

I knew it. Never give power to someone else. *Never.* They'll always use it against you. *Always.* Well, two can play at that game, matey.

"Says the boy who hears voices . . ."

"Voices?" asks Diana. "Didn't someone say that earlier?"

"Yes. Kyle's still hearing his voices that no one else can. Crying girls. And he has a phobia of storms and being locked in confined spaces. Thinks he hears this Claire girl that none of us can find all over the house. Crying and begging for his help. Not right in the head, is he?"

Diana turns to him. "Can you really? Hear her?"

Kyle sighs. And in that sigh I feel a moment of triumph. "Yes, I can still hear her."

"Why didn't you say?" says Len. "You could have led us to her."

"Because I've not been able to find her. And no one else can hear her. So I'm not sure if I was imagining it or not."

"Who couldn't hear?" asks Len.

"The lieutenant here and Sylvia."

"Well, you still should have said. We would have checked it out. We've got little enough to go on."

I stare at the three of them. My moment of triumph gone. They believe him. Those bastards believe him.

Before I can do anything else there's a scream. Maddening, ragged, desperate and frantic.

The three of them look at one another. I can hear them asking themselves where it came from, who made it, and then they're running from the room in search of the source.

But not me. I just want to sit here and drink. And the shattered decanter says I can't drink.

So I draw my knees up to my chin and close my eyes.

And wish myself anywhere but here.

I shout her name, check rooms behind curtains, nooks, and crannies, everywhere. *Monica! Monica.* Nothing. And I know, or part of me knows, deep down, that she's not there. I don't know where she is but I know she's gone. I can *feel* it. That attachment's gone. I can't feel *her* anymore. But still I keep looking, or running at any rate. Got to be doing something, moving. But soon I stop looking and then I'm just running. And running. Down the hallways, in and out of open rooms. Away from here, from them. From Ramona.

And from myself. Because I was stupid enough to think I could have been happy back there. No child, just me. And of course I can't and now I have to pay for that. But I don't want to, I don't want to feel all that guilt and loss. I know what it'll do to me. And I can't face that. Please don't let me have to face that.

I'm thinking all this as I'm running. To stop thinking about Monica being gone. But I can't. Like when someone tells you not to think of something and all you can do is think of that something. And I can't do it. I can't. Because I can't outrun myself.

But I'm going to try.

Round and round, up and down. Falling over on the stairs, getting up again, like I'm the kid, not the grown-up. Even when the house tells me I'm running in circles I lie to myself that I'm going forward. But no matter how hard I run, how far, it's there. In my mind. In me. The responsibility. The guilt. *The loss.* Always with me like a constant companion. And I can't shift it. So I do the next best thing. I can't outrun myself but I can tire myself out so I can't think anymore.

I run faster. I pretend the tears on my cheeks aren't there and that the part of my heart that's not pumping blood isn't breaking. My chest is burning, screaming for more air than I can take in. My legs are beyond aching. I'm beyond pain. I *am* pain. I meet none of the others. If I did

I'd ignore them. Keep running. Up, down, back and forth. Till my arms shake. My heart's ready to give out. My legs can't move anymore. But I keep going.

On. Up. Down. Back. Forward.

Tripping up the stairs, sending myself sprawling. Then up again, off again. Stumbling now. Crashing into things. Round a corner, down a hallway. My body's closing down, had enough. My heart's going to burst. I'm beyond my limit.

But I keep going.

Until I really, really can't go on.

Then I just drop. And lie there. My lungs are too small for the amount of air I need. Heart's hammering overtime, blood's pounding in my ears, ribs not expanding enough to take deep breaths, and my face is so contorted I'm ugly screaming. The pain's almost unbearable. I've pushed my body beyond its limits and I'm paying for my actions. I'm always paying for my actions.

I'm a broken machine of bone and blood and meat and I'm beyond repair.

This pain . . . this pain . . . hurts so much. And I deserve it. I *need* it. In its way, it's giving me a kind of peace. A good pain that kind of cleanses. This must be like what those religious people feel when they hurt themselves to be nearer to God. Joyous? I don't know.

But it doesn't last. My body starts returning to normal and I start to feel again. And all those things I ran away from are back again. Monica. Ramona. Love. Lust. Guilt. Loss. I'm a jigsaw that's been thrown over the floor but is now being reassembled. And all the same pieces are there and I know what the picture is and I don't want to see it. All that running and I'm back where I was. And so is the pain. And it's anything but joyous.

Then the last piece slots into place and the picture's complete. And it's me, Monica's mother. Monica's protector. Who I am. Who I always was. Nothing for me. No joy. No life. Only for her.

And I've failed. And I'm sorry. So, so sorry.

My body wants to move. My head doesn't. Maybe if I just lie here, everything'll go away. Every*one*'ll go away. And I can be like this forever. Until I'm not here anymore.

I've always paid for any bit of happiness I've had. My mother always hurt me, even when I was younger. Not physically, that was more my dad. But mentally. Emotionally. Sometimes she just did it with the tone of her voice, or even a shrug and a look away. And I'd feel that guilt, that depression, that I was doing something wrong and she was going to be angry and disappointed in me. And that would be that. I either couldn't do it or the joy would be sucked out so I'd hate doing it. And that would be a loaded gun pointed at me and ready to fire the next time I thought about trying to enjoy myself.

She always hated things that made me happy. Anything, no matter how small. Going out with friends. Laughing. Reading a book or a comic. Even if she didn't try to stop me—though she usually did—she would give me those angry eyes and that disapproving voice and tell me why I was wrong and why people who liked those things were always wrong. And she'd hint what would happen to them. And there would go the joy.

And it wasn't until years later that I realized why she was like that. All she had was her fear of God. She'd had the joy drained from her and couldn't bear to see anyone else being happy. Especially her own daughter. But it was too late, she had infected me with it by then. Her fear. Her disapproval. Poisoning me from the inside.

And things didn't get any better with Monica. Anytime I tried to do something for myself she would stare at me, and I'd see my mother's eyes again, in that tiny body. Judging me. Hating me.

And with those pieces back into place now, I understand. I can feel it now. *Really* feel it. And I know I have to pay for my pleasure like I've always had to pay for it. But this is the worst it's ever been. And I know what I have to do. It ends here. One way or the other, it ends here.

"Cerys."

I look up. And there's Ramona standing over me, a bundle of something in her arms. My stomach lurches and I immediately know what it is.

"I found her, Cerys. I found Monica."

I slowly get to my feet and she passes the bundle over to me. For a second my heart soars like it's been impaled by a shard of hope and opened up to the light. But I know I'm just lying to myself because there's no hope here. There never has been in my life and I know better than to think there should be any now.

I take the bundle. It's the sheet from the bed we made love in. I can feel what's in it by the weight. I'm used to carrying that weight all the time. Permanently resting on my hip. I open it. And there she is. I'm expecting this but I still gasp. Still shake. I close it again.

"Where was she?"

"Corner of the room," Ramona says quietly, almost reverently, like we're in a church.

"I searched there."

Ramona nods. "She seemed to be buried into the floor. Curled up. Like she was, I don't know, nesting."

I nod, even though I don't know that I'm hearing her right. I steel myself, open the sheet again, look at her. She seems content. Smiling.

"She seems at peace," Ramona says.

I say nothing.

"Happy, even. Dare I say it."

"What would you know?" My voice louder than I was expecting.

Ramona looks confused. "What?"

"What would you know about her being happy? About a baby, a child, being happy? You killed yours."

"Now hold on." Ramona's voice getting angry too.

"Killed yours 'cause it was getting in the way of you living your life."

"That's not what happened."

"And now you're telling me that my daughter, my *child*, is better off being dead. Is *happier* being dead."

"That's not what I said, she just . . . her face, it looks at peace. That's all I meant. Like she's happy. Like she wants you to be happy too." Her voice drops. "Cerys."

Ramona approaches me, hand outstretched.

I recoil from her touch. "Don't touch me. Stay away."

"Cerys, I'm—"

"Don't touch me." The words hissed out.

Ramona retreats. I look down again at the bundle in my hands. My daughter. My dead daughter. Dead because I decided to enjoy myself instead of taking care of her. I keep staring at her, and these thoughts come into my head. "What if she was right, my mother? What if I had no business being happy? What if all I was meant to do was to care for this child? Well, I ballsed that up good and proper, didn't I? So what do I do now?"

"What d'you mean, what do you do now?"

I look up, unaware I must have spoken those words aloud. Ramona's still watching me.

"Cerys, let me help you. I know this is an unbelievably sad time for you, I know this is a horrific thing that's happened. But let me help you. We can get through this together."

She moves toward me once more. I move away from her. I don't want her touching me. Her body's a powerful thing. I can't let it take me over again.

"Why d'you flinch away from me? I'm trying to help you."

I think of laughing but can't trust what it'll come out as. "Help? You want to help? It's too late for that, *lover*." Ramona looks like I've just slapped her. Good. I want her to share my pain. "I've failed, haven't I? Failed."

"No, you haven't."

"Yeah, I have. I had one job, that's all. One job. Protect her. Nurture her. And I let my own needs, my own filthy pleasure, come first. And now she's gone. Taken from me to teach me a lesson."

"You can't believe that?"

"Oh, I can believe that. Because it's true."

"But it's not, it's—"

"It's what? This has been my whole life. Failure. And guilt. Guilt. And failure."

Ramona shakes her head. "No. That's not true, Cerys. You're entitled to a life. You're entitled to be happy. Everyone is. It's just . . . bad timing, that's all. It's this house." She moves closer to me once more. "But hey, come on. We're together. You and me. We can get through this. Once we get out of here we—"

"*We*? You and me? What happened to, 'I don't want to be exclusive'? 'Let's just enjoy the here and now'? Oh no. Just because this has happened you're saying what you think I want to hear. But I know what'll happen. Once you're tired of me, I'll be dropped. And don't say I won't. Don't lie to me."

Ramona stares at me. And I look at her. Really study her. And god, I want her. Like I just had her, like she just had me. And I know in that instant that'll never happen. She's given me a glimpse of a different road, one that a different me could travel down. But the real me, the me who's always been here, who's lived my life, will never go down that road. Because that guilt, that loss, will always be with me. The failure to be Monica's mother will always be with me. I turn, walk away down the hallway, clutching Monica to me, away from the light of the stairs, away from Ramona.

"All I have is ghosts," I say. "The past. I have no future."

And I take Ramona's knife out of the back pocket of my jeans, turn, and smile at her.

It's always been leading up to this moment. One way or another. My road was always leading here. Either in this house or not. There was nowhere else for it to go.

"I don't care about any other killer in this house. I'm responsible for my daughter's death. And I know what to do."

I'm not doing this out of sadness, although I suppose it is a sad thing that I'm doing. And I'm not doing it out of love, even misplaced or thwarted love. I'm doing it out of hope. Because I've lived with hope and it's the cruelest of all emotions. It always lets you down. Or rather it lets you see things as they really are. Hopeless. So I do what I do through hope. Or hopelessness.

I pull the knife across my throat. Fast, deep.

Ramona runs toward me and I see her turn red with my blood.

I feel, or think I feel, Ramona's hands on me, trying to stop the blood. Push it back in my body. But it's hopeless.

I think I see Monica. No. I *do* see Monica. And she's smiling. And she's saying something. *I just wanted you to be happy*, she says. *Don't worry about me, I'm gone and happy. And now it's your turn to be.*

Oh god.

I claw at my throat but it's too late.

I call out to Ramona but it's too late.

I want to live but it's too late.

Too late—

See? What did I tell you? Eh? Eh? She did it. And there's your evidence, right in front of you . . ."

Len's having a field day. Hearing screaming, we all ran upstairs to find Ramona in a hallway cradling Cerys's dead body, the two of them saturated in blood, knife at her side, a blood-soaked bundle in her arms. It's a horrific scene, more blood than I thought a human body could contain and a gaping wound the width of Cerys's neck, like an extra, ragged mouth. The wound's stopped gushing now, though, and I wonder why, then realize it's because her heart's stopped. It says something about me and what I've been through these last few hours that I'm not as shocked as I once would have been. Or should have been. Now there's only that feeling of low-level terror mixed with tiredness. Like, there's one more gone and it might be me next but you know what? Let it happen. I'm too worn-out, too numb to care.

Or perhaps that's what I'm telling myself. Perhaps I do still care. Very, very much. And my body, my mind, just doesn't know how to cope with that. So it makes me tired and tries to shut me down. Or maybe it's all the adrenaline filling my system, ebbing, flowing, ebbing, flowing, until in the end I'm too wrung out to keep being surprised and scared. I don't know. All I know is that Cerys is the latest one to die, Ramona's holding her, and Len's screaming in what he believes to be some kind of unhinged triumph.

"For fuck's sake, Len, stop . . ." Kyle's apparently had enough as well.

But Len's having none of it. He turns on Kyle.

"Stop? Stop? When I've finally unmasked the killer among us?" He gives the kind of laugh you'd never use for a joke. "You thought I was imagining things, didn't you? Being paranoid, because this house was making us all paranoid. Scared of each other, scared of our own shadows. But I told you there was someone, right in our midst, working against us. And there she is." He gives a needlessly elaborate flourish toward Ramona.

Tears are falling down Ramona's cheeks. From what I've come to know about this girl in the short time we've been here I hadn't pegged her as a crier. She seems genuinely upset. "Shut up. Just shut up. She's dead, you fucking asshole, can't you see that?"

"Of course I can see that. And I can also see that you killed her. There's your knife, the one you stole, to prove it. Just next to her. And there's her blood all over you." He looks round at us. "Case fucking closed."

"She killed herself," says Ramona, in a voice more full of emotion than she's exhibited so far. "And I couldn't save her. Nothing I could say or do would save her. I was too late. Even though I was right here, *right here*, I was too late . . . for her and her daughter . . ."

I notice the bundle Cerys has been cradling. And understand. "Oh my god . . . the child's dead too . . ."

"You killed the kid as well, then?" Len, of course. "Two for one? Didn't think we'd see?"

"That's enough, Len," says Kyle.

"Enough, is it? I unmask the killer in the house and all you can say is that's enough?"

Ramona's too far gone to fight back. Her head drops and she begins crying again. Kyle and I look at each other. Out of everything that's happened in this house so far, this suddenly seems the most real. Someone is dead. Unfortunately we've become accustomed to that. But this is the first time someone got close enough to them to mourn their loss.

I walk away, down the hallway. It's like I'm intruding on private grief. Kyle does the same. We share a look.

"D'you think, is it her?" His voice is low, so Len won't hear. "Could Ramona have done this?"

"I don't know," I reply, equally quietly. "I mean, I trust Len about as far as I can throw him, but he did say that about the knife. How she'd stolen it. We both missed her doing that. But . . ."

Kyle sighs. "This is well out of control now," he says. "I don't know what we can do. You're a businesswoman, aren't you? You boss people around, can't you take charge? Do something?" He sounds so young when he speaks, like there's more than just years between us, there's life experience as well.

"I reached the limit of my comfort zone when I first arrived here. And the limit of my expertise. I haven't a clue what to do next."

"What are you two whispering about?" Len stares at us. "Tell me."

I notice he's picked up Ramona's blood-dripping knife and from the way he's holding it, it looks like he's threatening us with it while he talks.

"We're just discussing what you said," says Kyle. "How you've unmasked a criminal mastermind."

"Criminal mastermind? There's no such thing. That's all bullshit. Occasionally you'll find one who might be averagely clever, but mostly they're thick and prisons are full of them. And all that plotting and planning you see in books and on the telly? Bollocks. There's nothing elaborate about it. Criminals commit crimes because they want something, and something—or someone—else is in the way. Simple. Criminal mastermind . . ."

"I was being sarcastic."

Len's so angry it feels like he's going to use the knife on us next. "I should get a medal for cracking this one." He barks an unpleasant laugh. "One last case. And they thought I was too old. Well, fuck them." He turns, throws the knife as far as he can down the hallway, where it's swallowed by the darkness.

"That's if she did it," says Kyle.

Len points at where he's thrown the knife. "If? *If?*"

Ramona speaks without making eye contact. She's beyond exhausted. "Why the hell would I do that? We'd just had sex. We were going to see each other when we got out of here . . . We . . ." She starts sobbing again, near silently, shoulders shaking.

Kyle looks back at Len. "So that's why they got rid of you, Len. Wanted some alone time. And now this fucking house has claimed another two."

"It isn't the house, you moron. It's *her*. She did it."

"If she did it, Len," I say, "then you have to prove it. To us. Because I think Ramona's innocent."

He stares at us like he's ready to explode. Kyle and I don't move. Just then I become aware of a presence behind me. I turn. Jimmy Saint has wandered up to join us. He looks rough, vague. He's not walking straight and then I remember all the whiskey he put away downstairs. But it's more than that. It's like he's come unmoored.

"Have I missed something?" His voice is as vague as his manner. Like a ghost speaking.

"Cerys and Monica are dead," I tell him. "And Len thinks Ramona killed them."

"Ramona?" Jimmy says, as if hearing the name for the first time.

"The American bitch right there," shouts Len, gesturing.

That gets Ramona's attention. She gets to her feet, face wet from tears and blood, a mask of anger. Her voice is ominously quiet. "What did you call me?"

"Called you what you are. You heard me."

Ramona stares at him with such hatred that I wouldn't give Len much for his chances. She moves toward him.

Clearly Len agrees, because, having gotten rid of the knife, he looks round for something else to defend himself with. His eyes fall on Jimmy's open holster. Before the captain can respond, Len grabs his gun and points it at Ramona.

"Stay where you are. I mean it. You think I wouldn't use this?"

Jimmy has just noticed what's happened. It's like he's moving in slower motion than the rest of us. Kyle and I both instinctively jump backward at the sight of the gun. Ramona stops moving, but it's clear she still wants to hurt Len.

"Look at her, look at the way she's staring at me," says Len, a twisted smile on his face. "That's what a murderer looks like. Anyone doubt it now?"

"I'd be staring at you like that if you'd just spoken to me that way," I say. "Your problem with women back again?"

He swings the gun on me. "Shut up, you fucking bitch." Then straight back to Ramona. "You. Move."

"I'm not going anywhere with you." Ramona's hands are fists, waiting for the opportunity to strike.

He aims the gun at her face. "Turn around, and move. I won't say it again."

Ramona, seeing she has no choice, reluctantly turns away from him. Len is immediately on her, grabbing her hair from behind, twisting a huge hank of it so that Ramona cries out in pain, contorts her body. She's shouting at him, trying to fight him off but he just pulls all the harder. With his other hand he pushes the gun roughly into her rib cage.

"Now walk."

Kyle runs forward, makes to grab him. But Len's too fast. Without letting go of Ramona's hair, he swings the gun round to him.

"Back off, sonny, or you'll be next."

Kyle, seeing he has no other option, backs off. "What the fuck is wrong with you?" he shouts.

"Shut up." Snarling now.

And that's when Ramona makes a move. She reaches behind, twists the hand that's holding her hair, screaming from what is a clearly painful move, trying to maneuverer her body away from him and the gun and stamp down on his instep at the same time. But Len's too savvy for that. He lets go of her hair, grabs her wrist, and twists her arm up behind her back. Ramona screams again, gasps in pain. All the while he holds the gun in place.

"Want to make a game of it, do you? I'll give you a game, darlin' . . ."

Kyle's now rooted to the spot. So am I.

"What are you going to do now?" I ask. "You can't go anywhere, you can't leave the house."

"I'm going to get you your proof." He twists her wrist harder. Ramona gasps from the pain. "I've got a suspect to interrogate. And when I'm finished, I'll know where the missing girl is too."

He makes his way backward down the hallway, never taking his eyes off us, never releasing his grip on Ramona. Ramona just stares at us, helplessly, fearfully.

"We'll get you back," I say to her. I don't hear her reply.

They disappear into the darkness.

We're silent for a moment. Each of us processing what we've witnessed in our own way. We're left standing over the bloodied bodies of the mother and daughter. I honestly don't know what to say.

Jimmy Saint speaks first.

"Maybe Cerys did kill herself," he says.

We both look at him.

Jimmy sighs. "Maybe she killed herself because she couldn't protect her child. Maybe she failed and couldn't face herself because of it."

Kyle and I glance at each other. We don't speak. Can't speak.

Jimmy nods. A confirmation, like he's heard something we haven't said.

"We need to get weapons," says Kyle, "some kind of weapons. Get that knife back, find another. Go after Len, stop him from doing whatever he's got planned with Ramona. We should—"

Jimmy keeps talking, like he hasn't heard Kyle. "She killed herself because she couldn't protect her child. Because she failed as a protector." Another sigh. "I know. Because I failed. My duty is to protect. To be a shield. And I've failed. So what's the point?"

I frown. "The point of what?"

"Of me. Of her. Of . . ." He gestures round. "Of this. Of anything. What's the point? There is no point." Another sigh, another look down at Cerys's and Monica's bodies. Then back to us. "I'm going now. Goodbye." And with that he turns and walks away.

"Jimmy, what . . ."

Somewhere in the house a gong sounds.

RAMONA O'ROURKE

I'm almost twisted double by the gun digging in my side and this asshole nearly yanking my hair out by the roots. Stumbling and falling, the only thing holding me up, as he propels me through the house, is his grip on my hair. God knows where we're going.

And I'm goddamn terrified. I've been threatened by men before, with knives, guns, whatever. Comes with the job. But I've always been in charge, able to defuse a dangerous situation. I've done self-defense. Or always had a security guy to hand. But this old bastard caught me when I was off guard and vulnerable and blindsided me. So yeah, terrified. And angry with myself for allowing him to do this.

He knew I was off my game and used that against me. Ex-cop. Knows how to hurt. Guess that's the same in any country. He might be old but that's some muscle memory he's got. And I can tell I'm not the first woman he's manhandled.

I guess I'm angry at the others, too, for not stepping up and stopping him. Yeah, he has a gun and told them I'm the killer, but couldn't they see what had just happened? Cerys had just killed herself. Like I've always said: you can only ever rely on yourself.

"So, you taking me to where you killed the others? Your *lair*?"

"Shut up." He's snarling now. Mouth pressed against my ear. I can smell his bad breath. Pushing the gun harder into my ribs.

We reach an open doorway and Len pushes me through, letting go of my hair so I stumble and hit the bare floor. Hard. Elbows first. The pain's like an electric charge all up my arms. The room is empty apart from a couple of old bentwood chairs with a table between them. It's a blank room otherwise, depressing and institutionalized. Damp and cold, a room without hope. An interview room. I wonder if this is Len's room.

Still holding the gun on me, he points to one of the chairs. I rub my head where he pulled my hair.

"Put your arm down."

I don't. I gently rub my damaged scalp, check my fingers for blood. There's a little. "Bet I've got some huge bald spot on top now thanks to you, shit for brains."

"I said put your arm down."

He's standing over me, pointing the gun from his hip. Wow. Paging Doctor Freud. His mouth twists like he's mashing his teeth, unable to find the words he wants in there. His eyes never leave mine. He stares at me with distaste. Whether that's because I'm covered in blood or just because I'm a woman I don't know, but I guess it's a combination of the two.

"Why?" I say. "You're going to kill me so it doesn't matter whether my hand's up or not."

"Shut up." Then a pause. "What are you talking about?"

"This. Dragging me here to kill me. Giving the others that performance about me being the killer. Perfect way to get me on your own without them following. You couldn't have made it more obvious."

A look of disgust hits his face. "Bollocks. I'm not a killer. You are."

"Yeah? You got any proof for that, ex-cop?"

"You were crouching over the body with a knife in your hand."

"I was holding my lover's dead body, you fucking moron. She'd just taken her own life. The knife was next to me." I'm getting angry, reliving the scene, and I shouldn't. He's holding a gun.

He stares at me. I swallow, blink, hold his stare and throw it back. "I didn't kill her," I say. "I haven't killed anyone."

Another snarl. "Exactly the kind of thing I'd expect you to say."

I keep staring at him. He points the gun at the chair. "Sit."

There's no point arguing so I do so. Keeping his eyes and the gun on me all the time, he sits down on the other chair at the other side of the table. Holding the gun on me, he never stops staring.

I'm used to being stared at by men. Mostly their faces are expressionless as I do my work in front of them. They think those blank stares hide everything. But they're shitty poker players. It's Tell City with those guys and I've learned to recognize them all. They can't hide what they want to do with me or to me. Some of them just desire me. That's OK, that's the rules. It's fantasy, they know that, I know that. Their little imaginations run through scenarios while I perform, they file them away in their mental wank banks, then they give their old lady my face and moves later. Pretty harmless. Kind of sweet. Might even help their relationships. But then there are the dark ones. I don't see behind their eyes into their souls, any of that bullshit. They have this aura coming off them. Hatred. They want to blame me for all the fuckups in their lives. I become all the women who ever fucked them over. And they want to take all their hurt and all their failures out on my body. Hurt me bad for all the things those other women did to them. And I'm kind of getting that vibe from Len. But something stronger too.

"So you've got me here, Len. What are you going to do now?"

"Interrogate you." His eyes never leave my face, gun on me the whole time. A small smile flickers over his face.

And then I understand. It's not just me. He hates women. All of us. And now I'm really scared.

"So what will you do when you find out I haven't killed anyone? Let me go? Say sorry? Kiss and make up?"

"Don't be disgusting. I'm going to get the truth out of you."

I almost smile. "No, you're not, Len. It's clear you've made up your mind. I'm guilty and that's that. You know, you were born too late. You'd have made a great witch finder."

His finger tightens around the trigger of the gun. He snarls, eyes jumping with what could be madness. I'd better be careful or that gun'll go off and that'll be the end of that. And me.

"Sarcastic bitch. I ask questions and you answer them."

I say nothing. Now's not the time to speak.

"Why'd you do it? Why'd you kill all the others? What are you getting out of it?"

"That's three questions, Len. So in order—I didn't, I didn't, and nothing."

He reaches across the table, the gun poking in my face. "Tell me." He's really annoyed now, his voice rising. "Tell me why you did it, who you're working with, and where the girl is. Tell me." He smacks his thigh with the palm of his hand. I try not to jump. "*Tell me.*" Really angry now. "Who's Charles Boyd? What's he got to do with this place? Why are we all here?"

I stare at him.

"*Tell me . . .*"

Angry now, shouting.

Then he's up and out of his seat, around and behind me. Leaning down next to me, his mouth by my ear. The gun on my neck. And his breath.

"*Tell me.*"

"You need to drink more water, Len. Or maybe floss more regularly. Your breath . . ." I sound flippant but I'm shaking fit to burst inside.

There's a sharp hiss and he's upright, arm raised ready to hit me. I brace myself but nothing happens. Instead he sits back down opposite me.

"You know I used to be a copper, right?"

"You've kind of mentioned it once or twice."

He continues, voice ominously quiet. "Or cop, as you would say. And I was bloody good. High arrest rate, strong conviction rate. I was good at giving evidence in court as well. Never lost my cool, or my nerve. Dressed smart in my suit and tie, my colleagues nicknamed me the Accountant. Bland and unthreatening. Totally trustworthy. I realized early that's what worked. Don't stand out. Don't talk, just listen. How you learn things. How you get confessions."

"You don't seem to be following your own advice now, Len."

"Doesn't matter, does it? 'Cause I know you're guilty. I caught you with the murder weapon and that girl's dead body. Red-handed. Red everything, the amount of blood you spilled. So just confess. To me. Now. Here, in this room. And that'll be the end of it."

"I've done nothing to confess to." He's seriously starting to scare me now. I've got to do something. Anything. I've tried being flippant and it didn't work. I've got to try something else. I've got to be clever.

Len smiles, nods in resignation. He says, "If Plan A didn't work, I'd use Plan B. Not as clever as sitting there in my suit, waiting for them to trip themselves up. But more direct."

He studies the barrel of the gun. This has taken an even worse turn, if that's possible.

"As long as I didn't leave a mark on their face or their hands and arms, as long as they could walk when they left the interview room, then job done." Another laugh without humor. "Because who'd believe them? What, old Len, he did that to you? Boring Accountant Len? Never. So I always got away with it. And every time it got results. *Every* time." He pauses, thinking back.

My heart's hammering. Got to think of something, do something.

"You see now, here, in this room, I'm God. I control you. Your life, your death. Whether you get to leave or not." He leans forward, face right into mine. "But I'm a benevolent God. If you do what God tells you, tell God what he needs to know, then you get to walk out of here. Free." He sits back. I get the feeling I'm not the first to hear that speech. "So what'll it be?"

I've got to find a way to end this bullshit now. Got to. If I tell him the truth again, he'll just dismiss it. Get angry and probably hurt me. He just wants me to confess. And I'm not going to confess to something I didn't do. So I've got to say something else. Something that uses all the skills I've accumulated working in front of men all those years. Something that'll save me. That'll allow me to walk out of this room. And I don't know what that's going to be until I open my mouth and the words come out. So here goes.

"Who hurt you, Len?"

He stares at me, not taking the words in. I continue.

"Who hurt you? You didn't start out this way, Len, did you? Something happened to you. Or someone, more like. Made you the way you are now. Made you want to turn invisible so you could hurt people. Who was it?"

I hope I've pitched this right. Tone of voice, eye level, everything. I hope. I wait for him to reply. I'm holding my breath. Nothing. But something seems to have shifted behind his eyes. Like a rock dislodging itself from a cliff face. I go on.

"I mean, we've all had someone like that. Someone who makes such an impact on us they change our life. They damage us. Hurt us. You're no different. With me it was my dad. I hated the hypocritical bastard. Always will. Cerys had her parents. They treated her like shit too."

"So why did you kill her?"

Right. He's not giving in yet. It's the same question but asked in a different way. A calmer way. And I respond in a calmer way. "I didn't kill Cerys. She killed herself. Took a knife to her throat and killed herself. And I wish to God she hadn't." I can feel tears prickling at the corners of my eyes. I try to ignore them, be stronger than that. Not sure I can be. "She'd just found some kind of happiness with me. And then her daughter died." I continue. "She couldn't take it. Thought she was being punished and had to punish herself in return. That poor kid . . ."

No reply.

"She killed herself because she couldn't believe she was allowed to be happy. Someone hurt her years ago to make her feel like that. And this house makes everything worse."

"What d'you mean?" Actually listening now.

"There's something here. Some*one* here, maybe. And it's doing things to us. Manipulating us."

"Bullshit."

"You say that but I know you don't mean it. Think about it. Everyone who's been killed has been killed by the thing they are or the thing they wanted."

"Stop trying to mess me about with this bullshit." He shakes his head but he's still listening.

"Desmond. He wanted to violate Monica. Instead, it was him who was violated. Repeatedly. Iain. A thief. Lost his hands. Sylvia. She kept saying all she wanted was to be in her living room drinking a cup of tea. And Cerys—" My breath catches. "Cerys just wanted to be happy. And when she couldn't be, she took her own life."

Len says nothing.

"What about Amanda?" he asks eventually. "She was the first to be killed."

"I think she was going to tell us something before she was killed. Someone did that to stop her. It's just a theory, Len. But it's a better one than you blaming me for this."

He regains some of his old anger at that, the light reigniting behind his eyes. "You would say that, though, wouldn't you?"

"Oh, stop it, just *stop* it. I'm a stripper. A dancer. I don't know where this Claire is. I wish I did because I know what it's like to be helpless, to be vulnerable, and my heart breaks for her and I want to help her. I don't know who the hell this Boyd guy is. But somewhere in this house someone is playing on our fears, our wants—our *hurts*—and using them against us. Or if we're carrying some guilt it somehow knows how to target that. Think about it. What d'you want?"

"I want to go home and see my dog. Get this bullshit over with."

"So that's one thing. Now maybe you're feeling guilty over something? Or someone? Carrying that hurt with you. Like the rest of us. Whoever put us together in here must know what. And that's what they're playing on. That's how they're scaring us."

He just sighs.

"If something, or someone, is going to get you, it's not going to be me."

I sit back as much as I can in the chair and wait.

Len's eyes are sad but still never leave me, never stop pointing the gun. Eventually he speaks and his voice is considerably smaller.

"We don't have words for pain, do we?" He pauses and I wonder if I'm expected to answer. I don't. He continues.

"There's not a language to use to talk about pain, is there? I mean, I could bring this gun up, smack you in the face with it. Rake the barrel along your cheek. Dig it in. It would hurt. Definitely."

And to prove his point he brings the gun up fast. I flinch. Boy, do I flinch. He moves it slowly away again.

"But how would you describe it if I did that? It hurts. That's all you could say, isn't it? And those two words, *it hurts*, have to do all the work of conveying how much pain I've put you in. Because pain is never just one thing, is it? You're scared about whether you'll get out of here alive. And if you do, whether you'll still have your looks. If you can still earn a living. And the fear of what else I could do to you. You've got all that going on in your head and all you can say are two words. *It. Hurts.* And you can't push that onto anyone else. It's all yours and you have to cope with it yourself. Alone." He sighs again. "It hurts."

Eventually Len's gun hand drops. Then he throws the gun on the table. His body slumps, head down. He gestures toward the door.

"Go on."

I wait a few seconds to see if this is a trick, realize it isn't, then stand. He doesn't move.

I walk slowly toward the door. He still doesn't move.

I leave the room and walk away.

Fast.

She's broken me. A few little words, that was all it took. A few little words. And the bitch broke me. I shouldn't have let her do it, get to me. But how was I to know she was going to do that? Doesn't matter. She's done it. And that's that.

I stand up, look down at the gun on the table. Look around this grim, depressing room. The kind I've spent most of my life in. The nearest thing I had to a home. I don't know where to go or what to do next. I feel lost.

No. She couldn't have known. How could she have known? Couldn't possibly have known. No.

What did she say? This house—or someone in it, she said—might be doing something to us. Giving us what we want but exploiting our weaknesses. Sounded like bollocks at first. Something she'd say to wriggle out of her guilt. But her words got to me. Made me think. And I hate to admit this, she might be right.

Who hurt you?

I sit down again, close my eyes, open them again and the room has changed slightly. Like it's no longer disused and musty. The table's still there and I'm still at this side of it but on the other side, slumped over it, is a body. I know this body. Still see it in my dreams. Even after all this time.

Who hurt you?

A man. Young, Black, bruised and bloodied. A drug dealer from Lewisham, South London. Responsible for the deaths of at least two teenage girls. Both white. Denied it, of course. Said he didn't know he was selling bad stuff, the pills must have been contaminated when he got them. Didn't know with what. Nothing to do with him. He just sold them. The two girls? Nah. He'd given them out for free, get them to come over. Take them out, show them a fun time. Did it matter they were underage? Nah. Kids that age, they're all doing it. He had.

I wanted him to admit what he'd done wrong, confront it, apologize. See the error of his ways. So I set about making that happen. Plan A hadn't worked, so it was time for Plan B. Unfortunately he had this congenital heart defect I didn't know about. Couldn't keep up with the workout I gave him.

I open my eyes. He's gone. And I want to be too. Back home with Kenny. I hope he's all right, I worry about him. I hope my neighbor is looking after him. I miss him. Just him and me in my little bungalow in the Hythe in Kent. And my allotment. It's not much to most people but it's all I need in the world now. It is my world.

We look after our own, my boss said when he saw the body in the interview room. Don't worry. You did us a favor. One less piece of shit on the street. A shame we can't do this to all of them, isn't it?

Ramona didn't know anything about that. But she knew the truth.

Who hurt you?

She knew the truth.

I leave the room, don't glance back at the boy's body. The hallway's dark, like it could be night again. I don't know where I'm going but I start walking.

Did this for months after that kid died. Walked the streets I'd once been in charge of. My kingdom, my domain. Now they weren't my streets anymore, they were somebody else's. I knew I no longer belonged there and that scared me. *They* scared me. So I had no choice, quit the force. Couldn't stay on when I'd lost my nerve.

But I couldn't get away from him.

Every time I closed my eyes he was there. His bruised, bloodied body. That expression of surprise on his face when his heart gave out. Always there. When I slept, when I woke. Sometimes when I was out I'd see him. And he'd stare at me. That expression of surprise. *Why'd you do it, man? Why?* His last words. I never stopped hearing them.

We look after our own. Don't you worry. And they did look after me. An accident. All hushed up. Forget about it. Not worth remembering, scum like that. Did everyone a favor.

Why'd you do it, man? Why?

This corridor really is dark. So dark it doesn't matter whether my eyes are open or closed. I keep moving forward.

My wife's long gone. Said I'd become a different man. Said something died in me when that kid died but I couldn't tell her. I think something was born in me then too. Or started growing, like a creeper or weed, wrapping itself round what was left. I grew to hate her, my wife. And her life. She'd always had it good. I always shielded her from my work, from what was really outside. And I grew to resent that. Because she hadn't been touched by it. Hurt by it.

But she was hurt by me. Words, actions. Then finally fists. The thing growing inside me lashing out. Letting her know how much I hated her. And all those like her who had it easy. Who had never seen what I had seen.

Poor Kenny. I just hope Judy from next door is taking care of him. Caring for him's a big responsibility. And I don't take it lightly. He asks nothing of me except to be fed, walked, and taken care of. And I ask nothing from him except company. He'll be missing me. I can see his big, sad eyes. We've never been apart this long before. I want him next to me, like always. He's a good lad. The best. I miss him. So much.

Why'd you do it, man? Why?

Who hurt you?

I had kids. Two. I'm dead to them now. *She* saw to that. I suppose I don't blame her. Not really. But still. My kids. And they hate me. They've got kids of their own too. So I hear. Never seen them. Never will.

The thing that grew in me kept me apart from everyone and everything else. Didn't trust myself anymore. I settled into my allotment. Tried to find joy in nurturing things, making good things grow from dirt. The opposite of how my life used to be.

My detective intuition was long gone. Or at least long buried.

Oh, Cerys, you poor kid . . . I'm sorry. You didn't deserve that.

I can't see a hand in front of me. That's what people say when it's a bit dark but it really is dark here. No cliché. It's pitch-black. I'm still walking.

Then I hear it.

A growling. A howling?

Kenny?

Must be. He's here as well. He's come to join me. I can't see him, but I can hear him.

"That's it, boy. I'm here. I'm coming . . ."

Another growl. I walk toward it.

"Don't be scared, boy, I'm here . . ."

This house. It was this house that did it. Brought it all back to me. Brought *me* back to me. All the stuff I'd buried. The quiet life I lived, just me and Kenny, all gone in less than twenty-four hours. A crime to solve, a puzzle, I should have been in my element. Old Len should have come back. Clever Len, the Accountant, who could tie suspects in knots and make them confess. And he was here at first. Invisible Len. But that didn't work. So along came Plan B Len.

You can't have one without the other.

That's why I had to leave the force. That aggression, that *hatred*. I saw who I really was.

Who hurt you?

Me. I did.

I can't face the others. Not now. Not after all this. I've gone too far. I still want to think of myself as a good man. Because I can't think the opposite about me. Can't. Even when I see the truth about myself.

I'm sorry, Cerys, for blaming you. And Ramona.

The growling's getting louder. I must be getting nearer. Another step, two.

"That's it, boy, I can hear you. I'm here."

Nearer still. The darkness all-enveloping.

"I'm sorry . . . I'm sorry . . ."

The dog growls again. Louder this time. Much louder.

There's tears on my cheeks. And I'm sorry. I'm really sorry. I should have been one kind of person and I've revealed myself as another. And I'm sorry.

Another growl.

"I'm not a good man. I'm not . . ."

Another growl.

"I thought I was but I'm not . . . forgive me, forgive me . . ."

I can feel the dog's breath on my face. Stale meat and blood. It's a big dog. Very big. And it's still growling.

"Hello, boy. Hello . . ."

I see a flash of white teeth in the darkness. I see red.

I feel pain. Sudden, quick.

Cleansing.

The dog howls, roars. Rips and tears. I don't move. I take it. I might be smiling.

Why'd you do it, man? Why?

Come on, boy. Let's go home. Take me home . . .

I walk away from that room half expecting to feel a shot between my shoulder blades. But only half, otherwise I'd be running out of there. I don't think Len will, though. I think he's too broken for that. Too hurt, I guess.

Thank god I managed to get through to him. Otherwise I might not be here. I'm thinking about what I said in there, about this house. And what it's doing to us. Or someone controlling everything, pushing us toward thinking certain things, taking certain courses of action. I've got to find the others and compare notes. See if we can find a way to stop it. When I say others, I mean Kyle and Diana. I'm not including UK GI Joe in that. He can rot in hell for all I care. Useless moron.

The watch on my wrist tells me more time than I thought has elapsed. We've only got an hour and a half left. Have I really been stuck in that room with Len for so long? Or is this place playing tricks again? Maybe I'm the only one left now. Not a happy thought.

Then I hear something. I stop. Listen. It's music. And not any old music, but the kind you play in a strip club, runway and pole music. Def Leppard? Yeah. A lot of girls like to use that kind of thing. Even I've been known to work to "Pour Some Sugar on Me" on occasion. Depending on the crowd—not usually the most discerning of gentlemen—that stuff generally works. So why am I hearing it here?

All the doors look the same on this floor. None of them seem big enough to host a strip club. But I can still hear the music. It's Azealia Banks now. Good bump and grind stuff. And I've identified which door it's coming from. I open it, enter.

And immediately I'm at the side of the stage and the music is so much louder. And it's not just any stage, it's the club I started out in. The one I ended up queen of, before I moved on.

The one that was too close to home.

The lights hitting the stage seem extrabright. Is there an audience be-hind them? Can they see me? I mean, my first question should be what's this club doing here or is the house playing tricks on me. But no. It smells like a club, cheap beer and nervous sweat and cheap perfume, and I can hear voices behind the lights. Can they see me? And the next question: Do I want them to see me?

I shield my eyes, look out front. Yes, they can see me. And yes, they want me to dance.

I step onto the stage, telling them I'm not here to dance and asking if they know the whereabouts of a girl called Claire Swanson, but they're not interested, can't hear me above the music, above their own cheers. I keep talking, describing her to them, but they ignore my words, let their impatience show. This kind of club, women should be seen and not heard and definitely naked, not dressed. They want me to dance, pointing to the pole in the center of the stage. I'm not dressed for this; a bloodstained T-shirt, jeans, and trainers is not stripper gear. And I have no intention of stripping. But they keep screaming for me and, I don't know, somehow it kinda seems like the right thing to do.

So I walk to the center of the stage and grab the pole. My music starts and I'm away.

Again, I'm not stopping to wonder why I'm here or this place is here. Somehow this whole scenario makes a kind of sense to me. Maybe it'll reveal its answers if I go along with it. So I do.

I'm good on the pole. No false modesty, but I always have been. And they're still cheering, even though I'm not undressing. Maybe this audi-ence has become a little more sophisticated in my absence. Maybe they now appreciate skill and athleticism.

I'm well into my routine now. Lost to it. Just my body and the pole. Me moving around a fixed, reliable point. To be able to perform to the best of my ability I have to depend on it. Its solidity allows my confi-dence to shine. And again, no apologies for that. I've worked hard to be the best I can be. It's not wrong to want, to expect, to be appreciated for that.

And then it all stops. The music, the lights, everything. Like a big cosmic plug has been pulled and the club has become frozen in time and the only thing still moving is me.

But not for long. A spotlight goes on over the dark mass of heads in the audience and I can make out who's been lit. I get down from the pole, breathing heavily. I stare out.

My father.

"You're dead," I say.

He smiles. "Yet here I am."

"Still got your head, I see."

He shrugs.

Is this really him? Or is the house playing tricks on me again? Someone made up to look like him?

"You believe it's me," he says, reading my mind, "and that's the only thing that matters."

He's right. Even putting aside everything else that's going on, I do believe it's him. Don't ask me how, but I do.

"What d'you want from me? Why've you followed me here?"

"To see what a mess you've made of your life. How you've wrecked yourself."

I laugh. "Wrecked myself? Saved myself from you and your bullshit, more like." He's making me angry. Always did know which buttons to press. "I've got money now. I own property. Doing this"—I gesture round the room—"controls people like you. Exploits people like you. And you know what? I love it. Love the feeling it gives me, knowing that you hate it and there's nothing you can do about it. Because I'm out of your grip forever."

"And you're happy?"

I'm screaming now. "Yes, I'm fucking happy. More than you could ever imagine. I make more money than you ever could in your life. And if that doesn't make me happy, I don't know what will."

"So you hate me, then?"

I pause, rein my anger back in. "I used to. All the time. And you deserved it, what you did to me, how miserable you made my life. But in a way you saved me, because you hurt me so much I turned that hurt and anger outward instead of inward so I guess you helped me find the strength to become what I've become." I laugh. "So call it what you like. You little man. You nobody."

That struck him. He stands up, angry now. Pointing, gesticulating wildly.

"Don't talk to me like that, you have some respect for your father!"

"Fuck you."

"You patronize me, belittle me, try to emasculate me. You're a whore. Nothing but a whore."

If I'd stopped to think in that moment, I'd have realized that this conversation was going exactly the way I'd always imagined a final conversation between my father and me to go. Always *wanted* it to go. He was saying everything I expected him to say and I was saying the words I'd rehearsed in my head for years. Yeah, I should have thought about that but I was too caught up in the moment. Too happy to be winning.

"You're pathetic," I say, still laughing harshly, "going to strip clubs, watching women undress, thinking that gives you power over them when it's us who have power over you. Pathetic. It just shows you're a nobody. A nothing."

At last, *at last* I've won. And there's nothing he can do about it. I'm so exultant, so luxuriant in my triumph that I don't notice what he's doing. Bringing up a shotgun and this time, he's aiming it at me.

Yeah, this conversation's gone exactly as I hoped it would, played over and over, thousands of times in my head. But I forgot one thing: it's gone exactly the way *he* wanted it to go as well.

I'm rooted to the spot, too stunned to move. He doesn't speak, just pulls the trigger and back I go, swept off my feet by the force of the blast, smashing into the back of the stage, slumping to the ground.

I'm almost too surprised to feel pain at first. But then it hits me. I look down. The blast's near torn me in half. My insides are outside now and I know there'll be no putting me back together.

I'm dying. I know I'm dying.

But at least I got to stick it to that hateful fuck one last time.

I blink. Everything is fading to black. The strip club, too, slowly disappearing, being replaced by some characterless, dingy room. I smile.

I see what the house has given me. The conversation I'd always wanted to have with my father. The "fuck you I win" one. And it chose the best possible place to have it in. So yeah. Fuck you, I win.

I try saying it out loud, but my voice has gone.

I look up. My father's gone but there's a shadowy figure at the far end of the room holding what I think is a gun. And it's trained on me.

I try to smile, but all I can see is Cerys's face, how happy she looked when she smiled.

And before I have time for that image to hurt me—

The gun fires again.

THE BEAST IN THE CELLAR

Right. OK. Couple of things we need to discuss here.

Time for you all to become reacquainted with Professor Beast in the Cellar. No talking at the back and make sure your pencils are sharp. Yes, take notes because there'll be questions at the end.

To start, let's address the untimely death of the unhappy lesbians. Now, some of the brighter or more alert among you may have spotted what you think is what's known in storytelling as a trope. Or if that trope gets over-used, a cliché. The prevailing thought is, apparently, that gay characters can be included in a story but they can't be happy. Or at least can't have a happy ending. Or they're the first to die. And die tragically. So why is that? Well, some would say it's because we as a whole, as a race of people or a species or whatever, despite what we say, are still not wholly tolerant of same-sex relationships. This may be down to cultural conditioning from an early age that no matter how hard we try we can't completely break in later life. That may go for all whether gay, straight, or whatever. Write that one down, please. Some might say that we are tolerant but it ups the emotional ante if two gay people go through near insurmountable hardships to get together, face all kinds of prejudices only to have that happiness dashed at the end. Ramp up the crying. Cue the big cheap emotional ending and the invoice is in the post. That's the trope/cliché.

And consequently, and understandably, there are people who get angry about that. Thinking storylines like the tragic lesbians have no place in contemporary culture and that people, regardless of gender, sex, race, or whatever, should be equal when it comes to happy endings. And there may also be some people who have read what happened to Cerys and Ramona and decide to jump up and down and get angry about it. Cerys just found happiness! And now she's dead! You hate women! You hate women being happy! With other women! Yeah, well to those so inclined to that kind of refrain I say, pipe down! Hold your horses! Think before you start screaming about inequality! I know it's difficult, but try to. We all love our rights, especially the one to be offended.

However, that's another story.

Yes, Cerys died moments after she found happiness. Love, even. She also died moments after her daughter disappeared and she felt overwhelming guilt as a result of that, because she was off enjoying herself and for once, possibly the only time in her life, she ignored Monica. Was it her fault? Was that direct cause and effect in action? I'd say that depends on how you see Cerys. Is (or rather was) Cerys just Monica's carer? Or was she a person in her own right, with her own wants and needs, her desires and hopes and dreams? And if that's the case—and why wouldn't it be—why shouldn't she have enjoyed herself? She deserved as much as anyone else to go and live as fulfilling a life as possible.

Or perhaps not. Maybe Monica died because Cerys enjoyed herself. But if that's the case, would it have made any difference whether she was with a man or a woman?

Again, I don't make these rules, I'm just here to . . . I don't know. Ask questions? Give commentary? Be hilariously brilliant? The last one, obviously. I'm not controlling any of this. I'm just following events as they unfold same as you are. Yes, I do know a bit more about what's going on than you, but that doesn't mean I've got any influence over it. Take my word for that.

And of course, there's another, more obvious, reason why Cerys's and Ramona's deaths don't fit that trope/cliché thing. They're not the only ones to have died. And again for the hard of understanding at the back:

They're not the only ones to have died. They're just the latest ones.

I mean, Len's gone and he definitely wasn't a tragic lesbian. Although where did the dog come from? Was it here all along? Has it just got in through some massive dog flap?

More questions . . .

Actually, thinking of Len for a moment, he had a good point. Just the one, mind. I'll give him that much. But no more. We don't have words for pain. No words at all to describe pain. Think about it: You break your leg or your arm, or you're covered in bruises and cuts and burns. A doctor asks you to describe the pain. What do you say? It hurts. Or, it *really* hurts if it really hurts. But the doctor can judge how strong the pain is. Not from your words but from other things. How you look, the way your body's contorted in agony, your face all scrunched up into the kind of grimace that only a subscriber to a really weird website would find attractive. Which parts you can't hold up or are hanging limply. The doctor picks it all up from that. Body language in its purest form. He might also ask you where all those injuries come from. Well, that's a different matter. Words hold a different power in the answers you give—or don't give—to that question.

So getting back to it, how do we use words to describe things we can only feel? We could get all poetic about it. How much do you hurt? Well, it's like someone took a rusty carving knife and sliced into the side of my body and started sawing away but it was blunt and tough to cut through but they kept going and each thrust backward and forward increased the agony and I could feel it as it happened and wanted to cry out but couldn't because . . . You get the idea. It hurts. It *really* hurts.

You might say it's the same for love. We all know how love feels, right? But words sometimes don't seem adequate enough to do the emotions you're experiencing full justice, do they? And what about when love and hurt get mixed up together? What then? Are words any good? And what if you tell someone and you're not believed? What then?

But I'm digressing.

There have been a lot of deaths so far in the house. And you're still here. And those deaths have been messy. They've been real. People have died, blood has been spilt, pain has been caused. Lots of pain. Lots and lots of terminal pain. Lots of hurt.

And those deaths have left gaps. Real gaps among the ones still living. Whether those people were liked or not, or loved even, their presences were felt and their demises left gaps. No one is just continuing on as if nothing has happened. And that's the way it should be. I once read a book, long ago, where strangers in a strange house like this one died one by one under horrible circumstances. And yes, they were killed. But no one seemed to get hurt. The butler even apologized for breakfast being a bit late because his wife was murdered during the night. Well, that isn't *this* house. Not at all. This is real.

There's a girl missing. And she's going to die if she's not discovered in the next couple of hours. That's a fact. And this girl has a name. Claire

Swanson. She's not a faceless victim. She has a life that's been abruptly interrupted. She has family, friends, who will miss her if she isn't found and rescued. Some may never recover from that grief, never be able to cope without her again. They're going to experience hurt. *Real* hurt. Their lives will be an unimaginable black hole of grief so huge, so intense, it will define the rest of their lives.

So this lot had better sort themselves out and get a move on.

Because no matter what time it is, it's always later than you think.

Here ends today's lesson.

We followed Len as he dragged Ramona away, waiting until he'd rounded a corner of the hallway before setting off. Neither of us fancied getting shot. But when we turned the corner, it was like they had both disappeared. Kyle checked the floor for blood, as Ramona seemed to be wearing a lot of it, but there were no traces. It was as if the house didn't want us to find them. We were both spooked by this, probably more than we wanted to admit to each other, so when the gong sounded again, we headed back downstairs to the relative safety of the dining room.

Now, I slide the cage door of the lift across, step into the hallway, walk straight toward the dining room. Kyle is behind, closing the cage door and hurrying to keep up. When I reach the doorway to the dining room, where the gong sounded, I stop so suddenly he almost comically careens into my back. "Someone is expecting us."

"And just us, from the look of it . . ."

I didn't realize I'd spoken aloud. But Kyle's right. The huge table has been laid at one end for what looks like afternoon tea. There are two tea-pots, two sets of cups and saucers, two plates, two knives, two three-tiered sandwich and cake stands loaded with stuff. Only two.

"Afternoon tea?" he says. "Wait, what time is it?"

"God knows. Morning? If dinner was last night and all those hours have elapsed then, yes, that should be it. Afternoon tea? Are they just messing with our minds even more? And . . . Oh. I get it. Tea for two." I give a quick, alarmed glance at Kyle. "Like they're not expecting anyone else to join us . . ."

I don't wait for his reply. I hear him call to me as I run up the stairs, taking them two at a time until that proves too much for me, slowing down as my breathing intensifies. My heart had already begun hammering, now it's pumping all pistons.

I reach what I'm looking for. The paintings. I scan my eyes over them, trying not to linger on the more horrific deaths in the ones I've already seen. I'm looking for Ramona, Len. Jimmy Saint. And I find them. And wish I hadn't.

"Oh god . . ."

Ramona's now lying on the stage she was cavorting on in midperformance in the first painting, pole behind her, multicolored lights still playing across her body. Just one difference. She's dead. The painter has caught her in midwrithe, lying in apparent agony, mouth open and seemingly screaming. She's been shot, by a weapon that's completely eviscerated her.

"Oh god . . ." I can't think of anything else to say. My heart's now pounding from more than running upstairs.

I look for Len next. When I find him, whatever hope I may have had sinks. He's still on his allotment as before, but it's weed-choked and untended, the flowers and plants decaying and dead. And as for Len, he lies twisted on the soil, his innards ripped out; a dog, blood and gore smeared all over its snout, sits next to him looking pleased with itself.

And Jimmy—Jimmy's painting is the same. It hasn't changed. Is he still here? Has he managed to get out? Has he found Claire? Or has he just drifted off somewhere on his own to wallow in self-pity? I don't know. Don't know what it means. But the other two . . .

I slump to the floor. It's too much. All too much. I have to get out of this house. Just get out and run. As far away from it as possible. Put distance between myself and . . . this. Whatever this is. Death. That's what it is. Death.

Something twists inside me, bubbles up, tries to escape. Frustration, fear, anger, whatever. All of that. I want to scream. Need to scream. I feel so impotent, so scared. I want to run but I can't move. I've got to get out of here but I can't move. And I know I can't escape. But I still need to go. It's like I've been given an incurable cancer diagnosis and I want to outrun it. But I know I can't get away from this place. So I just break down.

And that's how Kyle finds me.

I feel his arms round my shoulders. He doesn't try to move me or get me up, he just holds me, sits with me. Says nothing and waits while my tears bear themselves away.

"They're gone," I say eventually, "Gone . . . we've failed them . . . all of them . . . we should have gone after them, we should have done . . ."

"We can't blame ourselves. We haven't time to feel guilty. Besides,

Jimmy's painting's still intact, so that's hopeful. And we're still here. Let's concentrate on that."

I give a slight nod. Or maybe a shrug. I don't know. But I think I acknowledge his words.

"Come on," he says, gently lifting me to my feet, "let's go downstairs. Eat something."

I allow myself to be led. Slowly, step by step, until we're in the hallway again. I still see the paintings. Still feel guilt over their deaths.

"I can't go back up those stairs," I say. "I can't."

"I know. Let's have some tea." Kyle tries to smile. "That's supposed to cure everything, isn't it?"

Any attempt at returning a smile dies before I even attempt it.

He leads me to the table, sits me down. Pours me tea. I hate tea. Never drink it. Coffee and coffee only. Espresso, black. The smell hits my nostrils and to my surprise I realize that it isn't tea in that pot. It's coffee. Exactly how I like it. Like someone knows me.

"It's coffee . . ."

"Yeah," says Kyle. "Too strong for me." He pours himself a cup from the other pot. "Tea. Builders. Like I have at home when I'm writing an essay. Wow. This is . . . spooky."

I feel panic begin to rise in me once again. "It's beyond spooky. It's . . ."

"Yeah. Fucking terrifying. They know us. Whoever's behind all this, they've done their research and they know us. And how to manipulate us."

"They're giving us food and drink in the middle of the night—if it is the middle of the night—to keep us going. Proper food, not some snacks, like earlier. And they knew it would just be us two coming in here. They know who's dead and who's not."

"And they know Jimmy wouldn't be joining us." Kyle stands up, paces round the room.

"What are you looking for?"

"Something we should have done earlier. Cameras. Microphones. Wires. Anything to show how they're observing us. They know where we are all the time, don't they? What we're doing, how we're behaving, responding. And look at this." He sits down again, examines the food on the stand in front of him. "This is for me. Has to be. Tuna and sweet corn mayonnaise sandwich. In a baguette with salad and pickle. How do they know that? How do they know that's my go-to at the uni sandwich bar?" He looks over at me then. "What have you got?"

I notice the stand for the first time. Considering what they gave me for dinner I'm expecting more of the same. Something small and delicate to decorate the plate. Tiny chess pieces I can move round. Or even, at a push, small pieces of sushi. But that's not what's there. There's a pork pie. A pasty. A doorstop of a ham-and-cheese sandwich on white bread with butter. I stare at it. Something connects. Something deep and rooted in my past. They know me. Oh god, they *really* know me. I feel disgusted with myself, ashamed, at how hungry it makes me feel and how much I want to devour it.

"Doesn't look like the kind of stuff you'd normally go for," Kyle says.

"No," I say. I'm still staring at it. It's doing something to me, unlocking something within. A memory. A deliberately submerged memory. More than one. I start to tremble. My hands shake.

"You OK?"

I still stare at the food. The memories return.

Of me at school. At home. Eating. Always eating. The bullies calling me fat, calling me . . . awful things. Just awful. But not me. Not *Diana*. No, they called Janice Crewe those things. The girl I used to be. The loser. The loner. The fat girl they all laughed at. Picked on. Even the ones who were supposed to be my friends. The girl who hated school. Who couldn't stop eating. The unhappy girl with the empty heart who tried to fill it. Hiding herself away and getting bigger and bigger. And hating herself more and more. The girl who would have abuse hurled at her from passing cars as she walked home from school. The girl who hated her life but was too scared to end it.

That's who the food's for. Poor Janice Crewe.

"Diana?"

Kyle's trying to talk to me but I can't hear him. Not above the shouts and the insults. They're deafening. The names. *The names* . . .

"No . . ."

I close my eyes. I'm not Janice Crewe. Not anymore. Janice Crewe is dead. *Dead.* I'm Diana Landor now. *Diana Landor.* Janice Crewe was a sad loser. Everyone hated her. Everyone should have hated her. But everyone loves Diana. Men love me. Employees fear me. Women want to be me. I'm the GirlBoss Extreme. I'm Diana. *Diana* . . .

I open my eyes. Stare at the food.

And I'm so hungry. So, *so* hungry.

Before I know what I'm doing my hand is out and I've got the pork pie and I'm cramming it into my mouth as hard as it'll go. Not bothering to chew, just wanting to swallow it as fast as possible, quickly, hurry, so I can cram the next bit in. And the next. And the next. My lips are so stretched they're straining but they'll hold. I've had much more in my mouth than this. It takes a lot for them to split. I know.

"Diana?"

I can't be dealing with Kyle and his concern now. He'll have to wait.

"Have your dinner," I say to him between mouthfuls, "don't bother about me."

He's still staring at me. "Your accent's changed," he says. "You've gone all northern."

He's right, I have. Because I'm not Diana Landor anymore. I'm Janice Crewe.

Hello, Janice, nice to see you again, knew you were in there somewhere . . .

I close my eyes again. Stop eating. Stop . . . whatever it is I'm doing. Cramming food inside me. It's not who I am. Not anymore. No. *No . . .*

I spit everything that's still in my mouth out on the plate. Stare at it. My heart is hammering once more, like I've just run a marathon. A lump of half-masticated food lies there. Disgusting. The kind of stuff I would once have eaten, then forced my fingers down my throat to bring straight up again. I've saved myself the trouble. I've stopped right in time.

I take another swig of coffee. Kyle's still staring at me. Saying nothing. Bet I know what he's thinking. How he hates me now. How he could never find someone like me, as fat and ugly as me, attractive. Because only the thin girls get the boys. And the men. The blade thin girls get the best men. That's the law. And now he's seen the pig inside me, he'll never think of me like that again. I stare at the table. Can't meet his gaze.

"Sorry."

My voice is so small I can barely hear it.

"Nothing to be sorry about."

His voice sounds warm but I still can't look up at him.

"Hey, it's been a long day. A long, horrible day. Probably the worst day of my life and yours as well, I bet." Kyle gives a small laugh. "At least

I hope so. You want to eat? Eat. It's getting on for nearly eight o'clock and God knows what'll happen then. So eat. You'll need your strength."

I manage a glance up at him. He's eating his tuna baguette. Drinking his tea. Now I feel so embarrassed, so stupid. Pathetic.

"Hey." He reaches his hand across the table. Takes mine. It's like he can read my mind. Like he knows me, knows who I am. Who I really am. "It's fine. It's all fine. Come on."

I nod and suddenly want to cry. But I stop myself. This time. He knows me. He sees me. And he actually seems to accept me. God knows why, but he does. And that just makes me want to cry again. But I manage to hold it in. Just.

Kyle checks the watch on his wrist. "Come on. It's late. We don't have much time left and we still haven't found that missing girl. We've allowed ourselves to get distracted by all the deaths and trying to keep ourselves safe, which is understandable, but we're here to find the girl. She needs us. We've got to put everything else that's happened, everyone else, out of our minds and concentrate on that. It'll be eight o'clock soon and we have to find her. So come on, get your head in the game. One last push. Yeah?"

I realize again that he's talking to me. Looking at me. My eyes are still on the putrid mound of food on my plate so I return his gaze. I'm not sure what he said, but it has to be better than sitting here.

"Yes."

"Good. Let's think. We've been all round the house. Or everywhere we could go. And we haven't found her. Jimmy and I found some stuff that might be used to keep her captive in that secret room but we couldn't find any more secret passages. The only place we haven't looked is the cellar."

I frown. "We went down there."

"Yeah, but we'd only reached the bottom of the stairs before we had to run back up to see Jimmy. I didn't see a thing, did you? So what d'you think? We'll try there?"

I feel like this is all happening to someone else. Like I don't know who I am anymore. But I know I don't want to be alone. And I don't want to sit here.

"OK."

"Right." He stands up. "Let's go."

THE BEAST IN THE CELLAR

Ruh—roh...

CAPTAIN JIMMY SAINT

Look at this little chap. A man of action. An Action Man. Military garb; rank, captain. Like me. Or like I'm supposed to be.

The attic seemed like the best place to come to be alone from the rest of them. I'm supposed to be a protector. And I've failed. I've failed at everything since I've been in this house, every obstacle that's been presented to me I've failed to overcome. Others have fared better. Even let me take credit for things I had nothing to do with. And I let them. Because I'm a failure.

Protectors are supposed to protect. That's my purpose in life. My occupation, my obligation. Otherwise what is the point of me? What good am I for? Nothing. A waste of a uniform. A waste of training. A waste of trust. A waste.

Ramona. I could have intervened when Len dragged her away. But I didn't. I just stood there, numb, mute. Watched him drag her off to god knows where after he took my gun from me. I couldn't look at the other two after that. I could feel what they thought of me, knew what they would say. So I walked away. Better than hearing bile and hatred hurled at oneself, have all of one's failings and deficiencies pointed out at top volume. Besides, they can't say anything that I've not accused myself of already. They couldn't be harsher on me than I am on myself.

The uniform is a first-class replica, though. And he's quite a substantial chap, too. Bit dusty now from the attic, smells a little mildewy and moldy but still intact. You can put him in various heroic poses. Leading his troops into battle. Standing, arms on hips, surveying the land before him, ready to make life-and-death decisions, the right decisions. Here he is with his—

His gun. His tiny replica pistol. On his hip where it should be. The fingers of his hand perfectly curled and shaped, ready to receive it. Trigger finger permanently extended. Almost makes me smile. And then I remember myself. My uniform, like this doll's, is a first-class replica. But this doll is more of a captain than I am. He has a gun. And all the natural authority that it confers. I don't even have that anymore after allowing Len to take it. All I have is an empty holster—

My hand goes to my side. Flips open the leather strap. I gasp. Literally. And my heart skips a beat, as they say in cheap novels, but this time it's actually true. It's there. It's back. My gun. I take it out, study it. Caress it. The cold metal fits neatly into my hand. I feel it warming as my body heat slowly transfers itself onto and into it, as if it's melding itself with me. I don't stop to think where it came from, how it got from Len to here, or why I didn't have it earlier when it could have been useful. I just hold it, feel it. Stare at it. My trigger finger extends into it. And I know this sounds ridiculous, like something the poets or hack writers would say, but the more I look at it, the more it feels like it's looking at me. Looking into me, even, if you'll excuse all that spiritualist mumbo jumbo. But that's what it honestly feels like. And it's a good feeling. For the first time in a long time, certainly since I entered this house, I don't feel alone anymore.

I palm the gun and think of Ramona. Is it too late to save her? Should I run back downstairs and intercede with whatever that old man's forcing her to do? I am a protector after all. And with this in my hand I feel like a protector again. Or at least capable of being one.

I make for the door, gun in hand. And stop.

That's too obvious. Running downstairs, gun blazing. He might see and hear me coming. Decide to do something with the girl. And then I'll have failed again. Before I've even started. No. Not an option. And besides, didn't he take my gun? Is it this one, or is this a different one? A new one given to me? By whom? The house?

I check the timer on my wrist. It's later than I thought. That poor girl still hasn't been found and she should be the number one priority. We're running out of time, out of options. I can't be sure those downstairs are still searching for her. They seemed to have given up, riven with arguments among themselves. I can't rely on them. It's down to me, now. I'll have to find her on my own.

I look around the attic. And a thought occurs to me.

Kyle and I found the secret passage that went down to the hidden room where the killer's tools were stored. What if there were other secret passageways where his (I say it's a man; I don't know, of course, but I find it near intolerable to consider a member of the fairer sex to be capable of this) further machinations had taken place? Perhaps even Claire herself?

The passageway opening is still here. I fondle the gun in my hand. The way ahead holds no terrors for me now; in fact, it is darkly inviting.

A final look round before I leave. I cross the floor, pick up the doll. Pose him into a heroic stance, brandishing his pistol at an unseen enemy. I leave him standing on the floor. Facing the doorway. Ready to hold off any potential attackers. I smile, feeling confident he'll do his job.

Just as I'm confident I'll do mine.

I enter the passageway. Ready, this time, for whatever I encounter.

The cellar looks the same. Same wooden staircase, same bare overhead bulb casting more shadow than light. Same horrible old Bakelite wall switch that I thought would electrocute me when I flicked it downward. But something feels different. Like the air has changed.

OK, that sounds ridiculous when I say it aloud. But it's how it feels. You know how sometimes you can go back to a place you've been to and you associate it with a certain atmosphere and you're expecting the same kind of atmosphere to pop up again? But it hardly ever does, because everything's changed in the time you've been away. It's moved on but your memory hasn't. And now you have to see that place from your current perspective, not the one you once had. That's what I mean by the air having changed. I mean, I know that mainly happens to places you haven't visited for a few years and I was only on the cellar steps a few hours ago and only managed to just get to the bottom before I was called back up, but I still get the feeling that something's changed in that short space of time. Maybe I'm projecting things on to it that aren't there. Maybe the scream I heard confused my memory. Perhaps it is the same and it's me that's changed. Yes, even in that small space of time. But I don't think so. Don't ask me how, or why. Don't ask me anything about this house.

Last time it felt like a cellar. This time it doesn't. The steps, old and wooden, are the same. Rickety. Unsafe. I walk down very carefully, testing each one before fully committing my weight.

"What are you doing?" asks Diana behind me.

"Making sure the wood doesn't give out from under us. Last thing we need in this place is an injury."

Behind me I feel Diana doing the same.

"Funny," I say. "But it seems longer now, don't you think?"

"How?" I hear the catch in her voice. Like she's so far on edge the slightest thing could trigger an outburst. And we don't need that. Mainly because I'm barely holding it together myself.

I haven't admitted it, but this place, this passage of time, this night if it is that, is taking its toll on me. I just want to put my head down and sleep for a couple of days. But I can't with the clock almost run out. The end almost in sight. I'll sleep when this is all over and I'm home again. Although it feels like home has never been farther away. The time spent in this house feels weird and twisted, stretched and snapped back, so much so that I've almost forgotten what home is like.

I reach the bottom of the stairs. Diana is a step behind me.

"Now what?" she says.

"Good question."

We pause to take in our surroundings. Shadows cast by the weak bulb over the stairs stretch in every direction. Peter out into total darkness. The floor feels like flagged stone. There are faint sounds echoing around, back to us. *Drip, drip, drip.* Like slowly leaking pipes. I touch the nearest wall. Stone also. Cold, damp to the touch. And something else. I shudder, pull my hand away.

"What?" says Diana.

I look at my fingers. I'm almost expecting to find some kind of damp residue from the wall I just touched. "Nothing." I don't want to panic her.

"Tell me."

"It felt . . . I don't know, like there was a pulse or something. A vibration coming from the stone. Within the stone."

"You mean it's alive? The house is alive?" Panic rises in her voice.

"No, that would be ridiculous." I try to make my voice as reassuring as possible. I turn away so she can't see that I'm lying. Alive is exactly what the wall felt like. "Just . . . humming. Like there's something behind it."

"Like blood pumping, you mean."

"I was going to say like machinery, actually." No, I was going to say it felt like blood pumping. It had rhythm, a pulse. But I don't want to tell her that.

She reaches out a tentative hand for herself. Touches it.

We both stand still, hardly daring to breathe. Diana's eyes widen.

"I can feel it . . . It's . . . alive . . ." She pulls her hand away.

"No, it's not," I say, as forcefully as I can. "We're down here in a scary, dark cellar in a twisted old house and the slightest thing is setting us both off. The wall is not alive. The house is not alive. That's impossible."

"But . . ." Panic wells up. Threatens to overwhelm her.

"Your mind's playing tricks on you," I say, putting as much authority into my voice as I can. "You're imagining things. Everything we've been through today, I'm not surprised. No. This house isn't alive."

Diana stares at her hand. I don't move. She keeps staring. It's not until she hasn't spoken for several seconds that I see she's crying. Standing there, barely moving, just sobbing. I put my arm round her shoulders.

"I just want to go home . . ."

I'm about to say the same thing when I hear a noise over the echoing drips, coming from somewhere deep in the shadows.

Diana jumps away from me, screams. "What was that?"

"I don't know. It sounded like—"

There it is again. It sounds like stone being moved. A great, heavy slab being ground with great effort against another great slab of stone. An ancient door closing. Or opening.

"I don't . . . I don't want to be down here. No. I . . . I can't . . ."

Diana turns, heads toward the staircase.

"Wait, we have to . . ."

The noise again.

"I can't stand this anymore . . . I can't, I can't . . ."

She runs away, back up the stairs.

I try to call after her, tell her we stand a better chance staying together, not to leave me down here on my own, not to run back into the house, all of that and more, but I'm shouting into dead air. The door at the top of the stairs slams shut. She's gone. And I'm left alone.

The noise has stopped. I look at my hand, the one that touched the wall. There's something dark on it, like a kind of dust. Oily dark dust. I smell it. Like old pennies. Iron.

Like blood.

My heart skips a beat. I wipe my hand on my jeans. I don't want to go on. I just want to go to sleep and wake up and have everything be all right and all this be over. But I know I can't do that. Not yet. First I have to find the girl. Then I have to get out of the house. And if I have to do that on my own, then so be it.

I look around once more, trying to get accustomed to the gloom.

At the base of the stairs I find an old-fashioned flashlight. A torch with a handle, and a compartment for a battery the size of a child's head. God knows how long it's been down here or whether it actually works. I pick it up, switch it on. The beam is weak at first but after a shake it becomes stronger. It's not much but it helps. I play it round.

If I had to draw this cellar, I'd need a lot of ink. Bottles of it because the cellar seems mostly composed of shadows. The walls are, like I said, stone. Interspersed with old, crumbling brick. Not so much a mash-up of styles, more a lack of them. Overhead there are pipes, rusted and corroded, dripping. It couldn't be more Gothic, but a more modern take on the Gothic. Somewhere Batman would prowl on the hunt for one of his deranged nemeses in Gotham City.

I glance over my shoulder at the steps back up to the house, wishing I could go up them and join Diana. But I can't. I have to confront what lies ahead of me.

I move forward.

I slam the door behind me, then push my back against it, panting hard. Eyes closed, legs shaking, heart slamming. The stairs felt much longer coming up than going down. Like the house didn't want me back up again. Like it had me where it wanted me, down there for good.

My heart begins to slow, breathing coming easier; with my physical strength returning, my mind goes to what I've just experienced. The house is alive. The house doesn't want to let us go. Has no intention of letting us go. And Kyle's still down there, he—

I've closed the door behind me. I turn, grab the handle intending to shout down to him. Get him back up here, make one last look for a way out. There has to be one. Has to. Just somewhere small that the house, or whoever's in the house, controlling the house, has overlooked. One tiny little place. And I'll find it. And I'll be free.

I check my wrist. Less than an hour left until eight o'clock. My stomach churns at the thought of what will happen if I'm not out by then.

I pull the handle, ready to call out to Kyle. But the door stays shut. I must have jammed it when I leaned against it. I can't have locked it, there's no key to turn. And Kyle wouldn't have locked it from the inside. I pull harder. It won't budge. There's not even any give around the frame. It's like I'm pulling on a piece of wall. Exhausting myself, I stop. No time for this. I need to escape.

Start with the front doors. Maybe there's a way to open them. Maybe we've missed it. I walk down the corridor toward the main hallway at the front of the house.

One thing I've always been good at in life is moving forward. From fat, unlovable, unwanted loser Janice Crewe to sleek, thin, gorgeous, successful Diana Landor. Never look back. Never. That's what I do now. Kyle's a nice lad and we clicked, definitely. Might have even had something outside of this house. But it doesn't matter. Diana Landor has to get away. And Diana Landor always gets what she wants.

I reach the double doors. Try them. They won't budge.

I don't waste my time on them. I have an idea. If I follow the wall from the front doors round the house, there might be another way out. An opening on the outside wall that spells freedom. None of the others found it but then none of the others were looking there. I've got less than an hour and a hell of a lot of determination. Here I go.

I work my way along the wall. It stops before the adjoining wall for the library. I enter the library. Start again from there. The wooden shutters are still up at the windows. I try them, not expecting them to move. I'm not disappointed. I work my way along until I'm in the corner of the room. By one of the bookcases that line the walls. It's at a right angle. I work my way along it. Yes, I know it's just books, or just looks like books, but how many times have these old houses got some door in them that swings open to reveal a secret passage? The captain and Kyle found one. It can't be the only one.

I press and pull the spines of all the books I touch. I press and twist the wooden shelves and ends, hoping for a secret button. Nothing. I keep moving toward the door, ready for the next room. Except when I get in the hallway there isn't a next room. Not immediately.

I go back inside the library. Mentally measure the space between the wall with the books on it and the hallway. My heart leaps. There's something hidden in there.

Feeling a surge of excitement, I go back to the wall of books and begin my search all over again. Pressing, prodding, pulling and twisting. The ones I've already done, the ones I haven't done. All of them. My enthusiasm is waning when I hear it.

Click.

Very faint, but definitely audible.

Click.

I retrace my hands, running them over the section I've just done, feeling for any slackening, loosening of the books or the shelves themselves. And I find it. A vertical space in the wooden shelving. It's slight, barely enough to get my fingers between, but I'm determined. I ignore the pain as the skin round my nails is pulled back as I stick my hand down the side, trying to get a grip on the wood, swing it outward or inward. The crack grows as the shelf begins to move. Slowly, though, incrementally. I can just get both my hands in now, make enough purchase to pull. My fingers are slippery with blood but I ignore that and the pain because I'm not going to give up now.

It doesn't move without a struggle, without the wood screaming. It mustn't have moved in years, decades even. The hinges are rusty, the wood warped in its frame. But I'm determined.

Eventually there's enough space for me to look inside, see space behind the shelves. Smell the cold, stale air beyond. I allow myself to feel hopeful and almost laugh at the thought that fat useless Janice Crewe couldn't do this. I squeeze myself inside the hidden room.

There's a light switch. Old Bakelite, like the one in the cellar. I switch it on. Another bare overhead bulb. But this feels different from the cellar. It's not old stone, it's brick. Old, yes, but not as old as below. I glance upward. There are wooden beams laid across, like the struts from the flooring upstairs. And it's a corridor. Which means it must lead somewhere. My heart leaps once again.

"This is more like it . . ."

I hurry ahead.

After a while the corridor begins to twist. I have no option but to follow it. Whether it's bending inward toward the rest of the house or outward to freedom I no longer know. I just keep going.

I also lose all track of time. My initial excitement wears off, the adrenaline spike lowering. My fingers are really hurting now. Throbbing with pain. They're hideous to look at. It'll take more than a manicure to repair them.

Desperate to find out where this corridor is leading me, I hurry on. As the earlier euphoria dissipates I feel the beginnings of a depression settling. But I don't give in, tell myself this has to lead somewhere. No one would put a secret passageway in a house that led nowhere. It *has* to lead somewhere. It must.

And eventually it does.

A door, wooden, heavy and thick. A bit like the front door. My adrenaline spikes again. The front door. An exit? I turn the rusty old handle. It opens. Smiling, I step through.

It's dark behind the door. And I'm still inside the house. An impotent, hopeless panic wells up inside me and I want to scream. The weak light from the bare bulbs strung along the passageway barely penetrates in here. It feels old and damp, musty. Like an older part of the house like—

Like the cellar.

I shiver at the thought.

I search for a light switch but there isn't one. There is something, though, that my damaged fingers brush against, sending needles of pain through my hands. A candlestick. And a box of matches next to them. Someone has been thoughtful.

Fumbling, my fingers barely responding, I light the candle. You know in old films, where someone holds up a match or lights a candle and suddenly this dark room is absolutely flooded with light? Well, that doesn't happen here. The light it throws barely reaches the wall I'm standing next to. I squint, trying to accustom my eyes to the gloom.

The room is rectangular, two longer walls either side, two shorter ones at either end, one holding the door I've just come through. There's something I can't make out at the other end, an object set up on the floor. I move nearer to investigate.

As I do I hear a sound behind me and turn, quickly. The door has slammed shut.

Panicking, I run to it, but there's no handle. I try to pry the edges open with my bloodied fingers, my ruined nails, but it won't budge. The door becomes slippery with my blood and I cry out in pain.

"No . . . no . . ."

Useless. I turn back to the room, feeling panic and hysteria rising within me. I grab the candlestick, fingers crying in agony as they curl round the metal, try to find another way out of the room. But the object at the far end grabs my attention. I go and look at it. And gasp.

"No . . . no . . ."

I stagger back in shock and fear. My heart is a massive boulder that's plummeted to the pit of my body. My legs are water. I'm shaking all over.

"No . . ."

Desperately shaking. Like I'm shaking the soul out of my body and looking down on myself thinking, this can't be happening, this can't be happening, not to me *not to me* . . .

Because there, in front of me, is my painting. Or rather a new one. I'm sitting at my desk in my office, leaning back as I was before. But it looks like I've been crushed. My blood decorates the room like a demented Jackson Pollock. My eyes are marbled with red from the burst blood vessels. I'm lifeless.

"No . . ." I'm sobbing now. Really sobbing. I fall to the floor in a heap. "No . . ."

It's all I can say, all I can think of to say. Because I know what's going to happen now. I'm going to die.

And I think about all the things I'm not going to be there for, the stupid things I hated before but now would trade anything for. Weekly meetings. Coffee runs. Parties with people I hate. All the things I was desperate to get out of this house and do even though I never enjoyed them. I would now. I'd even go back and see my family if I get out of here. And I can't . . . I can't . . . I can't believe they're all going to go on without me. That I won't be there. I'll be . . . nowhere. Nothing. I'll have just ceased to exist. Like a deep sleep you fall into and wake up not knowing who you are or where you are. Except this time I won't be waking up. This time I'll sleep on. And I won't dream. Never again. Just nothing.

It's not fair, it's not *fair* . . .

I couldn't sob any harder if I wanted to. But I don't want to. I just want to live.

Then I hear a noise. Stone grinding against stone. Moving slowly. Like I heard in the cellar. The noise that made me run back up here has found me.

I look round and quickly see what's causing it. The walls. The two long walls. They're moving inward. Slowly grinding their way toward the center of the room. Toward me.

And there's nothing I can do about it.

I could almost laugh. Crushed between two walls. Made as thin as could be. Oh, the irony of getting everything I want.

And poor Janice Crewe. What have I done to you?

I close my eyes. Hope, hope, *hope* that at least I'll be able to dream.

CAPTAIN JIMMY SAINT

I'm back in the secret passage again. The stretch that Kyle found particularly claustrophobic. But I'm sure I've been in worse places. Yes, the roof is closing in over my head. The corridor narrowing on either side too. But I can always go backward, I tell myself. Even as I make my way forward. I can always go backward.

Except I'm not sure I can. I've been in this passageway for what seems like hours and perhaps may be hours. Or perhaps is even more than hours, I don't know. Time seems to have something of the elastic about it in this house. And I've tried going backward a couple of times, just to retrace my steps, memorize them, like the lair of the minotaur. But it felt as if the architecture was changing behind me as I went. Left turns that should have been right turns in reverse had disappeared. Replaced by straight stretches. And straight stretches had turns in them. If I'd gone backward I'd have gone a completely different route. Yes, I know that sounds ridiculous, but I swear that's what's happened. Or feels like it. Like I say, time and space feel elastic in this house. And, if I'm honest, reality feels rather adjacent too.

However, I'm somewhat calmer now. The amount of distress I displayed earlier was unmanly. This letting-it-all-hang-out idea may be currently fashionable, sharing one's feelings and all that, but it's not for me. This walk has helped refasten those emotions back in place. Take one's mind off one's problems by doing something physical. Like negotiating this passageway.

I'm not imagining it, it's definitely getting smaller. Walls narrower, roof lower. I'll be on my hands and knees before I know it. Or rather I won't. Because up ahead is a doorway.

It seems to have suddenly just appeared, which would be in keeping with this house. But it's definitely a door and there's light coming from behind it. There also doesn't seem to be any alternative but to head toward it. The corridor ends at the door. So, nearly on my hands and knees, I push the door open and enter.

It's a bedroom. A child's bedroom it seems. A single bed, posters on the walls of a football team, a Formula One car, and what I presume are some characters from a popular science fiction film. There are books and a CD/radio/record player. Toys strewn across the floor. It's the room of a boy—I presume—trying to feel as if he's grown-up but unable to let go of his younger self. It's not a room that shares any architectural features with the rest of the house. The door I've just come through is completely flat, featureless, with a nondescript handle. The window on the opposite wall is rectangular, covered by thin, floral, closed curtains. Low ceiling, single light fixture. Deep pile, fitted oatmeal-colored carpet. It looks more like it belongs to a semidetached seventies house. And the room doesn't feel contemporary, either. Rather it's from several decades ago. But not abandoned, because it feels lived in. As if the occupant will be back at any minute. There's something else. This room, somehow, feels familiar. Not pleasantly so.

Registering my rising discomfort, I look for clues as to why that might be. I explore, pick things up, study them. There are play figures, dolls, matching the science fiction characters on the wall. The books on the shelf are a mixture of well-worn children's adventure stories followed by science fiction. Sherlock Holmes. Some Stephen King. Some Agatha Christie. A *lot* of Agatha Christie. One is open by the bedside. I pick it up. *And Then There Were None.* Even I know that story. Ten strangers in an old dark house being picked off one by one. Just like we are. And the twist in the novel is— I smile. The twist. Oh yes. That would make sense. Perfect sense. I replace it where I found it.

The wallpaper is familiar. But the pattern seems small. I look at the floor once more. And my heart skips a beat. There I am. Again.

I bend down, pick up the doll. It's an Action Man, dressed exactly as I am, gun in hand. Not just held, though, but pointed. At the door. The same way I left the doll upstairs. Strategically placed to protect the occupant of this room, ready to fight to keep them safe.

There's something inside me trying to get out. I close my eyes, knowing no good can come of freeing it. But this memory, emotion, whatever, is persistent. It wants to be free. And the barriers I've put up against it seem at this moment quite breachable.

Standing facing the door. Gun drawn. Ready to protect.

I'm . . .

I close my eyes.

Gun drawn. Protect.

Ready.

No . . . don't . . .

The room plunges into darkness. The same room but now it's nighttime. The door is ajar and weak light spills in from the landing outside. I hear movement. Stealthy movement. Someone not wanting to be heard.

I know . . . I *should* know . . . who this person is . . .

The door is opened and someone creeps quietly in. A man. Middle-aged, paunchy, unremarkable in dress and manner. He smells of alcohol and cheap fried food. And disappointment. And something else, something curdled and sour. And wrong.

There's a boy in the bed, sleeping. Or pretending as hard as he can to sleep. Eyes screwed tightly shut.

"Charlie, hey, Charlie boy . . ." the man whispers, an urgency in his voice. "You awake? Come on, time to wake up. Time for . . ."

The boy tries even harder to pretend to be asleep. He's clutching tight to the Action Man. Gun drawn. Things begin to make sense now.

The man slowly pulls down the duvet to uncover the boy.

"Come on, Charlie, I need . . . I need . . . Come on . . ."

Oh god. I know what's going to happen next. And I'm powerless to stop it.

This is a memory. A memory I've been trying to suppress in order to not have to deal with it. But it's not my memory. Because I'm the one holding the gun. The one who should have been able to stop all this. To protect the boy from this horror.

The man grabs at the boy's pajamas. "Come on, son, help your dad out here . . ."

I want to close my eyes once more but know it'll have little or no effect. I'm condemned to witness this.

When the boy doesn't respond, the man becomes rough, aggressive.

"Come on. You're not helping. Want me to get angry? Eh? Do you? Wake up, then. I know you're pretending. Don't make things worse for yourself than they already are, come on . . ."

The boy finds his voice. It's small, broken. Scared. "Please, please . . . leave me alone, please . . ."

"Leave you alone? Leave you alone? That what you want, eh? That what you want?" The man's aggression is rising, breathing heavier. "Want your dad to leave you alone? Bet you do. What's the matter with you? Eh? Eh?"

The boy holds out the doll in front of him, like a vampire hunter brandishing a crucifix. The man swats it aside.

"Don't give me any more of this shit. Outside now." And he grabs the boy, pulling him from the bed.

I stare, rooted to the spot, as the boy drops the Action Man on the carpet. The man pulls the boy out of the room. I can hear the rain outside, coming down heavy. There's the rumble of distant thunder too.

"Beast . . . *beast* . . ." Cursing the boy as he drags him downstairs.

Of course I know what's going to happen. My memory tells me. I once again look at the Action Man lying on the floor as impotent and useless as I am. And guilt washes over me, because once more, I've failed to protect the boy.

The boy's cries get fainter and fainter as he's dragged out into the night and the storm hits.

No. *No.* I can't let this happen. I may have failed in the past but I won't let it happen this time. I'm a better fighter than this man and he doesn't scare me anymore. I'm going to stop this.

I turn back toward the door, making to follow them, intending to stop him. Once and for all.

"No . . . stop this, stop it right now . . ."

I rush toward it, ready to administer the kind of beating someone like him should have been given years ago. "Scum like you don't deserve to . . ."

I stop. Everything's gone. The room is light once more, just as when I entered it. I wipe my brow. I'm sweating, shaking. Breathing like I've run a marathon. Adrenalized from what I was going to do to that abuser, now with no outlet to expend it on.

But I feel better than when I first entered the room. Not happy, that's not quite it. Just better. Stronger, more confident. A sense that I know who I am, that I've got purpose. I am the protector I believed I was. Or hoped I would be.

I glance back at the bed. That poor boy. So desperately in need of justice. Of help. But that was years ago. There's nothing I can do about that now. I can, however, do something about finding Claire Swanson. She needs my help. She needs protecting.

My hand automatically goes to my holster at my side. And my gun is still there.

I'm ready.

This torch could give out at any moment. It's flickering, surprised to be pressed into service one more time. And it barely illuminates much. Like the bare bulb over the stairs, it creates more shadows than light. As I swing it about, the shadows move. If I wasn't scared enough, these shadows, like sinister expressionistic dancers in their shifting fluidity, would do it for me. But I have to press on. So I squint into the light and go.

I try not to touch or rub up against the stone walls. Difficult, because some parts of the cellar are narrow, but not impossible. I imagine they're contagious and I'll catch something from them. Yeah, I know. Stupid game, stupid way to think when someone's life is at stake. But right now, anything that concentrates me and keeps me moving helps.

I haven't come across anything of note yet. It's cold, yes, dark, obviously. Dank and with a dampness I can feel in my chest as I breathe. Like an airborne virus infecting me, spreading its rotten spores from inside. I can't play a game like I'm doing with the walls. I have to breathe, so I have to endure it.

The torch shows up patches of moss and damp on the dark stone walls, crusty fibrous lichen growing down where they join with the floor, which feels more like hard-packed earth underfoot than stone. The overhead pipes occasionally run down into the floor, joints bloated with corrosion and rust, moss growing around them, seeping and dripping something that may be rusty water or may not. I don't get near enough to find out.

I walk for what seems like ages. It feels like the cellar extends the whole base of the house, if not farther. Like I could just keep walking forever and never find the end or my way back. At that thought I spin round, panicking, trying to make out the way I came, see the stairs. But they're long subsumed by darkness. I have to trust they'll be there again when I need them. I don't dare think about the alternative.

I wonder where Diana and Jimmy are. Have they found Claire? Or a way out? Or have they suffered a similar fate to the rest of the guests? I shake and my stomach curdles as I think that. Feel a sense of loss for both of them and hope that the worst hasn't happened. But I have to face it. I might be the last one left. It might all be down to me. And that's a responsibility I really don't want.

As I walk, trying not to brush against the walls and think too much about what particulate I'm breathing in, or the fates of the others, I think instead about my university course. Gothic literature. This cellar could be the kind of place I've written dissertations on. Of course, at degree level a cellar is never just a cellar, and a writer would never intend it as such. That's what our lecturers tell us. And since the majority of the authors I study aren't around to ask, I have to take their word for it. Cellars, basements, dungeons, whatever, the beneath-ground bits in Gothic fiction are all symbolic of other things. We're encouraged to look at them in psychological terms. Just as the old dark houses or castles aboveground are the physical, visible manifestations of the writer's psyche, so the floor beneath is the subconscious underpinning of that. Downstairs id, upstairs ego, if you want to get Freudian about it. And I have done. In an essay I got a first for. Like I said, I don't know if that's what the writers originally intended, but walking through this hideous cellar now all I can say is, if this was a novel they wouldn't be right in the head.

Any further thought along those lines is halted because I've reached something. An archway. It's old, the stone crumbling, but it's not covered in whatever the walls were previously covered in. I point the torch through the arch,but the darkness is impenetrable. I look for alternative routes. To the left of the arch there's what seems like another archway, but it's bricked up. As if it has been for centuries. And another one next to it. At the opposite side of the arch there's another. And another. I walk in a circle and realize that where I was previously was just one long passageway. I've now emerged from that into a circular chamber with doors all around me. But only one of them is open. The way ahead is kind of chosen for me. With no other options, I step through it.

And the air changes immediately. Much drier. Dusty, even. And it's lighter than before. There doesn't seem to be any source for the light, no bulbs or anything, cracks in the stone with illumination from somewhere else, but it's definitely brighter. I don't need the torch as much. I check my surroundings.

At either side of me are rows of stone arches, similar to the one I've just stepped through, but much smaller. Like cubicles on some kind of medieval accident and emergency ward. I swing my torch into the first one. There's a stone altar, or bed or something. Big enough for a body. It's empty. But there's some debris at the base of it on either side. I crouch down, examine it. My heart skips. Plastic sheeting. Like the kind the captain and I found in that secret room, but old, filthy, torn, with dried dark smears on it. Like something's been ripped from it. Or someone.

"Oh god . . ."

I shine my torch toward the far end of the stone cubicle. There's an old oxygen cylinder and mask. Just like we saw in the secret room upstairs.

"This is where he kept her . . . And we're too late . . ."

Heart hammering, I rush out of the cubicle and into the next one. It's the same layout. Stone slab, plastic sheeting, oxygen tank and mask. No body.

I do this four times. The same every time. Then I realize: There's no body here. But why would there be? The police have found the other girls. And they were too late every time.

Thoughts race. Were the girls found here? If so, does that mean the girl is here? If they were here . . . It must mean that.

I dash into the next cubicle my pulse pounding, the unfamiliar feeling of hope rising within. She's here. I'm sure of it. I've found her. I've saved her and it's all over. I smile as I reach the entrance, enter, and—

Nothing. Just an empty stone slab. No plastic, no tank, no mask.

I stare, not comprehending. It doesn't make sense . . .

I check the cubicles on the other side of the room. They're all empty too. Stone slab, nothing else. I walk out feeling dazed. Cheated, even.

I was so sure I had her then, so sure . . .

I sigh. Hard. Slump into a heap on the floor, raising a cloud of dust as I do.

She's gone. I've failed.

I don't know what to do now. Genuinely. Do I keep looking down here, do I go back, what? I thought I had her, I allowed myself to hope. And this is like a slap in the face.

And then I notice something at the far end of the room. I stand up, swing my torch round to get a better look. Another staircase. Leading down.

I go nearer. It's not like the first staircase I came down, all rickety wood. This one's stone, each triangular step ancient, worn in the center like some spiral staircase in a cathedral or castle. And it's leading downward.

I've got no choice. I've come this far. Torch in hand, I descend.

I have to stoop and it may be my imagination but it feels like the walls are closing in on me. I feel the first familiar tingling of claustrophobic panic. My hands tremble, my chest tightens. Ignore it. Keep going.

Down and down. Crouching as I go. It feels like I'm descending into something much deeper and darker than the bowels of a house. Something much more primeval, if that doesn't sound too pretentious. I am a student, remember.

The pressure changes the farther down I go. The air becomes heavier, oppressive. It's already hard to breathe because of my claustrophobia but this is making it even worse. I'm not imagining it. It's physical not mental.

Occasionally the battery in my torch flickers, the light weakens. Threatening to leave me in this crypt-like darkness. But it holds up. Just.

I reach the bottom, swing the torch round. Crypt was right. Catacombs, even. The archways upstairs were nothing compared to this. The ceiling is so low I can barely stand upright. The walls are built from curiously round-shaped pieces of stone. They throw odd shadows as the torch moves over them. There are archways along the walls again, like upstairs. But smaller this time. The effect it gives is like some ancient burial chamber, something Roman or even before that. Pagan, perhaps. I point the torch ahead of me. This catacomb stretches on into darkness. An infinite number of archways.

Before I can look inside one, my attention is taken by the stones the wall is made from. I move in closer, reach out to touch. And recoil, quickly. They're not stones at all. They're skulls. Ancient human skulls. And the walls are built from them. This isn't a crypt. It's an ossuary.

I want to get out of here. Immediately. Get back to the main house.

In comparison to this, the upstairs doesn't seem so bad after all. But my curiosity gets the better of me. I shine my torch into the first archway. And wish I hadn't.

There's a body in there. Lying perfectly still. A big man. I can only see him from the soles of his feet. Trainers. Old, worn, and *smelly* trainers. I enter, shine the torch over the rest of his body.

"Oh god, oh no . . ."

It's Desmond. The first of us to be killed.

He's lying on a stone bed similar to the ones I found upstairs. Not breathing, unmoving. Like a waxwork. I reach out a tentative hand, touch him. Cold skin. Not a waxwork. And something else about him. Last time I saw him his insides were outside. Somehow he's complete and intact once more. Like he's waiting for something—or someone—to bring him to life again.

I try the next one. I have a horrible feeling I know what to expect. And I'm right. There lies Iain. Exactly the same as Desmond. Inert. Like some horror film corpse about to be reanimated. With his hands reattached.

Panic threatens to overwhelm me now. I'm alone in a catacomb at the base of a house with dead bodies. Is the killer nearby? Is he or she watching me? I turn back toward the stairs. I have to get out of here, must get out. I can barely breathe now.

But I have to go on as well. Just a little bit more. A little. Reluctantly I look in the next chamber. There's Sylvia. Then Monica. And Cerys. And Ramona. And Len.

I'm shaking now, almost in tears. There are ten open chambers. I reach the eighth.

And slump to the ground once more.

Diana.

"Oh no . . . no . . ."

I'm openly sobbing now. I can't help it.

There are two chambers left. I have to look, I have to know. The first one is empty. Does that mean the captain is still alive, somewhere in the house? Or has he managed to escape?

And the other one is empty also. Because I'm standing there looking at it. My burial chamber. Where I'm supposed to end up.

And suddenly I'm back in my dream again, in the coffin with a storm raging, unable to move no matter how hard I twist and writhe, dirt being shoveled down onto me. Getting into my mouth, my nose, inhaling it, swallowing it. I'm there again.

"No . . . no . . ."

I turn and run. Back the way I came, up the stone staircase.

And the storm is following me. I can *hear* it. I can *feel* it.

Up and up, until I'm in the strangely lit chamber with the empty alcoves. Straight through, back to the seeping, damp walls. Along and along, feeling like it's never going to end, like I've given up all hope of ever getting out and then the torch dies.

I scream out loud, plunged into total darkness. Again and again, screaming. Blocking out the storm, trying to breathe.

I have no choice. Blind instinct drives me on and I stumble forward to where I think the stairs might be. Hope the stairs might be.

And then salvation. I see a small chink of light somewhere ahead of me. I run toward it. And make something out of the gloom before I reach it. The staircase. The chink of light is the open door at the top leading to the rest of the house.

I take the stairs two at a time, tripping and falling, feeling splinters from the old handrail embed themselves in my skin. But I keep going until I reach the top of the staircase and turn the door handle.

Locked.

No . . . no . . .

I push the door hard, as hard as I can, turning the handle every which way. Then when that doesn't work, kick it. Hard as I can. Throw my whole body against it. It looks easy in the movies, but old, heavy wooden doors are much stronger in real life and all I get for it is a coruscating pain in my shoulder. Everything I try makes no difference. It's like the door has made up its mind and nothing I can do will make it budge.

I slump down, back against the door, onto the small wooden landing. Sobbing once again. The storm smashing against my mind. I close my eyes.

This is it. This is my coffin. My darkness. My end.

I cry but the storm's too loud in my head to hear my own sobbing.

Oh dear. Oh, poor Kyle. He's really been through it, hasn't he? And now he's stuck in the cellar. Oh dear. Mind you, what was it he said about Gothic castles and houses and Freudian literary criticism? Want me to elaborate on that? Well, I'm going to whether you like it or not, so there.

Right. Here we are again. Professor Beast in the Cellar will be taking this lecture, class. Pay attention at the back or it'll be the blackboard cleaner for you. Quiet, now? Good. I'll begin. The id, the ego, and the superego in the literature of Gothic houses. That noise was me tapping my pen on the lectern.

Sorry, what? What did you say? This wasn't what you signed up for and can we go back to the dead bodies? Not yet. This is interesting. At the very least you can drop it into conversation with your friends in the pub and make them think you're clever. Or that you should get out more, one of the two. Here we go.

Kyle touched upon it, and so he should, being a student of Gothic literature. Blame Freud. I usually do. In early psychoanalysis he used the structure of Gothic literature to explain his ideas. Gothic being a literary celebration of the dreamlike state and Freud being numero uno in explaining dreams, or so he thought. Every passageway became a vagina, every sword (or in our case, I suppose, candlestick) became a penis. Poor fella was obsessed. Then Jung came along and built on this. In his explaining, the castle—or old dark house—became the ego; the dungeon—or cellar, shall we say—the id; and the monastery, the superego. Now the brighter among you will have noticed we haven't got a monastery but there is another location coming up soon that could do the job so bear that in mind.

But, you might say, I'm still none the wiser. What's an ego? What's an id? And didn't Freud once say that sometimes a cigar is just a cigar? Well, yes. He did. As to the other questions, the id, in Freudian terms, is the instinctual part of the unconscious that contains the source of bodily needs and wants, all our basic desires. It's with us when we're born. Libidinal energy. Purely hedonistic. As for the ego, it's the part of us that faces reality. It's what I think of when I talk about I or me. Or what you think of when you talk about I or me. It's the conscious bit of ourselves. The bit we present to the world. Now there's also the superego. That's the bit with all the morals and standards that tells us how to behave with other people. The part of us that polices us, if you like. You got it yet? Right. The ego negotiates between the animalistic desires of the id and the moral and social standards of the superego. That's what makes a person whole.

Now before you dismiss all this as pointless psychoanalytic babble, have a think. Was Kyle right? We've all seen what's on the surface here. The house. We've been all around it. You've also ventured down below into the cellar. Now, you could, if you were a student like Kyle, make the argument that the house is the consciousness—the ego—and the cellar the subconscious—the id. So where's the superego, then? Well, as I said, there's another location coming up soon. We had a glimpse of it earlier. And since our secular society doesn't need a monastery, it might be just the place to control our moral and social standards. Police them, as I said. All this would make sense to a student like Kyle.

But, you ask, is any of this important? What does all this nonsense have to do with finding Claire or stopping her would-be killer? Well, as usual, that's up to you to decide but bear something in mind. In literary criticism terms, as Kyle knows, if you give a single element a fixed meaning, then that becomes a metaphor for that thing, or metaphorical. You can then call that allegorical. The most common instance of allegorical analysis in Gothic literature is the double, or the divided self. The Other, as it were. Write that down.

But yes, you're right, none of this might be of any use to you. Sometimes, like the auld fella said, a cigar is just a cigar and an old dark house is just an old dark house. Up to you to decide.

So here endeth the lesson. Class dismissed. You may leave this classroom and go about your business, skipping down the hallways clutching your folders to your chests and smiling like they do in films but never in real life. And as for me, no more rambling on. You've had enough of literary criticism or Gothic allegories, you want to get on with the action.

You want to find out what happens next. And I have to admit, it's getting exciting, isn't it? The questions are ramping up again.

Why is the cellar door locked?

What exactly did Kyle experience in the cellar?

And, if I may modestly say, where was *I* while Kyle was doing all this running about downstairs?

All good questions. Might be time for some answers.

Or at least some different questions.

Now do excuse me, I have to go and get set up for the next bit. Anybody want to give me a hand?

Thought not.

The storm inside me begins to subside. Like it's moved from directly overhead but I can still hear it—feel it—as it rumbles away. For the time being, anyway.

Slowly, I pull myself back to my feet. I'm tired. So, so tired. The storm coupled with what I discovered in the cellar has left me completely drained. I don't think I've ever had a migraine but people have described them to me and how they feel afterward and this, I suppose, must be what it's like.

I try the door to the hallway one more time, not holding out much hope. It doesn't open. So I sigh and look downward once more. I have no choice and I know it. I can't stay here. So I have to return to the cellar. Steel myself for whatever else I find down there and hope—there's that bastard word again—that I can find another way out. There must be a way. Captain Jimmy and I already found one secret passageway, old houses like these are supposed to be riddled with them. There's bound to be another. I hope.

So down I go again. I know which stairs to avoid putting too much weight on, which ones are sturdy. They feel surprisingly familiar now, like I've been up and down them more than I actually have. I reach the bottom. The abandoned flashlight is still there. I pick it back up and give it a hard shake until it again throws out a cold, weak beam. Taking a couple of deep breaths to steady myself, I set off into the cellar again.

And stop. I can hear something.

Sobbing. Crying for help, to be released. Echoing off the walls from far inside the cellar.

It's her. The captured girl. Got to be.

Something surges within me. I hate to name it hope but that's what it feels like. If I follow her voice, I can find her, free her, and get out of here.

There she is again, begging now for help, sobbing.

I set off once more, my energy renewed.

It's been minutes not hours since I last walked this stretch but this house plays tricks on you. It feels like hours. The thing on my wrist tells me there's only about fifteen minutes to go before Claire's time is up. But it feels like it's been fifteen minutes every time I've looked for a while now.

The walls still smell of iron or blood. I avoid touching them. The corroded pipes still drip and the air feels just as damp and harmful. I retrace my steps from earlier, following the voice. It's no easier, nor pleasant. But like walking down the stairs, it feels much more familiar. Not just like I've been here before, but like I'm more connected to it than I first recognized.

What a horrible thought.

After winding my way through narrowing and widening hallways, I arrive at the stone archway. Part of me is surprised that it's still there, just as I left it. I check the chambers containing the dead girls' trappings, hoping to find clues to a live girl there. Trappings? Remnants? Traces. Like trace memories. I stop walking. What do I mean by that? Why did I think that phrase? I don't know and a sliver of panic inserts itself between my ribs. My mind is thinking things that I don't understand, yet on a subconscious level feel right. Like I don't know myself. That should scare me as much as everything else in this cellar.

But the girl's not here. Which, given that those girls are dead, should be an encouraging sign.

I see the stairs leading downward and steel myself to descend once more. The sound of sobbing gets louder the farther I go, the deeper I go. I don't want to see the bodies again but know I have to if I'm going to rescue the girl. And I haven't got much time. Fifteen minutes to be precise.

So down I go.

The bodies haven't moved. Not that I'd have expected them to. I make my way past them, following the voice, trying not to look at them. I point the torch ahead of me. And there, at the end of the chamber, is a crouching figure. My heart skips a beat. The figure is bent double and the weak torch beam throws up a grotesque hunched shadow on the far wall. It looks like some kind of deformed creature devouring its prey. I don't want to go any farther. I stop, ready to turn back and run, voice or no voice.

But it's too late. I've attracted the creature's attention. It turns toward me.

"You just going to stand there, or what? This thing's heavy, you know. Give us a hand."

THE BEAST IN THE CELLAR

Guess who?

I stand there, unable to move. I have to admit, the voice doesn't match the shadow. To say the least.

"Here, hold this . . . come on . . . God, you ask for help, no one volunteers. Typical."

I move closer, shine the torch on the crouching figure. It's not a deformed monster, nothing like that. It's a boy. A small boy. Struggling to pull up a huge stone flag from the floor. He's doing his best, but I don't think he can hold it for long.

I put the torch down, pointing the beam to where the stone is, get down on my hands and knees with him. Questions can wait until later. And there are questions. Plenty of them.

"Get that side. Now push it open. Go on, push . . ."

I do so. And the stone begins to move. I manage to get my fingertips underneath, get some leverage, and push it away from the floor.

It's coming now. Underneath is an opening, down into darkness. But this thick, dense piece of stone is heavy. Massively heavy. Between the two of us I'm not sure if we can hold it. But we have to. The voice is coming from down below so we've no choice. With a final screech and a heave, we manage to push the stone over. It crashes onto the floor with a mighty, reverberating sound, dust rising all round.

The boy sits back, exhausted. So do I. Arms shaking.

Eventually I can speak again. "Who are you? And what are you doing down here? I haven't seen you before."

The boy just smiles. "You must be Kyle, right?"

"Yeah. Who are you?"

He gives me a kind of half smile, like he knows things well beyond his years. Things about me, I mean. I have the time to study this boy properly now. He's dressed in T-shirt and jeans, but not contemporary. As if from the eighties, or an episode of *Stranger Things*. He can't be more than ten,

I think, although I've never been very good at picking out kids' ages. Maybe even younger.

"I said, who are you?"

Before he can reply, we hear the voice again. Sobbing once more. Always sobbing. He looks down into the hole we've just uncovered.

"She's down there, isn't she?" I say. "The girl. We've got to get her out."

"There's a set of steps," he says and looks at me. "You first or me?"

I can't let this kid go first. Whatever else he is, he's just a kid. "You stay here," I say. "I'll go."

I swing my legs over the hole we've just exposed, shine the torch down. He's right, there's a wooden ladder. I lower myself down. The wood's solid, holding. I grasp the torch and descend.

I don't know how long I'm climbing down, but it feels for a time like I'm suspended in darkness between two worlds. Just me, my rubbish torch, and the ladder. And nothing near me. The boy above, the voice below.

Eventually the ladder stops and there's something beneath my feet. Hard-packed earth, it feels like. I step off the ladder onto it. Swing the torch around. I'm in yet another stone chamber. But this feels different from the others, like it's pressurized, harder to breathe in. Like I'm deep sea diving and need a special suit or a diving bell to properly function.

And there's something else. It sounds stupid, but I can feel the place in my chest. Like I'm standing in front of a massive bass speaker at a rave or a stadium rock gig and its pulsating rhythm gets right inside me. It takes my breath away it's so deep, but, for all that, there's something within me that responds to it.

I find what I think is the source of the pounding. At the side of the chamber is a huge, rusty, old boiler. Massive. The kind they'd use in an old hotel or ancient block of flats. The rusty corroded pipes I saw upstairs lead into and out of it. Steam pushes out of its riveted joints and panels. It pounds like a huge heart and it feels as if it could blow at any second. This must be what made the house feel alive.

But I can't waste time on that now. Because in the center of the chamber on a raised stone plinth is a wooden box. Oh, let's be honest, it's a coffin. What else could it be? And from that coffin I can hear sounds. Sobbing, yes, and rustling, like the sound of plastic sheeting being moved.

"Help me, please . . . help me . . ."

I cross to the coffin, hands on the lid to pry it up.

"Don't worry, it's OK, I'm here. I'm getting you out . . ."

And then the storm starts up again. So sudden, so violent, that I'm thrown away from the coffin, onto my back on the packed earth floor. Hands over my ears, trying to block out the noise. How can the storm get down this far? How?

"Because it's inside you. And you carry it with you. Always."

I open my eyes. It's the boy, standing over me.

"I thought I told you to stay put."

"You can't tell me what to do," he says. "You're not my real dad." He smiles. But I sense something behind that smile, some kind of sad knowledge.

"What . . . what . . ."

"The storm might pass, but it never goes away completely, does it?"

I pull myself up onto my knees. Trying hard to cope with the noise in my head. "Who are you?"

The boy shrugs. "Who I'm supposed to be. Just like you."

I put my hand on the coffin, manage to get to my feet again. The storm is indeed subsiding. I turn to the coffin, try lifting the lid off once more.

"Don't worry, soon have you out of here . . ."

The boy looks puzzled. "Soon have who out of there?"

I turn to him. "The girl. The one we've all been looking for. She's been stuck in a box and she's running out of air. I've got to get her out before that air runs out. Want to give me a hand instead of just standing there?"

"You think there's a girl stuck in that box?"

"Of course there is."

"What's her name?"

"It doesn't matter what her name is! Just help me . . ."

"You don't know her name? Or you can't remember her name?"

"It . . . it doesn't matter. Just help me."

"There's no girl in there."

I turn to him, exasperation giving way to anger now. "So who is, then, brainiac?"

"Who it's always been. You."

I stare at him. Completely lost now. "I genuinely have no idea what you're talking about. Now just—"

But the sound of machinery stops me from talking. In a shadowed corner that the torch beam had failed to penetrate are the pull across bars for a lift cage. Just like the one upstairs. And from the faint light above it that's getting brighter, that lift cage is descending.

I stare at the boy, back to the coffin, back to the lift. "How can the lift come down here?"

"Did you never think to look? See if there were any buttons for lower floors?" says the boy. "Would have saved you an awful lot of trouble."

"There were no other buttons. I'd have seen them. It didn't come down this far."

The boy just shrugs.

The noise of the approaching lift increases. The light from within it gets stronger. It arrives. Both the boy and I stare at it, expectantly.

The cage door opens.

CAPTAIN JIMMY SAINT

I am lost and alone in this crooked house.

The darkness of this passageway has enveloped me entirely. I no longer know where I'm going, nor where I've been. Or even how long I've been here. I step slowly, carefully, in case the floor beneath me should suddenly disappear. I hear no sounds. Apart from my own breathing and movement. I stretch my arms to either side, front and back, above my head. There's nothing there. No walls, no ceiling. Just the floor beneath my feet. And the gun in my hand.

I should be fearful of this but strangely, I'm not. I'm calm. And alone with myself and my thoughts only, I've had time to reflect on why this should be. As I've said earlier, I'm not given to all this self-reflective nonsense. I'm also not a religious man. I've seen too much in this life to believe that there's a divine creator planning things and guiding us toward absolutes. *Everything happens for a reason* goes that trite saying. No, it doesn't. Nothing happens for a reason. Conversely, everything happens for no reason.

But I am calm in this darkness, because I believe I finally know who I am. And what I am.

I'm Captain Jimmy Saint. I'm more than a uniform. I'm a protector.

And should never have doubted that. Because I know now that I'll eventually find myself back in the light. I will be where I am supposed to be. I am a protector. Of this I have no doubt.

Until such time, I keep walking.

You're dead."

"Apparently not." Amanda walks out of the lift, toward me. Slowly, taking her time. Her body silhouetted against the light from the cage, her face unreadable.

Involuntarily, I take a step back, away from her. "No, you're dead. I saw you die. I watched you bleed out. I checked your breathing. I covered your body with the tablecloth." She doesn't respond. "What's happening?"

She ignores my question, turns her attention to the boy instead. Smiles at him. "Hello, you little beast."

He nods and smiles at her.

I look between the two of them. Confused, to say the least. "Do you two know each other?"

"In a manner of speaking," says Amanda.

"OK." I pace the floor, trying to put things together. "OK. You faked your own death, didn't you?"

She turns back to me. "Obviously."

"Why?"

"Because it was necessary, of course. To set the template for the game. To get you all going. To wrong-foot you, get you scared and scurrying round the house on the hunt for a murderer. And it worked."

I've backed away so far I've reached the far wall, away from the unsteady boiler. I'm on the other side of the wooden coffin. I point the torch straight at Amanda. She doesn't flinch or try to hide her eyes. Just keeps staring at me. Then the penny drops.

"You killed them all. Didn't you?"

She smiles at that. A slow smile. An unpleasant smile.

"Well, I think the captain's still here somewhere. And there's you, of course."

"So you . . ." I try to put it all together. Remember what Diana and I were talking about earlier. About what the house—or whoever was be-hind this house—was doing. And how they were doing it. "So. You were behind all the deaths. And you . . . let me get this straight. Everyone who died got what they wanted. Or what they deserved. Is that right?"

She nods, smiles. Like she's bowing before my superior deductive powers. A real insincere gesture.

"Desmond wanted to penetrate, he got penetrated. Iain was a thief who couldn't keep his hands off other people's things, so got them chopped off. Sylvia just wanted to go home. Cerys . . . wanted to be happy?"

Another nod.

"And the others? I wasn't there for them."

"All got what they wanted. Take my word for it. A kind of happy ending in a way."

Her words hit me like an electrical charge. Such a huge admission of guilt. So huge. Yet I have no idea what to do with this information. So I ask the only question I can think of. "Why? Why did you do it?"

"The game."

"You'll have to do better than that. This was never a game."

Amanda leans one hand against the casket. Relaxes. What light there is glints off her Gothic silver jewelry. Makes the skulls smile. She looks like she belongs to this place. And this place to her.

She smiles. Her face looks like one of the skulls on her fingers. "Of course it's a game, Kyle. What else could it be? It has a setting and rules. And I have to abide by them just as you have to. An old dark house. Ten strangers for dinner. A faked death at the beginning so I can keep going, and then they get knocked off one by one."

I'm still having trouble getting my head round any of this. I've never had a serial killer confess to me before. I'm not quite sure what the eti-quette, for want of another word, is for doing this. "So this whole thing. The house, the dinner, the introduction. And then your death. All staged."

She nods.

"And the paintings? That must have taken some effort."

She smiles. "Worth it, though."

"How did you move around the house?"

"Same way you did."

It's still too much to take in. "But . . . why?"

"To find Claire Swanson. And to find who had taken her."

"Oh, that's complete bullshit and you know it. You don't kill a whole load of innocent people, go to all this trouble just to find out where someone is. There's more than that. There's something wrong with you. Something twisted. Something that, I don't know, happened to you when you were a kid that made you behave like this."

"And if that's true, and I'm not saying it is, is that any of your business?"

"Yes. Your explanation's bullshit. After everything I've been through, you owe me the truth."

Another smile. "The diabolical mastermind revealing her plan? That's what you're owed?"

"Yeah, it is."

She steps forward to me and whispers, almost like a lover. "Maybe I do this because I like it." She steps back again.

Her words send a shiver down my spine. It sounds like the most truthful thing she's said. I shake my head to get her out of there.

"Why this girl, why is she so important? Are you related to her or something? Is this some kind of revenge?"

Her features become deadly serious. "It's more than revenge. I want her found alive. And I want to know who took her. And the others."

"And do you know now?"

"I do."

"Who, then?"

"That's something I'd like to know as well."

We both jump on hearing the voice. Turn to see where it's come from. I recognize it straightaway.

"Jimmy? How did you get down here?"

Jimmy Saint steps out of the shadows by the boiler. "Secret passages everywhere in this house," he says. "So. Amanda. It was you all along."

She shrugs. "Always the one you least expect."

"Never mind her," I say. "Give me a hand to get this coffin lid open. The girl's in there."

"Really? You've found her?"

"No, he hasn't," says the boy.

The captain looks at him, puzzled. "And who are you?" Before the boy can answer, Jimmy's expression changes. "Wait, I know you . . ."

"Never mind that," I say. "Give me a hand." There are still sounds emanating from the coffin. Weak, but still there. "She's dying," I say. "She's in there and she's dying. We've got to get her out."

Amanda doesn't move. Neither does the kid. Jimmy looks from one to the other, confused.

"We've got to get her out!" I'm shouting now.

Still no one moves. The boiler pounds fit to burst. The storm is overhead.

"If you're not going to help me, Jimmy, at least get ahold of Amanda. Stop her going anywhere."

Jimmy shakes his head as if coming out of a trance. "Yes. Right." He unholsters his gun, walking quickly toward her. "Stay where you are. We're going to free Claire Swanson and hand you in to the police." He brings his gun up to cover her.

"I don't think so," Amanda says.

She's fast, I'll give her that. She's on him before he can move. And surprisingly strong, punching him in the face and taking his gun off him before he has a chance to fall backward and hit the hard-packed earth.

She turns to the kid. "Come over here, you little beast, you're with me."

The boy does as she says.

Just then I feel a rumble under my feet. An earthquake? What? I look at Amanda. She seems concerned about it too. Before we can speak dust and small rocks fall on my head and shoulders.

"What's happening?" I say.

"Seems like the house is collapsing," Amanda says. "The fall of the house of Boyd . . ."

I hold on to the lid of the coffin, my footing unsteady, and try to wrench it free. "Then I'm getting Claire out."

Amanda looks panicked. She's twisting around like she doesn't know what to do.

"And you stay where you are," I shout over the noise.

"This has gone on long enough," she says. "I'm leaving." She turns to go.

"Come back. You can't just—"

Jimmy makes a lunge for her but she's too quick. She turns, fires the gun. He spins once, then hits the floor. Hard.

I just stare at her, jaw open. "What the fuck have you done?"

"Don't need him anymore," she says. "And I don't need you." She points the gun at the boiler. Fires, hitting the rusted old plates head-on, then grabs the boy and makes for the lift.

Steam starts pouring out of the bullet hole, the impact spreading, the metal tearing and rending, and the noise intensifies. I see the lift moving upstairs, taking the two of them away, and return my attention to the coffin.

But I have no time to do anything because at that moment the boiler blows.

And everything turns black.

PART THREE

THE BEAST IN THE CELLAR

Well, did you see me? Yep, there I was. Little old me. Or rather little young me. I'm quite giddy now, making that appearance after being hidden away for so long. I can see how this sort of thing can go to your head. I mean, now that I've popped up in this and been seen I should capitalize on it, shouldn't I? Open garden fetes, and supermarkets, things like that. Public appearances at nightclubs when I get older—if I get older—with ex–Love Islanders or, oh god, that bloke with the glasses from the Halifax advert, and all of that. Oh yes, it's all ahead of me.

What? What d'you mean, it makes no sense and what am I on about? I've just appeared in the narrative instead of sitting here chatting. Duh. And now I'm famous. I— What now? Oh. Right.

You'd like to know what's just happened. I see.

Well, that was the end, my friend, and all that. Short answer, you got what you wanted. There have been a series of murders in this house and we've been trying to find out who the murderer was. And now we know. So that's that. End of story, as they say. All wrapped up neatly. Murderer found. And you can all go home now. I mean, that's what you came for, isn't it? You wanted a mystery. You wanted murders. You've had your mystery, you've had your murders and now it's been solved. And not only solved, but with a proper plot twist as well. A proper twist! The first one dead was the murderer! How cool is that? I mean, what more do you want?

Oh. I see. That kind of ending isn't good enough anymore. Fair enough. I'm not sure it ever was, to be honest. I mean, I get why people want satisfying conclusions. Satisfying conclusions with neatly tied bows. Especially in stories like this. Because these stories deal with big things, with life and death. And real life is random. Life is messy. We're born, we live, we die. We all have the same story with a few variations in the telling. And it means nothing. Everyone knows the ending and there's not going to be some kind of last-minute twist. Not in real life. So we look to our stories for that. We want a narrative that creates order out of chaos. That gives life and death meaning and structure. We want to believe that there's *something more*, one way or another. So yes. You get your ending, you have your twist. You've got your money's worth. What else is there?

Well, there's real-life events that cause real-life damage. And there are real-life psychological scars and consequences to those events. And those things go beyond neat endings. Beyond twists.

I bet you've probably worked out this story isn't over yet. I mean, this is the start of Part Three, that's kind of a giveaway. And I wasn't being totally truthful about not being in it anymore. You'll see me again. Just to say goodbye, if nothing else. So if you want to know what happens next, what *really* happens next, not the neat crime-thriller-mystery-crowd-pleaser ending, but the real one, then read on. Back to where we started.

Hello? I know you're watching . . . Yes, you, behind the mirror. I know you're watching me. Course you are. You wouldn't put a mirror in an interrogation room if you couldn't hide behind it, so I know you're there. I've sat here long enough, get back in here and talk . . . *Now* . . . Because you're wasting time. She's out there, dying, and I know where she is. You've got to find her. You can save her, if you get a move on . . . This is urgent, come on . . .

"Don't ignore me, *please* don't ignore me . . . I escaped from that house, came straight here, and . . . and all the others . . . all the others are dead. Murdered . . . All of them . . . And you've done nothing about that. *Nothing*.

"Oh, wait a minute, wait a minute . . . this paper suit you've given me, being left in here on my own, you don't think I'm a witness, do you? You think . . . you think I'm the killer . . . Is that it? My god, you think because I'm the only one left alive that I did it . . . And then there was one and it's me . . . The prime suspect. The *only* suspect . . .

"Well, that's bullshit, and you know it. I mean, for god's sake, I even told you who did it. One of the other people. Gave you their name and everything so why don't you go and arrest them? Get a confession. Go on, instead of doing this to me . . . go on . . .

"Stop pissing about in there! Stop ignoring me! Hello?

"Hello?

"Oh god . . . Fine. Fine. Leave me here, do what you want, just get back to the house. *Please.* Go to the house. With the bodies. Find the girl. That's all you have to do. Go to the house with the bodies, find the girl . . .

"Please, before it's too late . . ."

I'm exhausted. I know, because I can see my reflection in the mirror I'm shouting at. Exhausted and wired at the same time. I slump back down on the chair behind the table. Beyond tired, but my heart is hammering. I'm wearing a paper suit because they've taken my clothes. I don't know how long I've been sitting here, but it feels like forever. But at least I'm alive. I keep telling myself that. At least I made it out alive.

I've given them everything. Told the two detectives my story for what seems like the hundredth time and all they did was look at each other, get up from the table, tell me they'd be right back, and leave the room. Nothing since.

They didn't believe me. It's obvious now, thinking back. The fact they've left me here for so long proves that. Oh god, oh god . . .

I feel lightheaded, I'm blinking fast. Taking lots of shallow gulps like I can't get enough air into my body.

That's me, what they think I am. The prime suspect. The *only* suspect.

I have to get out. Can't stay in this room any longer. I have to make them see, make them believe. I have to—

There's a knock on the door. I sit up straight, taking heaving breaths. Expectant. The door opens.

And in walks Amanda.

KYLE TANNER

I'm on my feet straightaway. Back over to the mirror on the other side of the room. "Are you there? Are you watching? This is her! This is who killed everyone! She's here, now! Come on, arrest her, she's a murderer!"

Amanda says nothing. Her face, her posture, gives nothing away. Then she smiles, and we sit down opposite each other. She puts the heavy file she's been carrying on the table.

"Hello again, Kyle," she says.

"Why are you here?" Then to the mirror, "Can't you see her? She's right here. And she's a murderer." I wait for someone to come running through the door but it doesn't open.

My head is swirling, throbbing, as if the falling ceiling of the cellar in the house has just hit me. I stand up, intending to make for the door, but suddenly feel too woozy to make it. I look at her. Try to take her in. See her properly for the first time since she set foot inside the room. She's toned down the goth image she had in the house. Not as extreme but still there. She's also wearing a lanyard like the police detectives.

Something strikes my chest like a wrecking ball.

Oh no . . . Oh god . . .

She's one of them. She's *in* with them. That's why they didn't believe me. That's why . . .

It hits me then. I'm fucked. Well and truly fucked. She's making me take the blame. For the murders, for Claire Swanson, everything. She's planned all this, whoever she is.

And why me? What have I done?

"Sit down again, please," she says. "I want to talk to you."

"No . . . it's you. You're the killer, you confessed down in the cellar. You're not going to blame me . . ."

She gives a small, tight smile. "Yes, Kyle, I'm the killer. It's me. I killed all those people in that house. You've got me."

She holds out her wrists, as if for me to handcuff them. I'm on my feet at her words, throbbing head or no throbbing head. Yes, got her. *Yes.* "You hear that?" I shout once more to the mirror. "She's just confessed! Come on, what's the matter with you? Why aren't you in here grabbing her? Come on!"

Then even as I say that I'm hit by another thought. Oh god . . .

If she's behind this and the police don't believe me, could they be in on this too? Maybe she's not just fooling them, maybe they're protecting her as well? Could the whole thing be one massive stitch-up? Is that why they're not running in here?

This is too much for me. I feel so powerless, don't know what to do next.

"Where's the kid from the cellar? And the girl?" Nothing. *"Answer me!"*

Amanda ignores me, opens the file she's brought in. It's quite thick. How could she have managed to put together a file so thick in such a short space of time? And what's in it, anyway?

She extracts several sheets of something. Places them on the table between us. "Could you look at these photos, please, Kyle?"

"Why? What are you . . ."

"Kyle? Could you look at the photos, please?"

I glance at them, then away again. There's too much happening before me to do this.

"What d'you see? Look at them properly, please."

She's got authority in her voice and this time I find myself doing as she asks. I look at the photos. They're all grainy CCTV blowups of this hooded figure attacking this girl in the street and dragging her away.

I close my eyes. And can feel the storm building up again.

"What do you see, Kyle?" she asks.

"Some guy attacking a girl."

"And you've seen these photos before?"

"Yeah. You showed us them in the house."

"And d'you know her name?"

I shrug. "Whatever her name is."

"Claire Swanson."

"Sure."

"So considering everything you've been through since you last saw these photos, do you notice anything different about them now? Anything new that stands out?"

A distant roll of thunder. I blink. Can feel that familiar headache coming on. And I've still got that kind of nauseous brain fog from seeing Amanda in this room. "No. Nothing else."

Amanda leans forward, concern on her face. "Something wrong, Kyle? You feeling OK?"

"Yeah, I'm just . . . I'm fine. Fine." Don't show any weakness in front of her. Answer her questions, wait until the detectives return. Play along until I can think of some way out of this.

"Can you look again, please?"

I look again. And I hear a voice:

"Is this Ashburton Crescent?"

"No, Hilltree Grove."

I try to blink the headache away.

"Please keep looking, Kyle. Look closely."

"Oh. I'm meeting my girlfriend here. Bloody satnav, eh? What can you do?"

She looks nervous. Her hand in her pocket, grabbing something. Keys probably. Backing away.

I look up, shake my head. It's really throbbing now. Ready to burst like that boiler in the house. "What? What's happening?" I close my eyes.

She's definitely nervous. And that excites me. Oh yes.

I open my eyes. I'm breathing heavily now, feeling like I'm going to be sick. Is this a migraine as well? Feels worse than that. My eyes close once more.

And I'm on her.

Up close, there's the terror in her eyes, caught forever in that frozen second where she experiences her old life jump from its expected trajectory to this new one. That disbelief that this is actually happening to her and not some other person. A whole lifetime of change all in that one second. I hold hard to her frozen body. One arm round her. With the other I punch her in the face. Once. Not enough. There's still light in her eyes, voice in her throat. Twice. Her eyes roll backward, head back with the force. Her body goes limp and I catch her.

My head . . . my head . . . "What the fuck is happening? What am I . . . what am I seeing?"

The storm breaks right above me. I can't question the logic of that now. All I can feel is the thunder. Penetrating through me, into me. To my bones. Lightning too. Hurting. Hurting.

"You can see it, can't you, Kyle?" she says.

"See what?" The pain is near intolerable.

"See Claire Swanson. That's her name. Claire Swanson. The one you've never been able to say because to you she's never been a person. Look again. It's Claire Swanson. When you took her."

"I didn't . . . take her . . ."

"Yes, you did, Kyle. That's you in the photos. You're even wearing your hoodie. The one that's been taken away for forensic analysis, the one with traces of Claire's DNA on it."

"What . . . what's happening? You were in the house. *I* was in the house. You killed all those people . . ."

"In a manner of speaking, Kyle, yes."

"You admitted. *You just admitted it again . . .*" Why is no one running in? Why? "*Why are you not doing anything?*" I scream at the mirror. Something else occurs to me. "And how did I get from the house to here?"

"You've always been here, Kyle." Amanda's voice, as calm and dispassionate as her expression. "We gave you twelve hours, Kyle. Twelve hours to tell us where you'd left Claire Swanson. Twelve hours. And you've run out of time. And I want an answer. Now."

The storm . . . So bad . . . stopping me from thinking straight . . . "What d'you mean I've always been here? No. We were in the cellar. Of the house. And then the boiler . . ."

"You were never in the house, Kyle. There was no house."

My head starts to spin. My breathing increases. I try to stand, to get out. She reaches across the table for my wrist, holds it firmly.

"Stay where you are, please."

I stare at her, too confused to move.

"Where is she, Kyle?"

"Where's who?"

"Claire Swanson. Where is she?"

"I don't know . . ."

She tries to hide it but I catch her making an exasperated gesture with her eyes. "Come on, Kyle. No more games. Where is she?"

"*I don't know* . . ." I'm yelling now. Both at her, trying to understand what's happening, and at the pain in my head. "I don't know . . . Why are you asking me?"

"Because you abducted her. You took her."

I sit back, like I've just been punched.

"I . . ."

"You know it's you. I can see it in your eyes. When you looked at the photos just now, you recognized yourself. You realize that, don't you?"

I look at the photos again, replay the thoughts I just experienced . . . "No . . . no, it's Charles Boyd, he did it. She's in the house . . . the cellar . . ."

She settles back in her chair. "Let's talk about Charles Boyd. When he was a child, he experienced trauma. Life-changing, life-defining trauma. Horrific trauma, the kind we can only hope we never have to go through, so bad most of us would hate to even acknowledge it exists. And this abuse, this systematic, regular abuse, was perpetrated by his own father."

I say nothing.

"It became so bad, so horrific," she continues, "that Charles Boyd's personality shattered. Fractured into splintered personalities, each one separate, each one different. What we call dissociative identity disorder. DID. It's not that common, affects only about three percent of the population. And these different personalities, alters we call them, have different personality types, or archetypes. These alters can be male or female and everything in between, old or young, fictional or real, even ghosts or animals. They manifest in various forms for a reason. The brain creates them either to help or react against the host. Some are gatekeepers, preventing traumatized alters from fronting."

"Fronting?" I don't understand what she's talking about and yet part of me, somewhere deep inside, somehow, does.

"Appearing. Taking over. There are persecutors who revel in the trauma, protectors who try to guard the host from trauma. Even taking the place of the dominant personality themselves. You met one in the cellar. The boy. He's a trauma-free version of the host, Charles Boyd. His personality, had it continued to grow and respond normally without the abuse."

"But he was a little kid."

"Because that's when he physically stopped growing. It's the easiest way for him to manifest. His mind continued to develop, though. There are nurturers like Ramona, protectors like Jimmy. And there are some we call demonic." She leans forward. "Like you, Kyle."

I say nothing. I want to argue, shout and rail against her. But I don't. I listen.

"I specialize in cases such as these. That's why the police brought me in. I'm Doctor Amanda Drew. I needed to know which of Charles Boyd's personalities had abducted Claire Swanson. And I didn't have much time to do that. So I hypnotized Charles Boyd. DID sufferers are easily hypnotized, I should say. Very susceptible. And within that hypnosis I created an environment that he would be familiar with. An Agatha Christie story. The old dark house. Ten guests who don't know one another at a dinner. A murderer on the loose. And a countdown. Charles Boyd loves that kind of thing. Responded to it well."

"But you killed them, I saw it . . . You confessed . . ."

"In a manner of speaking," she says, smiling. "While the scenario was playing out in Boyd's mind, I interrogated each different alter as part of that scenario here in the interview room. And when I was convinced they hadn't done it, I sent them back into his subconscious."

"I saw them lying there, in the cellar, like a whole load of Frankenstein's monsters waiting to be brought to life again."

"Yes, exactly. For this scenario to work, they had to be killed and the remaining ones be given no choice but to find the killer. Those remaining identities would be whittled down until only one remained. And that one, he or she, would be the killer."

She stares straight at me, deadly serious.

"And that's you, Kyle."

I keep staring at her.

"The house was a construct so there was no need of words in the pages of the books in the library. But to keep the conventions of the story there had to be a library. And the parts of the house at the edges of the constructed narrative didn't need to be as well drawn as the other places. Which is why the kitchen was a little basic, shall we say. The rooms you all woke up in are what you'd imagine your rooms to be like.

The paintings were a flourish of the story. You thought you saw someone in the garden. I sensed that whoever was saying that was trying to shift the blame away from themselves so I brought the shutters of the house down."

I look around the room, expecting to find myself back in the house once more but the walls don't move. I'm still in the room. And this time I know, *I know*, she's telling the truth. And that exhausts me.

"You shot the boiler in the cellar, it exploded. The roof caved in," I say. "Then I ended up here."

"The roof didn't collapse, Kyle. The house—the construct—started falling apart when you started to remember. I needed a way to get out and still question you. So by shooting the boiler in the construct, I just hurried the process along. Kept you alive in the house to be brought out and questioned here."

I say nothing. I don't know what to say.

"You were the only one who heard Claire Swanson crying, Kyle, because you were the only one who knew what her cries sounded like."

"But . . . I . . . I'm a student. I have flatmates. Classes. I remember them."

"You also remember attacking and abducting Claire Swanson, Kyle."

"But . . ." My head drops forward. I place it in my hands. "No . . . no . . ."

She's studying me intently again. "What triggers you, Kyle? What gets you angry, what scares you? Is it the storm?"

"The storm . . . And what the storm brings . . ." I look beyond her because I can see something beyond her. Hear something beyond her.

"What is it, Kyle? What can you see? What can you hear? What do you hear when you're alone, in your dreams? What do you experience?"

I can't move. The soil is being shoveled down on me. And I can't move.

"Burial? You're being buried alive?"

I must have spoken aloud. "I'm in a coffin and I can't move," I try to stop myself from talking but I can't. It's like I want to tell her this, make her understand.

"Is that right?" she asks. "You're being buried alive? Is that what he did to you? Is that what you revisit in your dreams? You're locked in a box? You're being buried?"

"Soil's raining down on me, getting in my mouth, my eyes, my nose . . ."

"It's his punishment for you, isn't it? The captain can't save you. He's only an Action Man doll. Useless. And there's no one else in the room, is there? And your mother's no good. She knows what he's doing and she lets it happen. Rather you than her, isn't it? As far as she's concerned. No wonder you hate women, Kyle. And when you fight back, he takes you outside? Into the garden."

And suddenly I'm crying. Tears running down my face. "No . . ."

"To the hole he's dug specially. When you misbehave. When you really annoy him, yes? That was you in the cellar, wasn't it? Not Claire crying but a small child. *You* as a small boy. *Charles Boyd* as a small boy."

I want her to stop talking. I put my hands over my ears, shake my head, but I can still hear her, like she's gotten inside me.

"The storm," I say. "The night of the storm. That was the worst. He left me there all night because he got so drunk he forgot to come back and get me. And that storm, all night it went on. All night . . ."

And my eyes are closed and my ears are blocked, but I can see it. See it like it's happening now, right in front of me. Like it's never stopped happening to me. I'm back there and I'm screaming and crying. Pulling at him as he leads me out into the garden, trying to get away. I can smell whiskey on him. He hits me round the head. He's already . . . been in my bedroom. I fought him off this time and he truly hates it when I manage to do that. Because something inside him knows that he won't always have this power over me, that one day I'll be stronger than him and he really dreads that. Fears it. One day I'll fight back. So to stop that he has to teach me a lesson I won't forget. And there's the hole in the garden . . .

"No . . . no . . ."

Sobbing now. Sobbing and sobbing.

"He took your power away, didn't he?" Amanda again. I must have been speaking aloud once more. "Put you in the ground. Left you helpless. And that's the ultimate trauma for you. It's what you've been acting out ever since."

I'm still sobbing. "I'm Kyle Tanner, I'm a student, I study English . . ."

"No, Kyle, you've hidden your secrets from yourself, buried them so deep because you can't bear to think of yourself as a bad person. And in your head you're not Kyle, are you? You just hear that storm, feel the soil falling on you, and you need to make it stop. Project it on to someone else. Find someone who'll take it away from you and leave you free of it. When it builds up until you can't stand it anymore, that's what you do, isn't it? Find someone? And that's why you do it."

"No . . ."

But there's things dancing around her words. I'm sitting in the car waiting for someone—I don't know it's going to be this girl—to walk past. She doesn't have a name. She's just the vessel for me to pour all that fear into. Because the old bastard is laughing at me once more, I can hear him. Belittling me, scaring me. Making the sky above crash and shake. And I have to make him stop. So I will, the only way I know how.

I hate this so much and I love this so much, what he's done to me, what he makes me do. And I can't stop. It gets stronger every time and every time I have to get rid of it. And every time it gets harder. I see it fully this time. And I *feel* it. The powerlessness, the fear.

The hatred.

Inside me, always there, curled like a poisonous snake in the pit of my stomach, ready to stretch out and strike.

The doctor's voice: "You hear that storm inside yourself, don't you, Kyle? A boom of thunder, and you're ready to go."

She's right. I am ready to go. To get rid of that fear, that powerlessness. To regain control. Of myself. To make myself too big for him to hurt me. Ever again.

"And it has to be a woman, doesn't it, Kyle? A woman who reminds you of your mother? The mother who wouldn't help you? Someone you can control, exercise power over, make them experience what you had to go through, what *he* put you through."

And there she is in front of me. The woman. And I can feel the anticipation, it's getting me hard.

I'm trying to talk to her. And she shouldn't be afraid of me, because I'm a student like her. I'm Kyle Tanner. She's probably seen me in the Students Union bar. We might have even chatted. I might have even bought her a drink.

She doesn't seem to remember me. She seems wary. But I can deal with that. Because I'm a nice guy, I'm no threat. She's safe with me and I'll make her realize that.

She's going to walk away. I can tell. I can't have that. If she goes, she takes that power with her. And I need to have it. I need to take it from her. I *have* to have it.

I ask her a question, pretend I'm lost. And she points, the way I want her to. And that's when the snake uncoils and strikes.

And she's mine.

Bundling her into the car, driving off. I can *feel* the sense of exhilaration as I drive away, breathing so heavily my chest could burst. I laugh, thin and high-pitched. My hands are shaking on the wheel. I must remember to slow down, not to attract any attention.

I think about what lies ahead. Giddy with the sense of fun and anticipation. I giggle.

With her in the back of the car I can feel that power building inside me once more. She's mine to do whatever I want with. Play, hurt, make scream, make laugh. Whatever. And I'll feed on that until the storm diminishes. But the power play won't stop there. There's the police. The taunting. It's all part of the control. Not enough to know I'm doing what I'm doing. I have to be seen to be doing it too. I have to show *them* how clever I am.

"Because he's long gone and you have to let someone know, don't you?"

I jump, stare at the doctor. Smile. I say, "You get it, don't you? You get what's going on here."

"The riddles to the police? I get it. You have to show them how clever you are, how powerful, don't you? You have to let the world know."

"Why not? I am clever. I'm cleverer than all the rest of them."

And as I say it I feel it. All those others in the house. All of them. "None of them managed to get to university. None of them have a degree. They're all . . . nobodies. Not like me."

"No, Kyle, they're not like you. So where is she, Kyle? Where is Claire Swanson?"

I smile. No words, just a smile. And I can feel it, that power coursing through my veins. And in that moment—*this* moment—I'm who I'm supposed to be. In control. All powerful.

"Where is she, Kyle?"

I smile. "I'm not going to tell you."

"Kyle, please listen—"

But I don't listen. I'm round the table before she can move, grabbing her by the throat, pushing her chair over, dragging her away. Her eyes are almost perfectly round, she's so surprised.

Before she can react I slam her up against the wall, choking her.

"Still got all the answers? Have you?"

I squeeze harder.

"Have you?"

That power. That *control*.

There's no longer any storm, there's no soil falling anymore.

There's just power.

And there's nothing else like it in the world.

CAPTAIN JIMMY SAINT

I can move. I'm still alive.

I try to sit up. It hurts but I manage. There's rubble everywhere. But I seem to be mainly unhurt. What can I remember? Getting shot? And then . . .

Nothing.

I'm still in the cellar but there's not much of that left. There's a light in the darkness above. Small. Like the end of a very long tunnel. Although who knows how long the tunnel is, in this house? Everything's relative. All I know is I need to move toward it. I'll find my destiny there. My reason, my calling.

I stand up. There's blood on my uniform, a hole on the outside of my left shoulder. Luckily the bullet has only nicked me. Looks a lot worse than it is.

I see my gun on the floor, pick it up. Feels good to have it back in my hand again.

I can hear something as well. Sounds like . . . screaming? Shouting? Whatever it is, that's where I'm needed.

So, gun in hand, I run toward it.

I've got one arm wrapped tight around the doctor's throat, cutting off her air supply. Her naturally pale face is going red. Not a good look for a goth. I could almost laugh. And then I hear this voice:

"Kyle! Let her go! Now!"

I look to where the voice is coming from, expecting one of the detectives to have entered the room. But I'm not in the room anymore. I'm back in the house. And in this instant I know who I am now. My illusions have disappeared. The captain and I are still in the house. We will always be in the house. And the house belongs to Charles Boyd. It's his body. That's what we're fighting for control of now.

We're in the hallway. And Jimmy Saint is by the front door, his gun drawn and pointed at me.

I slowly back away from him, keeping the doctor held firmly in front of me. I stop, feel my back against the lift doors. They're closed. I can't go any farther.

"Thought you were dead, Jimmy."

"Rumors of my death have been greatly exaggerated."

"How did you get here? Another secret passage? You do get about."

Jimmy looks disheveled, to say the least. The explosion in the cellar hasn't left him unscathed. He's battered, his clothing ripped, body bleeding. But still able to hold a gun on me.

"Let her go, Kyle. Or suffer the consequences." He aims his gun at me to emphasize his words.

"You're going to have to be a really good shot to get me from there, Jimmy. And not to kill the doctor while you're at it. I assume if she's killed in the house, she dies outside of it?"

"Jimmy's not on his own this time, though," says another voice.

I turn to my side. The boy from the cellar is standing there. The little beast, the doctor called him.

"What the fuck d'you want, kid?"

"To get rid of you," he says. "To get my life back. For everything to be OK again. But we can't always get what we want, can we? So let go of the doctor. And we can talk."

I laugh.

"Don't kill him, Captain," the doctor manages to gasp out. "I still need to talk to him. We still need to find out where Claire Swanson is . . ."

Jimmy holds his gun still. I notice his hand is no longer shaking.

"Let her go, Kyle," says the boy. "This won't get us anywhere."

There's no way I'm letting go of my hostage. I might not survive if he pulls the trigger from such a close distance.

"Stand down, Kyle," says Jimmy. "Now. That's an order."

"No."

"It ends now, Kyle. Let her go."

"And then what? You shoot me? Lieutenant?"

He smiles. It's grim, hard-edged. "I know who I am and what I'm here to do. Question is, do you?"

I stare at him. At that moment, out of the corner of my eye, I see the kid make a move toward me. I twist away from him but in doing also loosen my grip on Amanda Drew. She twists away from me. I make a grab for her but I'm not quick enough. The captain is, though. He fires. Bull's-eye.

My arms go weak. Amanda Drew runs to the boy. "Good shot," I say.

He says nothing, holsters his gun. "It's over, Kyle."

I slump to the floor, too weak to stand. Getting weaker by the second. Fading.

"No . . . no . . ." The power ebbs from me with each heartbeat. It feels like I'm dying. Then the storm starts up again. Right overhead. Thunder crashing, lightning flashing. I close my eyes against it.

When I open them again, I'm back in the interrogation room and the captain and the boy are gone. Doctor Drew is sprawled on the floor, rubbing her throat. The detectives have returned and one of them is on me, gripping my wrist, forcing my hand up behind my back, hurting me, incapacitating me. I manage a weak smile.

"Just like Len did with Ramona . . ."

"It's over, Kyle." The doctor's kneeling over me, supported by the other detective. "Give up her location, Kyle. We can still save her. And we can get you help. It's not too late. Come on, Kyle. Just tell us."

I'm broken. Physically, mentally, everything. I have nothing left. No self-belief, no illusions, nothing. I would cry but they would be tears of blood. "I'm nothing . . . nothing . . ."

"Just tell us. And we can get you some help."

"Look at me." I'm sobbing blood. "Look at me . . . there's nothing left of me . . ."

I don't mean to trail off into a self-pitying whine but it just happens. I can feel myself disappearing. Maybe for good this time.

"Where is she, Kyle?" The doctor sounds tired. Beyond tired. One last chance. One last hope.

"If . . . If I tell you where she is, will you make it stop? The storms, the burial, all of it? Will you . . . ?"

"Yes, Kyle. I will. I promise."

I close my eyes, nod. And I see the girl. No—I see Claire Swanson. In that coffin, buried alive, the mask over her mouth, the air close to running out. The terror she must be experiencing. I know all about that. I'm no stranger to it. She'll be wondering if her next breath will be her last one, hoping that someone will come and save her but knowing, deep down, that no one will. That she's about to die. Not someone else, not one of the other people. *She's* going to die.

"The trees at the Riverside Walk by Cowick Park. South entrance. She's there. You've still got time."

And now I have nothing left. Nothing at all.

Doctor Amanda Drew straightens up. "Thank you, Kyle."

I close my eyes.

Hoping the storm will pass.

Forever.

EPILOGUE

CHARLES BOYD

My name is Charles Boyd and I live in a house alongside other people.

My name is Charles Boyd and I am a house that other people live in alongside me.

Kyle's punishment has become my punishment. And I have to accept that. Live with it. Just as I have to accept I live with him.

The house I live in is for people like me. Or, rather, people like Kyle. Somewhere away from the rest of society where we can be worked on. Understood. Made better, if possible. It's a very secure house. I can't get out. Neither can any of the others. And some of them have tried. It's the kind of place that tabloid readers are encouraged to think of as a soft touch. That because we're not in some damp, rat-infested cell we're being pampered. Because we've got doctors trying to understand us and not prison guards punishing us we're getting away with murder. Literally. Obviously it's nothing like that. I have to live, every day, knowing I have the blood of four young women on my hands and I have no memory of the act of murder, no recollection of the planning and anticipation, no sense of whatever feelings I may have experienced afterward. But those hands looked like my hands. That face looked like my face. I have to look in the mirror every day and see my face. And know that it's not just my face. It's the last face these women saw. Apparently that isn't punishment. That is considered, by those other people, as somehow getting away with it. They should try living inside my skin sometime. I guarantee they'll soon feel different.

Four women. That's right. They managed to save Claire Swanson, to get to her in time. Just.

I don't think *save* is precisely the word. She's going to be scarred for life, one way or another. Traumatized. What she has been through could only be the start of her troubles. I'm speaking from experience here. Hopefully she'll get help to cope. The kind of help I wish I'd had. The kind of help that I didn't know was available to me then.

Once Claire Swanson was found I was arrested and formally charged. Kept on remand until the trial. On suicide watch from the start. Trying to come to terms with what Kyle had done while wearing my face. The other prisoners and the majority of the guards didn't understand or didn't want to. They made my life . . . difficult. Eventually I was moved to a secure hospital to await trial.

The trial. Juries don't like or trust dissociative identity disorder as a defense. Even with Doctor Drew trying to explain things. I got life. Which is right. Especially after I heard Claire Swanson give evidence. Hearing and watching this frightened, fractured girl explain to the jury what I'd done to her. And explaining to me what I'd done to her. I know it was Kyle but it was, as I said, my hands and my face. So I had no choice but to shoulder the burden of responsibility. Horrific. Utterly horrific. I could barely listen. Heartbreaking doesn't begin to cover the emotions I went through. I wanted to try to make amends to her in some way but of course I was the last person she would want trying to do that. I listened while experts explained in forensic detail just what I, or Kyle, I kept telling myself, had done to those other girls. It was so, so *evil*. Honestly? If I'd been on a jury listening to that evidence and hearing the DID defense, I would have given me life too.

Doctor Drew argued that prison wouldn't benefit me or those locked up alongside me and that a secure hospital was the best place I could be incarcerated. The judge agreed. With the proviso that if I didn't respond to treatment, then it would be back to prison.

So here I am. I'm not going to name the place but I'm sure you know what it's called. It's famous, if that's your idea of fame. Infamous, perhaps. Notorious. No. That makes it sound glamorous. Makes *us* sound glamorous. And we're anything but that.

So I live in this house and the other people live within me.

The therapy programs help. To control myself, they encourage only the positive alters to appear. Or when I'm stressed and can't cope and the situation demands another aspect to appear. If I'm feeling confident, then it might be Ramona. Jokey or flirty, then it's Iain's turn. Nurturing, then Cerys is at the ready. If something officious needs doing, then Sylvia pops up. It must be disconcerting to say the least to hear different voices come out of my one mouth. Even the baby, Monica, has a voice. I still struggle to understand it. The Beast, as he used to call himself, has come out of his shell a lot more. I believe the staff enjoy talking to him. More than me, from what I can gather. Oh yes, they're all still inside me. They didn't really die in the house. That was just for Doctor Drew's narrative, to make it work, to find out where Claire Swanson was. They're part of me. I can banish them or bury them. But they can only die if I die.

Since Doctor Drew's little game I've been encouraged to see my body as a house. And I do so. But it's different to how it was previously.

It's a much happier place now. It's usually daytime. High sun, the odd cloud, but nearly always a blue sky and a warm breeze. We sit outside, on the lawn. Making peace with one another. Inside, the shutters are all open. And we all have our own rooms.

We banished Desmond. He was no longer needed. Fulfilled no useful purpose. He was a demonic influence, an aggressor. We reached this conclusion gradually, with Doctor Drew's help. She demonstrated how we could all work toward making him irrelevant. She helped us to remove his presence. It wasn't easy, but he's gone now. And we don't miss him. His room is bricked up and there he'll stay. Hopefully. He may come back, there are no guarantees, Doctor Drew says. The brickwork is a reminder of who and what he was and that we don't want him back. And if we can't see or hear him, then he'll know he's not wanted or needed and stay where he is. Hopefully.

I don't think anyone will take his place. I hope not. The long-term idea is that as I come to a greater understanding of myself, the other people will decide they'll be better off somewhere else and leave. But if that does happen we'll keep their rooms vacant, not bricked up. Just in case. If they come back and can't get in, that would be worse.

As I said, the Beast is no longer in his cellar. He's decided he wants to be called Charlie to differentiate from me, Charles. He's a positive soul. A good addition. I like having him around.

Which means there's a vacancy for the Beast in the Cellar. No prizes for guessing who took that position. Who we buried.

There's quite a lot of debate surrounding Kyle. And this is where Doctor Drew and I disagree. She wants to work with him. And I understand that. On one level I know that, more than any of the others within me, he's the one who needs the most help. And Doctor Drew sees that he gets it.

And he does, but never one-to-one. Always with at least two other people in the room. She works with him, the long-term goal being to persuade him to ultimately leave forever. I think that's high risk. However, I'm still not comfortable handing over my body to him. He's strong. Stronger than people think. He's also manipulative. Saying what he thinks they want to hear, convincing them he's getting better when I know he's not. When I'm sure he's just sitting there, biding his time, gathering his strength. Getting ready to go again. I've told them this. Repeatedly. They note my concerns, they say. Are aware, will be vigilant, and will proceed accordingly.

However, when Doctor Drew isn't around, I take no chances with Kyle. He's chained up down in that cellar, firmly chained up. As far down as I can get him. Buried alive, I like to think. I see it as a place with moldering stone walls, a dungeon with dripping water and rat infestations, the kind of place the tabloid readers wanted to send me and the other people, not just Kyle. And that works for me, because the more sessions I take part in with Doctor Drew and others, the more I stick to my medication, the more I respond to the various therapies I'm offered, the further down I feel him slip.

But.

I can still feel him sometimes. When there's a storm overhead, thunder and lightning crashing, I feel him. Or when the darkness overwhelms me, and all those unwanted memories threaten to flood back, I feel him. Or when sleep paralysis takes over my body at night and I feel boxed in and I can't move and I'm too scared to shout out and I imagine a shadow at the foot of the bed, I feel him.

That's when his chains begin to loosen. His personality begins to re-surface.

I have coping strategies. Things and procedures Doctor Drew put in place to help me deal with that eventuality. And so far they've worked.

But sometimes, just sometimes . . .

He's there, in my head. Like his ghost is free and rising to the surface. And it wants to replace me. Is *going to* replace me.

It's clever, it knows how to do it. How to fool the doctors and the rest of the staff. How to sound like Charles Boyd and do all the things Charles Boyd does. Working slowly and patiently toward my eventual release, when I'm deemed sane and no threat to the rest of society. When the nightmares have gone and I no longer hear the screaming. And Kyle's been there all the time, pretending to be me. Biding his time. Patient.

But I would know, wouldn't I? I would know that was happening. And I would stop it.

Wouldn't I?

And you would know too. You would know when you're talking to Charles Boyd and when you're talking to Kyle Tanner. You would know the difference.

Wouldn't you?

But I've reached the end. And I'll leave you with this thought: As Edgar Allan Poe once said, "All that we see or seem is but a dream within a dream . . ."

Fish tacos for dinner tonight. Looking forward to that.

Goodbye.

For now.

Acknowledgments

Firstly, a big thank-you to Chrisse and Beth for letting me borrow your initials. You can have them back when I'm done with them.

Thank you to two wonderful people, editors on either side of the Atlantic: Lara Jones at S&S US and Katherine Armstrong at S&S UK. Thank you both for picking this book up and the faith you've shown in C.B. Everett. Not to mention working really hard on it. And a big thank-you to S&S people: Libby McGuire, Dana Trocker, Maudee Genao, Camila Araujo, James Iacobelli, Laywan Kwan, Paige Lytle, Liz Byer, Louise Davies, Gail Hallett, Karin Seifried, Stephen Sharrock, Isabelle Gray, Julia Marshall, Pip Watkins, Rich Vlietstra, Sarah Harwood, Dom Brendon, Maddie Allan, Olivia Allen, Heather Hogan, Mat Watterson, Alice Twomey, Nicholas Hayne, the reps team, Rachel Aitken, Dan Ruffino, and everyone else at S&S US, UK, and Australia. I've enjoyed doing this. Let's do another.

My agent James Wills at Watson, Little for telling me that the ending doesn't work "but I've got a couple of ideas, if you're interested . . ." The ending works a treat now.

Sharon Lettern for giving me loads of neuroscientific information. Can't say more than that—spoilers if you're one of those people who skips to the acknowledgments first and haven't yet read the book.

The four writers I shared this book's progression with as I was working on it: Mark Billingham, Mick Herron, Susi Holliday, and David Quantick. It's about a 2:2 draw between "WTF" and "Oh. Interesting" in their reactions. I'm not saying which is which, though.

And for my wife, Jamie. For everything, really.